THE HEADLONG FURY

A Novel of World War One

J. FRED MacDONALD

ARCHWAY PUBLISHING

Copyright © 2014 J. Fred MacDonald.

All rights reserved. No part of this book may be used or reproduced by any means, graphic, electronic, or mechanical, including photocopying, recording, taping or by any information storage retrieval system without the written permission of the publisher except in the case of brief quotations embodied in critical articles and reviews.

Cover illustration by Charles Nicholas Sarka first appeared on the cover of *Leslie's Magazine*, February 8, 1917 where it was entitled: Civilization?

Archway Publishing books may be ordered through booksellers or by contacting:

Archway Publishing
1663 Liberty Drive
Bloomington, IN 47403
www.archwaypublishing.com
1-(888)-242-5904

Because of the dynamic nature of the Internet, any web addresses or links contained in this book may have changed since publication and may no longer be valid. The views expressed in this work are solely those of the author and do not necessarily reflect the views of the publisher, and the publisher hereby disclaims any responsibility for them.

Any people depicted in stock imagery provided by Thinkstock are models, and such images are being used for illustrative purposes only. Certain stock imagery © Thinkstock.

ISBN: 978-1-4808-0611-5 (sc)
ISBN: 978-1-4808-0609-2 (hc)
ISBN: 978-1-4808-0610-8 (e)

Library of Congress Control Number: 2014904361

Printed in the United States of America

Archway Publishing rev. date: 4/24/2014

DEDICATION

This novel is dedicated to the millions of men, women, and children killed or wounded a century ago while engaged in a horrific global war that even today is neither sufficiently explained nor widely understood.

PROLOGUE

Battered and bleeding, Philip pressed himself close to the bottom of the muddy gulley where he was hiding. His body was wracked with pain, but his will to survive was strong. He stayed low, hoping the person who had just tried to shoot him was not following with pistol drawn.

It was almost 3 o'clock in the morning. A few minutes earlier he had leapt from a moving train, throwing himself into the dark void of the early morning. It was not the normal way for a visitor to arrive in Lyon in Central France. But when there was a distinct threat to his life, Philip had no choice. He was tossed about like a child's beach ball, bouncing and flipping through space before rolling to a stop at the base of a large tree. As he spit blood and dirt from his mouth, he grew increasingly apprehensive that he would soon be murdered.

From a reliable friend aboard the train, he was informed that the German government had placed a large bounty on either his capture or his death. The warning was accompanied by speculation that agents from throughout Western Europe were trying to find him. His life could not be guaranteed if he stayed aboard the Paris Express on its run from the French capital to Marseilles. So he decided to launch himself from the train after it stopped in Lyon and then pulled away for its non-stop race to the Mediterranean coast.

Call it foolhardiness or bravery, his escape from the passenger car was extraordinary. Philip had to time his jump perfectly. The train could neither be traveling too fast—that would be suicidal; nor too slowly—that would allow a would-be killer time to follow him off the train and continue the hunt on land.

Philip thought he heard gunshots before hitting the ground, but he couldn't be sure. Similarly, he thought he was the only person to exit the moving train, but he could not be certain. That's why he was cautious in making his way back to the Lyon station.

He rested in the gully for about a half-hour, scanning the darkness for any sign of a pursuer. No one emerged from pitch-blackness. Still cautious, he limped to another obscure position, this one near the bottom of the elevated railway roadbed. Here he lay for another quarter-hour: still in pain and still looking for a possible assassin to emerge from the morning obscurity.

While he sat gazing for human movement, Philip wondered how in the world he ended up physically pounded and hiding in a filthy hole in the middle of France. Only two weeks ago he had arrived in Paris as an idealistic and, as he now realized, naïve young university professor of history. All he wanted to do then was conduct research for an academic book and live in the French capital for a year. But here he was, involved in espionage work for the French government and scrambling to avoid foreign agents and private killers out to win a jackpot in German money for his elimination.

1

He could never forget his arrival on French soil.

It had been a rough passage. The fact he was crossing the Atlantic Ocean on the swank liner *La Savoie* made no difference when the sea became angry. For four of the eight days it took to get from New York City to Le Havre, the French Line vessel was relentlessly tossed by large swells created by spring storms. In the dining areas crew members had to strap tables, chairs and bar stools to the floor. Most passengers became seasick, however, compelling them to avoid all public meals. They remained in their cabins and suffered the agonizing effects of *mal de mer* in private. It had not been a pleasurable voyage, but it finally ended. And he was ready to forgive Poseidon and go about his business.

Although he was now safely docked in France his legs remained wobbly and his stomach queasy. But he was thrilled to be walking down the gangplank and relieved to be on solid ground. This was not just any ground, however. For the first time in his life he was setting foot in France.

The port of Le Havre was a whirl of activity. Stevedores unloaded trunks and suitcases as fast as the tall steel cranes pulled them from the ship's hold. Disembarking passengers wearing large coats and wide hats unsteadily descended, some then plunging into the arms of waiting relatives or friends, others frantically looking for assistance in moving their belongings to nearby passenger trains.

He eventually found a porter with a handcart who gathered the young man's property and rolled it to the next train leaving for Paris. The smokestack of the mighty locomotive channeled its plumes of steam skyward as the engineer waited for several hundred people from *Le Savoie* to place their possessions in a baggage car and then get into one of the dozen or so passenger coaches. After tipping his helper several francs, a generous gratuity by French standards, the visitor from America quickly entered a Second Class car and found a seat.

The coach was crowded: too many foreign visitors wearing too much clothing. It was, after all, almost summer; but many passengers were dressed as if they were headed for Siberia, or at least the Swiss Alps. Philip found himself seated next to a young Parisian woman heading home. Because he was fluent in French, he fell comfortably into a conversation with her. He was particularly interested in recommendations she might provide about her hometown—good restaurants, where to shop, must-see sights of Paris, how to use the new subway system.

He was weary, but all he had to endure now was the railroad trip of 142 miles, and that would take only four hours.

He thoroughly enjoyed the scenery flying across his window seat. He loved gazing at the flat green countryside with medieval villages dotting the landscape. He also liked the short stop the train took in Rouen, the city where Joan of Arc was burned at the stake in 1431. Then, more bucolic scenery as the train wove its way along the Seine River.

Everything about the rail trip pleased him. This was the real France—something he had spent years studying without actually touching or smelling—and he was speeding through it on his way to glamorous Paris.

It was almost a religious event for Dr. Philip Michael Belmont, Ph.D., an assistant professor of history at the University of California at Berkeley, and expert in French history. The date was June 15, 1914, and he had just arrived for a year of research on what would be his first book. Philip was writing about the diplomatic maneuverings behind French naval support for the Thirteen Colonies in their Revolutionary War against Great Britain. He wanted to know what Louis XVI and his advisors were actually planning when they intervened in a distant colonial rebellion and helped the upstart Americans gain national freedom.

Philip had come a long way to get here. He began life on the South Side of Chicago, the son of a successful merchant and a Russian-born housewife. His father taught him the value of hard-work. From his mother he learned to embrace the foreign in life with curiosity and appreciation. His own native intelligence brought him a good public education, then a scholarship and graduate fellowships for advanced study at the University of Chicago.

As a child growing up in the ruggedness of a big industrial city, he gave little thought of becoming an intellectual. He appeared to prefer physical activity to the cerebral, almost-priestly existence of those in academia. Philip loved all types of competitive sports, from individual activities such as track and gymnastics, to team sports like rugby and baseball. Above all, he enjoyed the energy that flowed from gentlemanly rivalry. Whether he was personally involved, or simply watching others play, honest competition always brought out the best in Philip.

He had one passion, however, and it was definitely not scholarly research or field sports. He loved airplanes. Flying was a fad sweeping up American men in the decade after the Wright Brothers started an aeronautical revolution at Kitty Hawk, North Carolina. As a young man Philip loved to watch the amazing aircraft—monoplanes, bi-planes, and tri-planes—that flew frequently above the shores of Lake Michigan. He especially liked the gala nine-day air meets held in Grant Park where as many as three million spectators came to see pioneering aviators compete for cash prizes in events such as highest altitude; speed races for bi-planes and single-wing aircraft; and duration of flight—solo as well as with a passenger. In August, 1911 he was at the airfield in Chicago when Harry N. Atwood landed on his way to setting a world's record for piloting a bi-plane from St. Louis to New York City, a distance of 1177 miles, in eleven days.

While in his late twenties, a girlfriend pushed Philip even farther in this direction when she dared him to become a pilot. He had frequently thought of becoming a flyer, but studies always seem to interfere. Never one to avoid a personal challenge, however, he decided to learn how to fly.

Following several months of professional instruction and practice flights in a wide range of available aircraft—American planes manufactured by the Wright and Curtiss companies; imported French aircraft from the Farman, Blériot, and Antoinette corporations—he became a fully-qualified pilot of heavier-than-air flying machines. Although the state of Illinois did not officially issue pilots' licenses, he carried one of the early licenses issued by the Aero Club of America, a pioneering private organization dedicated to promoting aviation globally.

There was something exhilarating about cruising among the clouds high above the ordinary. Philip called it air sailing, and it never failed to refresh his spirits. He enjoyed the wind blowing in his face, even on a cold day in Chicago. In the remote solitude of the clouds he was at one with the creatures of the skies. It gave him a sense of detachment from everyday concerns.

As an antidote to his penchant for sports and aviation, Philip enjoyed the study of history. The subject had grasped his imagination early in life, and he never shed its influence over his thinking.

He traced this passion to the World's Columbian Exposition held in Chicago in 1893. Philip's parents had taken him there several times to enjoy the excitement of the event. The Midway Plaisance with its large crowds on warm summer days; the massive Great Wheel designed by Mr. Ferris offered expansive views of the city and countryside; and White City—the collective term used for the large collection of neo-Classical exhibition buildings, all finished in white stucco and illuminated at night by bright electrical lights—everything about the World's Fair impressed this boy from the crowded and industrially-darkened South Side.

But it was the array of colorful historical exhibits that seduced Philip. Here is where he lost his heart to Clio, the Greek muse of history. *Viking* was a detailed recreation of a Viking warship from the ninth century. It sat in nearby Jackson Park lagoon and attracted modest crowds at an Exposition designed to celebrate Christopher Columbus, not Leif Erickson. In the Machinery Building young Philip saw the actual cotton gin invented by Eli Whitney, the device that changed the course of U. S. history by making it relatively easy to extract seeds from cotton balls. The Transportation Building featured the first steam locomotive used in the United States, the *John Bull*. It was imported from England expressly for the Chicago event. Even the revered Liberty Bell, crack and all, was shipped from Philadelphia for public display.

Overarching the entire Fair, of course, was the recognition that this was the 400th anniversary of Columbus and his discovery of America. To drive home the theme, the Exhibition displayed accurate replicas of the Spanish explorer's original ships, the *Niña*, the *Pinta*, and the *Santa Maria*.

From these encounters early in his life Philip eventually announced that as much as he loved sports, he was considering becoming a professional historian. And now in his early thirties, the Berkeley professor of history had come to France to do the proper research and begin writing his first monograph. He left behind his parents in Chicago, but he promised to write a letter once a week to share his adventure. He had no need for extra funding since the University of California and several academic foundations had awarded him generous financial support for a year abroad. And with no wife or serious love interest back home he was coming to romantic France unattached and open to whatever happened.

After another hour of pastoral spring scenery and casual conversation, the train began to slow as it approached its destination, the Gare St. Lazare. First came the industrial installations that ringed Paris, followed by rows of apartment houses that typified housing in the *banlieux,* the suburbs surrounding the city; and then into the stone architecture of the French capital itself. Philip was intoxicated by everything he saw.

Finally, the train entered the massive shed that sheltered the loading platforms of the St. Lazare station. This is it, he thought to himself, this is the *Gare*, the railroad station with its noisy crowds, its sulfurous odor of locomotive exhaust, and the expansive grid of steel support beams under which he and thousands of others were now walking.

As people rushed from the train and headed for the exits and a sunny afternoon, he placed his belongings on a luggage cart and followed the human stream out of the building. Here he took in his first panorama of Parisian life. *Fantastique*, he muttered aloud. Everything he had read about the city—and he had read a lot—was confirmed. Beautiful, elegant, colorful, alluring, his mind raced for synonyms. He concluded with exciting and *très* exciting. In an instant Paris was his city. And happily, it would remain so for the next year.

Philip sought out one of the commercial vehicles poised outside the station ready to scurry arriving passengers to their destinations within the City of Lights. He passed up several taxi-autos in favor of a slower horse-drawn conveyance. All the better to see and feel the city, he reasoned.

He negotiated a price then hoisted his trunk and valise into the carriage. "Here is where I would like to go," he said while handing the coachman a card containing the address of his new residence near the Place Danton in the 6th arrondissement.

Philip leaned back in the comfortable leather seat just as the driver patted his horse with a small whip and began winding through the urban traffic. As the coach moved forward at the speed of one horsepower, the newcomer plunged into the ambience of Paris.

"Welcome to my hometown, monsieur. My noble steed Étalon and I are happy you have chosen our carriage to transport you," said the coachman. "Let me guess. You are from America, and this is your first visit to Paris."

Philip laughed. "How did you know? Was I so obvious?" he replied. "I'm just so happy to see the beautiful old buildings, the statues, the crowds on the sidewalks, the shops and markets. Your hometown is magical," he exclaimed.

"Ah, our visitors are all like that. But especially you Americans. At a minimum you're bedazzled, at the maximum you fall quickly and madly in love with Par-ee," the driver answered. "But, that's good. Paris is a seductress, monsieur. Enchanting to strangers, there's no doubt; but we who live here are also in love with her."

As Étalon pulled the carriage through the streets, the driver continued his unofficial greeting. "Please. Don't let me diminish your enthusiasm," he remarked. "Paris is unique, especially in the hopefulness born on a bright and warm afternoon like this. Only once in your lifetime will you enter this city for the first time. So, while I point out a few renowned sites relax and enjoy the moment. It's unforgettable. Absorb it because you will remember your grand entrance forever."

Philip was pleased. Not only had he engaged a driver, he apparently had also selected an empathetic guide who began describing the highlights as they passed by. "We are heading toward the river, the Seine, so I will show you some of the city landmarks, if you would like," he said.

"You must know that Paris is divided into twenty arrondissements," the coachman remarked. "Well, not all these administrative areas are created equally. If you visit the 12th or the 20th, for example, you would swear you were in any big city in France. But where you are now, in the 8th and heading into the 2nd and then the 1st, this is the heart of the greatest city on the planet. Here is where history was made. And, I dare say, it is still being made.

"To reach your destination in the 6th arrondissement, we will be traveling along our glorious Seine. These are all remarkably historic sections of Paris. You have chosen your destination well, Monsieur America."

Philip relaxed and watched as his unofficial tour leader showed him the attractions. "If you look down this street to your left, the rue Auber, you can see our Opera House. It's big and imposing. Some people call it gaudy, but I think it's beautiful—even if it was built by our late, unlamented Emperor Napoléon III. Those who have money can see the finest performers in Europe: drama, dance, music, everyone famous plays the Opera House. Maybe someday I can afford a seat," the driver explained with resignation in his voice.

A few minutes later the driver pointed to a large neo-classic building in the center of a crossroad. "Straight ahead of us is *La Madeleine*, the Church of St. Mary Magdalen," he explained. "It's about seventy years old, but it appears as if were built at the time of ancient Rome—or even earlier in the Athens of Socrates. It is another attempt by our architects to construct Paris as a modern version of classical European glory. I love *La Madeleine*. It's a gorgeous building as well as a sacred church.

"Now we'll proceed along the rue Royale with its fine shops and *chic-chic* prices. Someone like me could never afford to buy in these stores. But, it's impressive, no?"

As Philip gazed, the tour guide continued. "Next, we get ironic. We are entering the Place de la Concorde, the Place of Harmony, as you would say in English. It was originally called Place Louis XV, but to be more timely the name was changed in 1789 to Place de la Révolution.

"Concorde is such a beautiful name for this gigantic open space. But this is where the Guillotine worked overtime during our Revolution. The radicals set up the great slicing machine right over there," he said while pointing to the part of the Concorde where the beheadings took place. "In those days Parisians called it *le Rasoir National*, the National Razor. And it shaved many a head. But don't worry, the street cleaners have removed the bloodstains," he added with comic precision.

"In 1795 the new government sought a less energetic revolution. So in a gesture of reconciliation and national unity, the Place was given its present name, de la Concorde. But the government failed to include the upstart Corsican, Napoléon Bonaparte, in its calculations. So much for French foresight!" he concluded.

Philip embraced his role as a tourist, although he already knew much about the places being described. Part of the happiness he now felt was generated by the enthusiasm in the coachman's running commentary.

The driver passed through the vast expanse of the Place de la Concorde. He called attention to the large obelisk in the center of the site. "That wonderful Egyptian monument is from the time of Ramses—something like the 13th century B.C.," he proudly announced. "It came to us as a gift from Egypt in the 1830s.

"Oh, look to your right. Do you see the large boulevard, the one flowing into and out of the Concorde? That is our most beautiful avenue, the Champs-Élysées. It's the main thoroughfare of the 8th arrondissement, and some say it's the most elegant street in Paris. I think it's more beautiful than that. If you look up the Champs when Étalon passes by, you will see the Arch de Triomphe rising up in all its glory."

Philip was impressed with the Champs-Élysées. In the distance he could see a multitude of pedestrians on the sidewalks, while horse-drawn vehicles, automobiles, trams, and taxis crowded the wide boulevard as it sloped uphill toward the Arch.

"So many famous sites just here on the Place, and so much impressive Baroque architecture surrounding it," continued the coachman. "But in the distance you can see something that is neither. There above the trees," he said pointing to his right, "you can see Mr. Eiffel's tower which at twenty-five years of age is a mere baby on our horizon."

"Ah, but what a baby," Philip responded.

"The Eiffel Tower is on the other side of the Seine in the 7th arrondissement. It's quite an architectural accomplishment. People like me love it because it's so bold. It commands the skyline testifying to French industrial achievement. Others despise it. I've heard it called an inverted exclamation point, a pile of scrap metal, a gaudy steel joke, and worse. No one in Paris is neutral about *La Tour Eiffel*," said the driver.

The coachman turned left and headed along the quays of the Right Bank of the Seine River. He took Philip past the Tuileries Garden, the Louvre Museum, and several unique bridges that led over the river and into the Left Bank. He also showed the young visitor some of the city's largest department stores. Frankly, Philip saw these latter structures as rectangular stone boxes built for the efficiency of modern commerce: functional, but not as attractive or intriguing as what he had already passed.

About a mile along the Right Bank Philip glimpsed the enthralling Cathedral of Notre Dame in the distance. "I know what that is," he said. "It's Notre Dame. Will we pass it?"

"No, sorry, we turn before we get to the Cathedral. You're going to the Latin Quarter where many university students and young intellectuals reside." explained the driver.

"Too bad," said Philip with disappointment, "but I'll be here for a year. For certain, I'll get to Notre Dame. And I want a closer look at the Eiffel Tower, too. I can't miss that monument."

There was so much for him to absorb in so short a time. He was attracted to everything, from the patient fishermen along the river to the grand apartments in which wealthy Parisians resided. Then there were the bridges spanning the Seine as it sliced Paris in half. Simple bridges, elaborate bridges, wide and narrow bridges: bridges of all types. And he shared his excitement with the coach driver.

"Ah, very perceptive, young man. I'm pleased you noticed the different types of bridges we have," the coachman responded. "We could have approached the Place Danton from several directions, but Étalon and I came along the river so we could introduce you to the quaintest of all the Parisian bridges. We adore it. It's not far from here."

"You call your horse Étalon. I don't know the word. What is the English translation of his name?" Philip inquired.

"Ah, Étalon is our word for the horse who makes many baby horses because he is a great stallion," answered the driver. "He is the daddy horse. I believe in your language you would translate the word as stud.

"Well, 'Stud' is old now, but he has a long memory. By calling him Étalon I remind him of better days when he was a horse of some repute. But let's not dwell on the subject. Too much talk about his glory days makes Étalon sad."

Philip smiled and sat back. He was in no hurry. In fact he was still mesmerized by the postcard-like imagery before him. Now it was the small steamboats, the *bateaux omnibus* plying their way up and down the river to move Parisian commuters from one end of the city to the other, and to show Paris to visitors in the warm springtime.

"Here it is, monsieur, here is our favorite bridge the Pont Neuf—our New Bridge which is actually very old. In my opinion, this is the most intriguing span across the Seine. It appears so simple, no *frou-frou* here, no complications. Yet, like the city itself, passing over the bridge is an intriguing experience," he remarked. "This bridge was opened in 1604. Crossing it is my personal communion with the history of France."

As the coach driver continued talking, Étalon pulled the carriage to the right and onto the bridge. "It's built in two separate spans connected to the small island, the Île de la Cité, set in the middle of the river. From the Pont Neuf you can see beautiful views of the riverbank with human architecture and natural beauty in abundance."

Philip expressed his agreement.

"You know," continued the coachman, "this once was the most popular spot in the city. Everyone came by here at one time or another. They used to say that if the police were looking for a suspect in Paris, they need only watch the Pont Neuf for three days and their man would be sure to pass by."

"Is this true?" asked Philip.

"Well, monsieur, that's what they say," the driver responded with a sly lilt in his voice.

Étalon plodded across the Pont Neuf and into the Latin Quarter. A few narrow side streets, then across the wide Boulevard Saint-Germain, and it wasn't long before Philip found himself before the place that would be his home, the Hôtel des Deux Cygnes located at 17, rue Gasconne.

"This is your destination, the Two Swans Hotel," announced the coachman as he reined his horse to a halt. "Place Danton is just down the street, and here's the address you gave me."

After the two men unloaded the luggage and piled it on the street Philip thanked the driver and tipped him for his service and his exceptional tour of the city. He added a few centimes for an extra bag of feed for Étalon.

Philip watched as the carriage pulled away then turned to feast his eyes on the Two Swans, his residence for the coming year. So this was his new Parisian home.

It wasn't exactly like the grandiose hotels he passed on his carriage trip through the city. It was an old apartment building with thick stone walls. A pair of small swans delicately painted above the entrance was charming, but a sales brochure described the Two Swans as quiet and comfortable, the perfect residence for intellectual pursuit in the heart of the Latin Quarter. It was also affordable. And, besides, before making his reservation he had been guaranteed a private room with a lovely view of the renowned Church of San Sulpice which was nearby.

He had chosen this residence in part because it was close to the Diplomatic Archives of the French Ministry of Foreign Affairs where he would be conducting most of his research. He also liked its academic location near to two great universities: the Institut d'Études Politique de Paris, the Paris Institute of Political Studies, or what the students called Sciences Po—and one of the oldest universities in Europe, the venerable University of Paris, popularly known as the Sorbonne.

When he entered the hotel, he discovered how misleading the sales brochure had been. There was no glamour here. The furniture in the lobby was old and well-worn, some might say shabby. The wallpaper was peeling in places and several broken windows needed replacement.

Then there was the concierge, the superintendent in charge of the hotel. She was an elderly, unfriendly woman named Madame DuBois. She spoke French with an unfamiliar accent. It confused Philip. He could understand most of what she said, but her odd pronunciation created occasional words he couldn't understand. And, unfortunately, she spoke no English.

After stumbling through the registration procedure, he followed her up a narrow flight of unstable wooden stairs that squeaked as they climbed the two flights to his room. Fortunately, the hotel did have a handyman who, for a few centimes, moved the visitor's baggage up the stairway and into the room.

In truth, "room" was too flattering for the space he was allotted. It was more like a large closet with very little inside. There was a narrow bed with a sagging mattress, a small desk with an oil lamp for nighttime studying, and a boxy wooden armoire that was the totality of his closet capacity. The fact that the floor sloped slightly toward the center of the building was another disappointing condition. As for the promised window overlooking beautiful San Sulpice, his window offered only a limited view of the apartments across the street and the rooftop of an old church two blocks away. San Sulpice was viewable only from the other side of the Two Swans.

Then there were the facilities at the end of the hall. The toilet was shared by the other tenants on the floor. It consisted of a hole in the floor with two raised ceramic islands on which users placed their feet to avoid the flood that occurred with every flush. There was a small sink with running cold water, no bathtub, no shower, and no warm water.

When Philip inquired about bathing, Madame DuBois explained that the hotel provided only the bathroom sink or a ceramic basin he could bring to his room should he prefer to bathe there. She suggested he visit the public bath house on the next block where for a small fee he could shower or take a bath. But, she added, should he insist on washing in the hotel, it was possible to order a tub from a nearby bathing company. If ordered before 8 o'clock at night, a bathtub could be delivered to the hotel early the following morning.

This was not what he expected, but he had little recourse since he was expected tomorrow afternoon at the Diplomatic Archives located in the Quai d'Orsay. He hoped to introduced himself and get a quick start on his project. First, however, he had to be presentable. He surrendered himself to reality and ordered a bathtub to be delivered early in the morning.

Unpacking was easy. He unloaded his trunk into the armoire. The rest of his belongings he left in his suitcase on the floor.

Philip fought against the disappointment he was beginning to feel. He muttered a lot to himself to vent the rising frustration. A soft rap on the door, however, diverted his self-pity.

"Hello. So you're our new tenant," said a young man standing at the threshold. "I'm Thad Lanyard from across the hall. I'm from Oz. I mean, I'm from Australia. Sorry, but I'm the one with a view of the Church. You get the rooming houses across the street and some plain old rooftops," he jested. Philip looked up to find a man in his late twenties extending his hand in greeting.

"Oh, hi, I'm Phil Belmont. I'm from California," he responded as he shook hands with the Australian. "I'm moving in, but I'm a little upset about this miniscule room I've leased for the next twelve months. Looks like I won't be entertaining friends for a while," he added sarcastically.

"Oh, you'll get used to it. The body adjusts to sagging furniture— and to cold weather later in the year," Thad explained. "It may be a bit dreary, but just think, old man, you're in the most dynamic part of the most electrifying city on Earth. This is Paris, mate. You're living in the Latin Quarter. This is the navel of the earth, the center of the universe. The food is delicious, student life is exciting, the women are gorgeous, and the cafés blend intellect and fine alcohols to create the most brainy intoxicants. Once you get out and into the neighborhood, it will offset any misgivings you have about the beautiful Deux Cygnes," he promised with an unbelievable confidence in his voice.

"In fact," Thad continued, "once you've unpacked I'll treat you to a glass or two at my favorite watering hole, the *Au Carrousel Bleu*. It'll pick you up. And it's less than five minutes from here. Besides, they serve excellent food as well. You'll really like it."

Philip accepted the cordial invitation. Already he was buoyed by Lanyard's happy adaptability and his refusal to bemoan the human condition.

In short order, Phil washed his face and hands, and was following his Aussie friend toward the bar. As they walked, Phil learned his new acquaintance was twenty-eight years old and a graduate student in economics at the Sorbonne. He had been in Paris for almost a year working toward a doctoral degree. His goal was a government career in finance back home in either Canberra or Sydney.

As Thad explained it, he had come to Paris to get a different perspective on his field of study. Where most Australian students sought advanced degrees in British universities, he felt a doctorate from the University of Paris would bolster his appeal in the job market back home. He calculated that he would finish his exams and his dissertation in another eighteen months. "I'll be graduating as a proud member of the Class of 1915," Thad boasted.

As they traveled through the narrow streets of the Left Bank, the two men continued to introduce themselves in greater detail. They slipped in and out of English and French until they reached their destination. "Let's not be rude to the students inside, Phil," said Thad, "let's speak to each other in French when we're in the bistro." Philip agreed and besides, he concluded, Lanyard's Australian accent was sometimes difficult for an American to understand.

When they opened the front door and walked into the restaurant the aroma of garlic and onions frying in butter was overwhelming. "Oh, I must have died and entered heaven," Philip he said. "All of a sudden I'm ravenously hungry."

"Now you know why this is my favorite spot in Paris," Thad noted. "Just wait until you taste it. As the French would say, *C'est formidable*, It's tremendous. But first, let me show you around the place. You have to see it. It's as socially interesting as it is gastronomically appealing." Thad then led him through several large rooms when he saw dozens of young people dining and drinking. A few were actually studying.

The ambience was one of friendly informality. And it was very international as Philip overheard students speaking in many languages.

"Oh, the French like to bring bright students from their colonies to Paris to study," Thad explained. "You'll find Africans from Senegal, Algeria, Tunisia, Congo, and Morocco. There are East Asian students from Indo-China. A few come here from North America. They come to study from Guadeloupe and Martinique and even from Quebec, although Canada is not part of the French Empire. I like to think of Paris as a glorious cassoulet percolating with a wide variety of edibles, a great stew filled with ingredients gathered from all corners of the world."

After finding an open table and browsing through the menu, the two men ordered dinner. Phil selected a white fish that the Aussie guaranteed would be scrumptious. Thad ordered poulet roti, roasted chicken, with a double order of *frites*, French fried potatoes. Dutifully, the waiter brought a bottle of Chablis, vintage 1910, with which to enrich the dining experience.

"Thaddeus! Thaddeus! *Mon ami, comment allez-vous?*" someone shouted from across the room. Thad was soon greeting and cheek-kissing with an apparently good acquaintance. "Jean-Pierre, my friend, I want you to meet the latest person to check into the glorious Two Swans. Phil Belmont just arrived a few hours ago from California."

Thad turned and introduced Philip to Jean-Pierre Trenet. "Phil, this is another student of history. Jean-Pierre is working on his undergraduate degree in French history at Sciences Po. He knows a lot about Napoléon Bonaparte."

"Yes, yes, that's my field of study. He was the Little Corporal, you know—although he was actually a General, and even an Emperor. He was so influential," Jean-Pierre exclaimed. "You are a student of French history, too?" he asked.

Philip nodded in agreement. "My field is the *ancien régime*, especially the reign of Louis XVI."

"*Magnifique*," Jean-Pierre remarked. "It's nice to meet another history addict. We French have plenty of history to share. There's no scarcity, especially here in Paris," he added.

Philip explained his academic goal for the next year and how he hoped to begin archival research tomorrow at the foreign ministry archives in the Quai d'Orsay. This impressed the young French student even more.

"I can see one problem, immediately," Jean-Pierre exclaimed. "Your name is not quite French; it's too much American. We French prefer long names, names with lots of syllables, names with character. I know you English speakers prefer the informality of Thad and Phil and Bill and Bob. I guess I'd be Johnny in such clipped speech. But if you will stay here for an entire year, you need a fine Gallic name. Tell me, what is you middle name?" he inquired.

Philip was amused at this disarming student. "Well, my full name is Philip Michael Belmont," he said. "At the University of California I am Professor Belmont to my students, and simply Phil by my colleagues."

"*Parfait!* You already have a fine French last name. So, from now on you shall be Philipe-Michel Belmont," said Jean-Pierre. Then, pouring a tiny amount of Chablis into his right hand, the personable young undergraduate made the sign of the cross above Philip's head and declared, "By the power invested in me by the President of our Third Republic, Mr. Raymond Poincaré—and with the approval of vintners throughout France—I award you the extended and proper French name of Philipe-Michel Belmont, honorary citizen of France and historian *extraordinaire*."

Everyone seated around Philip's table laughed out loud at the antic ceremony. It was a wonderful welcoming gesture, and the visiting professor appreciated it deeply. Before coming to France, Philip had concerns about his private life. Would he fit it? Could he make friends? How would the students and other faculty react to him? His uncertainty now dissolved. He was glad to have met Thad and Jean-Pierre and to be ushered so ceremoniously into Parisian student culture.

Thad interrupted the levity with an idea. "Wait a minute, Jean-Pierre. I have an idea. Because you are the Chairman of our *Jour de débat*, the Debate Day programs held here at the *Au Carrousel Bleu*, maybe you can persuade Phil, I mean Philipe-Michel, to participate in the next session," he said.

"A wonderful idea," responded the Frenchman. "Yes, Philipe-Michel Belmont, every Wednesday evening we students gather here in the ballroom to discuss pressing topics of the day. We call it the *Jour de débat*. It's a pun on one of Paris' leading newspapers, the *Journal des débats*. We empanel great minds from the Sorbonne and Sciences Po to debate a wide range of issues, usually political and cultural. And we would love to have you participate. We've never had an American debater. You would be making history. And how appropriate is that?"

"I would be flattered to be a part of your discussions," Philip answered with obvious pleasure.

"Then, if it wouldn't be too much trouble, could you do it the day after tomorrow?" asked Jean-Pierre sheepishly. "You see we need a third participant for our next debate. And it's only two days from now."

"Well, what is the question before the house?" the professor inquired before committing himself.

"Oh, forgive me for being vague," Jean-Pierre remarked. "Wednesday night we are discussing colonialism and the question we are debating is: Which country has the most successful program of imperial rule? We have someone arguing for the French Empire, naturally. There's another person speaking in favor of the British Empire. But our German and Italian defenders both have exams on Friday and can't make it. And the Russians and Belgians, well, no one is prepared to defend the indefensible. But, we would enjoy having someone argue the American case because, clearly, the United States is a new imperialistic power of growing importance. Can you do it?"

Philip didn't think long. "Yes, I can do it," he answered. "In fact, I would be happy to present the case for the American Empire."

"Perfect. You are now our third panelist," Jean-Pierre said. "The debate begins at 8 o'clock. You and the other two presenters should prepare an opening statement of about five minutes each. And then we open the floor to comments and questions.

"Oh, thank you very much, Philipe-Michel. And thank you, Thaddeus Lanyard, for bringing him to us," Jean-Pierre exclaimed. As the energetic student organizer walked away, Philip felt pleased. He actually looked forward to the encounter.

Not long after Philip agreed to the debate, the waiter brought dinner. Philip began eating immediately. But not Thad. Instead, he sat staring at a single French fry he had taken from his dinner plate. "Before

I start eating," he said in a tone filled with mock pomposity, allow me to introduce you to the lowly *frite*, the inimitable French fried potato." With this opening, Thad began a pseudo-intellectual disquisition on the superiority of the French method of preparing fries.

"You know how mealy the English make their obese fries. They're so unlike real French fries the Brits call them by another name. They call them chips. The English have ruined half the planet by bringing these big globs of deep-fried potato pulp to places like Australia, New Zealand, South Africa, and Canada. Wherever the map is colored pink and under London's imperial control you will find the fat and pulpy fried potato that is the British chip.

"We of the Empire usually drown these greasy items with an ample dousing of vinegar—malt vinegar, preferably—in an effort to kill the taste of cooking oil. We eat our chips because they are ubiquitous. But, we pray that someday France will conquer Great Britain and eventually the entire British Empire. This is the only way to rescue the lowly potato. Our battle cry is "Ennoble the *Frite*, Obliterate the Chip."

"You in the United States must have an opinion on our battle of the French fry. I ask you, Dr. Belmont, what do you have to say about U. S.-Potato diplomatic policy?" he inquired wryly, inviting Philip into the faux discourse.

Philip snickered as he began to elucidate on the American approach to French fries. "Well, Mr. Lanyard, we in America very much enjoy the potato fried deeply in hot oil," he began. "But in recent times we've discovered a better way to eat said item, be it emaciated in the French style, or bloated according to British designs.

"We have a new condiment, and it complements the French *frite*. We Yanks love this modern enhancement which we embrace as ketchup or catsup, however one spells the name. It is a sweet, tomato-based puree, poured in its glorious red thickness from long-necked glass bottles, sometimes directly on top of the fries, often next to those golden brown potato sticks, and occasionally 'on the side' on a small plate. No matter its proximity to the fries, ketchup demands greater participation by the *frite* eater. No longer just pick-up-and-eat food, the consumer must add an intermediate step of slathering his or her fried potato in the delicious brew.

"This scarlet goop is ambrosia. It merges the acidity of tomatoes with myriad exotic spices and a smidgeon of vinegar. The recipe constitutes a red tide of wondrous taste, a veritable flood of tomato-y tartness that enhances the natural *frite* while lubricating its luscious slide down the eager throat."

"Oh wait. Hold on for genius," Thad interrupted as he grabbed his head. "I feel a rhyme coming on. Ode is on the way." Holding a skinny French fry in front of himself, he employed a reverential tone as he recited.

ODE TO A FRENCH FRY

Oh, wee fry, sliced from the 'tato
Which guise do you take?
Which mode do you follow?
Are you thin—like the French?
All-sizes—à la Yank?
Or perpetually plump, as they make you in Brit-o?
Do tell me, dear *frite*,
I ask as no prank-o,
Which style do you like?
Which has most flavo'?
Frenchie or Brit?
Or Yank, in goo of tomato?

Poetic eruption now over, the two new friends laughed heartily then turned their attention to the task at hand: devouring the crispy, thin French fries before they became too cold.

Following the tasty but poetically-challenged dinner, Thad was up for more food. "Room for dessert, Philipe-Michel?" he asked. "The sweets here are excellent, but I have a great idea. Let's walk over to Les Halles for a dessert. It's on the Right Bank, about a fifteen-minute stroll from here. The journey will do us good after such a big meal. And Paris at night in the springtime is glowing with traditional gas lamps and modernistic electric lights.

"Come on, you'll love it. Les Halles is a massive distribution center for the food that feeds this city daily. There's nothing like it anywhere."

"Well, I can't stay for too long. I have a rendezvous with a bathtub early in the morning, and I really want to introduce myself at the American embassy and the Quai d'Orsay tomorrow," Philip explained. "But I can use a promenade. Let's split the tab here, and I'll treat you to dessert in Les Halles."

"That's a deal," said Thad as they gathered their coats and paid the bill.

The short trip to Les Halles was refreshing. The two friends walked down the Boulevard Saint-Michel, the renowned Boul-Miche that was the main artery of the Latin Quarter. As they neared the end of the street's downward slope toward the Seine, off to his right Philip eyed the awe-inspiring Notre Dame Cathedral brilliantly lighted against the night sky. Instead of turning toward the famed church, however, Thad led him straight across the short expanse of the St-Michel Bridge and onto the Île de la Cité.

They went directly across the small island, passing large government buildings, then over another short bridge, the Pont du Change, and into the bustling ambience of the Right Bank. A few minutes later they arrived at Les Halles.

Philip had never seen anything like this large marketplace of wholesale and retail foods. At once, it was a central depot for the fresh meat, fruit, vegetables, and dairy products required daily to feed Paris. And the 2.8 million citizens of the city loved food. Annually, the markets of Les Halles provided hungry Parisians with 251,000 tons of meat, 42,000 tons of fish, 21,600 tons of poultry, 1470 tons of fresh game, 11,300 tons of shellfish, 23,000 tons of vegetables, 20,000 tons of fruit, 14,700 tons of butter, 24,500 tons of eggs, and 16,800 tons of cheese.

"This fantastic market covers twenty-two acres of prime real estate," Thad pointed out. "It contains ten different pavilions, and each pavilion has 250 small stalls for the sellers. And the entire enterprise is located under that large zinc roof above us. It's not beautiful like Notre Dame, but it's efficient."

Philip agreed. It was an amazing site. "But let's find a shopkeeper who's selling desserts at this hour," he said. "It doesn't appear to be the busiest time for the marketplace. I hope we can find someone who's still open."

"You're right, the markets come alive in the early morning and stay that way all day. At night the merchants replenish their supplies for the next day," explained Thad.

The two men walked around the massive facility looking to satisfy their intensifying craving for sweets. Most stalls were closed. Those still doing business were mostly selling vegetables, meat, and flowers. Eventually, however, they discovered the small pastry shop of François Bertrand. Technically, it wasn't located in Les Halles. It was actually across the street from the marketplace, very near the historic St. Eustache Church. But it was the only pâtisserie still selling sugary confections at this hour.

Unable to decide upon which pâtisserie to buy, Philip and Thad finally opted to buy several confections: two pieces of chocolate flan, two cream-filled éclairs, an apple tart and a small raspberry-coated gateau. Philip paid, and the pair ambled into the Paris night gorging themselves on tasty delights.

"What a city! It even tastes delicious," said Philip.

"Let's take a peek at the old church," he continued. "I know a lot about this place. It's from the 16th century. But during the French Revolution radicals conducted an atheistic worship service here in honor of Reason. The participants replaced the spiritual with the rational. God replaced by Logic. And that's how modernity was born."

After exploring St. Eustache, Philip and Thad continued their journey back to the Two Swans. This time, however, they opted to return via the Pont Neuf just south of the Boul-Miche.

Somewhere in the midst of their passage over the Seine, the two men heard a muffled cry and the sound of flesh being struck. They ran toward the sound. "Quick, Phil, over here," Thad cried out. "Over here! Two guys fighting. Quick!"

As they ran toward the noise, they sighted two men engaged in a vicious brawl. Light from a nearby street lamp showed one man with a bloodied face. Wildly swinging his fists, he was unsuccessfully trying to punch the other man. But the second fighter masterfully used his feet to deflect these blows and to kick his opponent's head and body.

"Watch out for that kickboxer. He fights savate style," warned Philip. "One slap to the head with those shoes he's wearing can be lethal."

The noise made by Philip and Thad as they ran screaming toward the struggle apparently startled both fighters. The kickboxer quickly ran away, but his wounded rival was too stunned and disoriented to flee.

"Are you all right?" Thad asked him.

The battered man said nothing for a while. Wiping his face and clearing blood from his mouth, he finally thanked the pair for their intervention. But he refused medical attention. And when Philip suggested calling a policeman, the man rapidly walked away and faded into the darkness.

"Welcome to Paris for a second time," said Thad sardonically. "This is the part of the city you'll never find in the guidebooks."

The remainder of the walk back to the Two Swans was upsetting for Philip. He was clearly shaken by what he had just witnessed. He didn't know if he should be scared or dismissive. He wondered if this was commonplace, or perhaps an aberration, a one-time confrontation with ugliness.

"Trust me, I've lived here for many months," Thad explained. "What we just saw is a reality for Paris and for every big city. Probably for every town and village, too. Paris is an exciting city. But you can't get too swept up in the romance of the place. Parisians are real people, and real people fight and injure each other. Sometimes they even kill each other. You just have to be careful and try to avoid conflict."

"I guess I was too naïve. All this historic charm, excellent food, and friendliness confirmed a pre-conceived fantasy I believed," Philip confessed.

"Well, get over it, mate," said Thad. "This is a town of real people. And when bad demons take control of human beings, regardless of beautiful buildings and antique statuary, those possessed sometimes beat each other rather savagely. That's what you just saw."

2

Bathing had never been a particularly fascinating ritual for Philip. But this morning it was all different. At 7:30 a man carrying a zinc bathtub came to the door of his room. He also had with him a large canister of warm water—or at least it was warm when he left his store several minutes ago.

"Your bath is ready for use," the delivery man declared when Philip opened the door. "Where would you like me to place it?"

Philip had a little difficulty understanding the visitor because he carried the bathing vessel upside down with his head inside the tub. Philip invited him in and asked that he put the tub in the center of the room. The man then poured in his lukewarm water supply and went downstairs for more unheated water with which to fill the vessel. It took a several trips downstairs to gather enough liquid to make bathing possible.

"Here are some towels, a sponge, and a bar of soap," he said as he handed Philip the bathing materials. "I'll be downstairs. Just call me when you're finished."

"Oh, for running hot water and indoor plumbing!" Philip said aloud to himself. Still, he plunged into the water which by now was tepid at best. He didn't spend too much time in the tub. After a few minutes of rapid lathering and scrubbing, he was out of the water and drying himself. This was an important day, and he was anxious to get it underway. And besides, by this time the water was downright cold.

The delivery man came back upstairs and scooped out water and poured it down the toilet drain. He accepted payment from Philip, plus a generous tip for such unprecedented service. The zinc-tub experience convinced the American visitor that from now on he would use a public bath house instead of renting a portable metal tub.

Soon, Philip was dressed and out the door. Before going to the Quai d'Orsay, however, he planned to visit the Embassy of United States on Avenue Kléber. Here he needed to collect the papers providing him official access to the Archives. Back home in Berkeley Philip had already filled out and mailed the required applications and paid for the processing of his documentation. He was hoping for no complications when he picked up his finalized materials in Paris.

Madame DuBois, the concierge, had given him directions for getting there by way of the city's expansive underground railway, the Métropolitan. The Métro was only fifteen years old and limited in its coverage of the city, but already it moved hundreds of thousands of Parisians daily. As he descended the stairs of the St-Michel station, Philip was still a bit uncertain about his understanding of the Métro.

Twenty minutes and one transfer later he walked up the stairs at Place de l'Étoile and learned that his concierge was a good teacher. He was standing on the Champs-Élysée facing the Arch of Triumph, the victory arch begun by Napoléon Bonaparte as a tribute to his own military achievements.

The Arch sat in the center of the Place de l'Étoile, the Place of the Star, the traffic round from which twelve major avenues spread like wide beams of starlight radiating into the neighborhoods of the Right Bank. Avenue Kléber was one of the streets emanating from the Étoile.

As he neared the American embassy, Philip could clearly see another stellar Parisian site, the Eiffel Tower, rising in the distance. He couldn't understand the controversy generated by the Tower. It was so technically striking in its construction, a bold amalgam of steel and modern design. But for critics to call it a pile of junk metal and urge its removal was unbelievable. Seeing it in person, even from a mile away, he easily understood the Tower as a monument to French leadership in this era of industrialization.

It required no more than a half-hour to collect his documents at the embassy. A quick lunch, another adventure on the Métro, and he was soon strolling along the Quai d'Orsay headed toward the large building that housed the Ministry of Foreign Affairs. The tall walls of gray stone gave the Ministry the appearance of a fortress. But Philip was undaunted because he was holding official papers that would allow him to breach its walls.

As he neared the side entrance that led to the Diplomatic Archives room, Philip jumped back suddenly. An expensive black automobile swerved directly in front of him and entered the Ministry courtyard. Once he caught his breath, the near-miss made him wonder just who might be in that impatient vehicle: Was it a king or a president? Perhaps an ambassador or a foreign minister? Maybe it was just an official of the French government here for an important meeting on policy matters— or late for lunch? Perhaps, it was the Minister of Foreign Affairs himself, Gaston Domergue.

Philip realized that he was entering the building containing the foreign affairs offices of one of the European Great Powers. France was one of the six most important nations in Europe, an integral part of the balance of power that maintained global stability through a system of offsetting military and political alliances. The so-called Great Powers—Russia, Germany, Great Britain, Austria-Hungary, Italy, and France—were actually arrayed against each other in two blocs of three: a Triple Alliance of Germany, Austria-Hungary, and Italy, and a Triple Entente that linked France, Great Britain, and Russia.

It was a precarious arrangement and subject to change, but it worked. Furthermore, Philip realized that because many of these nations had contentious imperial holdings around the planet, any European conflict could fast become a worldwide conflagration involving military forces in Africa, Asia, and the Americas.

The web of alliances and ententes that wove the Great Powers together had kept Europe from total war ever since Napoléon was crushed at Waterloo in 1815. Proof of the effectiveness of this balance lie in the fact that a century of European boundary disputes and colonial confrontations had failed to ignite full-scale combat on the continent. The balance of power had been tested in the Balkan Peninsula as recently as a year ago when two international wars were confined to the region.

Still, there were many in Europe who doubted the long-term stability of this balance-of-power situation. Too little was known about the interlocking diplomatic agreements that bound together the Triple Alliance as well as the Triple Entente. Too many secret clauses, too many unknown obligations, too many devious potentialities: such a system may have kept the peace in Europe for a century, but it offered no guarantee of always doing so.

As he marched up the stairs to the Archives, Philip was relieved that his academic interests would take him away from contemporary politics. The Foreign Minister who most interested him right now was Charles Gravier, the Comte de Vergennes, an aristocratic statesman who conducted foreign policy for Louis XVI in the 1770s and 1780s.

Philip presented his papers to the clerk at the reception desk and was promptly handed a half-dozen new forms to be completed. It was his first encounter with the *la mentalité functionaire*, that mindset of government functionaries methodically devoted to regulation and protocol, even to the point of abandoning personal judgment. When Philip observed that much of what he was filling out had already been answered on earlier forms, he was reminded in a stiff monotone that "These are *les règlements*, the regulations, Mr. Belmont. Please complete all the forms."

After a half-hour of hand-cramping composition, he finished the applications and passed them to the receptionist. Another wait followed. A bespectacled old man eventually emerged from an adjoining room and handed Philip his *carte d'identité*, a small card bearing his name and address, plus his photograph and signature. "You must show this card to our security guards each time you enter the building," the official explained.

Philip thanked the bureaucrat and turned to enter the doors marked Research Room. "Monsieur, your card, please," demanded an old man sitting behind the reception desk. The man had been watching the entire registration ordeal. But he still had his job to do. After perusing the identity card Philip had just received, the receptionist finally waved him into the Archives.

The room was a large library space with several rows of wooden tables where seven or eight scholars were already poring over boxes of paper documents. The bookshelves built into the wooden walls contained rows of oversized folios and bound volumes. Out of sight, however, were the archival gems, the correspondence and personal papers which, when read and placed in proper order, would answer the historical questions confronting Philip.

This was the historian's dream, a research facility dedicated to the investigation of original sources and serviced by clerks who fetched and returned documents as requested.

He spent the next several hours checking the availability of materials. Rigorously, he perused the catalogues, dismissing the irrelevant and ordering the items he wished to see. In essence, he was plotting his schedule of inquiry for months to come.

During a break outside the Research Room, Philip flexed his aching fingers. They were almost rigid from so much writing. "Hand cramped?" asked a young woman who had also been researching folders of documents.

"Yes. It's this fat fountain pen of mine. I need a new one. My hand gets stiff too easily with this old thing," Philip remarked as he shook the circulation back into his hand.

"Hello, I'm Anna Liese Bjork. I'm from Norway. I'm here working on my doctoral dissertation," she said.

Phil introduced himself and soon the two were talking about their respective projects. But Phil was more interested in the fact that Norway was such a new nation. He questioned Anna Liese about that fact.

"Yes, we've been an independent country for less than a decade," she said. "We were an independent kingdom once before, but that was a long time ago. For 500 years we were controlled by other countries. Sometimes by Denmark, sometimes by Sweden, and sometimes by a merged Denmark-Sweden. But rather than wage a nationalistic war to keep us within Sweden, the king in Stockholm relented in 1905 and allowed Norway to become independent. We changed the name of our capital city from Christiana to Oslo, and here I am, a free Norwegian citizen. As I tell people, I'm proud to have been born in Christiana, but prouder that I now live in Oslo."

"Wonderful," replied Philip with a wide smile. "Welcome to the reality of national independence."

After a few more minutes of casual conversation, Philip and Anna Liese returned for more reading and note-taking.

After another hour of selecting documents, Philip decided that he was finished for the day. He officially placed a request for the materials he wanted to see tomorrow. Walking home, he was satisfied that he had planned his work, and that the following day he would start working his plan.

Although he remained very excited about his topic, within a few days scholarly investigation became routine. Already by Wednesday afternoon, his pattern was established. Up in the morning, get to the Quai d'Orsay in the early afternoon, conduct research until the early evening. It was a manageable schedule that allowed him to assess the documents and begin writing the book he hoped would enhance historical understanding—and advance his young academic career.

When he arrived at *Au Carrousel Bleu* for dinner and his debut as a debater, Philip was convinced that his social life in Paris was also set for a while. The food and drink were wonderful again. But the din inside the *Carrousel* was almost deafening because the bistro was filled with people drinking and chattering in anticipation. He was amazed that the *Jour de débat* attracted such a large crowd of students plus a few older men who appeared to be professors.

When he spotted Thad Lanyard, Philip motioned for his buddy to join him. "Would you like another glass?" he asked as the young Australian seated himself. When Thad nodded his agreement, Philip ordered a demi, a half bottle of the cheery red wine Thad was already drinking. "I'll have some with you, too," he explained. "But not too much. The last thing I want to do is face a public debate when I'm blotto."

"How are you feeling, old boy? Ready to take on the greatest minds in France," Thad joked. "It should be a lot of fun this evening. Lots of the people I've talked to are anxious to witness a true American intellect at work. You Yanks—or as the Frenchies prefer to call you, Sammies—are a bit of an oddity over here, you know."

"I hope they're not disappointed," Philip replied. "I did a little reading in some of the books I brought with me. Even read a few newspapers since so much of the colonial predicament involves current events."

As the friends conversed, Philip recognized the event organizer, the effervescent Jean-Pierre Trenet. "Ah, Citizen Philipe-Michel Belmont, are you ready for the debate?" he yelled from across the room. "You're on very soon."

"*Bien sûr*, yes indeed," Philip hollered back. "I'm ready, and I'm pleased to be here."

"It's quite an atmosphere," Thad noted. "We have students tonight from every political persuasion. You may get questions from the floor from royalists or socialists, traditional Marxist Communists or Marxist-Leninist Bolsheviks, maybe even a republican or two. As long as it's not one of those damned anarchist with a bomb in his satchel. It's difficult to argue with dynamite."

Suddenly Philip heard a man clanging a bell. It reminded him of the town criers of earlier times. "Oyez. Oyez. Oyez. Hear ye, hear ye," said the bell ringer as he clanged for attention. "The *Jour de débat* is about to begin. Please remove yourselves and your libations to the ballroom. The debate begins in five minutes. Tonight's topic: Which imperial nation runs the most effective empire? Oyez! Oyez! Oyez! Hear ye, hear ye. In the ballroom in five minutes."

Almost everyone in the *Au Carrousel Bleu* grabbed a glass or a bottle—some more than one—and headed for the large room at the rear. The ballroom was already humming with raucous observers as he entered with his fellow debaters. Philip ducked instinctively when a paper airplane came floating directly toward him. In fact many of the assembled seemed to enjoy folding sheets of paper into little aerodynamic gliders and lofting them willy-nilly into the air. Philip probably liked airplanes more than anyone in the room. After all, he was a trained pilot. But it was a bit ludicrous to be entering an academic debate with toy planes cruising by in all directions.

"*Calmez-vous, calmez-vous,*" Jean-Pierre demanded of the audience. "Calm down, please. Let me introduce the principals for this evening's discussion." Despite his plea for attention, the crowd was still talking loudly and swallowing alcohol. But at least the paper air force that once controlled the ballroom skies unilaterally disarmed as Jean-Pierre continued his attempt at a formalized introduction.

"To present the case for the British Empire, permit me to introduce Veronique Bompard from Sciences Po. She is in her final term, and at the end of this year she will receive her degree in, what else, the Science of Politics. Although she is French like most of us, she will try hard to convince you that the British colonial model is the superior model."

The students hooted in exaggerated approval, although a few whistles and thumbs turned downward revealed a lack of unanimity with Mademoiselle Bompard's premise. This was, after all, France, and the rivalry with Great Britain in colonial matters was almost two centuries old. London and Paris may have been linked in an Entente for the last decade, but the audience reaction demonstrated that the Anglo-French rivalry was only dampened by this understanding, not eliminated.

"Our second debater is new to the *Jour de débat*. Please welcome Professor Philipe-Michel Belmont, honorary citizen of France, but actually Professor of History at the University of California in Berkeley, United States. The good professor will support the position that America is the world's best imperial power."

Again the boisterous assembly roared its approval, punctuating the noise with hand gestures and foot stomping. Several in the crowd, however, appeared to be sitting on their hands in an obvious gesture of disdain. Philip tried to be unaffected by these critics who were already contemptuous of what he would say.

Jean-Pierre continued, "Finally, our third presenter this evening is Thierry Gaspard, a graduate student from the Sorbonne who is finishing his doctoral thesis on the topic of French colonialism in Indo-China. He will present the argument that France maintains the best empire."

THE HEADLONG FURY

This time the hometown crowd erupted. Screams of support filled the room. A group of students in the back began singing the *La Marseillaise*, the French national anthem. Soon, the entire meeting room vibrated with the song. Philip recognized a tough crowd when he saw one.

Veronique Bompard's presentation began predictably with the assertion that the sun never sets on the British Empire. She pointed out that today in the year 1914 Great Britain held political sway over almost thirty-five percent of the Earth's habitable land and twenty-seven percent of its 1,623,300,000 people. That means, she asserted, every day more than 438 million people go to sleep in the embrace of this vast Empire.

She spent time tracing the rise of London's colonial policy from the settlement of New England in the 17th century and India in the 18th century, to recent acquisitions in Africa. She displayed maps of that continent overwhelmingly colored in British pink. "They are the greatest civilizers. They have brought English common law, social organization, and industrial economics to peoples who never knew modernity," she continued. "The poet Rudyard Kipling was correct when he wrote that Britain must 'Take up the white man's burden, send out the best ye breed, go bind your sons to exile to serve your country's need.'"

She concluded her remarks, arguing "Granted, the British have had to fight to maintain some of their holdings, the Boer war being an example from less than fourteen years ago. But when allowed to take root and mature, the liberality inherent in Great Britain's colonial rule will remake the political world, fashioning it according to the rational, democratic standards of the British constitutional model. If Canada is the shining example of what Britain can do beyond its island borders," she added, "then the planet will eventually be made up of Canadas, scores of Canadas. And we all will be better for it."

The presentation was rather pedestrian and most people in the audience began to clap politely. Three young men in the front row, however, jumped up from their chairs and hoisted a large banner above their heads. In large block letters it declared "Down with British Imperialism!"

"What about Ireland?" one of the men yelled at the students. "Get the Brits out of my country. Ireland for the Irish!"

The demonstration unsettled the onlookers. Some in the crowd signaled their agreement with the protesters while others whistled and booed and yelled for everyone to sit down and be quiet. What had begun as a courteous response from the audience had devolved into a noisy nationalistic *manifestation*, or as the French abbreviate it, a *manif*.

The disruption continued for about ten minutes. During the time the Irish patriots and their supporters sang a few songs about their love for Ireland and the bold Fenian men who would someday rescue the island from the grip of British tyranny. Their point finally exhausted, the protesters walked out of the room to boisterous cheers and jeering.

Once the students calmed down, Philip stepped forward as the next presenter. He made no reference to what had just happened, but instead went directly into his case for the superiority of U. S. imperialism. He argued that as a democracy and a constitutional republic, the United States was best able to bring to its subjects the promise of eventual liberation and responsible self-governance.

"I realize that the Philippine insurrectionists led by Emilio Aguinaldo did not appreciate American colonial authority when it first arrived," he contended, "nor did monarchist supporters in the Hawaiian Islands who protested the American conquest of their kingdom. But the potential for obtaining social freedom and economic modernization was well worth the sacrifice."

"If you like," Philip continued, "the history of the United States as it spread from the original Thirteen Colonies to the mighty bi-coastal power it is today is a tale of imperial expansion. The United States has relentlessly moved beyond its original frontiers and appropriated the wilderness. Consider the dynamic of our empire: the Louisiana Purchase from Napoléonic France, the Gadsden Purchase from Mexico, then the acquisition of Alaska from Russia. Supplement this with the annexation of both the Republic of Texas and the Republic of California—and add statehood for New Mexico and Arizona two years ago.

"You can plainly see our march from one coast to the other is all about territorial growth and the spread of freedom and democracy because, except for barren, frozen Alaska, everything I just cited is an integral part of modern America."

Philip continued, "We next took American civilized standards beyond North America and established them in the Pacific Ocean and the Caribbean Sea—from the Hawaiian Islands to the former Spanish colonies of Guam, the Philippine Islands, and Puerto Rico. Then it was into Samoa and Wake Island. And don't forget the American territory in Panama where later this year a mighty new canal across the isthmus will be opened for international shipping. The parade of American Empire was late in arriving, ladies and gentlemen, but it has been inexorable since it started.

"And the appetite for imperial enlargement continues in the United States. People today expect that the expansionist U. S. will eventually make inroads into Africa, South America, and East Asia. And if Pancho Villa and the corrupt regimes in Mexico cannot stop threatening us, Mexico may be the next target for Yankee colonialization. The potentialities are endless.

"Certainly, American imperialism is an economic adventure. But it is also selfless growth in the name of sharing our values of constitutionalism, democracy, and republicanism with everyone interested in the good life.

"Wouldn't you want to be conquered by modernity, then trained in representative government and eventually granted independence, ready now to join the comity of nations as an equal partner?" Philip concluded. "This is our moral purpose and such a noble destiny makes the U. S. empire the greatest."

Philip's remarks found support among the spectators as moderated cheers and hosannas followed his presentation. The American visitor was proud that he could represent his nation so positively. But he was aware that many students appeared unmoved by his argument.

The final presenter was a Thierry Gaspard, a graduate student determined to prove that France was the best colonizing nation. He began by dismissing early French ventures in expansion. Gone was New France in North America, and attempts to settle southern India. Gone, too, were some small islands in the Caribbean and elsewhere. And since the Fashoda crisis in the Sudan sixteen years ago, he admitted, France had abandoned its hopes to control Egypt, the Sudan, and the upper Nile. Gaspard argued that all these holdings and plans had been lost to British military power, but more specifically, he blamed these failures on the internal weakness of French domestic politics in the 18th and 19th centuries.

"But when you ask which is the greatest Power at administering overseas territories, France is without question the leading power," he continued. "We all know the phrase *la mission civilitrice*, the civilizer mission. That is what French imperialism is about: bringing the superior standards of our nationality to the underdeveloped nations. It is our burden and glory. And now that the Third Republic has resolved the internal problems of the past, we are once more a mighty people and the strongest colonial administrator.

"French colonials are citizens of France if they learn our language and commit themselves to our laws and our standards. We have students here tonight who come from French colonies. And we have recently welcomed a black man from Senegal into our Chamber of Deputies as an equal member. Can the British match this achievement? Will the Americans accept voting representatives from their colonies to be full members of Congress in Washington?

"Eventually our movement into Western and Central Africa will reap for France the benefits of raw materials and capital for economic expansion. Soon, we will be revered in Asia and Africa as the great conduit to modern social living. We are respected, my friends, like no other nation. *Vive la France!*"

Thierry Gaspard's final interjection brought the audience to its feet. More singing of the national anthem ensued. Several audience members jumped up and down with prideful glee. Yells, rhythmic applause, and screams of joy indicated that the students had already decided the winner of the debate.

It took a few minutes before the clamor subsided and Jean-Pierre could open the floor to questions. "Make your inquiries brief and to the point," he admonished the crowd. "And please identify yourself before asking your question."

Thus began almost two hours of vigorous interrogation within a theatrical atmosphere that involved the onlookers as much as the debaters. People in the room seemed to relish their role in this intellectual dance, as both questioners and those who answered were roundly derided or cheered, and sometimes both, simultaneously.

For Philip, for example, there was the student who identified himself as Georges Sainte-Ville who attacked his argument as well as his reputation. He claimed that Philip was being insincere, that he could not really believe what he had just expounded. "What you presented was a case for American conquest." With the encouragement of much supportive noise, he insisted to Philip, "Don't try to fool us. The United States is out to take over the Earth."

A young woman named Marie-France du Maurier asked about the Monroe Doctrine and its recent supplement, the Roosevelt Corollary. "First, your President Monroe says all colonizing foreign nations must stay out of North and South America. Almost a century later your President Roosevelt says the United States will intervene in Latin America when necessary, but no European power can ever do that.

"So now France must go through Washington whenever a country in Latin American refuses to pay its debts? Must the United States become Europe's new bill collector in North and South America? This is hypocrisy," she continued, "You have, in fact, sent your Marines into Cuba and Nicaragua. They are there today. You have deployed your military in Chile and Haiti. You even created the nation of Panama by tearing away the northern provinces of Colombia and turning them into an independent country. Doesn't this mean that you Americans want all of Central America and South America for yourselves?"

A Leninist student from the Sorbonne, a young German man named Klaus-Dieter Hochmeister, accused the professor of being "an exploitive capitalist imperialist." In rebutting Philip's argument, he argued that imperialism was nothing more than the final stage of capitalism, a point in the Marxist-Leninist dialectic where monopolizing corporations have grabbed the reins of the state and now seek to control colonial holdings, indeed the world, for their selfish purposes.

"This will be your end as a capitalist nation state," he warned Philip. "The people of this globe will no longer tolerate America's bayonets and military boots. The colonies will rise against you, as they will against all capitalists. Imperialism has taken capitalism one step closer to its inevitable extinction."

This was the cue for a group of five or six others to come to their feet and hurl leftist slogans at Philip. He retained his composure, however, and responded in a calm voice. He had never faced a classroom like this while teaching at Berkeley, but he realized losing self-control would only embolden his hecklers.

Philip answered Sainte-Ville and Hochmeister as well as he could, and then turned to confront a French republican named André Gaillard who brought up the racial question. "You want to spread the gospel of Americanism internationally. Fair, enough, Professor Belmont," he began. "But most of the Earth's population is not Caucasian: it's brown and black and red and yellow, at least that's how Western society colorizes human physical differences.

"In this regard, the American record is disgraceful when it comes to your native peoples. Consider what you have done to the aboriginal people of North America: slaughtered them, denied them their history and culture, and herded the survivors onto barren reservations in deserted parts of your country.

"When it comes to Africans trapped in American enslavement—and even after their emancipation—your performance has been horrid. I need not expound on this because everyone here knows America is a racist society.

"And if we focus on people with brown skin who occupy your Southwest which your country forcefully stole from Mexico, or those Asians who came as inexpensive laborers to build your great railroad lines and farm your great Western lands, the United States has been overtly unjust and discriminatory.

"So my question is: How do you explain your nation's record with non-whites when you tell people with dark skins that they should welcome American colonialism?

"Yours is a society built on racist practices," Gaillard contended. "America still does not allow democratic rights and civil liberties to people whose skin is not white. How can you expect people in Asia and Africa and South America to embrace your imperial promise when your domestic record is so abysmal?"

As the audience again rose to its feet to support the questioner, Philip searched his mind for a supple answer. He didn't know what to say. Like many Americans, he had never really viewed the history of his country from such a perspective. He found himself at a loss to defend the indefensible.

"Young man," began Philip after a lengthy pause, "I'm compelled to yield to your argument. You are right, and I am wrong. Too much of my country is racist and hypocritical. We Americans have expanded at the expense of people with non-white skin. We have conquered and humiliated them, brutalized and killed them while seizing their lands and their dignity. It's a bad record unworthy of a moral colonial power. I must accept your criticism as valid."

This time the audience sat in startled silence for a few seconds, then erupted in cheering. "Wait, wait a minute," Philip implored the crowd. "Do not applaud me for being honest. A debate is a learning event, not a test match of slick argumentation or competitive pride. When you entered the university to study, you willingly renounced ignorance and abandoned preconception. Your goal has always been to learn. Well, the same is true for your professors. They do not know everything. They understand that, and I have just proven it. Professors, too, must be willing to learn. And not just from books. Sometimes they can be educated by their students. No one in academia holds a monopoly on truth.

"Thank you, *Jour de débat*, I have learned much this evening. I hope you have as well," he concluded with humble frankness. Appreciative clapping and hooting followed his confession, but the audience was clearly confounded by Philip's reaction.

The three debaters fielded more questions in an attempt to explain or buttress their positions. But, clearly, it was Philip's self-effacing reply to André Gaillard that made the most indelible impression on the students. When it came time for the attendees to select the winner of the debate, despite their obvious bias toward Thierry Gaspard and his pro-French argument, they cheered loudest for Philip.

"Thank you students of the *Jour de débat*," proclaimed Jean-Pierre as he fought to regain control of the rowdy crowd. "I guess we know who your winner is. I can tell from the clapping that tonight's debate victor is our American professor and honorary French citizen, Philipe-Michel Belmont."

He then implored Philip to step forward and accept the evening's prize, a large bronze medallion bearing the profile of Léon Gambetta, a founding father of the Third Republic and a champion of social democracy. "Gambetta would have been proud of your honesty and your openness to knowing truth. I know we are. And we are pleased, Professor Belmont, to welcome you into the Grand Order of Gambetta, the highest honor we of the Sorbonne and Sciences Po can bestow upon a debater."

Philip was overwhelmed and frankly humbled. He graciously accepted the medallion and thanked the students, some of whom were still shouting "Bravo!" as he spoke. He was genuinely touched by the gesture.

As the crowd began to disperse, many people gathered around the various debaters, introducing themselves and seeking further elaboration. Philip dutifully responded to his eager interrogators, even suggesting books they might read for more information.

"I'm very pleased to meet you," said an older man who approached the American professor with his hand extended in greeting. "My name is Alain Laroche. I am a professor of modern history at the Sorbonne. I was most impressed by your response to the critic who attacked American racism and imperialism. Thanks to you this evening, I learned something, too, about academic integrity and honesty. I'll try to remember that truth is not exclusively mine."

"Then we both learned something," said Philip. "I know I won't forget what happened tonight either."

"I am hoping, Professor Belmont, that you might be able to attend one of my seminars to talk with my students about your insight on becoming a historian," Laroche inquired. "I realize that you are relatively new to the profession, not a worn-out old shoe like me, but I think my young scholars could learn from your approach. There are about a dozen people in the class. We meet on Monday mornings between 10 and noon. I would appreciate it if you could come to one of the meetings."

"Well, thank you for the kind offer," Philip answered. "I would like very much to accommodate you. But what would you want me to speak about?"

"Most of the students are interested in careers in history, so if you could share your tips and insights about the historian's profession, that would be wonderful," Professor Laroche responded.

"Sounds easy enough," said Philip. "My afternoons are committed to research at the Quai d'Orsay, but my mornings are open. I can probably fit it into my schedule. When would you like me to visit?"

The Professor checked his pocket notebook. "Well, if you could come a week from next Monday—that's the 29th of the month—that would work well for them and me," he said. "The students will be beginning their research projects about that time, so your input would be timely.

"The topic we're treating this term is Nationalism, so expect a lively discussion. Maybe not as raucous as this one tonight, but vigorous nevertheless."

The two men talked further, establishing specifics of the visit. Philip agreed to be at the Sorbonne on the 29th at 10 o'clock in the morning. Privately, it pleased him to think that he would be conducting a seminar at the University of Paris, an institution founded sometime around the year 1170. In comparison, his University of California was opened in Berkeley seven hundred years later.

Walking home with Thad after the debate, Philip was pleased with his performance. He kept flipping the heavy Gambetta medal into the air, satisfied that the students had learned something from his honest response. He had come to Paris as a student, himself. And with the invitation from Alain Laroche, Philip was pleased to discover that in Paris he could function occasionally as a professor.

That evening he had a chance to write his first letter back to Chicago since arriving. He described the highlight of his arrival and his first days at the Two Swans. He even wrote about bathing in a rented bathtub.

"But most of all," he concluded, "I want to say what a friendly and charming people the French are. They have welcomed me much more warmly that I could have hoped. Maybe they're hospitable because they live in such a wonderfully civilized city. Chicago is a booming, bustling, rugged place: a city of steel mills and cold temperatures half of the year. The Chicago life makes one tough and energetic.

"Paris, on the other hand, is a *Grande Dame*, a Great Lady who is sophisticated, refined, and cosmopolitan. The Parisian experience, I sense already, makes one wiser and more tolerant. This is as good as it gets—discounting, of course, my room in the Two Swans Hotel. If I had more time and energy, I would search for a new residence.

"Well, we shall see what happens. But at this juncture, I'm all for Paris."

3

This next day of research was like the previous days, except for one remarkable development. Philip had recalled a footnote he read while still in Berkeley. He searched his notes and found reference to a special tribute to the Comte de Vergennes that a legislator in 1827 placed in the record of parliamentary debates of the time.

Philip asked the archival assistant about accessing the obscure publication. She motioned him toward a bookcase where oversized bound-volumes of the Chamber of Deputies proceedings were kept. "You'll find the publication you want on one of those shelves," she informed him.

Indeed, the wall was lined with large volumes of parliamentary discussions from the 1820s through the mid-1840s. They appeared to be little used. In fact, with his fingers Philip was able to push away a thick patina of dust that had accumulated on the exposed page tops.

When he removed the heavy volumes covering the year 1827, Philip was startled by what he encountered. In the dark open space behind the books he found a number of wallets and purses. In fact, before informing the assistant of his discovery he retrieved a dozen billfolds and five purses that someone had obscurely hidden behind the old parliamentary papers.

He walked back to the assistant. "Excuse me, Madame," he said, "Has either the Archives or the Ministry had a problem recently with the theft of personal property?"

The woman's wide-eyed response betrayed her surprise at the question. "Why yes, sir, there has been a pattern of theft here among researchers, and even inside the Ministry with our own people. It's been going on for a while. But, how did know that? And why do you ask?"

"Well, I may have solved part of the crime," Philip replied.

He led her back to the shelf and methodically pulled out the loot and spread it across a nearby empty table. "It looks like your robber took money and other valuables from these purses and wallets and then deposited them behind these oversized volumes," Philip said. "You may want to look behind all them. Who knows what you may find."

By this time the other researchers had turned around to watch the ongoing drama. The assistant thanked Philip for uncovering the thief's hiding place. "We'll check behind every book once the research room closes for the day. Meanwhile, I have to bring these items to the proper authority." Carefully she placed the stolen objects in an empty box and rushed out a side door.

For his part, Philip was a little shaken when he returned to his research table carrying more hefty tomes of legislative debates. Diving back into 18th and 19th century history, however, had a calming effect on his nerves. Eventually, the entire research room reverted to normal.

Perhaps two hours after his discovery, the assistant tapped Philip on the shoulder and begged him to follow. As they walked through the side door and down a corridor of Ministry offices, he wondered if her bosses suspected him of being the thief or at least part of a robbery ring. Finally, she ushered him into a small drawing room. It was an elaborately decorated chamber with floor lamps, thick colorful curtains, dark wooden furnishings, and several lush Persian carpets.

The assistant suggested that Philip sit on the sumptuous sofa that occupied the center of the room. She departed, leaving him comfortably seated but alone and uncertain about what was about to happen.

In time the door opened and a distinguished man entered. He was tall, thin and about sixty years old. He appeared important in his suit and tie; very prosperous and possibly an influential official within the Ministry. "So, you are the young man who discovered where the Ministry rat hides our billfolds and purses once he has extracted the cash," he said in flawless English with a pronounced British accent. "My name is Camille Barrère. I am France's ambassador to Italy and my wallet was among the loot you just found. It was stolen two months ago. I just wanted to meet you and express my gratitude in person."

Philip introduced himself. "Thank you, Ambassador Barrère," he said in English. "I have heard much about you and your remarkable accomplishments in Rome. You've been stationed there for a long time."

"Yes, a long time. I'm in Paris now for special conferences. But I'm so excited that you located these items before I return to Rome next week. We have no idea who took them, but we're sure it's someone who works here, someone with access to our offices and our staff—including my office!"

Before Philip could reply, the door opened and another man entered—much shorter, but smartly dressed and authoritative in appearance. "Théo, come in and meet Professor Philip Belmont, the accidental detective who located our stolen possessions," said Ambassador Barrère to the new arrival. "And Professor Belmont, I would like you to meet my friend and fellow victim, Théophile Delcassé."

"I know Mr. Delcassé very well, or at least I know of you, sir," replied the young American switching back to French. "Your work here at the Quai d'Orsay when you were Minister of Foreign Affairs is well-known and appreciated in the United States. I am flattered to meet you."

"Thank you very much," Delcassé said. "But, I haven't been Minister of Foreign Affairs for nine years. I'm only here today for some policy discussions. I keep busy, however. But who are you, sir, and what brings you to study here in our little repository?"

Philip spent about five minutes explaining where he came from in the United States, what he was doing at the Quai d'Orsay, and how much he was impressed with Paris and France. He tried to play down his enthusiasm, but that was difficult.

Here he was, conversing in person with two of the most important diplomats in the history of France. It was Ambassador Barrère whose diplomatic efforts in Rome twelve years ago had calmed Italian fears about French policy and brought Italy and France into a state of rapprochement. Some even called it a realization of their Latin sisterhood. This was most significant because it diminished Italian dependence on Germany and Austria-Hungary, even though Italy remained a member of the anti-French Triple Alliance.

As for Delcassé, he provided amazing stability and direction for French foreign policy because he held the office of Minister of Foreign Affairs for an unprecedented seven consecutive years. No minister in the Third Republic had yet approached that record. During his tenure, moreover, Delcassé and his diplomats forged an *entente cordiale* with Great Britain, strengthened France's military alliance with Russia, and, of course, created cooperative ties with Rome.

If there was a military balance among the Great Powers today, it was because of Delcassé's tenure between 1898 and 1905. He envisioned and created much of the Triple Entente that now countered the Central Powers—Germany Austria-Hungary—and their threat to peace in Europe.

But both diplomats wanted to talk about stolen wallets, not Germanic threats to continental stability. They lamented their loss of hundreds of francs each, but they were pleased to have their billfolds which contained paper items and sentimental photographs that were irreplaceable. "My wallet, I love it," said Delcassé. "It was a gift from Camille years ago. The finest Italian leather craft. Directly from Rome. I'm very happy to have it back."

"I'm flattered that you're still so loyal to that old sock, Théo," the ambassador jested. "It may be time to get you a replacement.

"But I know I'm happy to have mine back. Madame Barrère was upset that I lost so much money in the theft. But I was angrier that someone we may trust with state secrets either picked my pocket or snatched this wallet from my office during one of my visits to the Quai d'Orsay."

The three men continued their friendly conversation, wandering to other topics and observations. Barrère even recommended his favorite Italian restaurants in Paris, and Delcassé insisted that Philip should get out of town on occasion and see the rest of the country. "People are so much friendlier when you get out of the big city," he explained.

"What do you mean, Théo?" asked the ambassador. "Everyone knows that if you scratch a Parisian, you'll find a Frenchman. The French are a warm and generous people wherever they are. Even in the center of Paris."

"Yes, I know," jested the Minister, "The person who stole our belongings must have been a foreigner. Most likely he was a German."

"Certainly, not an Italian," Barrère shot back before the two men chuckled. "Ah, Théo, in a former life I believe we were both on stage performing Molière farces at the Comédie-Française."

More conversation and clever banter ensued until the assistant eventually returned and escorted Philip back to his research documents. For the rest of the day, however, he found it difficult to concentrate. Finally, he folded his notebook and returned the bound volumes and private papers he had been inspecting. Not much on Louis XVI was accomplished today, but Philip was euphoric.

Outside he immediately noticed an unusual development. The police, some carrying guns and rifles, had cleared the area of foot traffic. They kept pedestrians behind rope barriers that had been strung between the lamp posts and trees along the sidewalks. He had intended to walk home immediately, but the crowd-control measures fascinated him. He decided that something was about to happen, but he just didn't know what. Curious, he decided to wait and see what transpired.

After a few minutes of waiting behind a rope, Philip spotted a black limousine exiting the courtyard of the Ministry. It turned in his direction.

When the automobile sped past, Philip thought he recognized the man slumped down in the back seat. He looked very much like Lord Edward Grey, the British Foreign Secretary, whose picture had appeared almost daily in recent newspapers. He was being whisked away from whatever business he had been conducting inside the foreign ministry. Philip wondered if Barrère and Delcassé were among those who met to exchange ideas with Lord Grey. He also wondered what they might have discussed. Because no reference to such a high-level conference appeared in this morning's newspaper, Philip concluded that it must have been a hastily-arranged, even secret consultation.

With so much on his mind the stroll toward his hotel passed quickly. He did stop, however, at a small bar and ordered a sausage sandwich and a cold draft beer. As he ate, he tried to draw meaning from the events of the day. The discovery of the wallets and purses still amazed Philip. Was money the only thing taken from these personal items? Surely, important people such as Barrère and Delcassé carried documents—perhaps confidential state papers—in their billfolds. If so, what secret state documents might have been stolen?

And what about the black automobile speeding from the Ministry? Why was Lord Grey secretly visiting Paris? What were two of the foremost diplomats of France doing there that day if not meeting with the British Foreign Secretary?

Philip was a bit confused by the events of that day. But when he finally reached the Two Swans he received another surprise. As soon as he entered the hotel, Madame DuBois yelled, "Professor Belmont, I have a special letter for you. Wait a minute, I'll get it." The concierge raced back to her room and soon reappeared carrying a large envelope. "A messenger delivered this a short while ago," she explained as she handed it to him.

Before he even opened it, Philip was impressed. The envelope was made of an expensive grade of paper and addressed in a beautiful calligraphy to Professor Philip Belmont. When he opened it, his eyes widened. From the Ministry of Foreign Affairs, it was a formal invitation to attend a grand reception and dinner on Saturday evening. The event was in honor of Myron T. Herrick, the United States Ambassador to France who was leaving his post after more than two years of successful service. The affair was to be held at the Élysée Palace, the residence of the President of France. Tuxedo mandatory. RSVP.

"Oh, my God," he said loudly. "Madame DuBois, where can I rent a tuxedo for Saturday evening? I've been invited to a reception and dinner tomorrow at the Élysée Palace. It's formal, so I'll need a tux for the event. And how can I contact the Quai d'Orsay immediately to tell them I will be attending? An RSVP card came with the invitation."

"There's no problem with either," she answered. "There are several tailor shops on the Boul-Miche. They all rent formal wear. I'm sure one of them can fill your order tomorrow morning.

"As for the RSVP, go to the Post Office right now. There's one in Place Danton, and it's open until 9 o'clock. You can send your letter of acceptance via the *télégraphie pneumatic.* That's a network of pneumatic tubes that spreads like a spider's web throughout the city. The post office will place your reply in the proper tube and it will be swooshed away to the proper destination. Then, as soon as your letter is received in the Post Office serving the foreign ministry, it will be delivered. It takes only a few minutes and will cost you less than one franc."

Philip was developing a greater appreciation of his concierge. And he was getting used to her accent. He thanked her and generously handed her two francs for being so helpful.

By Saturday evening, everything was in order. Freshly returned from the public baths, Philip was fastening his cuff links and inserting the black and silver studs that fastened his pleated white shirt. It had been a long time since he was dressed like this. Still, after he adjusted his bow tie and wrapped the cummerbund around his waist, he gazed approvingly at his reflection in the mirror.

A rap at the door interrupted his self-inspection. "Hey, Phil. You look great, my friend" said Thad. "I'm jealous. I've been here for more than a year, and no one has invited me to Raymond Poincaré's house. You've been here a few weeks and you're already dressing up like a penguin to waddle off and meet the President of France."

"Ah, don't complain, Thad, I'll put in a word for you," Philip answered whimsically. "I'll demand that they invite you next time. I'll say, 'Ray, you absolutely must invite Thad Lanyard to our next state reception?' Expect an invitation in a month or two. I'll even give you directions on how to get to his place."

The Australian smiled. "That's what I wanted to hear," he said. "By the way how are you getting there? You can't exactly take the Métro."

"No, I've hired a limousine to drive me there and then pick me up when the festivities are over," Philip responded. "In fact, the automobile should be here shortly. So, tell me, how do I look?" he asked as he made a swift turn to show off his formal attire.

"I already told you that you looked great. Now that I can see you in a brighter light, I'd say you look like a million dollars," Thad jested. "I mean, a million francs since you're going to a French event."

When his car and driver pulled into the reception area of the Élysée Palace, Philip was amazed by the array of luxury automobiles, most bearing small flags of various nations and each with a chauffeur patiently waiting for his passengers to return. The creamy white Rolls Royce Silver Ghost had a small Union Jack mounted on its right front fender. The Stars and Stripes adorned the fender of a shiny black Packard sedan. And the Swedish attendees, apparently, came in the Scania-Vabis Phaeton on which the flag of Sweden flew.

The raciest car, however, was a futuristic Italian model, an Alfa Romeo Aereodinamica, that resembled a small silver submarine perched atop four wheels. And, of course, there were many French automobiles—Hurtu, Alva, and Rolland-Pilain among others. This was guaranteed to be an event unlike anything the Berkeley professor had ever attended.

As he entered the grand foyer, Philip walked into a gala of pomp and formality. Distinguished gentlemen bedecked in formal dress. Women flamboyantly displaying their gorgeous gowns and finest jewelry. There were tuxedoed waiters moving about the several hundred guests with trays of red and white wines, various cheeses, and a variety of other hors d'oeuvres. There was also a cocktail bar for those with more specific tastes.

Conversations and music from a string quartet filled the room as people milled about, chatting with colleagues and friends, and sometimes introducing themselves to strangers. There was also a greeting line at the head of which were President Poincaré and his wife as well as Ambassador and Mrs. Herrick, all shaking hands and making small talk with a long line of passing well-wishers. Philip joined the line and waited his turn to meet the dignitaries of the evening.

When he got to the head of the line, the French head-of-state appeared confused. "How do you do, sir," he said, "I don't believe I've had the privilege of making your acquaintance."

Philip felt a little unnerved. He was no ambassador or important state official. But he shook hands and introduced himself. At this point Madame Poincaré whispered discreetly into her husband's ear. "Ah," the President said, "you are the American detective to whom so many French officials are indebted. Are you sure your name is not Sherlock Holmes?"

Philip smiled. "No, Your Excellency, just plain Philip Belmont. Or as some students at Sciences Po and the Sorbonne have rechristened me, Professor Philipe-Michel Belmont."

"Wonderful, for this festive evening Philipe-Michel Belmont it shall be. My wife and I hope you have a pleasant time tonight. Now allow me introduce you to this fine gentleman on my right," the President of France continued. "This is his Excellency, Ambassador Myron Herrick from your United States of America. He is the gentleman we celebrate this evening. He has been here for more than two years, but, his mission is ending soon. We will miss him terribly."

With that, Philip moved along the reception line to be greeted by the retiring American ambassador to France. "How nice to know you, Professor Belmont. I've heard about your exploits as a consulting detective at the Quai d'Orsay. I trust my staff handled all your paperwork in a satisfactory manner."

"Certainly, sir," Philip responded, "It couldn't have been better. I'm happy to meet you. And I'm sorry that someone so respected by his French hosts has to leave such an important post."

"Kind words, Professor Belmont. But I'm an old Republican warhorse and our new President, Mr. Wilson, is a Democrat. He has the right to select his own appointees. In fact, I submitted my letter of resignation when he was inaugurated in March of last year. I guess the stress of the presidency prevented him from accepting my offer and appointing a successor until a month ago.

"Such is life in an embassy," admitted Ambassador Herrick. "But my wife and I are booked to sail home soon, and we're looking forward to starting a nice long vacation. Our new ambassador, Bill Sharp, will be arriving soon to continue representing American interests. I'm sure he'll do a wonderful job."

Philip expressed his mixed emotions: sadness that a revered statesman was leaving government service, but happiness that Ambassador Herrick and his wife were about to enjoy a well-earned vacation.

"Thank you for the sympathetic words. I'm pleased that the Ministry was able to invite you on such short notice, and that you are able to attend. It's always enjoyable to celebrate with a fellow Yank."

As Philip turned to leave the reception line the ambassador added a final quip. "Try to mix in with the other guests, Professor. You just may find more stolen wallets. You may even discover the thief."

Philip smiled and waded into the crowd. From a passing waiter he took a glass of wine and surveyed the room. Somewhere out of his line of vision he heard someone calling for his attention, "Professor Belmont. Professor Belmont. Over here." He looked furtively in all directions until he recognized Camille Barrère moving toward him, trying to get his attention. "I'm so glad you were able to come," the ambassador said. "Théo and I needed to thank you more substantially than we did, so we asked the Social Bureau at the Ministry to expedite an invitation to you."

Barrère was attired in his finest ambassadorial garb. A black tunic with elaborately-woven gold brocade. Several large medals of achievement were pinned to the coat. And the ensemble was highlighted by a wide and brilliant scarlet sash that draped across his body from his left shoulder to the right side of his waist.

With his wide mustache and smartly cropped beard in the style of Henri IV, the first Bourbon monarch of France, Barrère appeared to be the epitome of French nobility—at least until Philip remembered that the ambassador was no aristocrat. In fact, he was the son of a school teacher who spent his youth in exile in London because of his father's subversive democratic leanings. He was also a leftist participant in the Paris Commune uprising of 1871, and that sent him back to London in exile from France for another seven years.

"Well, I thank you sincerely for your graciousness in inviting me," Philip said. "I know I'll never forget this night."

"Excellent, Professor. But now I must excuse myself. I'm looking for Théo. He's somewhere around here. When I leave, you will not be alone for long. There are others here who wish to meet you to express their gratitude for your investigatory brilliance. I'm sure they'll find you. Enjoy yourself, my young friend."

Indeed, as the diplomatic reception continued many men and women did come up to Philip to introduce themselves and express their thanks. Most were secretaries and Archives employees working behind the scenes at the grand reception. A few were ranking civil servants from deep inside the Ministry's bureaucracy. Also thanking him were two French ambassadors, the brothers Paul and Jules Cambon who represented France in Great Britain and Germany, respectively.

Philip enjoyed speaking with all of them. But he was particularly interested in what Jules Cambon had to say about the time he spent in Washington, D.C. as ambassador to the United States. That was sixteen years ago, but he vividly remembered his tenure there.

Cambon shared with Philip his explanation of why Grover Cleveland was a much better President than William McKinley. "As a historian, you should know that McKinley was a weak leader when compared to President Cleveland. I remember back in 1899 when I tried to negotiate an end to your Spanish-American War. I would have rather spoken for Spain to a victorious Napoléon Bonaparte, or for France to Otto von Bismarck, than ask anything of Mr. McKinley," Cambon explained. "Napoléon and Bismarck were masters, and they knew what they wanted. But McKinley was a weak man who was afraid to show his weakness. He was pitiful. He didn't command his government the way Mr. Cleveland did.

"Do you know how McKinley explained his taking of the Philippines from Spain?" Cambon continued. "After defeating the Spanish in 1899, the coward said he dropped to his knees and asked God what he should do. God told him to take the Philippines and uplift, educate, and further Christianize these uncivilized people.

"What cowardice! He would not admit that it was a naked power grab by the United States. Instead, he explained it as a Commandment from Heaven. Balderdash!

"What did he mean? God did not want Spain to educate and civilize the Filipino people? God wanted the Americans to do it? No, McKinley was afraid to be honest and explain that Washington planned to enter into the imperialistic race for colonies, and stealing Spanish holdings was a major move in that direction. Instead, he blamed the Almighty and insinuated that the United States was simply fulfilling a divine commandment."

Unfortunately for Philip, his lesson from Jules Cambon ended when the waiters began wandering through the foyer striking their chimes to signal the beginning of dinner. Conversations abruptly ended and people began crowding into the dining room. He and Ambassador Cambon parted company before he could ask questions about the two Presidents.

As gracious as the Quai d'Orsay had been to him, Philip knew he would not be sitting at the front tables. These prime spots were reserved for state officials of the highest levels. When he eventually located his assigned table and chair, he found himself among an array of *chargées d'affaires* and lesser officials from foreign embassies. Specifically, Philip was assigned a seat between a nobleman who worked at the German embassy and Countess Maria Ferraro, the young and attractive wife of the septuagenarian financial secretary at the Italian embassy. It was an odd blend of the profane and the beautiful. Freiherr Carl von Keitz was a stuffy nationalist who spent the evening boasting about the recent German military buildup and the necessity for the Fatherland to surpass British naval strength. Madame Ferraro was a lusty woman with a loud laugh and a flirtatious personality. For most of the meal Philip alternated between resistance to German military braggadocio and expressions of Italian sexual titillation.

At one point during dinner, beneath the table the beautiful Countess actually rubbed her leg against Philip as she asked him what would make him happiest during his visit to Paris. Calling upon a hidden reserve of tact, Philip deflected the advance while staying friendly and conversant. As for her elderly overweight husband, Count Ferraro seemed to bury his embarrassment in liquor and an excess of food.

Von Keitz was a different problem. After a few glasses of champagne, his tongue was loosened and he became decidedly undiplomatic. His anti-French bias became more pronounced, even obnoxious. For instance, when Philip mentioned in passing that he knew and admired Camille Barrère, the German declared, "I don't like him at all. He is a liar and a nasty man. And he hates Germany."

When Philip brought up the necessity of France to be strong as a counter to the power of her enemies, von Keitz angrily argued that Germany was the real victim. "These French have been abusing us for centuries. For many years, they used to pillage and destroy our people at will. They fought their foreign wars on our soil. But this is a new day. Germany will no longer provide the battleground for Great Power hostilities. We will no longer tolerate French arrogance."

Across the table the other guests did not recognize Philip's quandary. A Rumanian embassy official was too busy conversing with Turkish and Austro-Hungarian counterparts about the future of the Balkan Peninsula and the squabbling ethnic populations living there. When he wasn't gorging himself with multiple helpings of food, the Count was speaking to a Spanish financier about recent Italian trade statistics. Such arcane discussions guaranteed that no one was eavesdropping on Philip's conversations.

Meanwhile, Countess Ferraro kept up a steady barrage of romantic innuendoes and physical touching. Philip was becoming frustrated. He had to act soberly and dignified. After all, he was a guest of the French government and couldn't be rude. On the other hand, he dared not surrender to the woman's seduction. It was a difficult challenge, but one which he had to resist.

As for the German and his rant against France, Philip finally returned fire. "Let's face it, Herr von Keitz," he said, "Germany seems intent upon dominating the continent. Your economic prowess is unparalleled. Your naval expansion is recent and impressive.

"Germany has even been aggressive in colonial matters. In fact, you almost started a war in 1905 when your Kaiser Wilhelm inserted himself in France's plans to acquire Morocco. In recent years, your continental buildup has forced France to augment its land and sea power and extend its term of conscripted service. The British naval program has had to expand to counter your buildup. No one here wants conflict, but your policies are forcing France and the Entente powers to consider the possibility that Berlin is preparing to fight soon.

"To this add your alliance with Austro-Hungary, the most repressive nation on the continent," Philip continued. "In this age of nation-states, consider the nations Austria-Hungary is suppressing. Besides Germans and Hungarians, there are Czechs, Poles, Ukrainians, Serbs, Rumanians, Croats, Slovaks, Italians, and Slovenes. And there are probably others. When will this explode? Are you waiting for the old Emperor Franz Joseph to die before there is political change in Vienna?

"I read of a prominent Serbian official who suggested that Austria-Hungary, the Dual Monarchy, was not a Fatherland. Instead, he called it a prison of numerous nationalities all plotting to escape," Philip asserted. "And a historian I respect argued not long ago that your principal ally remains a shapeless and almost accidental collection of pieces rather than an organized and vital whole. He called Austria-Hungary an amorphous mass of Hapsburg family possessions.

"The Dual Monarchy is from another century, sir. But it's certainly not of the 20th century. The 16th century would be more accurate. It must be reformed, Herr von Keitz, before it's blown apart in bloody revolution. Only Germany can force such reform on its ally in Vienna."

Von Keitz became so frustrated he actually excused himself and left the table. For his part, Philip felt embarrassed that his anger led him to be so blunt. Still, as a scholar and an American citizen, he had to speak his mind when he encountered such assertive ignorance and blind bias.

"Oh, let him go," whispered the cooing Countess. "Talk to me. We have so much to speak about, and so much to share."

Fortunately, dinner was ending, and President Poincaré was on the dais lauding the guest of honor, Ambassador Herrick. This official ceremony allowed Philip to turn his attention from the libidinous Italian beauty and focus on Herrick and his well-wishers.

After dessert and coffee, the celebration was concluded with a performance of the *Star Spangled Banner* followed by the French national anthem. The attendees then rose and began leaving their tables and the Élysée Palace.

Philip was but one of the many who flooded out into the June night looking for chauffeurs and automobiles. It had been an exhilarating event, something he never dreamed of attending. Still, he was remorseful about his intemperate outburst against the boorish German bureaucrat. But it happened, and he was convinced that his assessment of contemporary European politics was accurate.

Heading home across Paris at night, Philip gazed at the beauty of the city. An array of lights illuminated the magnificent architecture and public art that the French had decided to live amongst. This was the height of civilization in the early 20th century. This was refined civic life. But he knew that Paris was not alone, and France was not unique. Berlin and London, Vienna and Rome, Florence, St. Petersburg, Athens, Belgrade, Stockholm, Warsaw, Madrid and Barcelona: Europe was filled with massive, glorious centers of organized living. No cowboy towns here, these were substantial and historically rich centers of human accomplishment.

Quite possibly Philip was more than a Francophile, he was a cosmopolite whose appreciation of Western society transcended parochial nationalism and embraced a wider continental perspective. As an educated man he loved the refinement and intellectuality that built and maintained a city like Paris. But as a historian he understood that civility was everywhere people came together to live and work and enjoy the commonweal. He knew, too, that creativity, the driving force of culture, was found in every nation and every great city.

4

It was Monday morning and that meant it was time for Philip's scheduled visit to Professor Alain Laroche's seminar at the Sorbonne. Philip was still tired, however, from his remarkable evening at the Élysée Palace. He got little relaxation on Sunday because he spent most of the day explaining details to curious friends, acquaintances, and even to inquisitive people he didn't know. On his way to the Sorbonne he was able return his rented tuxedo where even the tailor asked for details about the Élysée festivities.

As he walked up the Boul-Miche toward the university, he began to think about the seminar and its focus on nationalism. Philip was familiar with the conversational style of most academic seminars, so he wondered what role he was to play. He had not prepared specific comments, and Laroche had not made it clear exactly what was expected of him. But, he was a historian, and nationalism was part of his area of expertise. So, Philip decided, if he were asked questions or called upon to contribute ideas, he would handle everything as well as possible.

It was 9:30, the warm morning sun was invigorating, and the boulevard was crowded. Philip's attention was drawn to large groups of people surrounding the newspaper kiosks that stood at various points along the boulevard. Crowds of people were reading the headlines from an array of morning journals.

Philip twisted through the readers to see what was so interesting. In thick black letters all the papers were reporting one thing: the Austrian Archduke Franz Ferdinand and his wife, Sophia, had been assassinated yesterday in Sarajevo. Philip was able to buy one of the last issues of *Le Matin* to read as he hurried to class.

The story was gruesome. The archduke and his wife had apparently been shot dead by a young Serbian nationalist named Gavrilo Princip who was captured immediately after the murders. Franz Ferdinand was heir apparent to the throne of the sprawling Austro-Hungarian Empire. He and his spouse had been visiting the capital of Austrian-annexed Bosnia to review troops loyal to the Emperor.

The assassin's motive was apparently political. Still bitter about the Austrian annexation of the provinces of Bosnia and Herzegovina six years earlier, Princip hoped the killings would embolden Serbia to seize the two provinces in the name of Slavic nationalism and the creation of an inclusive South Slav state. According to the published reports, there were substantial indications that Serbian police officials in Belgrade assisted in planning the assassinations.

Philip understood immediately that this murderous event was significant. In a peaceful Europe it would have been a royal tragedy. But nowadays, in a continent woven together by international rivalries, intersecting alliances, unknown military obligations, and generalized fear, who could say what the killings might precipitate?

He was early in arriving at the seminar room, but the Professor was already discussing the assassinations with his students. And they were noticeably agitated. He nodded toward Philip then stopped the discussion to recognize his guest from America. Philip stood up after being introduced and acknowledged the light applause from the dozen students in attendance.

"Professor Belmont," Laroche said, "yesterday's developments in Sarajevo blend constructively with the focus of today's meeting. Our scheduled topic is nationalism: its roots, its history, its future. And, as you have already seen, the young minds in this seminar are deeply engaged in the subject. The assassination of the archduke yesterday has everyone in France, and probably everyone in Europe, searching for meaning. Would you care to share your interpretation of the event and its possible consequences?"

Philip responded as calmly as possible. He explained to the class that most likely nothing will happen, but that anything was possible given the tenuous nature of peace in Europe. "We live in Europe, but we have little understanding of the complexities within the political relationships keeping our lives peaceful," he asserted. "What arrangements lay buried in the Entente Cordiale between France and Great Britain? Are there intricacies we should know? And if we were told the details, are you sure we would know all of them?

"What is true for Anglo-French relations is even more valid for those arrangements between Germany and Austria-Hungary where the free flow of information is even more stunted," he said. "What do the Central Powers owe to each other? Can we ever learn the truth?

"And what is the true nature of the relationship between democratic France and Britain and decadent, autocratic Russia? What unreported obligations brought these unlikely bedfellows together? Then there is Italy: a friend of France, but an ally of Berlin and Vienna. Where do Italy's interests lie? What are her moral and military obligations to each side?"

A student interrupted Philip's discourse with a question. "Tell me, sir, do you think war is possible in a continent of workers? Doesn't socialist brotherhood transcend nationalism? If all workers refused to fight their brothers from other countries, wouldn't this invalidate treaties and secret alliances and put an end to war?"

Philip pondered the query for a moment. "I think you're asking the wrong question. Working class brotherhood is not at issue here. The real question is whether or not there is a boiling point at which the romance of nationalism—and make no mistake, nationalism is an emotional commitment—shuts down our willingness to reason. Have we reached that point yet? And if not, how much farther must we travel until we pass this point of no return?"

"What do you mean that nationalism is an emotional question?" asked the only female student in the seminar. "Are you saying that my French nationalism is similar to the love I feel toward my husband?"

"I'm saying exactly that," Philip replied forcefully. "The Western mind is divided between romance and reason: one is impulsive, needing no verification, no tangible evidence. Hate, love, fear, anger, faith and belief: these are romantic realities.

"The other part of the Western mind is logical, even mathematical. It demands accurate, verifiable substantiation with which to make decisions. The purest form of logic is mathematics—mathematics which is precise and able to be reproduced, every time reaching the same conclusion. Two plus two will always be four, and it's provable no matter what language you speak, no matter what your heart or your temper tells you.

"Romantic attitudes are emotional. When they're directed toward a political state, they sometimes attribute certain unprovable characteristics to race or ethnicity. In recent years we've encountered the politics of Pan Anglo-Saxonism and Slavophile notions of ethnic superiority. Why would British or Russian people conclude their nationality was superior to all others? The answer is that they *believe* it true, but they can't *prove* it.

"That's the crux: belief. In earlier centuries the Church was the focal point of belief. People committed their lives to Christianity's message which was romantic, not rational, because like love the spiritual message could never be proven. People were convinced that Christian faith was Divine Truth. They willingly made that 'leap of faith' by which they committed themselves to its interpretation of life and social responsibility even without solid proof.

"Over the past several centuries, however, the Church's appeal has diminished. The Church even exploded in a civil war—that's what the Reformation was about. Catholic versus Protestant, Pope versus Princes: this was a Christian civil war. And it weakened the Church at exactly the time the modern nation-state and science began to emerge as rivals to religious dominion.

"Faith has not perished, but it doesn't have the sway it once held. Where leaders once trembled at the power of the Church, today many nations have their own Christian churches—think Sweden, Russia, Great Britain—which are influenced by the State.

"In the political world people began to shift their emotional attachment from the religion of the *Bible* to a secularized worship of the State. And they often used the old religious model as an organizing principle. They wrote hymns to the State, songs we call national anthems. They observed secular holy days in the history of their State; one of yours is Bastille Day on July 14; in my country it's July 4. In the military, many have given their lives to protect the interests of the state just as a man might kill or die to defend his home and family or his God.

"And let's not forget that nation-states have sacred documents that are now enshrined in hallowed temples. In the United States, for example, original copies of our Constitution and Declaration of Independence are encased in Washington D.C. Members of the public come solemnly to witness these 'holy texts' and gain renewed commitment to the political arrangement they love and even worship."

"More than thirty-five years ago the British musical team of Gilbert and Sullivan introduced their wonderful operetta called *H.M.S. Pinafore*. One of the songs in the production was a spoof of nationalism and its emotional appeal. The question confronting us today is whether the intensity of nationalism in the next weeks will triumph over the cynical truth in those lyrics: I quote those delicious words from memory:

> He is an Englishman!
> For he himself has said it,
> And it's greatly to his credit,
> That he is an Englishman!
> For he might have been a Roosian,
> A French, or Turk, or Proosian.
> Or perhaps Ital-i-an.
> But in spite of all temptations
> To belong to other nations,
> He remains an Englishman.

The students laughed, but they were not convinced. One young man stood up and declared his loyalty to France. "The Boches would not dare to attack France. We are strong and we have powerful allies," he said. "It would be a disaster for the Germans, even if they brought the Italians and Austrians with them. They would be vanquished in less than four months. *Vive la France!*" Most of the students were in agreement with the sentiment.

Philip tried not to be pessimistic in his reply. "Let me tell you. Deciding to go to war is like jumping on a streetcar. There are so many situations that can spark hostilities; they come and go like metaphoric streetcars. It may be the murder of an heir apparent, or the rude treatment of a high official, the failure to pay a debt, or a military standoff in a foreign colony.

"A nation-state can let the streetcar go by, ignoring it and settling the divisive issue through rational diplomacy. Or, it can board the vehicle, call the international problem unsolvable, and roll off to war in search of resolution. But here's the problem," Philip warned, "when you jump on, it's difficult to get off; and you can never know exactly where the streetcar will take you."

"The Morocco crises in 1905 and in 1911 were streetcars that the Great Powers allowed to pass by. Two recent Balkan Wars were streetcars—again, no one got aboard and headed off to war. Well, here in the summer of 1914 there's another streetcar passing through the European capitals. Will the Archduke's murder be another Moroccan Crisis? Or will one or more of the Great Powers leap aboard this time and ride it toward an unknown destination?"

Another student, this time with a strong German accent, took issue. "You are implying that they are contemplating war in Berlin right now. That is nonsense. Germany is a peace-loving nation," he asserted over the noise. "We Germans would never be foolish enough to start a war. But if invaded or threatened, we would wage a *defensive* war! And if we did, our superior technology and well-trained manpower would naturally lead us to inevitable victory. My prediction is that a European war would be over by Christmas."

Such a chauvinistic comment prompted jeers from the others. This was clearly a pro-French group. Even the idealistic socialist who had asked about worker solidarity joined in hailing France and hooting at Germany.

Student emotions intensified as the seminar progressed. Some participants seemed ready to exchange blows. Eventually, Professor Laroche inserted his cooler head to announce that he was cancelling the rest of the today's meeting. He chastised the group. "Hopefully, you will have calmed down by our next meeting," he said sternly. "Intellectual pursuit demands rationality. I see none of that here today. So, go home and come back in one week; and be prepared to act like intellectuals, not spectators at a Roman gladiatorial contest."

Philip was impressed by his colleague's handling of the class. These were, after all, mature students. But, clearly, the tensions of the day and the nature of the subject under discussion created a volatile atmosphere. Had he allowed them mix it up for much longer, Philip feared it might have become a brawl.

Once the room cleared, the two historians retired to a small faculty lounge located within the Sorbonne. They discussed the seminar but gradually drifted to other matters. While they exchanged ideas Philip was pleased that he was in a respectful, collegial discussion held over cups of strong coffee.

"Oh, by the way, Philip, I want to give you a token of my appreciation for coming this morning," announced Professor Laroche. "You didn't get to complete the seminar, but that was not your fault. I liked what you said, and maybe we can do this again in a few weeks. If my students ever calm down.

"Meanwhile," he continued, "here is a small gift, an honorarium to thank you for participating." With that, Laroche handed him a pair of gold-plated cuff links with a sketch of the Sorbonne painted on the inlaid-porcelain center of each link.

Philip was pleased and sincerely thanked his colleague. In fact he needed new cuff links. He considered it a thoughtful and very practical gift.

Shortly after noon, Philip left the university and headed toward the Boulevard Saint-Michel. To his surprise, the entire street was now filled with boisterous young people bearing signs and yelling slogans and insults. Automobile and horse traffic was at an impasse because protesters had erected barricades across the roadway. The demonstrators were also smashing the paving stones into small pieces. They stored these fragments behind the makeshift barriers, apparently to be used as ammunition in case the police came at them.

The crowd seemed at mixed purposes. Some carried placards calling for the dissolution of the Austro-Hungarian Empire; others praised Serbia, Russia, and France. The most prominent signs proclaimed in the name of Young Bosnia that Bosnia and Herzegovina must become part of Serbia, and that Serbia should unite all Slavic peoples in the Balkans and create a nation state of South Slavs.

Some protesters chanted that Germany was behind the assassination in Sarajevo; that Kaiser Wilhelm wanted war but the Entente would crush any foreign aggression. Philip did notice a few socialistic reminders of class unity, but this handful of protesters had little influence on was happening along the street.

He stood and watched for a while, transfixed by the image of the barricades, those ad hoc street fortifications that French protesters had been erecting through more than a century of social upheavals. Constructed of wood and covered with tarpaulins, carpets, and anything else that was portable, the typical barricade stood about four or five feet high and appeared to be more inconvenient than impenetrable to the attacking police and military forces.

Farther down the Boul-Miche a large contingent of riot police milled about while awaiting orders. These were members of the *Gendarmerie*, the feared riot control specialists that operated under French military command. At this point they appeared content just to make their presence known to the protesters and to those who crowded the sidewalks watching this spontaneous civic drama unfold.

The situation was calm for about a half-hour. But Philip sensed restiveness among the activists. Eventually, a few small fires broke out behind the barricades, and several people started to throw rocks and debris in the direction of the police. Nothing struck the policemen, but these antics were provoking interest among the *flics*, the cops who were experienced at crushing such street demonstrations. Slowly, they began to form into smaller tactical units. Philip recognized that the authorities were preparing to launch these battle groups against the rock throwers and those huddled behind the barricades.

Just as he anticipated, several more fires and an increase in stone-throwing spurred the *Gendarmes* to action. A large number of police ran up the boulevard toward the trouble makers. A few of them turned onto side streets. The rest continued straight toward the barricades.

It was a frightening scene. The police wore black uniforms with protective helmets and face guards. They also carried round shields in one hand and wooden batons in the other. In Philip's historical imagination, they resembled Viking warriors pillaging Paris in the Dark Ages, smashing popular resistance with brutal force, crushing everything in their way. No police officer carried a sword or a spear, but the truncheons they swung were capable of crushing bones and smashing skulls.

Onlookers and protesters scattered in all directions. Philip stepped back against a shop window to avoid the police racing toward the uprising. He didn't want to be swept into this political confrontation.

Just when Philip was feeling lucky to have avoided the assault by the police, two large men in menacing uniforms stopped him. They asked to see the palms of his hands, obviously to learn if he had been heaving paving stones. His hands were clean, but the *flics* still dragged him away to a waiting van. They ignored his loud protestations. Indelicately, the police shoved Philip into the vehicle and sped off.

He was both irate and terrified, alternating between screaming at the driver through a small window at the back of the van and sitting with his head in his hands lamenting his situation. He didn't even have a fellow arrestee with whom to share his agony. He was alone in a paddy-wagon heading directly for jail.

Philip had never felt so depressed in his life.

The motor trip took about fifteen minutes. When the van finally stopped the door was opened and he was taken down a long tunnel with the arresting officers holding him tightly under the arms. Eventually, they pushed him into a small room and ordered him to wait quietly.

Several minutes later Philip was taken upstairs by a guard who placed him in another nondescript room where he sat until the door opened and two men entered. One heavy-set man was unfamiliar. But he knew the other, shorter person. It was Théophile Delcassé, the former Minister of Foreign Affairs whom he had met and spoke with several days earlier.

"Profound apologies, Professor Belmont," Delcassé said with sincerity. "I am very sorry you were so roughly treated. But we had to make it look like an actual arrest. We had to be forceful—but not too forceful, I hope."

Philip was totally confused.

"You see, Professor," Delcassé continued, "we need you desperately for a special task that must remain secret. That is why no one can know that this meeting took place. As far as Paris is concerned, you were arrested as a rioter and will be sent to jail somewhere in France.

"Oh, excuse me, Professor. Allow me introduce you to my colleague," said Delcassé. "May I present General Joseph Joffre, Chief of the General Staff of the Army of France. Although I have no governmental portfolio, I've been working with the General during these crucial days."

Philip was stunned. The famous Mr. Delcassé was impressive enough, but to arrive with the famous General Joffre was unbelievable. Philip's physical pain and psychological distress quickly evaporated. His mind now was racing to comprehend what was happening.

General Joffre spoke first. "Professor Belmont, you may be startled to know that we've been watching you closely for some time now. We conducted extensive background searches through the American embassy in Paris, and in Washington through the Department of State and Department of War. We are extremely impressed by what we have learned about you—including your distinguished academic accomplishment in the United States and the character you exhibited in returning the stolen items you found in the *Archives Diplomatiques*."

"And, by the way, we were also struck by the delicacy with which you resisted the overtures of Countess Ferraro," added Delcassé facetiously. "She is a notorious flirt—at least a flirt. We call her *la plus jolie de la corps diplomatique*, because she is truly the prettiest one in the diplomatic corps. And we are always diplomatic in our use of language. You understand, *non?*"

General Joffre returned to his discourse. "We now have great need of your service, Professor. Time is crucial for France. On such a short notice, only you can do what we need."

"You see, Professor Belmont, as strange as it may seem, you are now indispensable to the fate of France," Delcassé added. "I cannot tell you about the special project unless you agree to accept it. So, you must accept it blindly. But you must trust us as we are willing to trust you. It will be extremely dangerous, and no one can ever know of your work.

"France is placing her faith in the three people now in this room. If a thief can pilfer wallets from under our noses, no one in the Ministry can be completely above suspicion. And with spies and other enemy agents targeting the Army General Staff as well as our ambassadors and foreign operatives, General Joffre can't entrust anyone in his command with information so sensitive.

"But time is of the essence. You, Professor Belmont, are our only possibility for this mission."

Espionage was not Philip's calling. But with Delcassé and Joffre insisting on unwavering acceptance, he yielded. "When do I start?" he conceded. "But first, what do you expect me to do?"

"That's wonderful Professor," Delcassé responded. "We shall never forget you, although no history book will ever record your story. But, I'll let General Joffre explain the details since the project involves his military expertise."

"Professor, what I am about to tell you is the utmost of Top Secret," the General began. "Divulging it could get you killed; carrying it out will get you our private thanks but little more. However, though the people of France will never know what you are about to undertake, their lives depend upon your success."

Philip's curiosity was ready to explode. "Please, General, I will do it, whatever it entails. Please explain what you wish me to do."

Joffre took a deep breath before responding. What he then told Philip astonished the young American. "You see, we think the assassination yesterday may lead to something much more disruptive throughout Europe. Théo and I are afraid that the Austrians will react rashly to the murders. The imperial court in Vienna never liked the archduke, especially when he married someone who wasn't royal enough for the old Kaiser Franz Joseph.

"But the Hapsburgs dislike having their relatives murdered by scruffy young Serbian nationalists, especially in territories controlled by the Austrian police and military. Delcassé and I agree in thinking that Austria-Hungary may try to invade the southern Slavic areas of the Balkan Peninsula very soon. If that happens, the secret agreements buried in the Triple Alliance will probably be set in motion, and before you know it, the continent might well be plunged into open warfare. I pray that I'm wrong. But Théo and I concur that it's possible, even probable."

General Joffre continued his explanation. "Several weeks ago through Ambassador Jules Cambon's military attaché in Berlin, we came into possession of a supremely secret German document. The Boches would kill to keep it from our eyes. In a nutshell, we have a copy of a secret military scheme they call the Schlieffen Plan. It was drafted in late 1905 by the head of the German General Staff, General Alfred von Schlieffen. We have the original Plan, plus important modifications made by his successor at the General Staff, General Helmuth von Moltke."

"That sounds intriguing," Philip remarked, "but what is the Schlieffen Plan?"

"Oh, forgive me, Dr. Belmont," General Joffre answered. "In 1905 German military leaders devised a strategy for the European war they saw coming. They envisioned Germany locked in a two-front war against France and our ally Russia. To the Germans, the principal enemy would be Imperial Russia with its millions and millions of conscripts—the largest land army in Europe. But because France was militarily tied to Russia, the Plan calculated that Germany needed to launch a quick preemptive invasion of France that would knock us out of any war before the cumbersome Russians could fully mobilize. With France eliminated," he continued, "the Germans could concentrate on waging war against Russia.

"A year later the Schlieffen Plan was slightly modified a by the new Chief of the General Staff, General von Moltke. It now calls for German troops to launch their preemptive war against us by marching through neutral Luxembourg and Belgium and entering France through our northern border."

Delcassé interrupted Joffre. "The Schlieffen Plan is a frightening strategy," he explained. "But there is one vulnerability in the German scheme. We can stop a Boche onslaught in northern France, but to do that we must be absolutely certain that Italy will not honor its alliance commitments to Germany and Austria-Hungary. We must convince leaders in Rome that the Germans are deceitful allies.

"We figure the best way to accomplish this is to show the actual Schlieffen Plan to the highest levels of the Italian state," added Joffre. "Let them see the catastrophe Berlin is plotting. Italy is committed to assist Germany only in a defensive war. The Schlieffen Plan shows that the Germans are planning a war of aggression."

"Wait. What is aggression?" Delcassé interjected. "It's a matter of semantics in Berlin. The Germans will argue to Rome that we French provoked war by rebuilding our military, by creating the Triple Entente, by forcing Germany to defend itself by attacking France first.

"The leadership in Italy must see that this is a lie. They must read the Schlieffen Plan to see the cold calculation, the decade of premeditation in German preparations for war."

"We need you, Professor, to carry the actual document to Camille Barrère, our ambassador in Rome," Joffre asserted. "He must have this Plan to make his final appeal for Italian neutrality. If we can pull thousands of troops from our Alpine borders with Italy, they can help us stop the invaders in our northern sectors. Without these troops, I cannot guarantee victory. And France may be lost forever.

"Only recently we worked out an arrangement guaranteeing the neutrality of Spain on our southwestern border," Delcassé inserted. "Now, we need to get Rome's cooperation sewn up. And you will be our secret courier to accomplish this.

"No one will suspect a college professor from a neutral country. We have train tickets for you to leave for Italy within the hour. You will not return to your residence, you will not be able to pack a handbag. And you will not tell anyone what you're doing until Camille greets you at the Palais Farnese, our embassy in Rome.

"We have brought new clothing and other supplies for you. The tailor who rented the tuxedo to you provided your proper sizes. Everything is packed in a suitcase that we'll give you when you leave here. You must get this document to Barrère."

Joffre offered specifics about the mission. "We'll take care of your Paris apartment. One of our agents will visit the concierge at the Two Swans Hotel with a letter you will write on the way to the station. It will explain your decision to move to Bordeaux indefinitely for research purposes. The agent will collect all of your belongings and transport them to the Paris apartment we are leasing for you at the Hôtel de Crillon which is on the Place de la Concorde. You will stay there when you return from this assignment. No enemy agent will ever think to look for a university professor living at one of the most expensive hotels in Paris.

"Oh, one more thing," commented Delcassé. "You will be carrying this large envelope containing the printed version of the Schlieffen Plan. But we have edited it somewhat. If someone discovers your purpose and takes the document from you, there is nothing to be gained. The copy you will deliver to Barrère is on microfilm, a new process of photographic reduction our scientists have been quietly perfecting. The Plan has been photographed and the negative reduced to a miniscule size. It can be enlarged and printed in our embassy once you deliver it.

"Here is the microfilm," Delcassé said as he handed the treasure to Philip. "We have hollowed out a French centime and placed the film inside. Looks like a worthless coin, doesn't it? But it actually contains the future of France. We don't want to know how or where you hide it. Only you will know that. But Camille must receive what is inside that coin.

"He is waiting for you at the Farnese Palace. You'll have no problem finding the place. When you get to Rome, just ask anyone for directions. And when you reach the embassy, if you still have this printed version, you may burn it in the old coal stove they have in the kitchen. It should make enough heat for the chef to prepare a delicious *steak au poivre* dinner for you."

Philip smiled at the thought.

"Oh, by the way, here's an envelope containing 4000 French francs," said General Joffre pulling the cash from his tunic pocket. "It's more than you'll need, but it may prove useful. And remember, trust no one. Go as fast as you can and deliver the microfilm to Ambassador Barrère, personally."

"Our fate is now in your hands," added the former Foreign Minister. "May God go with you, my friend."

Philip took the hollow centime and the suitcase, then shook hands with the two French leaders and departed.

The Ministry automobile left the Paris jail with an important person sitting in the backseat. It was Philip Belmont, now a French agent with a monumental assignment. He had voluntarily accepted the task before him, but he had no idea of what he was getting into.

There was no talking inside the car as it headed toward the Gare de Lyon, the train station from which all trains departed Paris for destinations to the south. The driver stopped, however, not at the Gare but at the Métro station at Châtelet.

"For safety purposes, we don't want you to be seen exiting a government automobile at the railroad station, so we're dropping you here," said the driver. "Just take the Métro to the stop for the Gare de Lyon. That way you'll look like anyone else on the way to catch a train."

As he stepped from the vehicle with his valise in hand, Philip handed him the note he had just written informing Madame DuBois of his hasty departure for Bordeaux. It was beginning to dawn on Philip that this might be a treacherous assignment. He was sure the Quai d'Orsay was careful in arranging the task. But he was now wondering if government security was adequate or even trustworthy.

On the Métro headed for the railroad station he grew increasingly worried. Was there someone sinister following him? Had the Ministry secretly assigned a bodyguard to protect him? What were the dangers facing him? Would he be alone in facing them or were there French security agents in the shadows willing to risk their lives to keep him from harm?

He scanned the passengers and became suspicious of a few. One man seemed to be looking at him too directly. A woman with a large shopping bag was conspicuously eyeing him. Did she have a pistol in the bag? Another man was overdressed for the warm weather. Maybe he had a weapon hidden beneath his long coat. Philip was used to Métro travel where passengers sat motionless and stared blankly into space, avoiding eye contact or any sign of familiarity—except, of course, the ever-present young lovers who seemed always to be kissing and gazing romantically at each other. But on this short ride to the Gare de Lyon too many people seemed to be watching his every move, and that was unsettling.

The pressure intensified as the Métro approached his stop. Hôtel de Ville, St-Paul, Place de la Bastille: the stops came and went. His was next. Philip had to be careful that his mounting insecurity didn't cause him to stand out as someone different.

When the subway came to a halt he joined the herd of people pouring out the cars and heading toward the trains. Everyone seemed to have at least one piece of luggage. Some travelers wrapped their valises with cords to keep bulging contents from falling out. Others packed their belongings in large sacks, then wrapped them in bed sheets and secured everything with wires or ropes. Philip thought it was clever that the Quai d'Orsay had placed his clothing in a well-used suitcase. Its scuffed condition gave the impression of frequent train travel and abuse.

The Gare de Lyon was a massive building filled with hundreds of people in a hurry. Schedules posted on large boards listed departure times for local trains servicing nearby cities as well as the grand-lines with destinations in central and southern France and foreign countries. On the floor, it was a madhouse of people streaming in all directions. The only stillness in the station was in the long queues of people standing patiently in front of ticket windows. At the head of each such line overworked ticket agents frantically accepted cash and distributed train tickets.

Fortunately for Philip, he was already booked for a First Class seat and a sleeping space in the wagon-lit, the sleeping car. He had a lengthy trip ahead of him. It was 500 miles just to get to Turin in northwestern

Italy, and that would take almost seventeen hours on the Rome Express. From there he would have to transfer to an Italian train for another 325 miles to Rome.

As he perused the rail schedule looking for his departure platform, Philip continued to worry that he might be followed. He was suspicious now of the man standing in the corner looking in his direction. He wondered if the person who walked into the station behind him wasn't somewhere in the crowd scrutinizing his every move. He was certain that people throughout the Gare were looking for him.

His fear eventually overtook him. He decided that since he was the operative on this harrowing mission, and it was his life at stake, he would modify the journey to Rome to his own liking. To throw off his perceived followers, he made up his mind to take a different train. He would go directly south to coastal Marseilles, then turn east and enter Italy at Ventimiglia on the Italian Riviera. He felt it would be safer for him if no one knew his route.

He was scheduled to depart at 7 pm on the direct Rome Express. But the Côte d'Azur Express, a First Class-only Train de Luxe from Paris to Marseilles was leaving ten minutes later. He quickly entered the queue to purchase a ticket for the later train with a connection to Ventimiglia and Rome. Fortunately, there were few people standing in front of him.

As he moved steadily toward the ticket agent he couldn't help but overhear a nervous man talking in the line next to his. As Philip understood the conversation, the man was Italian in his late thirties and apparently traveling alone. What Philip could see was a man in great anguish. He was explaining to a ticket agent that he did not have enough money to afford passage on the Rome Express, not even a Third Class seat.

Philip was not fluent in Italian, and the man kept jumping from Italian to French and back to Italian as he mumbled aloud. But from what Philip could understand, the man needed to be in Rome as rapidly as possible. It had something to do about the declining health of his mother. When the ticket vendor refused to sell him a seat at a discounted price, the disappointed man left the line weeping.

Philip turned his attention to his own problem as an agent called him to the reservations window. He kept the prepaid Rome Express ticket since it would make those hunting him think that he had boarded the original train. But now he paid cash for the Côte d'Azur Express with sleeping car accommodations. As he left the agent he felt a bit more confident that this switch would send his pursuers, wherever they were, in the wrong direction.

Walking toward the platform for his departure on the Paris-Lyon-Méditerranée Railway, he was approached by the man who had been in tears a few minutes ago. "Monsieur, can you please help me. A few francs would allow me to buy passage to Rome. My mother is dying and I must be there as fast as possible. Please, anything would help."

Philip started to turn away, but then had an idea. "I'll do you better than a few francs, monsieur," he said. "How would you like a fully-paid First Class ticket on the Rome Express with a bunk in the wagon-lit? It departs the Gare de Lyon at 7 o'clock and arrives in Rome at the Statzione Termini tomorrow evening."

"Please, don't tease me. I'm upset enough without being mocked," the desperate Italian replied.

"This is not mocking. I'm very serious," responded Philip. "I have an extra ticket, and you may have it. See, First Class seat, sleeping car space. You may have it if you wish," he said as he handed the ticket to the surprised man.

After glancing at the actual document, the stranger embraced Philip and kissed him twice on both cheeks. "Monsieur, whoever you are, you are an angel. God must have sent you. I'm sure that after this miracle, my mother will fully recover. I don't know how to thank you. I would name my next son after you, but I don't know your name, and I'm not married."

"Not necessary," Philip explained with a smile on his face. "Have a safe voyage, and I wish your mother improved health."

The two men embraced once more then each went to his respective platform. When he saw the Rome Express leave the station, Philip was sure he had done a good deed. But he was still not safe. What if a spy had seen him change his route? The Italian had been so effusive in his thanks, maybe a would-be assassin recognized that Philip had switched trains.

Boarding his assigned passenger car, Philip found his seat in a compartment with windowed doors and padded seats. The room accommodated six passengers with three sitting spaces on one side facing three others. But the seats were comfortable and wide. And the room was off limits to smokers. His place was next to the outside window and facing south the direction the locomotive would be headed. This allowed him to gaze through the window at the French countryside in complete darkness, and to avoid the vertigo he always developed when riding backwards in a train.

In the next few minutes his traveling companions filed in. An elderly French couple, two Frenchmen who appeared to be salesmen, and a matronly woman who appeared to speak only Spanish: nothing too threatening there, Philip concluded. But he was still not confident, even as the Côte d'Azur Express left on schedule.

About thirty minutes outside of Paris, stomach pains reminded him that he hadn't eaten since breakfast. Fortunately, the deluxe train had a restaurant. A menu placed in his compartment advertised a full dinner for six francs. This only made him hungrier.

Philip excused himself and headed back toward the restaurant car.

It was a fairly tasty supper. But Philip was distrustful of the *vin ordinaire*, ordinary table wine, that too often he found to be *très ordinaire*, very ordinary. He gladly paid extra for a half-bottle of the best wine aboard. This was the most relaxed he had felt since leaving Alain Laroche's seminar earlier today. He sat back and enjoyed his comfort.

Eventually, a waiter approached and pleaded that there were many people waiting to dine and that if he were not going to order more food, would he please vacate the table. Courteously, the waiter pointed out that there was a small bar located in the next car should he wish more alcohol.

Instead, Philip elected to return to his assigned seat. He tipped the waiter, but was very careful not to give him the hollowed coin entrusted to him by Delcassé and Joffre.

As he returned to his seat it struck Philip that he had left his valise totally unattended in the room with five strangers. He was not used to being a spy, but he was beginning to react like one. What if they were operatives who stole his suitcase? They wouldn't get much, but it would mean that he was vulnerable.

Happily, when he opened the compartment door he saw that the bag in its proper place. Or was it? He carefully took it down from the rack as his fellow passengers stared at his every move. Earlier he had affixed inconspicuous strands of hair across the top and one side of the case. And as he examined it now, he could see clearly that these hair seals had been disturbed. Someone had opened his luggage.

Somewhat angrily he asked his traveling companions who had disturbed his valise. No one answered. The woman seated across from him muttered something in Spanish, but he didn't understand her. The salesmen looked at him then went back to discussing business. And the older French couple acted as if they hadn't even heard his question.

He stood up, grabbed his belongings, and walked out of the room. He would have to find another place to sit. He was walking toward the *facteur*, the porter, when he heard someone call his name. It was a female voice half-questioning and half-confident in its tone. "Professor Belmont, hello" the caller said. "Is that you?"

When he turned he saw Maria Ferraro waving at him. "This is a coincidence. Isn't it?" said the beguiling wife of the antique Italian embassy official. "We shared dinner at the Presidential palace and then meet on a crowded train heading for the Côte d'Azur," she added provocatively. *"Quelle coincidence!"*

But was it a coincidence? Philip knew that there were monarchist elements in the Italian government, especially in the military, who would love to team with autocratic Germany and Austria-Hungary against republican France. Maybe she was a royalist spy working for German interests. On the other hand, she might just be a lovelorn young woman looking for romance and this meeting was totally unplanned and without political implication.

"Ah, Countess, I didn't expect to see you again so soon. But it's always a pleasure to be with you—even on a night-train to Marseilles," Philip said as gallantly as he could.

She looked at him quizzically. "Why are you carrying your suitcase? Were you about to leave the train when it's going fifty miles an hour?" she inquired. "Come on, let's go to the bar for a cocktail…and, perhaps, even more."

He had little choice but to acquiesce. Following Madame Ferraro, he recalled the words of Delcassé who had called her *la plus jolie de la corps diplomatique*. She was, indeed, very pretty.

Over drinks and a few carefully placed touches and innuendoes, Philip learned that her husband had remained in Paris working on embassy finances while she was traveling to Nice with her parents. They had remained in her compartment when she stepped out to dine.

Thus, she lamented, nothing could really happen between her and Philip until she reached the French Riviera. But if he wished to leave the train in Nice and rent a hotel room for a few days, she would love to have supper with him some evening—or evenings.

Philip expressed a desire to accommodate her, but added that he was on his way to Marseilles on business, and eventually west to Bordeaux to research a newly-released collection of government naval documents. His schedule, he explained, couldn't allow for a layover in Nice no matter how pleasurable it promised to be. Perhaps another time, another city?

The amorous banter continued for a few more minutes until Madame Ferraro dropped her coquettish attitude and spoke frankly. "Look, dear Philip, you are a handsome and fascinating man, so I want to be honest with you. No flirting anymore. I must tell you squarely: you are in very great danger. Your life is at stake.

"Whatever you are doing—and I don't want to know—has made the German government determined to stop you. Berlin has put a price on your head of 500,000 Deutsche marks. And they have notified every crook, spy, and flirt, that you must be captured or killed.

"I don't know what you're up to, but I would be extremely careful. In fact, if I were not with my parents, I might even consider shooting you for the reward," she added, then thought better of it. She leaned over their table and pinched his cheek playfully, adding, "Ah, maybe not until I got to know you a little better, *mon petit chou*."

Philip tried to act nonplussed, but that wasn't easy. After a few more minutes of conversation, he escorted Madame Ferraro back to her family. "Thank you so much for the warning," he said. "I don't know what has upset the authorities in Berlin. There must be some mistake."

"Oh, *cara mia*, Berlin does not make mistakes in such matters," she whispered as they squeezed through the narrow passage way toward her compartment. Abruptly, she stopped and wrapped her arms about him in a passionate embrace. Pressing her body against Philip, she kissed him in the French style. "I will never forgive myself if you are killed," she said breathlessly. "You are such a virile young man. Killing you would be such a great waste. Please come with me to Nice. You will be safe there."

"I would love to follow you," Philip replied, "but I have to meet people in Marseilles, and then travel on to Bordeaux. So, I have to postpone pleasure and surrender to requirement. But when it's all over, I hope we can resume this conversation right where we left off."

She smiled. "Somehow, I don't believe you, you American devil," she remarked.

"Maria, is that you?" loudly came a question from inside her compartment. "If that's you, please come in."

"Damn, that's my father," she said with disappointment. "He and my mother like to keep me on a leash, even though I'm a married woman. Well, maybe it's because I am a married woman.

"Good night, sweet Philip, I'll look for you in the morning." She leaned into his body once more and reintroduced him to the bliss he was sacrificing.

Philip enjoyed the teasing repartee as well as the passion in the train corridor, but he was frightened by the threat against him. He was now fair game for anyone willing to pursue the German prize. He could be killed at any second.

His mind searched for an answer. Maybe changing trains in Paris had failed to deceive his pursuers. Maybe would-be killers were on board right now, just waiting for the opportune moment to strike. And according to the railroad schedule, the Côte d'Azur Express was due to stop in twenty minutes. That could allow even more bounty hunters to come aboard.

He checked his wristwatch. It was exactly 2:30 in the morning and his train was coming to a halt in the Gare de Perrache, the principal railroad station in the French city of Lyon. Philip was scared and time was fleeting. He quickly had to decide what he wanted to do.

Despite the early hour, many passengers with Lyon or Central France as their destination stood patiently, baggage in hand, waiting to depart. As the train rolled to a stop, a restive crowd on the station platform was set to board for the journey southward toward Marseilles and the Mediterranean coast. Both groups were oblivious to the death scenario developing in their midst.

In the few minutes between arrival and departure, Philip and several other passengers took advantage of the chance to leave the train to stretch their legs and otherwise refresh themselves for the remainder of the trip. Some rushed toward food sellers to grab a stale sandwich or a piece of fruit. A few entered station toilets. But most people scurried toward the newspaper stands, anxious to read the latest reports on the political crisis precipitated two days ago in Bosnia.

But Philip had a unique problem. Outside the train, he debated his next move. Were his pursuers still aboard? If so, how many were there? And how could he recognize any of them? On the other hand, were there German operatives or freelance killers waiting for him in the railroad station? Where were they? Who were they?

Philip grew increasingly apprehensive. When the engine whistle sounded, he carefully joined the others and scrambled back. He was among the last passengers to re-board the Express. By his calculation more people got on the train than left it, and that worried him immensely.

Lyon was the largest and most important city in this agricultural region, so it was not unreasonable to expect many travelers would be boarding, even at this early hour. But any of the new travelers could be a potential assassin intent on murdering him for 500,000 marks. For that matter, his potential executioner could be among the continuing passengers who had boarded in Paris or any of the several cities at which the train had stopped before reaching Lyon.

As he entered the coach he looked at the other voyagers. His mind raced for answers. How would he be slain? Stabbed? Shot? Perhaps strangled or poisoned? Maybe someone would just shove him off the speeding train.

Forced by the circumstances, Philip conceived a desperate plan of action. He would jump from the train. Once the Express left the station, but before it was moving too fast, he would throw his suitcase and then himself to the ground and hope for the best. The timing had to be perfect: that precise moment when the train was moving slowly enough that he would not be killed by the fall, but fast enough to make it fatal for a potential murderer to react and follow him off the vehicle. He had no other choice. He felt increasingly certain that he would not survive if he stayed aboard.

After a few more warning bursts from the steam engine the engineer shifted the locomotive into gear. The wheels spun spasmodically in search of traction. A few uncertain lurches followed. Finally, the locomotive gripped the rails and slowly began moving forward.

Because the train was already beyond the station platform, gathering momentum and moving into pitch darkness, there was no way Philip could know what he was about to plunge into. Still, he was determined to jump. He opened the door at the end of his coach and stepped to the bottom stair. The wind blew against him as he waited for what he calculated to be the optimal moment.

First he threw his luggage into the darkness. In quick succession he hurled himself into the same void.

When he hit the ground Philip bounced into the air, then fell heavily on his side and began rolling. The earth was hard and unforgiving, and more than once he winced in pain. He covered his head and face with his forearms, but he could still feel the bumps and scrapes punishing his body. Every part of him was affected as he tumbled over dirt, grass, rocks, and even pieces of lumber abandoned along the track. Fortunately, his momentum carried him away from the iron rails and the wheels of the passenger cars which might have severed limbs or, perhaps, his entire body.

After tumbling down a slight embankment Philip came to an abrupt stop against a large tree trunk. At that moment he thought he heard gunshots whiz past his head. In the darkness he saw no gunman or flash from a weapon, so he couldn't be certain. But hearing unusual sounds flying by his ears suggested that someone was trying to kill him.

Philip lay face down in the dirt. He was in great pain, but he was on solid ground. His neck muscles, his ribs, and his left ankle were especially throbbing as he brushed soil from his hair and torn clothing.

Fortunately, his nose was intact, but his hands and arms were lacerated. He was also spitting out a mixture of blood, dirt, and grass. Alive, but sorely wounded, he rose from the ground and limped forward in search of his battered suitcase.

Valise in hand, Philip staggered back toward the distant station lights. He reckoned that no other passenger would be coming after him, but to be absolutely certain he eased himself into a nearby muddy gulley and stayed concealed for a long time. During the next hour he saw no one emerge from the blackness of the early morning.

While he sat looking for human movement, he wondered how he ended up physically battered and hiding in a filthy ditch in the middle of France. Only two weeks ago he had arrived in Paris as an idealistic and, as he now realized, naïve young university prof. All he wanted to do then was conduct research and come to know life in Paris. And now he was scrambling to save his life.

5

Relieved that no one had emerged from the darkness, Philip finally walked back to the Gare de Perrache. He cleansed his wounds in the public lavatory and assessed the damage: scratches everywhere, bloodied arms and hands, clothing badly torn, dirt covering everything head to foot. He was a mess, but nothing appeared to be broken. He had a change of clothes, thanks to the suitcase packed by the French government. And he was also able to walk with only a slight limp as his ankle pain was subsiding. He was confident that if circumstances required it, he could run fast.

Philip spent the rest of the evening in an auberge near the station. He was injured by the fall, but he was able to shower and fall asleep in peace.

In the morning over breakfast, the professor-now-secret-agent contemplated his position. Here he was in Lyon, more than 300 miles from Paris, but still a long distance from Rome. And he couldn't rely on the railroad anymore. Everyone, he decided, was expecting him to be on a passenger train. He had to deliver the microfilm, but he was trapped.

As he ate his scrambled eggs and buttered baguette, an elderly man entered the hotel restaurant. A man in his mid-sixties, he was a large fellow with a great gray beard and a protruding belly. He was obviously familiar with the waitress and the cook because he joked easily with them, and they laughed and slapped him on the back.

Philip could overhear the conversation that flowed between the three. Apparently, the man was a barge captain on the Rhône River, France's longest and, arguably, most important waterway. And as Philip well knew, it was the only river in France that flowed into the Mediterranean Sea.

An idea took hold.

He approached the man who by now was seated and drinking coffee. "Excuse me, but I'm looking for a quiet river trip to Marseilles. Would it be possible to hire you and your boat to take me there?" he inquired.

The old man looked curiously at Philip. "Please, sit down, monsieur," he said in a friendly voice. "Let me get this straight, you're looking for a pleasure cruise down the Rhône to Marseilles, and you want to hire me and my boat? There are faster ways to get there, my friend. What about the train? The station is not far from here. Or, what about hiring a chauffeur and going by automobile? My barge is slow and you'll soon tire of seeing ancient Roman viaducts and purple fields filled with lavender."

"I know, sir, but I'm not looking for the beauty of the French country. I only want a peaceful journey free of complications. My nerves are on edge, and I need a leisurely journey to sooth my anxieties. Sight-seeing is secondary to me," Philip explained in as guarded a way as possible.

"Well, peaceful it will be. But such a trip will also be expensive. I have to return empty—with no cargo or passengers. So, you'd have to pay for a return voyage," he answered.

"Fine, how much? But first I must tell you, I need to leave now. I can't wait," Philip said.

"What's your hurry, young man? Are you some kind of criminal who's just escaped from prison? On the run, are you?" the boatman asked with concern in his face.

"No, sir, I'm not a criminal. I'm a professor," he said.

The man laughed heartily. "That's funny," he replied. "I've carried you academic types before. But the others always came with lots of books to read and plenty of pens and tablets with which to write down their deep thoughts. But you, by the looks of the blood and bruises on your face and hands, you appear to have been in a terrible fight.

"However, for 1200 francs I will take you south with no questions asked. Unfortunately, I can't take you to Marseilles. This river doesn't flow into Marseilles. But I can float you to the village of St-Louis-du-Rhône. It's a harbor town on the Mediterranean just a little west of your destination."

"It's a deal," said Philip. "I'll let you finish breakfast. In fact, I'll even pay for your breakfast. Let me go upstairs and get ready. I'll be back in a few minutes," he said excitedly.

With Philip out of the room, the old man chuckled, but with a little confusion at the back of his mind. He explained to the waitress that he wasn't sure if this self-described professor was on the level. But he was charging a high price and getting a free breakfast. He would leave for the Mediterranean immediately after his passenger came up with the money.

Philip returned, suitcase in hand. He handed the old man 600 francs for now and promised the balance at the end of the trip. The old man found that acceptable.

The two voyagers then left for the river estuary where the barge was moored. It was a long black vessel powered by a kerosene engine. Because it was flat bottomed, it was not particularly fast. Boats like this were built for transporting heavy loads of agricultural and industrial products, but to accommodate tourism in recent years many alternated between hauling commercial loads and sightseeing visitors.

"Come aboard, Professor," said the captain. "I am Moshe-Daniel Ginsberg, at your service." Philip introduced himself and helped untie the boat from the dock. Soon the boat was floating through Lyon with no sign of danger thus far.

Philip was well aware that he would be terribly late in reaching Rome—if he got there at all. But he had to protect himself and the microfilm at all costs. He had no choice now but to lay back and watch the Midi, the south central section of France, pass slowly by.

The elderly barge operator informed his passenger that the river trip would take about twenty-four hours. Luckily, he had a pantry with enough food for the trip. Once he had passed through Lyon and was well outside the suburbs, the two men fell into a casual discussion about the contemporary political situation.

Ginsberg was an inveterate Bonapartist who felt that only a new Napoléon sitting on an imperial throne would restore French glory and prestige. "We have a colonial empire, so why do we call ourselves a republic. Republics don't work in Europe," he complained. "We need an Emperor to match muscles with Wilhelm and Franz Joseph, the Tsar, and even that flippant Italian youngster, King Victor Emmanuel.

"France doesn't even have a sovereign as mediocre as that old fathead George V in London. He has no power. His parliament runs the British kingdom. But Georgie still calls himself King of England and Emperor of India. *C'est incroyable!* It's unbelievable!

"And who do we have?" he continued. "Citizen Raymond Poincaré, President of our third attempt at making a successful republic. How many republics must France try before we all learn that this form of government doesn't fit the mentality of the French people?"

"Well, you may get your wish, Mr. Ginsberg," said Philip. "If this problem in Sarajevo leads to a wider conflict, you may soon have to learn German to order your breakfast."

Ginsberg dismissed the notion of an impending war. To him the Balkans weren't worth fighting over. "Who wants that infernal region anyway?" he said. "Nothing but mountains and Bosnians, mountains and Albanians—more mountains, and more Montenegrins, Macedonians, Serbians, Turks, Kosovites, Bulgars, Croats, Slovenians, Greeks, Gypsies—even Rumanians and Moldavians. And none of them really gets along with the others. That area is such a small space for such a big mess. You know, these crazy people have fought two separate wars there in the last two years and very little has changed. Bah!

"And what are those damned Austrians doing there anyway?" he continued. "They know the Russians will intervene to keep their Orthodox Christian brothers and sisters from falling into the grasp of the Roman Catholics Huns from Vienna—especially since St. Petersburg sat silently when Austria annexed all those Slavs in Bosnia and Herzegovina a few years ago. Russia will not let that happen again.

"That's why we in France need a new Napoléon to protect our interests and settle matters if they ever come to a boiling point."

This was a political perspective with which Philip was not familiar. But at least it wasn't pro-German, and that gave him some comfort.

Along the way, Ginsberg docked his boat at several small towns. He had his own way of hurrying that included visits to familiar cafés and public houses no matter the time of day or night. Although it increased his exposure to possible attack, Philip used the time at each stop to scan newspapers to catch up on European political developments.

The barge trip was pleasant and uneventful. In fact, Philip was able to nap comfortably inside the boat. He also ate well because Ginsberg had packed tasty provisions. If he had been in the mood for relaxation, this would have been a restful vacation trip. But at the present he felt neither rested nor touristic.

Philip remained on edge, continually watching the riverbanks when he was on deck, listening for outside disturbances when he was below. He didn't expect to see a sharpshooter with a rifle aimed at him, but he still wondered if those were real gunshots he had heard last night when he jumped from the train.

Ginsberg was talkative only in spurts. He was too busy piloting the craft and sipping down bottles of locally-grown Côtes du Rhône wine.

Still, he couldn't resist matching his political wit with that of the professor. "You know that I support the return to another Bonapartist political state, right?" he asked Philip. "It would be the Third Empire, and it would bring us Frenchmen together in a powerful new nationalist arrangement.

"But some of this nationalism stuff is what the British would call piffle," he commented. "Can you imagine dying for your country? That's madness. You die because you are killed by the enemy when he puts a bullet or a sword through you. Only the living call that glory?

"And what about killing for your country? You are raised by your family and the state to know that murder is a crime against God. You kill a man on the street in Lyon, the police arrest you, and the state later executes you or puts you in prison for years. But when it's wartime, the state says you can kill as many of the enemy as you can. No limits on how many you may slay, just kill. And if you murder enough of them, the state will give you medals and promotions.

"This can only be understood as a form of insanity," he ranted.

"Well, it's part of a natural historical progression," Philip responded. "European society has moved in recent times to embrace more and more democracy. Monarchy and Empire are things of the past; their sway is coming to an end. It's acceptable if you have a monarch who's a figurehead like King George in London or Queen Wilhelmina in the Netherlands: on the throne but without substantial political power.

"No one dies for the sovereign any more. Now people die for their nationality or their nation-state. Those Bulgarians and Greeks who perished in the recent Balkan Wars died for their ethnicity, not their respective monarchs."

Philip continued his discourse. "An excellent example is the Ottoman Empire. Today, that once-great Empire is in retreat and Turkish nationalism is rapidly replacing loyalty to the Sultan sitting in Constantinople. Nationality has triumphed over monarchy and even religion as the centralizing force in modern politics. In fact, nationalism might be considered to be the new religion of the industrial age."

"You may be right," Ginsberg interjected. "At least I can see that happening here in France. We've been more or less democratic for a century, and increasingly we respond to the icons and relics of this France: the *tricolor* flag; national anthems that make us cry; warriors heroes from our recent and ancient history; cultural characters who act in a French democratic way. These icons helped to stabilize and define our society. And we venerate them because of their deeds.

"But isn't there peril in turning over the fate of Europe to people who once were peasants and factory workers and common secretaries?" asked the old man. "In such an environment elections give the fate of our civilization to the common man, the uneducated rabble, the Great Unwashed, if you will. Isn't that frightening?"

Philip thought a while as he poured himself a small glass of wine. "Well, isn't it scary to retain an incompetent Tsar or King or any autocrat who is unresponsive to the needs of his or her subjects? It wasn't a peasant who started the Franco-Prussian War or the Russo-Turkish War, or any other war for that matter. No factory worker ever precipitated a pogrom."

"True, but what do the common people bring to the table when they are given the chance to direct a state?" asked Ginsberg rhetorically. "This is the masses, Professor Belmont. It's mass man, and he is ignorant, impassioned, of minimal economic value, and usually unaware of the consequences of his politics."

"You're partially correct," my friend," Philip said. "But if mass man is ignorant, provide him with education. If he is more passionate that logical, teach him the value of reason and respect for others. And if he is unaware of what he advocates, help him to understand his political system, give him a stake in acting responsibly. It boils down to educating—but not indoctrinating—the masses.

"And while you're doing that, let mass woman participate in democratic politics," Philip added. "Let women vote and run for office. There is something less aggressive in the female character. We need this moderating temperament and wisdom in our democracies. In Great Britain and the United States there are substantial feminist movements working right now to bring women into the political process, to guarantee them the same rights men have taken for granted."

"Good points, all of them, Professor," Ginsberg answered. "But I fear that the unshackled common man and woman may one day produce uncommon savagery. I have seen mass man when he is filled with alcohol or drugs. I have seen him be brutal and dominating. I have seen him screaming foolishness while friends applaud his rant as insight.

"And when mass man wraps himself in a flag and calls his nonsense patriotism, reason has a difficult time resisting the emotion unleashed. I guess the problem, Professor, is that mass man, even with the education you want to provide, is still capable of horrendous actions.

"And nationalism is his political liquor," Ginsberg continued. "We don't see the problems in our own country because we're French patriots. Only the Germans have problems, or the British, or whoever. We don't see our own warts because we are blinded by our French preferences. Of course, it works the other way in Berlin and London. They see only French or Italian or Russian inadequacies, seldom their own.

"That's why I say down with nationalism," he asserted as he refilled his wine glass. "Ah, but wait a minute. There is only one nationalism I support wholeheartedly. Zionism, Professor Belmont. Zionism is the nationalism of us Jews."

Philip questioned the captain about Zionism. "Why now?" he inquired. "There's never been a nationalism based on a religious community that has been scattered for almost two millennia. Nationalism is ethnic and based on a common language and customs that are nurtured and shared by people from a confined geographical area."

"Well, I'll tell you," replied the barge pilot, "Jews in France, in fact throughout Europe, are coming to realize that our survival depends on gaining our own nation state. Christian Europe hates us; and, frankly, we are terrified of Christian Europe. That's what bonds us together as one people no matter where we live or what languages we speak.

"Just look at the Dreyfus Affair that France suffered through recently. That poor soldier, Alfred Dreyfus, was convicted as an enemy spy because he was an officer in the French Army and he was Jewish. The Roman Catholic officer corps couldn't stand the thought of a Jew commanding Christian troops. So they framed Dreyfus as a spy when the real enemy agent was that bastard Esterhazy. The generals knew that. But Esterhazy had a fine old Hungarian family name. His ancestors employed the great composer, Joseph Hyden. And Esterhazy prayed at a church, not a synagogue. So, they blamed the Jew!"

"But it was finally resolved in the French military and civil courts, wasn't it?" Philip interjected.

"Dreyfus' fate? No!" said Ginsberg. "That will never been resolved in the minds of French hotheads. To this day rightist newspapers insist that he be shipped back to Devil's Island. Others demand a pogrom to remove all Jews from the French military.

"But we won the day," he continued. "We Jews triumphed because of Teddy Herzl.

"Have you ever heard of him? He was my friend back in Paris years before I bought this boat and became a river rat. He died ten years ago, but we Jews will always remember him. Theodore Herzl was a distinguished journalist from Vienna who came here to report on the Dreyfus Affair. Herzl was a Jew. And what he heard in our courts and what he saw in the streets of Paris made him fear for the future of Judaism and its people.

"When he returned to Vienna, he and I continued to exchange letters for several years until his death. He once explained to me that we can't fight the anti-Semites and expect to win. There are too many of them, too few of us. The hatred of Jews is too engrained in Christian culture. So, he said, if you can't beat them, leave them. He knew it was time for the Jewish people to get out of Europe and let the anti-Semites stew in their own hatred."

The old man continued. "Like a modern Moses trying to lead his people out of bondage, Teddy was a Zionist urging us to make a new Israel and move there. He told us that we must find a homeland and do it soon.

"He wanted it to be in Palestine in the Ottoman Empire. I favor Palestine, too. But Jews are growing desperate. Some talk of building the new Zion in East Africa and even Paraguay, wherever in the world that place is. We need a modern Israel. We must gather together, reunite ourselves. Do you understand? Our lives are at stake here.

"Wait a minute, there's something I want to read to you," Ginsberg said.

He turned and entered his private room. He soon reappeared with a letter in his hand. "You see this? This is an actual letter from Teddy written a few years before he died. He sent me this copy of the letter he wrote in 1904 to Tommaso Tittoni, the Italian Foreign Minister. At this time Herzl was contacting all the Great Powers. Always, he made the same request: Save the Jews by helping us make our own safe homeland. Here, let me read it to you.

Theodore Herzl to Tommaso Tittoni February 13, 1904

Excellency,

During the meeting in Rome you honored me with, you invited me to formulate the Zionist demand. Permit me then to submit the following observations to Your Excellency.

The Zionist movement, represented by the annual congresses of delegates from all countries, has as its goal to create in Palestine the legally-assured home for the Jewish people.

As President of the Action Committee I have been in contact with governments interested in this question. I have tried above all to enter into a relationship with the Ottoman government. His Imperial Majesty the Sultan received me in a private audience and invited me on different occasions to return to Constantinople. I have not failed to go there, but the negotiations have not made any tangible progress. In seeking an explanation in international terms for this slowness, I am doing my utmost to obtain the consent of the interested powers.

The Zionist idea found its first support in Germany. In Jerusalem in 1898 in a serious audience with me and a Zionist deputation, His Majesty the Emperor promised us his goodwill. The German government's attitude of goodwill has not changed since. The letter that His Royal Highness the Grand Duke of Baden addressed to me on September 30, 1903 on this subject affirms it.

The British government has shown itself so favorable to the Zionist movement that it has proposed a large territory in the British possessions in East Africa for our colonization. In Austria the government regards our efforts with a kindly interest, as Counsel Mr. de Boerger said in his letter addressed to me on September 28, 1903.

But the most important support comes to us from Russia. In the month of August 1903 the Minister Dr. de Plehvé sent me a letter, a printed copy of which is found attached. Mr. de Plehvé has added that this governmental declaration is sent to me by order of His Majesty the Emperor with authorization to publish it. On December 6, 1903 the Russian government let me *know that the Russian ambassador in Constantinople has already received the order to intervene with the Sublime Porte in favor of the Zionist propositions.*

The Russian declaration of August 12, 1903 goes further than our own proposal. We have not asked for an independent Jewish state in Palestine; we are aware of the difficulties such a pretention would encounter. All we are asking for is the establishment of the Jewish people in Palestine under the suzerainty of his Imperial Majesty the Sultan, but under conditions of legal security. The administration of our colonizing would be incumbent upon us. To manage all the susceptibilities of all believers, the Holy Places ought to be exempt and retain extraterritoriality forever.

From the Ottoman government we will only ask for a Charter of Colonization for the Sandjak of Akka. For this Charter we pledge to pay the Ottoman Treasury an annual rent of one hundred thousand Turkish pounds.

Our proposals are not without serious advantages for the Ottoman government. But if it is so simple to enumerate them, it is difficult to speak without emotion of the miserable situation in which our poor Jews in Russia, Rumania, Galicia, etc. are mired.

Immigration to America is not a remedy. Particularly, in their political, social, and economic miseries they find even free countries, like the rest, beginning to close their doors to this immigration. Anti-Semitism makes life hard everywhere.

For Italy these struggles and miseries are only a faraway noise. Italy is not even touched by the Jewish Question, and it is for this reason that the government ought to render a great service to humanity by taking up the solution of this painful Question.

A letter from His Majesty the King of Italy to His Majesty the Sultan recommending our proposals and counseling in a friendly matter to take them into consideration will have a decisive effect for the reopening of our negotiations.

The Jewish people, dispersed, and despite such unhappiness always standing, vow their eternal recognition to Italy and to its chivalrous King.

Dr. Theodore Herzl

"Do you understand what Teddy was doing with this letter?" Captain Ginsberg asked. "He was trying to save our lives—trying to rescue his Jewish brothers and sisters from ghettos and pogroms, from accusations of blood libel and the idiocies found in the *Protocols of the Elders of Zion*, a pack of lies written a decade ago by the Russian secret police to justify persecuting Jews. One man, one lowly newspaper man from Vienna, contacting the heads of state of Europe with a simple request: free my people, let us find our own destiny away from the prejudices of Europe. What a *mensch* he was!

Philip was about to tell Ginsberg how impressed he was by Herzl's Zionist activities, but the boatman abruptly changed the subject. "Oh, here comes Arles. Get ready to go ashore. This is one of my favorite towns in all of Provence. We'll stop here for a few minutes. I have friends to greet. You can grab a bite to eat and read the latest newspapers."

Philip didn't mind the pause. He was anxious to see if anything had exploded yet on the political front. He tied the boat to the mooring post and the two travelers entered a small inn near the dock.

As Captain Ginsberg embraced his friends and everyone seemed happy to greet him, Philip skimmed through the morning journals. They were filled with speculation, but no solid moves had yet occurred in the affected capital cities. Austria apparently was demanding satisfaction from Serbia for the assassinations, but it was difficult to learn from the foreign reports exactly what Emperor Franz Joseph wanted from the Serbs.

However, many experts quoted in the newspapers feared the demand for satisfaction was not a diplomatic bluff. They speculated that the Austrians planned to launch a war against Serbia as punishment for its presumed role in facilitating the murders. Others felt Austria was using the assassinations as an excuse to deliver a crushing blow against the emerging economic and political strength of Belgrade. How then, some asked, would the Russians respond? And if Russia responded confrontationally, what would the other Great Powers do?

It was July 1, three days since the killings in Sarajevo, and Philip feared that Europe was stumbling toward a conflagration the size of which was open to speculation.

The final leg of the Rhône journey was the thirty miles between Arles and the Mediterranean. It was a particularly dangerous section of the river because the water level was low and the spreading delta created a flat swampy area called the Camargue. It was an unspoiled place famous for flamingoes and wild white horses, but not especially conducive to boat traffic.

Philip smiled as he assessed the untouched beauty unfolding before him. The old man, however, was oblivious to what he was passing. He was too occupied guiding his boat slowly and meticulously through the many shallow spots in the river.

It was early afternoon by the time Ginsberg reached St-Louis-du-Rhône and docked his vessel. "If you're going to Marseilles, it's only a few miles east of here," he advised. "Just follow the shoreline. You can catch the railroad there to Italy, if you're not afraid of falling off the train again," he said. "But if you're a great swimmer, you could make it to Rome a lot quicker by going straight across the sea in a southeastern direction."

Philip smiled at the thought of a lengthy ocean swim, but he sensed that train travel into Italy would not be safe. He had no doubt that enemy agents were waiting for him in Ventimiglia if not Marseilles.

"What about a boat trip to Rome?" Philip asked. "Can I hire a boat in the village?"

"That's a long haul for a fishing boat, and that's the only kind of craft you're going to find here. You can ask, but I doubt it," he said to Philip discouragingly. "Try the bars and brasseries along the docks. Tell them Moshe-Daniel Ginsberg gives you his seal of approval."

He paid the captain the remainder of his fare. The two men smiled at each other and Philip departed. It was a voyage exactly as he had hoped it would be, slow, but mercifully without incident.

As Philip walked from one tavern to the other in search of another bold skipper, he almost forgot the fears he faced a day ago. But each bar and each fruitless request only exposed him to more prying eyes and curious ears. When he finally found a boat owner willing to take him, it was not to Rome but only as far as Livorno.

"Rome is too far away. Too much water from here," explained the fisherman. "But for 700 francs I will take you across the Ligurian Sea and into the harbor at Livorno, or as American and British tourists know the city, Leghorn. From there you can get to Rome by train or automobile if you wish."

It sounded like a workable plan. Philip figured that once he arrived he would be home free. Just a short ride train ride down the Italian shore, he thought to himself, and he would be in *bellisima Roma*.

After a few preparations and a down payment of 400 francs, the two men set out. The motor craft moved fairly rapidly, so the pilot estimated arrival in about ten or twelve hours. That would put him there in the early hours of the morning. It wasn't exactly the time an average tourist went looking for a hotel room, but Philip was not on a pleasure trip.

Most of the time, he sat below deck in a small cabin lighted only by a few candles in glass containers. The smell of fish was pungent, the result of years of harvesting the sea of cod, branzino, loup de mer, squid, octopus, and other assorted creatures that made dining so wonderful in this part of Europe. Or so he heard, because the captain, a Portuguese mariner named Pedro Madeiros, had only packed chicken sandwiches and Vinho Verde. But Philip was hungry, and everything tastes delicious with a cool glass of Vinho Verde, that classic Portuguese "Green Wine," that was actually a tasty white wine.

While he was in the cabin, Philip made another instinctive revision to the scheme designed by Delcassé and General Joffre. Using a jackknife he found in a galley drawer, he pried open the hollow centime and removed the microfilm. Carefully, he reassembled the coin and placed it back in his pocket.

He removed his cuff links and pried off the decorative porcelain pieces with hand-painted images of the Sorbonne. He placed the microfilm inside one link and replaced the decorative glass. Then he sealed both cuff links with a thin layer of wax from a nearby candle. With so much open water around, waxing the links made Philip feel more confident about protecting his precious cargo.

Choppy waves slowed the boat for a while, but Captain Madeiros was able to speed up whenever he hit placid sections along the route. It was about 3 am when he pointed out the lights of Livorno. Philip gathered together his belongings and paid the captain the balance of his debt.

Slowly the fishing boat entered the harbor. The captain cut the engine and used the boat's inertia to float noiselessly toward the pier. Philip stood on the bow ready to depart.

Suddenly, gun shots rang out from the docking area. Someone on shore was shooting at them.

"What the hell is going on?" screamed Madeiros. "They're not shooting at me, they're aiming at you. Get off my boat before you sink it. Quick, get overboard. You're on your own from now on. Get off!"

With that the Madeiros pushed Philip into the ocean and kicked his suitcase overboard as well. He raced back to the cabin and restarted his engine. "Adeus, Professor, nice knowing you. I hope you can swim."

Philip was about fifty yards from the wharf, but he was alone in the dark water and still a bit unsure of what had just happened. His suitcase had quickly filled with water and sunk. But his concern now was survival. As he swam toward the shore, his wet clothing dragged against the water slowing his progress and sapping his energy. But he couldn't worry about that, he had to keep swimming forward.

Moving through the water, Philip heard more shots fired toward him from different directions. The bullets, however, seemed to be splashing into the sea some distance from where he was. Clearly, the would-be assassins couldn't see him in the starless night. Still, he had to be careful not to be noisy as he approached the wharf terrified and near exhaustion.

Rather than make for shore, however, he decided to paddle silently under the wooden dock and glide among the large pillars that supported the structure. This way he would have cover while he waited for the shooters to leave in search of his floating corpse or the water trail he would have left had he come ashore on the beach.

After about twenty minutes of treading water under the pier, he crawled onto a small platform and climbed up a flight of steps leading to the surface. Cautiously, quietly, he crept away from the dock. The gunmen appeared to be gone, but he was still being extremely cautious.

Philip was cold and soaking wet, but he decided to avoid looking for a hotel. After what had just happened, a public hotel would be an obvious place for killers to search for him. Instead, he walked until he discovered a secluded area in which to rest. He found a discarded jacket, but it didn't help much because he was still chilled from his morning swim. He found a dry place to lie in the high grass, however, and soon fell asleep.

In the morning sunlight he awoke to find himself in a small forested area not far from the harbor. He needed more sleep; he was hungry; and his clothing was muddy and wet. Nevertheless, he had to plot his next move. He still had a substantial amount of money, although it, too, was drenched. But wet or dry, he knew that cash always worked.

Most importantly, he still had the microfilm. His suitcase with the phony paper document was at the bottom of the harbor. Maybe, he thought whimsically, he wouldn't be getting that *steak au poivre* meal at the Palais Farnese after all.

Philip was feeling a little groggy, too. He had read many tourist booklets about France and Italy, but none had ever suggested the best way to enter an unfamiliar city was to swim in while dodging bullets in the morning darkness. He laughed at his unusual predicament. "I'll bet I'm the only person in the world right now to have come through such an experience," he said aloud to relieve the tension.

Dirty, unshaven, wet, and uncertain about what to do next, Philip decided that in this situation valor was better than discretion. He would risk registering at a hotel. He put all his money and papers in his trouser pockets and discarded his damp suit coat. His goal was to look as non-professorial as possible. Instead, he wore the old jacket he had discovered in a field earlier this morning.

Philip located a moderately-priced auberge, the Hôtel d'Angleterre Campari where for six francs he got a room and a bath. The manager, Luigi Paradiso, was skeptical about Philip's ability to pay. After all, the professor did give the appearance of a man down on his luck. But when he presented Paradiso with a 100 franc note, the manager reassessed his guest. As delicately as possible, he suggested to Philip that because the hotel was on the main street in town, via Vittorio Emanuele, he might wish to visit one of the several clothing stores that opened early in the morning.

"Signore, in Italy as in every country, clothes make the man," Paradiso remarked in French. "You are young, and underneath your present appearance, I think you are a handsome individual. But now you look like an unloved alcoholic, an *ubriacone*, a drunkard. Let society see you as you really are. Take the word of a man old enough to be your father: you can do much better than this."

Philip smiled and nodded in agreement. He knew that he was in need of a thorough cleansing and a new wardrobe. He considered Paradiso more like a talking mirror than a personal critic. "Thanks for the recommendation, Papa," he replied. "I'll start with a nice warm bath and a shave. Then I'll visit the via Vittorio Emanuele."

Philip was waiting at the door when the proprietor of the Moda Moderna opened at 9 o'clock in the morning. Still wearing his disheveled clothes, he felt odd as he searched for replacements. But he did not let his sartorial woes obscure his need to be careful. He continued to watch the store windows for possible assassins on the street.

Philip bought only enough new clothes to get him to Rome: no suitcase needed. He laughed to himself as he thought of the absurdity of a French secret agent stopping in mid-assignment to purchase a new outfit. He paid with French francs, then returned to his room and changed. It made him feel good that matters were getting back to normal.

It was a new man who came downstairs to enjoy a late breakfast. He was rejuvenated, although he was still running on adrenaline and nervous energy. Smiling broadly at Philip's improved appearance, Signore Paradiso greeted him and eagerly directed him toward the hotel restaurant.

"Ah, *signore, splendido!* Now you look like a *uomo distinto*, a man of distinction," Paradiso said. "If I had a daughter, I would introduce her to you in hopes that someday you would become my son-in-law."

"Thank you very much, *grazie tante*," Philip answered with an exaggerated bow to the fatherly inn keeper.

While he busily perused the morning newspaper and devoured his breakfast, a noisy group of English-speaking people crowded into the tables surrounding him. At first Philip was upset that the cacophony of so many different voices was interrupting his concentration. But as he overheard snatches of the various discussions, he realized this might be his salvation.

This was a large group of Canadian tourists from Cape Breton Island in Nova Scotia. They were on a guided tour of Italy, and they were on their way to Rome. The travelers had started in Milan two days earlier. Leghorn had been their destination last night. This evening they were scheduled to reach Civitavecchia.

Gregarious people that they were, it wasn't long before Philip was involved in conversations at several tables. With last names such as Pinkerton, MacInnes, McLeod, Nugent, Coakley, and MacKenzie, this was an admixture of descendants of Scottish and Irish immigrants who had stopped short of the United States and found refuge and prosperity in eastern Canada. They were farmers and coal miners, storekeepers and fisherman. They came from towns he had never heard of, places called New Waterford, Glace Bay, Port Hawkesbury, Wycogama, Sydney, North Sydney, and Sydney Mines. But they were friendly, and he liked them immediately. Fortunately for Philip many in the group spoke French—some well, others haltingly but understandably.

When they learned that he was alone and headed for Rome, they invited Philip to join their tourist expedition. "Come on with us," one man suggested. "It won't cost you a cent. We have some room on our bus, and you'll get a wonderful tour—or at least half a tour—if you'd like. We're going along the coast today. Lots of things to see, they tell me. We'll be getting to the capital tomorrow late in the morning."

Philip acquiesced and thanked his new friends. Without saying it aloud, however, he hoped he wasn't putting anyone in jeopardy. But he had to get out of Livorno, and this was a viable way to do that. Buried within a group of enthusiastic tourists from Canada seemed like an excellent hiding place.

It took a little arguing with the bus driver before he was allowed to board. But with twenty francs quietly slipped in the driver's palm, Philip won the argument.

Soon he was on a bus with an Italian female guide explaining that the travelers were now passing ancient Roman ruins. Then they were driving by archeological remains of ancient Vandal and Visigoth invasions. Next, it was remnants of Saracen raids against coastal villages. Of course, there were also green meadows and steep cliffs of significance. They stopped in picturesque towns such as Cecina and Piombino. Here the Cape Bretoners left the bus and followed their guide on short promenades around local historic spots.

Between Piombino and Grossetto, the guide pointed out the island of Elba that was visible off shore. "It was from here that the defeated and exiled Napoléon Bonaparte escaped in 1814," she explained. "He soon raised a new army and marched against his European conquerors. Unfortunately for Mr. Bonaparte, he and his army were crushed at Waterloo the following year. He was exiled again, but this time to the island of Saint Helena, a remote volcanic speck situated between the tip of South Africa and the tip of South America. From that location Napoléon never escaped alive."

Interestingly, as the guide spoke the Canadians dutifully turned the pages of their small, red copies of *Baedeker's Handbook for Travellers* focusing on northern Italy. And as their tour progressed farther southward, they switched to a second volume of *Baedecker's Handbook*, this one covering Central Italy and Rome.

Philip actually enjoyed his touristic excursion. After all, he was a historian, and he was learning things as the guide brought context to each of the sights along the way. Still, he watched the others with great care. He was never sure he was safe. Was someone following the bus? Was there someone onboard anxious to collect the German reward?

As he peered through the bus window he noticed a yellow Peugeot automobile with a driver and one passenger. The car had been behind the tourists for about fifteen minutes. Now, it pulled alongside as if someone in the Peugeot was trying to look inside the bus. Philip might not have been alerted had the car's driver not pulled back and continued to follow for another few miles. The suspicious driver then repeated his slow inspection of the bus windows.

Philip could not be certain this was a threat. But he could take no chances. Without making a scene, he left his window seat and moved to the rear of the bus where a space was open between two married couples. He introduced himself and soon was deep in a discussion of Italian art and architecture.

After several more short stops, one of them a break for lunch in Tarquinia, the group arrived in Civitavecchia. Philip joined the Canadians as their guide paraded them from the seaport whose harbor was planned by the Emperor Trajan, to the remnants of Muslim invaders who attacked the town in the 9th century, to the areas which showed traces of occupation by the French in the 1850s and 1860s. It was educational, but Philip remained focused on the fact that this village was only fifty miles from Rome. Tomorrow he and the Canadians would be there.

The tour was booked into the Albergo Termale Traiano. Of course, Philip's name was not on the list of prepaid travelers. He had to arrange for his lodgings separately. Fortunately, there was a small room available, and it came with an attached bathroom.

The tourists spent the remainder of the evening eating and drinking, smoking and singing in the hotel restaurant. One voyager had brought a small accordion from home so the room was soon filled with the music of hornpipes, jigs, and reels—and songs about wild colonial boys and forlorn sailors far from home.

As long as they kept buying beer and wine, the manager seemed indifferent to the boisterousness. In fact, the waiters encouraged more consumption and the visitors obliged. Philip may have been an outsider, but he drank and sang with them as if he were back in Chicago cavorting with old friends.

The group was still singing and drinking when Philip crept upstairs to his room. He flopped on the bed and was soon deeply asleep.

Sometime in the early morning hours, a knock at the door awakened Philip. "Who's there?" he inquired groggily as he stumbled toward the sound. He received no response. Without thinking he opened the door. A gun pressing against his stomach forced him back into the room.

Philip couldn't believe what he was seeing. Holding the weapon was Alain Laroche, the professor who had invited him to participate in his seminar at the Sorbonne only a few days earlier.

"So much for scholarship, Professor Belmont," Laroche said to the startled American.

"What are you doing here?" Philip asked. "And what's the meaning of the gun?"

"It must be obvious that history has little to do with this visit or this pistol, my friend," Laroche snapped. "I've had a difficult time finding you, but I'm here now.

"I've had people looking for you for days. How did you manage to escape them so often? My assistants must be losing their touch when an inexperienced Yank historian can outsmart all of them."

"I don't know what you're talking about," Philip answered. "Somehow, I never thought of you with a gun in your hand."

"Such brave talk. But make no mistake. I'm no gunslinger out of one of your cheap American cowboy tales. I'm a hero, Dr. Belmont, a loyal citizen of the German Empire in service to my Kaiser. I'll also admit that I'm a man anxious to become very wealthy by confiscating the microfilm you're trying to take to Rome. I don't know what's on that film, but I intend to deliver it to German Intelligence in Berlin."

"From what I saw in your classroom," Philip interjected, "I took you for a French patriot."

"I am a patriot, Herr Professor, but a German one," said Laroche with disdain. "I'm from Strasbourg. You know Strasbourg, the capital of German Alsace? But I am not one of those French crazies running around looking for revenge because the Fatherland annexed a couple of French province almost half a century ago. I am a man who's happy that his leader is Kaiser Wilhelm II, and not a spineless republican like Raymond Poincaré.

"But I didn't come here to discuss politics. I came here to get the microfilm. I know you've been carrying it in a hollow centime ever since you left Paris. I suspect that the coin is in your pocket. So, Professor, please empty your pockets and place the contents on the bed."

With a gun pointed at him, Philip obliged. Reluctantly, he reached into his trousers and pulled out coins and cash. He also placed his identification papers on the bed. But Laroche wasn't looking for documentation or even soggy francs. He knew exactly what he wanted.

"Under normal circumstances, I would take this wonderful little hollow coin and then kill you," said Laroche as he picked up the fake centime Delcassé had provided. "But I enjoyed your collegiality, your comradeship in historical study. I predict that you have a solid career ahead of you—once you return to America.

"I really hate to do this, especially because I know you appreciate my professionalism. I see you're even wearing the cuff links I gave you at the Sorbonne. I accept that as a sign of your appreciation and respect for my work. Academic brotherhood, isn't it intriguing? It transcends borders and beliefs just like those silly socialists expect trade union membership will prevent international wars.

"Besides, your life makes no difference to me. Berlin doesn't necessarily want you dead, just stopped. This centime will prove that your mission to Rome was a failure. So, in the spirit of professional brotherhood, you may as well keep your life. Go home and write many books about 18th century topics.

"And there's no need to alert the Italian police. By the time you report this incident to the Carabinieri, I'll be out of the country and well on my way to my reward in Germany. With 500,000 marks waiting for me in Berlin—less the share I promised my assistants who have been looking for you since Paris—I'll live a rich and comfortable life somewhere in the world.

"Aren't you going to check out the coin before you leave?" Philip said somewhat boldly. "How do you know the microfilm is there?"

"Not that tired old bluff, Dr. Belmont," Laroche replied. "It's the old stall routine: I get distracted while you get more time to think of a way to stop me. My sources are infallible. If they say the film is inside the hollow centime, then that's the way it is. No, you didn't remove anything. The ploy won't work. *Danke schoen*, *Herr Professor*. *Und aufwiedersehen*. Thank you and good-bye."

With that cold farewell, Laroche backed out of the room and fled down the hallway. Philip was badly shaken, but at least he was alive. Never had his professorship meant so much to him.

He feared for his life should Laroche change his mind and inspect the contents of the coin. He didn't need to summon a local police official; at this point he needed the protection of the French embassy. It was also urgent that he reach Rome because he had to report that Laroche was heading a ring of German spies, and that there was at least one German agent working inside the Quai d'Orsay—most likely in the photography section. Once the Sorbonne professor was out to sea, or crossed the Swiss or Austrian border, Philip understood, Italian law enforcement would never be able to capture him.

Philip quickly dressed and left his hotel room. He didn't bother to report the robbery to the night clerk. He also failed to inform his new Canadian friends that he was leaving their tour. Instead, he walked out into the early morning darkness and disappeared.

Philip walked for several miles into the night until he found a small trattoria that was open. At this point he still had no idea how he would reach the Palais Farnese. Inside the restaurant he found a few tired people eating and drinking coffee. Several of them looked young and athletic. He wondered if they might be the owners of the dozen or so bicycles he saw parked outside.

He was desperate. "Anybody here willing to sell me a bicycle?" he asked loudly in French. "This is no joke. I am willing to pay cash for one of the touring bicycles I see outside. Whoever is first to agree will get 200 French francs."

"Make it 300 and it's yours," answered a voice from the back of the room.

That was a very high price for a used bicycle, even a beautiful Italian multi-geared Stucchi racing bike. But Philip was in no position to bargain over the cost. "Sold," he replied.

The deal was consummated in a matter of minutes. Money was exchanged. The seller unlocked the bike and handed the lock and chain to Philip. It was only fifty miles to Rome, and Philip was now ready to pedal there on two wheels.

First, however, he had to wait for the first rays of daylight. No one in his right mind would bicycle along the rugged Italian coast in the dark. The roads were too winding; the cliffs dropping to the sea were almost perpendicular; and road traffic in Italy was always unpredictable and unforgiving.

At the initial glimpse of dawn, however, he began his trek. But before he rode very far he was overtaken by a group of bicycle enthusiasts, all members of the Touring Club Italiano. He learned that the group was in the final leg of the Milan to Rome cycling tour. Some of the Italians snickered at Philip for wearing street clothes while riding such a high-class machine.

He explained in French that he was dressed for a romantic rendezvous in Rome and that he would look silly calling on a beautiful young woman dressed in the racing shorts that avid cyclists liked to wear. "You know that old saying, clothes make the man," he noted.

"Hey, why don't you join us in our run to Rome," yelled one of the bikers. "We're in the final day of our tour. We'd love to have a novice like you join us. Maybe you can set the pace for us to follow. If you have the stamina, that is."

Philip felt emboldened by the challenge. "I'm no pacer. I can race any of you to Rome, even dressed like this. Want me to prove it?" he asserted.

"Ah, a French blowhard," said another Italian to his buddies. "These guys from up north always think they're superior to us. We'll show him."

The obvious leader of the Italian riders was more serious. "Wait a minute," he commanded as he brought the bantering to a halt. "If this guy rides with us, he must be with us. He has to join the Touring Club Italiano, or he's on his own."

With a broad smile Philip surrendered to the demand. "Sure, I'd be happy to join your bicycle Club, but I don't have a professional riding costume. I don't even have a pair of wind goggles."

"Well, dressed like a businessman and riding a Stucchi, you do look out of place," said another rider. "But there's no problem, Frenchie. Just pay the dues and we'll give you a silk banner you can hang on your back. That'll make you a member of TCI. As for eye protection, just squint and the wind won't bother you very much."

"Where do I sign?" Philip asked.

From of the rear of the group a bespectacled young man appeared with a small cloth banner. "I'm the treasurer. Just give me eight francs for the membership fee and two francs for participation in the tour, and you're one of us." he said.

"Agreed," said Philip.

"What is your name?" asked the treasurer. "What shall we call you?"

As he reached into his pocket and pulled out a damp twenty franc note, Philip responded, "Well, they call me Philipe-Michel. "Here, keep the change—for the Club. *Viva Italia!*" he said.

The group appreciated his gesture. "*Viva, Italia*," they responded in unison. The treasurer pinned the TCI marker to the back of Philip's jacket.

"OK, fellas and you, Filippo," commanded the leader, "Let's ride."

It was a flat and open run to Rome. Granted it was fifty miles of pumping, but Civitavecchia was a seaport and Rome was situated only sixty-two feet above sea level. It was a bicyclist's dream route. But that was unimportant to Philip because all he could think of was reaching the Palais Farnese safely.

By late morning, the riders approached the industrial outskirts of Rome on the southeast side of the city. They flew past the Testevere train station, the Porta Portunese, and the city's tobacco factory. In a few minutes, however, they were rolling past more glamorous sights. One rider pointed out Monte Testaccio, the Pyramid of Cestius, the Aventine, and eventually the Temple of Minerva Medica.

As the group rolled carefully across the Garibaldi Bridge to reach the left bank of the Tiber River, Philip asked the rider next to him for directions to the Farnese Palace.

"Oh, that's easy. When we get across this bridge turn left and just stay along the Left Bank for about a half-mile and you'll be in the Piazza. The Palazzo fills one side of the Piazza Farnese. The Palazzo is now the French embassy. There are shops, restaurants, and a few office buildings on the other side. And in the middle you'll see two granite fountains made with large tubs taken from the ancient Baths of Caracalla. But with all this wonderful Roman beauty around you, why do you want to go there? We're turning right toward the Coliseum, the Palatine Hill, the Roman Forum," the Italian said as the riders entered a busy part of the city.

"I'd love to ride with you all the way, but I'm going to meet my girlfriend in front of the Palazzo," Philip replied. "Love calls, you know!"

"Very well, lover boy," yelled the Italian rider as the street traffic, plus the rush of the wind, made it increasingly difficult to speak or be heard. "Turn here along the Tiber, look for via Giulia slightly off on your right. Take that street for one block to via del Mascherone, turn right and the Palazzo will be immediately on your left. You can't miss it. If you see the Vatican and Castel San Angelo, you've gone too far. *Buona fortuna*, Filippo, good luck."

With that friendly wish, Philip turned away from the bicycle club and started moving along the riverbank. It was a warm summer day, and he felt confident now that the French embassy was nearby. He slowed down to enjoy the scenery.

In a matter of seconds the familiar yellow Peugeot menacingly pulled up near him. Philip began to feel crowded, even threatened. He turned to see the driver. Unbelievably, it was Alain Laroche who began crowding him off the road. Laroche and Philip jostled through the streets of Rome, the automobile swerving toward Philip who managed with difficulty to dodge each assault. At one point the Sorbonne professor even pulled out a pistol and aimed it at Philip.

As he approached the sign directing him toward via Giulia, Philip rapidly veered away from the speeding auto and darted up the narrow street. Laroche missed the turn. But Philip knew he would back soon, this time with murder on his mind.

A moment after losing his pursuer Philip spotted via del Mascherone. He took a sharp right turn, then a sudden left and coasted into the Piazza. Immediately he spotted the French flag flying atop the Palace. Philip stopped his bike abruptly in front the embassy entrance. Allowing the bicycle to fall to the ground, he bolted toward the entryway.

He was shaken and exhausted from the long trip and especially from the harrowing chase through the streets of Rome. As he ran unsteadily toward the Farnese Palace, he almost collapsed. Had the French soldiers guarding the embassy not grabbed him as his knees began to buckle, he would have fallen headfirst onto the stone pavement.

"My name is Philip Belmont. I must see Ambassador Barrère," he gasped. "I must see him immediately. I have vital information. Please tell him that Philip Belmont is here from Paris." At this point, he fainted into the arms of the guards.

6

The soldiers immediately called for medical assistance. Although the doctor diagnosed stress as the cause of the fainting, Philip was placed in a wheelchair and taken to the embassy infirmary for closer observation.

While he was regaining his composure, Camille Barrère entered the room. "Ah, it's my favorite historian, Professor Belmont. What's happened to you, my friend?" he asked with concern. "You look depleted and very tired. Are you injured?

"More to the point, why aren't you dead? We heard from the Italian police that the Rome Express arrived with a body found shot to death in the seat we reserved for you. The train arrived at the Stazione Termini several days ago. We presumed that you were murdered by German agents, and that they had stolen what you were carrying. In fact, our medical officer was supposed to identify your body tonight in the city morgue.

"But, if you are able to walk now," Barrère continued, "Please come into my office where we can continue our conversation in private."

Philip rose to his feet a bit dizzy, but he managed to follow the ambassador upstairs to his office. "Here sit down on this sofa," Barrère said comfortingly. "I have many questions for you. But your health is important to me. If you become too exhausted, let me know."

"Thank you," Philip replied in steadier voice. "I've had a difficult adventure getting here. But, finally, I feel safe. Enemies of France have been following me and trying to kill me since I left Paris. I've traveled by many routes to get here."

"That's remarkable, and I am so glad to see you made it," responded Barrère. "But the question of the moment is: did you bring the microfilm? It is vitally important that I have that document as soon as possible to share with the Italian authorities," the ambassador pleaded. "Without those pages, France may be lost."

"Well, sir, first let me explain that Professor Alain Laroche of the Sorbonne's history department is a German spy," explained Philip as he began to remove his cuff links. "He is the leader of a team of assassins who have tried to kill me ever since I entered the Gare de Lyon. I decided there to change my direction, to abandon the Rome Express and come here via another route. It was a terrible decision. But, if you found a dead man in my seat on the Express, it must be the poor Italian chap to whom I gave the ticket provided by the Quai d'Orsay. All he wanted to do was visit his ailing mother. I feel terrible about that.

"As for Laroche, you'll find him in Rome right now. He tried to run me down with his yellow Peugeot not 200 yards from the Palais Farnese. That was less than a quarter hour ago."

Barrère picked up the telephone and called his chief of security. As Philip described Professor Laroche and the automobile he was driving, the ambassador relayed the information to the officer. "Now, call the Italian Ministry of the Interior and request that the capture of Laroche be considered a state emergency of the highest priority," Barrère commanded.

"As for the secret German document, here are my cuff links," said Philip as handed the pair to the ambassador. Look under the porcelain plates of each link; you'll find the microfilm under one of them. I switched the film from the hollow centime to my cuff link. Good thing, too, because Professor Laroche knew about the centime. He took it from me at gunpoint.

Barrère immediately called in an assistant. "Take these down to our photo lab," he commanded. "Remove the glass plates and print me three copies of the microfilmed document you'll find underneath one of them. Quickly, young man, this is a matter of life or death."

The assistant grabbed the links and ran from the ambassador's office.

"There is no way we can thank you or honor you enough, Professor Belmont. Be assured, you've played a vital role in saving France from conquest by the Germans. As the days progress, we are more and more convinced that we will be attacked by Germany. We are not certain, but policy moves in Berlin and Vienna suggest that we are headed toward a continent-wide conflict.

"If we can convince the Italians that this will be a war of German aggression—and the Schlieffen Plan clearly shows that to be the case—they will have no difficulty in refusing to cooperate militarily with their allies. We can then free up thousands of our troops on the Italian frontier and redeploy them north to attack Germany and to defend Paris.

"Above all, we must protect Paris. We failed to do that during the Franco-Prussian War, and the Germans laid siege to the city. They fired heavy artillery shells into the capital at will. Starving citizens resorted to eating animals from the city zoo. Some even trapped and ate vermin. We were defeated and humiliated. I know only too well because I was fighting there in the aftermath. It must never happen again!"

"Well, sir, I tried my best. It wasn't easy," Philip answered. "But it is finished, and I kept my word."

"That you have, my friend," Barrère replied. "But, no one must ever learn of it. To have had an American operate as you did is beyond extraordinary. It's a breach of American law and international law. It could place you in prison and draw the United States into a global war if Germany decides to implement the Schlieffen Plan. Rest assured, we will do whatever we can to honor you. But we'll do it quietly."

"I didn't do it for honor, Ambassador," said Philip graciously. "But there is one thing you could do for me. In my meeting with Delcassé, he gave me a falsified paper copy of the Schlieffen Plan. He said that if I arrived here with it still intact, it would be useful for starting a fire in the embassy stove that your chef would use to prepare a wonderful *steak au poivre* dinner for me. Well, I lost the paper document. It's somewhere at the bottom of the harbor in Livorno. But I would still love to taste your chef's best *steak au poivre*."

Barrère burst into laughter. "Your wish is France's command. I will have our wonderful chef prepare a feast for you. A fine filet mignon, a smooth brandy cream sauce, and topped with those scrumptious morsels of black pepper that set the mouth afire—plus, of course, the finest Bordeaux in our wine cellar. Come, Philipe-Michel, we will dine together," he said. "Let me telephone the cook downstairs and tell him to stoke the fire.

"But before we eat, I must wire Delcassé that you are very much alive and that you have successfully carried out the mission. He and I established a private way to communicate your arrival. When I telegraph Théo that I have received the *confiture de framboise au château*, the chateau-grown raspberry jam he sent to me as a gift, and that it was delicious on my breakfast baguette, the wire will appear as a simple note of thanks. But he will know that you have arrived safely and successfully. You see, Professor, to France you are a jar of raspberry jam."

Barrère summoned his communications director and ordered that the raspberry dispatch be sent as a non-classified communiqué to the Quai d'Orsay. As he explained to Philip, "If I make this a Top Secret telegram, we run a good chance of being electronically intercepted. But a plain old thank-you note? Who would suspect anything other than graciousness in that?"

The ambassador turned to his aide. "Please, make an appointment for me to meet with the Marquis di San Giuliano at 9 o'clock this evening. Tell the Italian Foreign Minister that the meeting is of the utmost importance."

He then placed his arm around Philip's shoulder and the two men walked off to dine together.

As much as he wanted to return to his research in Paris, Philip had to yield to his damaged body. He was sore and tense and generally fatigued. Besides, Ambassador Barrère had offered him a guest room in the Palais Farnese for as long as he wished to stay in Rome.

He did not see the ambassador very often during the next several weeks. Barrère was either working in his office or visiting the Quirinale, the seat of the Italian foreign ministry. But, the embassy provided him a staff car and a driver to take him wherever he wanted to go.

Rome in the warmth of summer can make human aches disappear rapidly. With a personal chauffeur as guide, Philip visited and enjoyed all the wondrous cultural sites. Surviving since ancient times were the ruins of the Roman Forum, the Coliseum, the Capitoline Hill on which Emperors once resided, the Circus Maximus where chariot races and other competitions occurred, and the Appian Way, the great Roman road that remained a functional street in the old section of the city.

From a later era, Renaissance art and architecture publically declared the rebirth of Greek- and Roman-inspired civilization a thousand years after the fall of Rome. This reincarnation was most evident in and around the Vatican City. Technically a self-governing political entity existing within the secular Kingdom of Italy, the Vatican was the home of the Roman Catholic Popes whose operative mandate was spiritual and no longer political. As a showcase of Renaissance art, it was a living museum constructed and decorated by Michelangelo, Bernini, Raphael, Botticelli, and a galaxy of other master artists.

Rome had a more recent level of artistry as well. It was found in monuments celebrating contemporary Italy. Especially imposing was the gigantic memorial to the first Italian monarch, King Victor Emmanuel II who accepted the national throne in 1861. Situated in the center of the city, the monument was a brashly large edifice that declared in no uncertain terms that a new era had begun and all visitors should know that they were now in the modern Kingdom of Italy.

To live among such man-made wonders was to appreciate the potentialities of human endeavor. Much as he loved Paris better than Rome, Philip's primal affection was tempted by the Italian capital. He adored the accomplishments of civic and artistic life that flourished in Rome. Here artistic order and human freedom coexisted productively. Here, too, art and commerce interacted in harmony. Rome offered homo faber (man creating) and homo sapiens (man knowing) in constructive, communal balance.

But always at the back of his mind was the steady cadence of war drums which intensified with the publication of each day's newspapers. While Philip relaxed and grew stronger, Europe was sliding toward the headlong fury that is full-scale warfare.

By the middle of July, matters had deteriorated badly. In Austria-Hungary government leaders, the driving force of the war party urging confrontation, were demanding the destruction of Serbia as an independent nation. Serbia, which had been autonomous since 1829 and an independent kingdom since 1878, was vilified for assisting in the assassination of the Archduke and his wife.

Camille Barrère was consumed by day-to-day diplomatic developments. Philip almost never saw his host unless he was darting off to confer with Italian authorities. French and Entente statesmen in the area also visited the embassy for strategy meetings. These were frightening times for France as well as the other European nations sliding inexorably toward a continental shooting war.

Still, in the midst of Europe's slippage toward conflagration, everything was put on hold on July 14th as the Palais Farnese formally celebrated Bastille Day, the independence day of France. Of course the festivities in Paris would be much more spectacular, but even in this French outpost in the center of Rome, Ambassador Barrère and his staff organized a memorable fête.

The first floor of the embassy was decorated in red, white, and blue bunting with French *tricoleur* flags plentifully on display. But the main festivities were scheduled for upstairs in rooms filled with Roman statuary, great works by renowned Italian painters, and massive French tapestries from the looms of the celebrated weavers of the Gobelin factory. The Palais was a virtual art gallery and today it was celebrating the birth of modern France—and modern Europe, for that matter.

The guest list was stellar. Apparently, Barrère wanted to drive home the message of French-Italian solidarity because many prominent Italian leaders were in attendance. Philip was amazed as he met important dignitaries such as Prime Minister Antonio Salandra; Foreign Minister, the Marchese San Giuliano; the former Prime Minister and financial expert, Luigi Luzzatti; and the venerable former Foreign Minister, the Marchese Visconti Venosta. The embassy even invited the German and Austro-Hungarian ambassadors to Italy. Philip was pleased that Barrère introduced him to each man as "a friend of France and a friend of mine."

Philip was most intrigued by eighty-five-year-old Visconti Venosta, a living link to the Risorgimento, the political and military movement that created the Kingdom of Italy. "May I ask you a question, sir?" the professor of history inquired of the elderly patriot. "You were involved in the founding of modern Italy. In fact, you were one of the Kingdom's first diplomats. How does Italy today compare to the new nation born a half-century ago?"

"Ah, I like your question, Dr. Belmont," the revered old statesman replied. "I think the major difference is that in 1861 the newly-born Kingdom was, as your question suggests, an immature nation with all the problems of infantile weakness and vulnerability. Today, when you look beyond the walls of the Palazzo Farnese you see a powerful adult country, a Great Power. Italy is now strong and robust in all ways. We no longer crawl as we did in our first years. Now we stride the planet alongside our friends. And France and Ambassador Barrère are among our best *amici*."

Philip found this a poignant comment, especially from a wise diplomat who was well aware of the current political climate.

"Attention, please. The Villa Medici musicians are here. The music has arrived," announced an embassy official shuffling through the crowd. "Please, ladies and gentlemen, please repair to the Grand Salon for this afternoon's concert."

"We're in for a delightful afternoon, Professor," Visconti Venosta promised Philip. "Have you heard these young musicians before? They are excellent. They consist of three of the music students who are winners of Prix de Rome scholarships awarded by the Paris government. The scholarships allow French scholars to study here in Rome for two years at the French Academy which is in the Villa Medici. Ambassador Barrère enjoys them greatly. He often visits there, at least when he's not tending to diplomatic priorities."

Philip watched as the musicians entered the ballroom and began to prepare their instruments: a violin, a cello, and a viola. Soon the trio was deeply involved in beguiling the audience with interpretations of chamber music by Mozart and Hyden as well as the Italian composer Vivaldi and the French composer Saint-Saëns.

"As excellent as the student trio is," whispered Visconti Venosta, "it will improve considerably with the addition of a fourth musician who will soon join the ensemble. In fact, here he comes now. Here is Camille Barrère and, look, he honors us today by playing his priceless Stradivarius."

Philip was surprised to see the ambassador enter the room and sit in with the original trio. He was unaware of the Barrère's musical prowess.

"You do know that Camille is a master violinist?" the elderly Italian inquired.

"No, not at all," replied Philip. "I knew he was a masterful diplomat. And I have seen the animal heads mounted on the walls of the embassy, trophies from his hunting excursions. But a violinist? I didn't know that."

"Oh, yes. Had Camille not become a statesman, he could very well have been a first-rate concert violinist. With dedication and a little practice, he might have been as good as our legendary Niccolò Paganini," answered the Marchese. "But not only is he a performer, he is a collector of rare violins and an expert on the history of Italian violin making. He has an Amati and a Guarneri del Gesù. And the instrument he is now bringing on stage is a very rare. It was crafted in 1727 by Antonio Stradivarius of Cremona, the greatest violin maker of all time."

"Seems like you are also a historian," said Philip. "With such an interest, you and Camille must have wonderful conversations about history and music."

"Indeed we have, young man, indeed we have. In fact, working together we made a little history, too," Visconti Venosta answered wistfully.

It was a thrilling concert as the string quartet performed impeccably. One of the chamber pieces was by the French composer Hector Berlioz. The Marchese pointed out that Berlioz had been a Prix de Rome winner and had studied at the Villa Medici in the 1830s. "Italy has been nurturing great music for a very long time," he remarked proudly.

Appropriately, the Bastille Day concert ended with a rousing version of *Le Marseillaise* performed by the "Barrère Quartet" and sung by an audience which stood throughout the emotional French national anthem. Only the German and Austrian ambassadors failed to join the singing.

Bastille Day at the Palais Farnese was a welcomed respite from the festering European crisis. As the political intrigue intensified, journalistic accounts increasingly focused on the byzantine web of ententes, alliances, and unknown military obligations that might ensnared all the Great Powers. No one knew exactly what the arrangements required of each nation. If Vienna moved militarily against the Serbs, surely the Russians would intervene, as they had it in past, to protect the independence of their Orthodox Slavic brothers—and to keep their Austro-Hungarian rivals from grabbing new territories in the unsettled Balkan Peninsula.

But if the Austrians moved, what pressures would that exert on Germany, the longtime ally of the Hapsburg Monarchy? Would Germany militarily back Austrian expansion in the Balkans? And if the Russians decided to stop Austria-Hungary would Berlin remain quiet?

From his cursory understanding of the Schlieffen Plan, Philip knew that if the Germans did go to war with Russia, they would have to invade France first. And what about the other powers: Great Britain and Italy? Conjecture was rife about Great Britain sending military and naval forces to support France. Some felt, however, that Britain would remain neutral in a continental war. Questions continued, too, about whether Italy would follow her Germanic allies into conflict against France and Russia and perhaps Great Britain. And while Philip appreciated the quiet confidence of Camille Barrère that the Italians would declare neutrality in a continental war, he was as confused and nervous as most Europeans.

He wondered also about the disposition of the weaker nations. What would the Turks do? What would Belgians do? The Rumanians? The Greeks and Bulgarians? The Swedes and Dutch? The Spanish and Portuguese; the Danes and Norwegians? Every European nation-state had an important decision to make if the Austrians used military force against Serbia.

It was a fluid situation and, frankly, Philip was pessimistic about the future. He feared a generalized surrender to nationalist passions. Throughout Europe, patriotic young men not already in uniforms were rushing to join various armies and navies. Newspapers long affiliated with socialism or monarchy, the Church or even anti-Semitism, were editorially rallying to their national flags. The nations seemed to be bracing themselves for a showdown.

As alarming as this emotion was, Philip was also concerned about the popular frame of mind he encountered during his weeks in Rome. The spirit of Futurism and its surrender to the thrilling seemed to foreshadow everything that was happening now.

Begun as an artistic notion of how to capture in painting, sculpture, writing, and other art forms the modern reality of speed and technology, Futurism had become a popular social philosophy. In an array of flamboyant manifestos and declarations, the Futurists expressed their disgust with rational compromise and civil standards. They damned museums and tourist guides, archeologists and professors. They shouted their preference for the noise and smell and the feel of race cars, machine guns, and fast airplanes. They despised university learning and urged education through fiery experience. Futurists condemned the stodgy and demanded the visceral in the name of a youthful alternative direction.

The leading writer to the movement, a poet from Milan named Fillipo Tommaso Marinetti, had written only five years ago in his controversial *Futurist Manifesto*, "We want to glorify war—the only cure for the world—militarism, patriotism, the destructive gesture of the anarchists, the beautiful ideas which kill, and contempt for woman."

Futurism suggested that people were bored by a century of peace and progress on the continent. The Futurists and the myopic politicians who turned the rhetoric of frustrated artists into romanticized political advocacy were essentially championing conflict because it was thrilling and virile while peace was tiresome and feminizing.

Was this insanity? Was it bravado or perhaps farsightedness? Whatever it was, it gripped the public mood and lubricated a terrifying public tumble toward global conflict. Philip was astounded that the European people who were capable of such wondrous achievement seemed now to be contemplating, even embracing destructive sensuality.

By mid-July Philip was ready to return to Paris and his research. By undertaking his hazardous duty for the Ministry of Foreign Affairs, he had done all he could to slow the mass march toward madness. He could do no more. It was time to return to his 18th century project and let the events of the summer take their course.

Maybe, he thought to himself, there are statesmen like Ambassador Barrère in every capital; men who would protect their beloved nations through skilled diplomacy instead of bombastic threats of war and mass death.

Ever cordial, even at a time of great tension, the ambassador met with Philip before he left the embassy. "We have enjoyed your company, very much," he said to the professor. "You will return to Paris a private hero, and a public unknown. But you knew that from the beginning.

"However, Alain Laroche will never be a problem again. He was captured by the Italian police last week and is being deported to France for trial. His espionage ring has been shattered. And I know you will be glad to hear that we discovered the wallet thief working in the Quai d'Orsay. He stole much more than purses and billfolds. We discovered that he took state secrets and sold them in Berlin and Vienna. I'm afraid he will soon be joining Laroche and his cohorts in the swampy heat of Devil's Island."

A few more pleasantries passed between Philip and the ambassador. Finally, Philip said farewell to Barrère and the embassy personnel, then entered a limousine for the short ride to the railroad station and his return to France on the Paris Express.

Compared to his Paris-to-Rome adventure, the return trip was a delightful bore. First Class accommodations, a comfortable sleeping bunk, and arrival at the Gare de Lyon refreshed and happy to be back alive and well.

Philip emerged from the station into the Paris summer and still found the city vibrant.

This time, however, a comfortable taxi ride took him to his new living quarters: the Hôtel de Crillon. Expensive, glamorous, overlooking the Place de la Concorde directly in the center of Right Bank opulence and power, it was no wonder Benjamin Franklin stayed at this hotel, Philip thought to himself. And all of this comfort came courtesy of the French government.

Tomorrow he would return to the Ministry Archives, but this afternoon and evening Philip wanted to explore his new locality. There was so much to appreciate here and in the arrondissements surrounding the hotel.

He meandered through the neighborhoods, viewing the architecture and the people on the streets, investigating the great variety of shops, and reading menus posted on the many high-class restaurants and brasseries. When he approached Brentano's booksellers on the Avenue de l'Opéra, Philip knew what he had to do. He treated himself to a beautiful new Swan fountain pen: thin, short, black with gold banding, and a safety screw-top that guaranteed no accidental spillage of ink. He wanted the finest for the research work to which he was returning.

He also bought several newspapers to catch up on recent political developments. Much of the reportage concerned the state visit of President Poincaré and Prime Minister René Viviani to St. Petersburg. The two French leaders had just ended three days of political conversations at the highest level in the Russian capital.

Philip knew what these meetings were about. Clearly, Poincaré and Viviani were conferring with their Russian allies about possible reactions should Austria-Hungary or Germany do something provocative. No doubt they were also discussing possible British involvement as well as the reaction in Italy should hostilities erupt.

In a shorter article bearing today's dateline of July 24, he saw a report that the Vienna government had issued an ultimatum to the leadership in Belgrade demanding that Serbia bend to a set of harsh Austrian demands. The most onerous, Philip thought, was the insistence that the Austrians be allowed to conduct within Serbia their own investigation into the assassinations—even though the murders actually occurred in Bosnia, which for the past six years was part of the Hapsburg Empire. Philip recognized that this was an impossible demand for a sovereign nation to accept.

As a historian, he knew that the escalation of diplomatic pressure could produce uncontrollable consequences. As he understood foreign affairs, when one government says A, it must be prepared to say B. Clearly, A was Vienna's insistence on concessions from Serbia. No one knew what Austria's next move would be should the Serbs refuse to acquiesce, but B just might be an Austrian invasion of Serbia.

In different circumstances it would have been relaxing to promenade farther down the rue de Rivoli toward the Louvre to visit the museum's superb collection of historic art. But the news of the day was too distressing. Instead of cultural delights, ugly politics imposed themselves on Philip's mood. Rather than a reinvigorating stroll, he went for an early supper at a small bistro near the Place Vendôme, then returned to his room at the Crillon.

For the next several days Philip confined his activities to archival research. He arrived when the Ministry opened and departed as the doors were closing. He made a conscious effort to bury himself in academic work and thereby avoid the frightening situation in contemporary European politics.

Complete escape, however, was impossible. Newspaper headlines, conversations overheard in restaurants, talk between passengers in the Métro, and even overheard chatter between companions walking on the boulevards: the approaching conflagration preoccupied a fearful Paris.

Philip literally encountered such public anxiety when he was swept into a massive political demonstration. It was July 27 and Philip was seated at a sidewalk café on the Boulevard Saint-Germain lazily people-watching on a warm Monday morning. What began as a distant noise rose in a crescendo until it was thunderous and headed in Philip's direction. When he walked into the street to look for the source of the din, he saw thousands of Parisians several blocks away marching toward him. Drummers were maintaining a brisk military cadence as men and women of all ages paraded down the boulevard carrying banners and individual signs proclaiming their commitment to peace and other issues.

The demands were clear: "Down with War!" "Working Class Brothers Will Not Fight Fellow Workers," "We Want Peace Now," "I Will Not Fight," "Repeal the 3-Year Draft Law"—the latter referring to the conscription law passed last year extending the military commitment of drafted young men from two years to three years.

Here was French socialism on the march. The working-class movement that proclaimed itself the political alternative to divisive nationalism was standing against potential war. As he waded into the marchers, Philip heard appeals for laborers of all countries to embrace each other in class solidarity. Marxist and Roman Catholic trade union organizations, often bitter rivals, were united in declaring that workers of the world would not die for capitalists or kings.

To Philip it appeared as if the entire French political Left was represented in this *manif*. Given the power the Left had won in French parliamentary elections last month, the insistence of the crowd stood a chance of affecting state policy.

He decided to walk with the protesters and soon found himself in the middle of a group from the CGT, the Confédération General du Travail, the largest trade-union organization in France. These marchers seemed to support the broad demands of the entire demonstration, but many CGT banners also called for a shorter work week, improved salaries, workplace improvements, and other narrower issues.

To fit in, Philip took a sign and carried it high as the *manif* reached the Seine and turned right. The protesters crossed the Pont de la Concorde, the bridge leading over the river and into the Place de la Concorde. There Philip saw thousands of people already gathered to urge the French government in a new direction.

For the first half hour, the crowd chanted its demands and moved signs up and down to attract attention. But the level of intensity rose considerably when a string of prominent leftist leaders appeared to speak to the group. Philip recognized only Jean Jaurès, the parliamentary leader of the reformist French Socialist Party. But the protesters knew all of the speakers and the approval was loud for each.

Clearly, however, Jaurès was the crowd favorite. When he came to the platform to address the gathering, he was thunderously received. He spoke about international politics and his fear that the armaments race masterminded from London, Paris, and St. Petersburg might lead to war against Germany.

Jaurès decried the militaristic tensions in modern politics. His prescription for peace that day was an immediate reconciliation of differences between France and Germany. He promised, however— and the protesters strongly concurred—that should war come the working classes of industrial Europe must refuse to follow the captains of industry and ultra-nationalistic zealots whose policies might destroy civilization.

Philip walked among the demonstrators for another hour. They were inspiring in their idealism, but as a professor of history, he saw little chance that working-class brotherhood would prevent a conflict should the momentum of events carry Europe into open warfare. The study of history generates a certain cynicism. It wasn't that collectivism couldn't stop the drums of war, it was that no unofficial counter-movement had ever accomplished this in the past; and it was likely that socialism would not be effective this time either.

Philip left the protest march saddened by what he had just experienced. These were conscientious people railing against a force they could not stop with parades and placards. If war came, he worried, these people would be trampled in the rush to join the battle. Nationalism had controlled the public imagination for a long time, and nothing had yet diminished its appeal. Socialism was a legitimate political reaction to exploitive capitalism in the 19th century. But this was a new century; and at times the collectivist philosophy seemed too class-focused, too industrial, and too void of universal attractiveness.

Alone in his room that evening, Philip wrote to his family. He confessed his attempt to avoid thinking about contemporary politics. But he was overwhelmed by the events of the past week, he wrote. He expressed a deep pessimism over the course of political events. His final sentences encapsulated the anxiety he was feeling. "Be assured, I will do everything I can to protect myself from harm and get back to America. But matters are running downhill here. I see nothing that can halt the precipitous descent into full-scale combat. It reminds me of those crazy Futurist artists and the attitude of reckless, nihilistic abandon they advocated. Unbelievable as it seems, many people here are in love with the idea of war. They seem to be bored with peace because it's cerebral, even tedious. But a dose of war will re-engage the senses and make life exciting again.

"What has happened to our civilization? Is boredom followed by conflict the future of all civilized living? Oh, my God, I pray not."

Developments the following day, however, made Philip shiver. The headline in *Le Temps* was frightening: Austria-Hungary had declared war on Serbia. The hotheads in Vienna had won the day, and combat would begin at any moment. The fate of Europe, if not the planet, depended on what happened next. Exactly one month after a single Bosnian extremist had murdered the disrespected Franz Ferdinand, the Hapsburg monarchy was willing to risk continental holocaust in order to squash the Serbian gnat.

It was clear to Philip that, at a minimum, the Austrians had jumped on the Sarajevo streetcar. Leadership in Vienna decided that this was the event on which they would ride to war even though they had no idea where such a journey would take them or anyone else.

He retreated to his room depressed, frustrated, angry, and scared.

That afternoon a messenger delivered a note for him at the Crillon. It was from Théophile Delcassé requesting a personal meeting as soon as possible. Philip noticed that Delcassé had signed the note as Minister of Foreign Affairs. Somehow, he had missed newspaper accounts of Delcassé's return to power at the Quai d'Orsay. As rapidly as possible, he left for the rendezvous.

The Ministry was close by, but given the urgency detectable in the note, Philip went by taxi. He was immediately admitted to Delcassé's office.

"Professor Belmont, it's nice to see you again," exclaimed the Foreign Minister. "I know Camille has thanked you officially, but I have been extremely busy and have not had the opportunity to add my appreciation until now. We had no idea you would face such hardships on your trip to Rome. But on behalf of myself and France, I wanted to say *merci beaucoup beaucoup*."

"It was my honor, Minister Delcassé," replied Philip. "And, I am pleased to see that you have retaken the portfolio of Foreign Affairs. These are critical times and France needs you and your talents."

"Ah, thank you. That happened two days ago. But, do you know that since 1911, I am the eleventh foreign minister?" responded Delcassé. "We've had eleven ministries in less than four years! That does not generate a stable foreign policy. In my prime, I held the portfolio for seven consecutive years, and we made outstanding progress. One can accomplish nothing, absolutely nothing, with only a few months—sometimes only weeks—in office. Hopefully, I can bring consistency back to the Quai d'Orsay and to French diplomacy. As you probably know from reading the journals, we need it badly right now.

"But enough of my desperation. I requested this short conference with you for no purpose except to express France's obligation for your remarkable assistance," Delcassé declared. "I will not have time in the future to thank you. We are in frightening times, my American friend. The government is already making plans to leave Paris and reestablish itself far to the southwest in Bordeaux should the Germans invade or threaten the capital. So much is at stake. We cannot afford to be captured by the Boches as was Napoléon III in 1870."

"The government planning to evacuate Paris: that's terrible news," said Philip.

"Oh, no, no, no. We are only making contingency plans. We are not ready to leave yet. These plans are for just in case," Delcassé interjected.

"Then let's hope the plans never need to be activated," said Philip. "Again, it was my honor to have assisted. And I wish you good fortune in your efforts to return stability to French foreign affairs and sanity to Europe."

Philip left the brief encounter with increased respect for the Foreign Minister and the task ahead of him. But he knew that Delcassé couldn't stop the dynamic now sweeping through the chancelleries of Europe. All he could do was work for the best interests of France and hope the Austrian action did not trigger belligerent responses elsewhere.

In the following days, however, Philip watched helplessly as the history of the world changed. In a relentless sequence of interrelated choices, a decision in one capital city triggered a counter-response in another capital. From the Austrian declaration of war against Serbia on July 28 there followed an order in St. Petersburg for the general mobilization of the Russian armies against Germany and Austria-Hungary. It was quickly modified to specify only mobilization against the Hapsburg monarchy—but on July 30 the Russians changed their mind and reinstated the original order for a general mobilization.

July 31 was an event-filled day. The Germans threatened consequences if Russia did not stop its military buildup along the Russo-German border. Then Berlin, locked in the rhythm of the Schlieffen Plan, refused a British demand to respect the neutrality of Belgium, a status Great Britain and other Great Powers had guaranteed since Belgium was created as an independent and militarily-neutral kingdom in the 1830s.

The Germans also delivered an ultimatum demanding that France announce its neutrality within several hours. The insincerity of this overture was evident in its supplementary requirement that France also surrender to Germany the strategic fortress cities of Verdun and Belfort as a guarantee that French non-involvement would be maintained.

Later that day Austria-Hungary declared its own state of general mobilization. But Serbia was no longer its only target. Austria was now preparing to wage war on the Russians because leaders in Vienna felt the Tsar would intervene on the side of the troublesome Serbs.

By August 1, 1914 the dynamics of continental destruction were unstoppable. First, France rallied in support of its Russian ally when the General Staff in Paris revealed that general mobilization was now underway. Five minutes later Germany announced mobilization of its armed forces massed on its Western and Eastern Fronts. And three hours after announcing general mobilization, the Germans declared that the Fatherland was now at war with Russia.

Sadly, newspapers this day reported that the strongest voice against continental warfare had been silenced. Jean Jaurès had been shot dead the previous evening by a French chauvinist.

On August 2 leaders in London began to assess the British position, this as German troops in the West commenced their march into neutral Luxembourg, obviously heading for Belgium and eventually France. The following day at 6:45 pm, Germany declared war on France.

On August 4, Berlin announced that a state of war now existed with Belgium, this as German soldiers blasted into that small nation in search of an entry point from which to penetrate northern France and drive directly to Paris. The same day, in response to German aggression—in particular what British newspapers termed the "Rape of Belgium"—Great Britain declared war on Germany and readied the small British Expeditionary Force for combat in France and Belgium. Two days later Austria-Hungary declared war on Russia, and Serbia announced that a state of war now existed with Germany.

Within one week the fragile balance of power that maintained the peace of Europe for a century was in shambles. What had taken careful diplomacy and enormous restraint to create crumbled precipitously. The continent now plunged into the most horrific conflict it had experienced since Napoléonic times. European civilization was locked in full-scale civil war.

As brutal as the week had been, one action stood out for Philip. In the midst of the political meltdown, the government of Italy announced that it would remain neutral in the unfolding conflict. It was a decision not unanticipated in Berlin and Vienna. But it still infuriated leaders in the Germanic capitals. By terms of the Triple Alliance, Italy's obligations to her allies became operative only if Germany or Austria went to war as a defensive measure. In this case, however, the Italian government considered Germany and Austria-Hungary to be waging wars of aggression.

It made Philip feel vindicated. Clearly, the Schlieffen Plan exposed the true character of the strategy. No amount of rhetoric from Berlin could alter what the German General Staff had planned for almost a decade.

Suddenly, Philip's situation changed. Academic research was out of the question. Access to the Quai d'Orsay and its offices were now restricted. Scores of soldiers with machine guns intimidatingly patrolled the grounds and the streets around the building.

Moreover, it was impossible by this date to book passage back to the neutral United States. Thousands of Americans trapped throughout Europe were scrambling to find some way to get back home. But it was difficult to reserve space since British, German and French ocean liners—the vessels that conducted most of the trans-Atlantic passenger business—were now either requisitioned for military purposes or were vulnerable targets for enemy submarines, destroyers, and battleships. Philip placed his name on a waiting list, but there were many hundreds of eligible people listed ahead of him.

On the battlefield the German military machine was formidable. Even though Belgian forces put up a valiant and unexpectedly-strong defense of their nation, and French and British troops were there to greet the invaders when they moved into northern France, the Germans fought their way at great expense toward the French capital. Despite the cost in human life, they moved toward Paris. A near panic gripped the citizens of the city throughout August as news reports traced the unstoppable advance of German military forces toward them.

By the end of the first month of combat, German airplanes were dropping leaflets on Paris announcing that the Kaiser's armies would be arriving by September 3. Following aerial bombardment of the city on August 30 and September 1—the first attack killing two civilians—vigilant Parisians studiously watched the sky for additional assaults by enemy airplanes as well as long blimps and longer Zeppelins—those oval-shaped, gas-filled bombing-stations that people were already derisively calling "sausages."

Adding to the confusion, reports of German spies operating within Paris were plentiful. Who could be trusted when everyone was a suspect? Stories circulated among the residents, such as the one about a young Alsatian woman in Paris who accidentally stepped on a man's foot causing him to curse at her instinctively in German. Recognizing the language, she followed the suspicious man to his home then reported his location to the police who soon uncovered a nest of spies operating from the residence.

Still, the citizenry held together and sought out the latest battlefront information. Newspapers became vital to the maintenance of mass sanity. Throughout those first weeks of war, all Paris devoured the news reports. Unfortunately, most of the reports were ominous for France.

Remarkably, the German advance through Belgium was slowed by unexpected military resistance. Three weeks and thousands of lives were lost by the superior German forces in overcoming this opposition. And when the resistance was finally broken, tens of thousands of Belgian soldiers fled southward where they fought alongside the French Army.

It angered Philip that General Joffre and other military leaders in Paris had gambled that while Germany was coming down from the north, France could strike toward the northeast. In August the French had 800,000 men deployed on their northern borders, but too many were used to invade southern Germany in a futile effort to reclaim Alsace and Lorraine.

Hadn't Joffre understood the implications of the Schlieffen Plan? Didn't he recognize that on their Western Front the Germans had amassed 1.5 million well-trained and well-equipped soldiers organized into seven armies with most of them marching through Belgium and heading for Paris? Apparently not, because the French General Staff committed hundreds of thousands of troops to the campaign to retrieve the so-called Lost Provinces.

For three weeks the French and Germans fought a series of engagements known as The Battle of the Frontiers. After initial success, French forces were mauled, especially by German machine gunners who were now fighting a defensive war. And while the surviving foot soldiers, the *poilus*, were retreating precipitously from the northeast, the German juggernaut finally passed through Belgium and moved now through the northern provinces of France toward Paris.

When British military assistance arrived in France in mid-August, it was cheered by fearful French citizens, especially the Parisians. But the British land force was small and poorly-trained. The British Expeditionary Force contributed only about 150,000 soldiers to the war in northern France and Belgium. And in the first decisive battle involving British and French troops, the Battle of Mons on August 23, the German Army prevailed primarily by the strength of numerical superiority. Anglo-French units were compelled to retreat southward in rapid order.

But at what cost? In some cases, rather than employ elaborate flanking maneuvers, the German troops marched straight through the enemy. As one observer recalled it, "The rifles blazed but the Germans walked into a wall of fire....the chaps opened up—and the Germans fell down like logs. I've never seen anything like it." Hundreds of British riflemen, trained as crack shots, fired once every four seconds at the wave of humanity thrown at them by German commanders. In one day of intense fighting at Mons, estimates placed German casualties between 6000 and 10,000. The British suffered 1642 killed that same day.

Matters became so fragile in Paris that the French government activated its contingency plan and on September 3 fled the capital. The government relocated to Bordeaux near the Atlantic coast and the Spanish border, hundreds of miles from the conflict. Moreover, by this date approximately one-third of all Parisians had abandoned the city, fearful that the invaders would be victorious.

By early September, German armies numbering more than a million men were nearing the Marne River at a point about twenty-six miles from the French capital. Enemy scouting units on horseback were actually spotted in Ecouen, only eight miles away. Paris was facing either siege or outright military conquest.

Between September 5 and September 12, the fate of France seemed to be teetering toward loss. While the exhausted French and British and German troops fought a last-ditch engagement that the newspapers called the Battle of the Marne, Philip labored feverishly in the city to assist however possible.

There was so much to be done. He had never been in such a terrifying situation, but he did not desert the city. Certainly, Philip had read of historic military attacks. But it was one thing to read about an invading army operating 200 years ago, and quite another to sit and wait in barely-repressed terror for the sound of the horses, marching boots, and the artillery of conquerors on the march.

Philip stayed in Paris where the only way to relieve tension was to work. He volunteered his services in a variety of endeavors. During the day he worked at a military hospital run by the French Red Cross. Here, injured soldiers were shuttled from the frontlines into the city to receive life-saving attention. Philip was no doctor, but he rolled bandages, carried stretchers, repaired the plumbing, swept floors, trained other volunteers in support skills—anything he was asked to do.

In the evening he was in the streets as part of a group of civilian monitors who used large megaphones to keep Parisians abreast of the latest battle developments. They also directed traffic on the streets and sidewalks, answered questions, and encouraged citizen optimism. With most members of the city police force now serving in the armed forces, these volunteers helped to preserve order in an increasingly tense city.

In trucks and automobiles and on foot these monitors kept the city from descending into chaos. Philip was assigned an old truck with which to patrol the neighborhoods around the Place de la Concorde looking for problems that needed immediate intervention. The vehicle was noisy and belched smoke, but his voice was louder than the sputtering engine.

The megaphone he carried was an amazing weapon of authority. A heated argument rapidly dissolved when Philip barked out a command to tone it down. Two inebriated men stopped their drift toward fisticuffs once Philip yelled from his truck, "If you want to fight, go out to the Marne!" Sometimes he had to resort to patriotic appeals to placate the malcontents, but Parisians usually cooperated at the first sound of his stentorian orders amplified through a megaphone.

One development continually bothered him as drove through the city's neighborhoods. With French military units engaged in a life-and-death battle nearby, why were there so many able-bodied soldiers still walking in the streets? These were not deserters or slackers, they were members of the Army Reserves based in the suburbs and ordered to remain in Paris and defend against invading Germans.

In his rounds Philip encountered hundreds of such troops. They were friendly and cooperative, and sometimes he needed a soldier or two to help enforce his orders to disruptive civilians. But at the back of his mind the question gnawed at him. With so much at stake, why weren't these military personnel at the battlefront?

In an audacious gesture reflective of the precariousness of the situation, Philip decided to find out why. On the rue de Rivoli he stopped a young officer who had just emerged from one of the few brasseries still open for business. He asked the soldier why he was in Paris when the battle was on the Marne. "I don't know why we're not out there," the soldier replied. "We're trained and we're rested. We want to fight, and those guys on the Marne must be exhausted by now.

"But don't ask me why we're not there," he added dismissively. "Go ask General Gallieni that question. He's in charge of the Paris garrison, not me."

It was a flippant response, no doubt meant to get rid of a pesky busybody. But Philip decided to take it literally. He jumped into his truck and began looking for the General's headquarters. It took him about an hour of false leads, but finally he found the command location near the École Militaire, the Military School situated in the shadow of the Eiffel Tower.

Boldly, and a bit naively, Philip drove toward the two soldiers guarding the entry to the facility. He announced that he was a trusted friend of General Joseph Joffre and was demanding to see the Commandant of the Reserves.

"You, a friend of Joffre?" a bemused lieutenant snickered. "Well, you can find Joffre somewhere near the Marne fighting the Boches." The other soldier was amused by the mocking tone with which Philip was being pushed aside.

The professor was used to brusque attitudes by this time. He refused to be intimidated. For at least ten minutes he continued to argue with the guards, insisting that he knew Joffre and needed to see General Gallieni immediately. It didn't work. The guards grew increasingly frustrated with Philip to the point where one of them actually discharged his rifle into the air as a signal that he had heard enough from this civilian complainer.

The sound of a rifle shot brought an unexpected response. Five or six soldiers ran toward the shooter. When they learned that the entire scene was caused by the incessant rudeness of one lone American, Philip was promptly placed under military arrest.

Peering from a jail cell, he continued to insist he was a friend of General Joffre. It didn't convince the man watching him, but it apparently had an effect higher up the chain of command. Somewhere around 7 pm a slender French officer, distinguished by a thick white moustache and eye glasses, entered the room where Philip was being held.

"I'm General Joseph Gallieni," he said to the prisoner. "If, as you claim, General Joffre were not such a close friend of yours I would not be standing here. I hate to say it, but your ranting has worked. I am here now. Tell me what is on your mind. You have two minutes to explain yourself, no more."

"Thank you, General," the surprised professor exclaimed. He introduced himself and stressed that he was a U. S. citizen with no interest except the survival of France. "I've been looking for you to ask one simple question," he said. "With the future of your nation in the balance, why are there so many reserve troops still stationed here in Paris? Why aren't your troops at the Marne battlefront right now?"

"Why? You ask why?" the General replied somewhat angrily. "I'll tell you why. The other officers have already moved every last military vehicle to the combat zones. They shipped troops and supplies east and northeast and even out to the Marne and beyond. As a result, I don't have the wheels to get my soldiers there. What can I do? Order a forced march of twenty-six miles in full combat uniforms? That would only tire my men and make them easy targets for enemy artillery and especially Boche machine guns."

"If I may ask, General," Philip interjected, "how many troops are available in Paris?"

Amazed by Philip's insistence, the exasperated General replied, "We have about 11,000 soldiers, but we can't get them to the fight. Do you know how frustrating that is for me?"

"Well, I have an idea that may help you," Philip brazenly declared. "I have a truck and I would be happy to drive some of your troops to the Marne—right now!"

Gallieni and his aides laughed heartily at the notion. "You want to take soldiers to the frontlines tonight? Be serious, Professor Belmont," the General answered.

"Don't laugh, General. I could take as many as five fully-armed men carrying extra ammunition. Now, how far is it to the frontline on the Marne? Let's say it's thirty miles. If I pushed myself, I could make two trips tonight. That would double the reinforcements I could provide. That's ten more armed *poilus* than the generals have on the line right now," Philip added.

"All right, stop playing arithmetic games," Gallieni said as he began to walk away from Philip. "You can transport ten soldiers at best. That's foolishness."

Philip persisted. "But, General, hear me out, please. Here's the point I'm trying to make: I am not alone. Do you know how many trucks there are in Paris? Better still, do you know how many taxicabs there are in this city, sir?

"I say, commandeer every taxi, every car, every truck on the streets. Fill them with French reinforcements and drive them to the Marne. There must be a thousand or more vehicles that could be enlisted. Each driver could make two trips to the Marne this evening and through the night. And how many men in battle gear can one of those big Renault taxis carry? Five? Maybe six if the *poilus* are small?

"With due respect, General Gallieni, make the calculation. Eleven hundred vehicles, two trips with five soldiers each time: that's 11,000 trained fighters moved to the battle overnight. And that's the number of rested men you have sitting in Paris or the suburbs itching to see combat. Could any French commander operating along on the Marne use an infusion of fresh troops at this time?

"You get your men ready, and I'll get the taxis to you," Philip declared with conviction.

The General looked flabbergasted. The proposition was so simple and obvious, yet he and his staff had totally overlooked it. Besides, what had he to lose? If the French and British defenders collapsed on the Marne tomorrow, he and his soldiers would be either dead or in German prison camps the following day.

"Can you do that, young man?" the General asked somberly.

"I am sure I can, sir. Just loan me forty of your soldiers with forty megaphones. And if you don't have enough megaphones in storage, get me some thick pieces of paper and we'll make our own.

"Here's how we will do it. We will start with the railroad stations and large hotels: telephone the taxi stands there and order them here immediately. Send your soldiers to commandeer taxis off the streets. Then send those taxis all over Paris and the suburbs looking for even more vehicles.

"Scatter your men throughout the city. Stop every cab and enlist the drivers in the cause. If there are passengers in the cabs, ask them to leave in the name of France. And if that does not work, pull them out if you have to.

"We'll order the vehicles and their drivers to your staging area here at the École Militaire. Then we'll disperse them to Gagny or Livry-Gargan where, I understand, most of your troops are garrisoned. The 7th Infantry Division, the 10th Hussars Regiment, the 103rd and 104th Infantry Regiments—they are mostly just sitting in the suburbs ten miles from here. As for your troops in the city this evening, order them back to their bases as rapidly as possible. Let's start them all flowing toward the Marne, General. As for the drivers, they won't complain. They'll be proud to help save their treasured city."

Gallieni thought a few seconds then ordered his aides to release Philip and implement his *ad hoc* plan immediately. "I never studied this tactic in military school," he said, "but if it works tonight, there'll be training manuals written about it in the future."

Within a half-hour, Philip had his contingent of soldiers, all carrying megaphones and spreading throughout Paris. The hotels and railways stations were a natural target, but the soldiers requisitioned the taxis and trucks moving along any street, even those that were parked at curbs. From the great boulevards to the narrow alleys, every four-wheeled automotive vehicle was ordered to the staging area.

Philip and his crew directed the drivers from all over the city to assemble at the École Militaire. Within ninety minutes, the area was filled, predominantly with red Renault taxicabs ready to participate in this unprecedented military plan.

Before the first vehicles actually departed for the battlefront, however, General Gallieni appeared at the Paris staging area. He summoned a group of drivers to gather around him, Philip included, and began to speak about the importance of what was about to happen this evening.

He spoke frankly, seeking to rally enthusiasm for the adventure. "Several days ago I spoke to the armies and the inhabitants of Paris, telling them that the government of France had left the capital and that I was charged with defending Paris from the invaders," Gallieni declared. "I said it then, and I say it now: I shall do this to the end.

"But now I ask for your help. You must act with bravery and cunning because you are now with me defending Paris from the barbarians. What you are about to do tonight is a civilian's idea. I have never conducted such an operation. But you are patriots and you are fighting for your lives and your way of life. Drive straight and drive fast, my brothers. We of the French Army salute you and pray for your success."

The men stayed silent, then burst into cheers until one of them yell out, "To your taxis! We're losing time!" That scattered the group as the drivers ran to their respective vehicles.

They raced the ten miles to the two loading areas in the Paris suburbs. Here, military officers directed them to form lines, bumper to bumper, stretching hundreds of yards. Methodically armed soldiers were ordered into the empty cabs. As each was filled, it headed for the Marne. Those directing traffic ordered the loading lines to converge into a serpentine caravan. The operation became so well-executed that a taxicab could be filled within twenty seconds, and in another ten seconds be in the single-file procession heading to the front.

Philip traveled to Gagny with one of the first departing Renaults. Soon, he and his military assistants created a rolling armada: the taxis of the Marne out on a little night trip. At Livry-Gargan, other Army officials organized the loading of troops into the Paris trucks and cabs and sent them on their rescue mission.

That night of September 7 to September 8, 1914 was extraordinary. Throughout the evening the drivers from Paris pushed themselves and their vehicles. Never had unarmed civilians been so intimately involved in modern warfare. Around the clock they loaded soldiers and deposited them near the battlefront.

The way to the fighting was not always smooth. A number of taxis went off the roadway in the darkness. Several developed flat tires. And there were a few instances of vehicles crashing into each other. Some drivers even stopped to buy dinner because in the heat of the moment, the French Army forgot to give provisions to the troops and drivers. It was, nevertheless, an inspirational event.

At the front, the taxis deposited their valuable cargoes, and then raced back to Paris for another load. Some drivers pushed on with tears in their eyes, others sang patriotic songs aloud to keep themselves from falling asleep. None complained, except for one driver who whimsically told Philip, "I'm only sorry our soldiers are so big nowadays. If we had *poilus* the size of Napoléon, I could get one or two more in my Renault."

More typical of what he heard, was the determination in the voice of a middle-aged driver who confided that in '71 during the Franco-Prussian War his father had to eat rats and dogs because the Germans laid siege to Paris and interrupted the supply of fresh food. "Mark my words," he asserted, "I will never allow my son and daughter to eat rats because I did not fight for my city. *Jamais encore.* Never again."

Philip knew that 11,000 reinforcements could not win a battle against the mighty German Army. But, he knew how important emotion was to the French soldiers. *Élan vital* was the vital spiritedness, the emotional superiority that was supposed to carry France to victory against the invaders. That spirit had been sorely abused by enemy machine guns in the first weeks of combat. But the inspiration drawn from the caravanning taxis and trucks of the Marne was incalculable. From highly-ranked officers to the lowliest *poilu*, the realization that Paris drivers were working with reserve soldiers to stem the German advance gave the French Army regulars a burst of energy and hope that proved crucial to reversing the German advance and pushing the Boches away from the cherished French capital.

In little more than a month since the invaders had brutally smashed through neutral Luxembourg and Belgium and into France, this was already a different kind of conflict. More than clashes between professional armies in the field, this war involved civilian combatants, working-class taxi drivers volunteering their services, ordinary men and women making bandages, people donating their own energy and time to resist the relentless invaders. And, of course, countless innocent civilians massacred by the Germans.

This was Europe's first total war. It engulfed entire societies in a life-or-death struggle. Cities and towns were no longer islands of safety. The brutality of conflict was palpable even in the most beautiful and sacred of places.

Everyone felt the agony. This was a common person's struggle, war made intimate and immediate. And it was savage. In the month of August the French Army sustained 260,000 casualties, including 75,000 deaths, and 140,000 killed or wounded in only the last four days of the Battle of the Frontiers. Ten percent of France's military officers were killed or wounded in the same month.

Returning to Paris after depositing his second group of soldiers, Philip began to assess the evening's events in historical terms. Something monumental was happening in Europe. He could not know the future, but the past informed his understanding of the way things were headed. The magnificence of the continent's civilization—that model of social betterment that empire-makers employed to convince their colonial subjects that French or British or German or Russian ways were superior—was disintegrating before his eyes.

Philip was reminded of something he had read in a London newspaper a few days earlier. With Britain entering a war that was already blazing on the continent, the British Foreign Secretary, Lord Grey, commented ominously. "The lights are going out all over Europe and I doubt we will see them go on again in our lifetime."

Philip prayed that this was not the case. But he feared the worst. He sensed that the mightiest and most-accomplished continent was killing itself. He wondered about the thin veneer of civility that protected socialized human beings from becoming rapacious animals. How thick was that coating? How animalistic could uniformed men become if they were freed from legal constraint and rewarded for killing as many people as possible?

By the time he returned to his hotel room, Philip was drained of all energy. He did feel pleased, however, that he had contributed everything he could in the defense of France. But he grew almost fatalistic. He felt like those casino croupiers who spin the roulette wheel and then drop the small wooden ball. With all bets down, they announce *les jeux sont faits*: the bets are made, the game is on. Nothing more can be done—whatever happens, whatever number or color the ball stops on is now in the hands of fate.

Fighting on the Marne would continue for several more days. Intense and horrific, men on all sides perished in large numbers. Advances and retreats by the warring armies were accomplished over muddy fields littered with human and animal corpses and shattered machinery. Philip knew that some of the poor souls he had taken to the front were probably among the casualties.

Not until the morning of September 10 was there good news in Paris. The exhausted German Army had finally broken. Enemy positions were abandoned as the invaders headed away from the Marne and from Paris.

By the evening of September 12 the Germans were in general retreat. With tired French and British troops in pursuit, the raiders were fleeing back to their fortified lines that ran through such French country towns as Verdun, Rheims, and Soissons. The capital was saved, but France remained a bloody battleground.

War is never glorious except to old men who have forgotten and young men who are inexperienced and know nothing of its realities. War is a death dance: human and otherwise. It is by definition uncivilized. And the victor is usually the side that kills more people. Philip was only too happy that his own nation was not a part of this unfolding debauchery.

7

When Philip volunteered to help the French Red Cross, he never anticipated such trauma. He had no training in medicine, but given the reality of their manpower shortages the French were not particular. They needed competent assistance, and Philip was willing to help.

How to dress a wound, how to decontaminate a festering inflection, how to nurse an emotionally-disturbed soldier back to some semblance of normality: he learned medicine on the job. This was his new university of life and death. He despised what he had to do, but it was essential. There is no doubt that without his intervention, and without the actions of countless others giving their time and energy, lives would have been lost.

This is a side of war seldom seen and never glorified. This is the world of the injured and maimed, the unfortunate people who stopped bullets and bayonets and shrapnel with their bodies, the misfortunate who cheated death but paid a high physical and emotional price in the process. It is also the morbid dimension of combat because many of the battered do not survive. They die on the operating table, on the ground waiting for medical attention, in stretchers while on the way to hospital, in post-operative recovery rooms, in the midst of emergency intervention when the surgeons learn they have run out of critical medicines.

Philip witnessed a depressing parade of human cruelty, as men with a multitude of injuries came under his care. Some had shattered or missing limbs; others had grievous open wounds; a few just sat and mumbled incoherently, the victims of shell-shock. Crippled, blinded, deafened, traumatized, infected: the varieties of hurt seemed endless. All had blood somewhere on their skin or matted in their hair, familiar signs of intense fighting.

Brave soldiers were often reduced to screams and trembling. Tears, not boasting, typified the reactions of men whom he handled. Wounds may have ripped apart the flesh, but for many of the survivors the war also broke open the soul. And Philip Belmont, American historian, was still not immune to the anguish such violation inflicted on the human spirit.

Some young soldiers cried on their death beds because they didn't want to die. Some cursed their leaders—President and Kaiser, King and commander—who guided them toward mutilation. None of the wounded sang a national anthem. And all of these men wanted to go home—home to family, familiarity, controllability. Instead, they were lying in an anonymous hospital ward that was throbbing with pain, a make-shift arrangement providing care to a non-stop flow of shattered bodies.

Fortunately for Philip, however, he was not involved with the funerary contingents, the civilians who tended to the final affairs of combatants killed on the front. That might have driven him over the edge of sanity. He tried hard to avoid military funerals, the kind that occurred regularly in the villages of northern France where townspeople buried their own sons as well as victims from throughout France.

Fighting inside a foreign country, the Germans were far from their support system for handling the dead. They often erected funeral pyres on which they cremated as many as 2000 of their own dead at one time. Other medical personnel told Philip about such occurrences. And in his later travels near the frontlines he once encountered such a site. It was a ghastly incinerated barn which had been reduced to an amalgam of ashes, charred bones, and melted buttons. For weeks the gruesome scene gave Philip nightmares.

His work in Paris, however, forced him to push horror from his mind. His concern had to be for the living and the barely living. One wounded soldier in particular affected Philip. He was a German corporal—yes, the Red Cross sometimes cared for wounded enemy soldiers—perhaps nineteen years old, whose life seemed ruined. A French mortar had burst near him and blew away his lower jaw. He was left with an upper jaw and a portion of his tongue intact. The explosion also cost him his left leg. Although ravaged by modern weaponry, his eyes betrayed a youthful innocence that remained unextinguished.

The soldier was difficult to understand because he could not articulate his words, and Philip could not speak German. Even with a translator, he was almost unintelligible. As Philip understood him, the young German wanted a volunteer to write a letter home for him. He wished to reassure his fiancée in Saxony that he was alive and would eventually return to her—and that he loved her very much.

It was wrenching as Philip listened to the translator read in French what the young man had just dictated. Tears swelled in the professor's eyes as he heard tender words such as sweetheart, kiss, love, and lonely. The brutalized soldier never once said Fatherland or Kaiser or Empire. Not once did he yell "*Nach Paris*"—the infamous German rallying cry of "On to Paris!"

This was personal, a letter filled with tenderness and vulnerability. The wounded man no longer cared about the words that seduced him into the conflict. At this point in his life, he was a human being who was suffering greatly and crushed with sadness. Philip turned away for a few moments in order to gather his self-control.

For weeks this procession of injury passed by on stretchers and gurneys and wheelchairs. Although each case had its own special challenges, Philip was almost becoming immune to the shock of seeing so much anguish so closely. That is until the day in mid-September when he recognized one of the stricken warriors lying before him.

It was his good friend from the Two Swans and the *Au Carrousel Bleu*, Thad Lanyard. The young Australian student lay before him minus an eye and a right arm. Tourniquets stopped external bleeding in several places, but what remained of Thad's lost limb was already inflected with gangrene. "Hey, Phil, is that you?" he asked as he peered upward. "Imagine meeting you here."

"Thad!" Philip exclaimed. "What's happened to you?"

The Australian smiled. "Oh, I got carried away a few months ago. In fact, just around the time you disappeared from the Two Swans." he said while wincing in agony. "I went and joined the British Army. Don't ask me how, but I ended up with the Royal Scots Fusiliers. Figured I'd look spiffy in a kilt. Didn't get too much training, though. Not enough time. Ended up just another Tommy carrying a rifle for King and Country."

As Thad spoke, his voice grew weaker. "No one told me about heavy artillery and red-hot shrapnel. I made it out of Mons in one piece, but I left behind a few body parts when the Germans bombarded us during the retreat to the Marne. We were outnumbered eight to one. We marched as many as twenty-six miles in a single day. But the Boches kept coming after us. We fought back ferociously, but they finally got me. Looks like I'm out of the war for a while."

Philip called for more medical help. "Just hang on, Thad, you're going to be fine. We're going to fix you up," he promised.

Doctors came and administered pain killers. A nurse bathed and disinfected his open wounds. As the trained professionals attended to Thad, the two friends talked about shared experiences. Thad smiled when he recalled the zinc tub being carted down the street. "That was a crazy sight," he said to Philip. "The guy carried it upside down with his head inside the thing—while he carried a pail of hot water. I don't know how he could see anything in front of him. I'll remember that fellow and his bathtub for the rest of my life."

Philip recalled good times at the *Au Carrousel Bleu*. "You were so right about the food there," he said, "it was excellent. And the *Jour de débat*. I don't want to think about it. Too much intellectual excitement for me," Philip jested.

The small talk and reminiscing made little difference. Thad faded fast. First he began to spit up blood. Then he couldn't see Philip. Then he couldn't hear his friend any longer. Thad died on a gurney in front of Philip's eyes.

For the record, he was listed as a British casualty, another life lost for the cause. But for Philip, Thad Lanyard was a wonderful guy, a gentle friend with unlimited potential who was now forever gone because of civic insanity. Philip cried uncontrollably over his dead friend.

He cursed the war. Profanity helped him recover his composure. By the time Thad's body was taken away there were at least ten new disfigured men waiting for Philip's assistance.

That's how he spent the next few days. Philip did the best he could, intervening and counseling, then watching as life and death conducted a cruel debate over the fate of each injured soldier. Eventually, death became more familiar; but it was never ever easy.

Somewhere in the late September, Philip received notification that his request for passage on a neutral ship to the United States could not be honored for the foreseeable future. French ports were filled with British troop ships and supply vessels. Passenger traffic between France and England was restricted due to German submarines operating in the North Sea. And although the German Army was no longer advancing, there was always the possibility of an offensive breakthrough. Coastal cities such as Cherbourg, Dieppe, and Le Havre represented prime targets for enemy artillery. As a result, land travel to the coast was monitored carefully by the French military.

When he took his problem directly to the crowded U. S. Embassy on avenue Kléber, Philip found little sympathy. The waiting room was crowded with Americans who shared his predicament. Some had been tourists who came to France at the wrong time and were now stuck. Others held tickets on luxury ocean liners, U. S. and otherwise, that were now operating under military control.

Many people also lacked cash because they could not convert their dollars into French francs or British pounds. Even more complications affected Americans with French bank accounts. They were unable to withdraw funds because the nation's banking system was in chaos. And those with German accounts had no hope of retrieving their money.

One staff secretary confided to Philip that even retiring Ambassador Herrick was unable to leave. In fact, she explained, President Wilson had to extend Herrick's status because his replacement, William G. Sharp, had arrived only recently. But the pressing responsibilities created by the war made it impossible to introduce the new ambassador officially. "Mr. Sharp still hasn't traveled to Bordeaux to present his papers officially to the French government," she explained, "and he can't be formally installed until he does."

While listening to the garrulous secretary, Philip felt a tap of his shoulders. "Excuse me, young man. Aren't you Philip Belmont, the history professor from Berkeley?" asked someone with a deep male voice. When Philip turned he found himself face to face with the retiring Ambassador. He was no longer the happy man honored at the Élysée Palace in June. Herrick looked underweight and fatigued, even exhausted. Moreover, his face betrayed deep concern. Still he seemed unbent in optimism despite the conditions in Europe and the momentous tasks those conditions created for him.

"Yes, Mr. Ambassador, I'm Philip Belmont," he answered. "We met in the receiving line at President Poincaré's reception held to honor your service as ambassador. I'm the historian who is here to do research on the Revolutionary War era."

"Ah, I remember now. You were looking into French motives in supporting the Thirteen Colonies during the Revolution. Wonderful topic, but this has become an unfortunate time to conduct academic research," Herrick replied.

"Wait. Aren't the French government archives now closed now?" the ambassador inquired. "You couldn't research the diplomatic documents, even if you wanted. If that's the case, what are you still doing in Paris?

"Oh, I understand," he continued. "You're stuck here and can't get out, right?"

"Well, sir, I've been doing a lot of things lately," answered Philip. "Mostly, volunteer work with people who refuse to see this great city die. I've done everything from directing street traffic to bandaging injured soldiers in makeshift hospital wards."

Herrick paused for a moment then asked, "If you have the time right now, Dr. Belmont, would you mind stepping into my office? I'd like to talk to you in more detail about your predicament."

Philip agreed and soon found himself sitting with Ambassador Herrick sipping a cup of American coffee and discussing the war as it affected France.

After a few minutes of explaining embassy activities since hostilities began, Herrick grew more serious. "As you may know, I planned to be out of Paris by this time. Bill Sharp was supposed to be in charge by now. But President Wilson has notified me that due to the circumstances in which we found ourselves after August 1, he wanted me to remain here as ambassador for a while. Bill is in town, but he's still not accredited. In fact, he hasn't even found a place to live yet.

"As you can see, the United States Embassy is still here and we're operating night and day. The Germans may have come close to the gates of the city, but the United States of America bends for no one, not even the Kaiser. Lots of other nations relocated their embassies to Bordeaux, but the U. S. A. is staying put. As I told a newspaper reporter last week, Paris doesn't belong only to France—it belongs to the world. And we Americans will not surrender any of it to barbarity.

"Right now, we're working to protect U. S. government interests and the concerns of our citizens. They might be tourists trapped here or members of the American community living permanently in France. Our embassy is charged with safeguarding their lives and property.

"But that's not all. Do you know that as the territory of a neutral nation we now legally represent the affairs in France of several other countries? Presently, we handle such matters for Germany, Austria-Hungary, Great Britain, Serbia, and Turkey—as well as Nicaragua, Guatemala, and Japan. It's often a madhouse in many languages around here, Professor."

Philip was impressed by the ambassador's frankness. "I know that since I've been working in the war effort," he said to Herrick, "I've heard French people speak very fondly of you and of the volunteer programs you've organized. They're especially impressed with the American Ambulance you created.

"Yes, the American Ambulance is a priority. That's 'ambulance' in the French sense, a military emergency medical facility, not a truck to transport you to the hospital when you break a leg. But I didn't create it. It's the product of the Americans living in Paris, and the philanthropy and humanitarian spirit of people back in the United States.

"The Ambulance is our medical volunteer service. Don't confuse us with the Red Cross. The American Ambulance is an independent entity run out of the American Hospital in Neuilly, a suburb just outside

Paris. The doctors and nurses working there are giving their time just as you've been doing. They're not at the frontlines of the fighting. Instead, they work on soldiers who have been brought to them with combat wounds.

"Of course, if an American citizen has a heart attack or fractures an arm in Paris, we'll be there to take him or her to the American Hospital. But most of our efforts lately have involved caring for badly injured French and British soldiers—even the odd German prisoner, too.

"Just recently, we began operating our own facility, the Lycée Pasteur, a new school building that the French government has provided to us. We've turned it into a center for treating war wounds. We call it the American Military Hospital. At present, we have ten Ford trucks making roundtrips to the Gare la Chappelle where injured soldiers arrive by train from the battlefields. The French military transports them to us. The Lycée Pasteur facility has 240 beds and maybe a few more if necessary. But we have plans in the works to expand that soon to 600 beds.

"And this is just the beginning, Professor," the ambassador added. "We hope to send our people out into the countryside to create medical treatment facilities closer to the wounded. That's why we're raising thousands of dollars right now in large U. S. cities.

"Here in Paris we have wealthy benefactors like the Whitneys—Gertrude Vanderbilt Whitney and Mrs. William K. Whitney—who are helping us meet our goals. And we've named the various wards in our Pasteur hospital after the cities and states that have contributed the most money for us. Already we have wards named for Philadelphia, Boston, Chicago, and New York City—as well as Rhode Island and Virginia.

"For our expanded plans, we need more trucks. You see, we make our own vehicles. We buy a Model T chassis and engine from the Ford automobile plant in Levallois-Perret a few miles from here. Then we bolt the body of a large, enclosed delivery wagon to each chassis. And voilà, there's an ambulance—in the American sense of the word.

"More Fords and more medical personnel stationed closer to the front will increase the survival rate. That's our goal. We can't fight in this war because the United States is a neutral nation. But we certainly can save lives."

Ambassador Herrick shifted his tone and spoke directly to Philip now. "How would you like to have an important position in the American Ambulance?" he asked. "I know you're not a medical professional, but we could really use your organizational talent and your enthusiasm—that is if you're not going anywhere for a while."

Philip slowly inhaled trying to catch his breath. "Well, as you know, I'm not going anywhere in the foreseeable future. And I am flattered by your confidence in me. But I just don't know if I could do the job as well as your people who are already handling it."

"Nonsense, Professor Belmont," Ambassador Herrick responded. "I know more about you than you've been telling me. I've spoken off-the-record with Camille Barrère and Théo Delcassé. They told me about your Italian interlude. And when Gallieni phoned me to express his personal thanks for the American educator who suggested the taxis of the Marne, I'll bet he was speaking about you."

"Well, sir," replied Philip, "Rome was beautiful in July; and, yes, I recently did a little organizational work for the General and his brave troops."

"Then, you'll accept the position? It's purely voluntary. We can pay room and board for you, but no salary. But we could operate so much more effectively if you were one of us," the ambassador said.

Philip relented and accepted the ambassador's offer.

"One more thing," added Herrick, "you'll need a passport. I know when you came to France you didn't need one. But the war is changing matters. Many countries are suddenly requiring passports for entry and departure. So, come back tomorrow morning and we'll issue you a passport—just in case you ever need it."

The American Ambulance was not new to wartime service. Volunteers from the American colony living in Paris had offered their services to aid the injured during the Franco-Prussian War. However, Ambassador Herrick envisioned a much larger operation this time. He planned for the mobilization of all Americans in Paris who had the skills and the inclination to save lives.

He also welcomed the support of people in the United States who wanted to participate in person or through cash donations. From its earliest days the American Ambulance accepted young men who would leave the security of life at home to journey to France to help the cause. The qualifications for new drivers were simple: American citizenship, good health, a clean record, and the ability to drive an automobile—with the skill to repair one as a definite advantage.

Hundreds came willingly to Paris to offer their services. From New York City to Honolulu, doctors, surgeons, dentists, nurses, orderlies, and even truck drivers made their way to France to join the Ambulance.

Many who came were young men from wealthy families, people who could afford to work for living expenses only. A good percentage were college graduates. Others left college early or postponed their careers to come to France. For adventure? For humanitarian principles? Out of a sympathy with the French? All of these motivations and others accounted for what one volunteer called "the possibility of having even an infinitesimal part in one of the greatest events in history—the possibility of being of some service in the midst of so much distress—the interest in witnessing some of the scenes in this greatest and gravest of spectacles—and above all the chance of doing the little all that one can for France."

At first, the life-saving activities were confined to the American Military Hospital in Neuilly. But once the Germans were routed at the Marne and pushed northward to the Aisne River—fifty miles from Paris—the Ambulance established auxiliary medical field facilities in villages and towns immediately north of the city.

It was difficult for many of the volunteers in these localities if they did not speak French. And it was extremely unusual to find villagers able to communicate in English. Philip's language skills enhanced his importance to the organization. Soon those skills came to define his role in it.

With idealistic volunteers arriving weekly from the United States, the Ambulance and its recently-created American Ambulance Field Service had sufficient medical personnel, but they lacked the ability to respond rapidly with translators. Before long, Philip was serving as the Coordinator of Translation Services. This placed him in charge of three other translators, but mostly it put him in a Ford truck driving throughout the expanse of battlefields reclaimed from the Germans.

One day he might be in Meaux negotiating between town leaders and Ambulance personnel seeking to establish a medical site there. Another day it might involve a road trip to Soissons to arrange the evacuation of a hundred wounded soldiers. With the Germans, the French, and the British now digging trenches along the Aisne, for a long time the killing grounds of north-central France would produce life-and-death emergencies that a proficient translator could assist in resolving.

And those killing fields were expansive. When the battling armies tried for weeks to outflank one another in what they called "the race to the sea," neither adversary could punch through the other. So, each side expanded its commitment to build and fight from trenches. By December 1914 there was a line of rival trenches extending from north-central France through southern Belgium and stretching almost to the English Channel.

Philip read about this new style of warfare emerging in northern France. His heart bled for the unfortunate people hidden in filthy man-made gullies shooting and dying in the name of one nation's superiority over another. The frontlines were now impenetrable earthen ditches dug seven-feet deep and facing each other across barren expanses of battle debris they called No Man's Land. This was evolving into a defensive war on both sides. In the operative phrase of the day, the new path to victory was to "bleed the enemy white." It was a ghastly tactic that sickened Philip.

Philip had great respect for the band of selfless young Americans with whom he worked in the field. These were idealistic men with no stake in this war except their empathy for people who were suffering. To a man, none had ever considered volunteering to assist the German army with its wounded.

Some Americans signed on with the Red Cross which operated as a political neutral. It offered medical assistance to France and Germany on an impartial basis. But the American Ambulance was not neutral; this organization worked in tandem with the French army to achieve a French victory. France, after all, had been attacked without cause. The land of Lafayette was being mercilessly assaulted by superior German forces, and it was now time to repay the American debt to the famous Marquis who almost 140 years earlier had cast his lot with General George Washington and the intrepid Colonial revolutionaries.

Among Philip's new friends were people like Roger Brown from Seattle and Terry Lemieux from Buffalo who put their medical careers on hold and shipped out for France in the first weeks of the war. Brown had graduated from the University of Washington as an internist in 1913. Through connections, he had become a popular young doctor serving the city's wealthier citizens. He was even engaged to marry the daughter of a prominent local banker.

For personal adventure, for the humanity of the cause, or simply for the love of God, Brown discarded the security of Seattle and rushed to France. He joined the American Ambulance and was now in the field stitching wounds and saving lives.

Terry Lemieux was already wealthy. A graduate of Harvard medical school, he had been a respected surgeon in Buffalo for eight years before the war broke out. Being of French-Canadian ancestry, he was drawn immediately to the plight of France. Within weeks of hearing about the Ambulance, he left his business and came to Paris.

Nothing in upstate New York had prepared Dr. Lemieux for the injuries he encountered in this war. He cared for trauma to every imaginable part of the body. Facial wounds and loss of limbs still affected him deeply. He hated performing amputations, but when the alternative was death, he sawed.

Sometimes the procedure made him ill. But Dr. Lemieux always explained his predicament with a favorite saying. "This is war, and in war human beings become inhuman and do inhumane things. My job is to repair victims and in doing so restore a little of that lost humanity." It wasn't exactly the Hippocratic Oath, but behind the frontlines the doctor found it inspirational.

In the midst of such depravity, something wonderful happened to Philip. On a visit to the American Ambulance hospital in the hamlet of Juilly, he met a nurse. She was 25-year old Mildred Thomas. She had come to France recently to offer her medical services. While the Ambulance preferred male volunteers at all levels of activity, her professional training at Johns Hopkins University, as well as her quiet demeanor, made her irresistible to the directors in Neuilly.

But Millie Thomas was not content to work in a formal hospital that received its wounded from a railroad depot. She wanted to work outside Paris, out in the field where medicine was in an hourly struggle against extinction. This was the place to be, she decided, where life-altering decisions were made instantly, where the caring touch of a woman's hand was so alien, yet so gratifying, to those lying in agony.

After employing considerable charm and argumentation, the Ambulance finally gave in to her. Millie was assigned to the field hospital in Juilly. She lived with a local family, the widowed Madame Challot and her teenage daughter, and she worked at the hospital located on the grounds of the College of Juilly, the local school for area children.

Although the village was located only twenty-five miles from Paris, it may as well have been in another country. Juilly was rural, small, and simple—everything Paris was not. Still, as long as she kept her head down attending to those who continued to be brought there by American Ambulance and French Red Cross drivers, she didn't miss big city life.

It was Thanksgiving Day and Philip had been invited to come to Juilly to share a holiday meal with other Ambulance volunteers. The invitation actually promised turkey with gravy and potatoes and cranberries. Just reading the menu made him hungry and nostalgic. In deference to the wounded awaiting intervention, however, the celebration was confined to no more than one hour—and no more than one glass of wine.

It had been raining for two days and the dirt paths that passed as roads in this area were muddy and treacherous. Philip was careful to drive slowly. When he reached the College the festivities were half over. His discontent at being late evaporated when he first saw Mildred Thomas. She smiled when he entered the room filled with holiday cheer, then looked away. He did not avert his gaze. He found her beautiful and so feminine dressed in her white nurse's gown and cap.

When she slowly turned her head and looked back at him, Philip approached her and introduced himself. She hurriedly filled a plate for him and the two ate and conversed for the remainder of the celebration. It was a tender respite from the brutishness they both witnessed every day.

How do people fall in love? How does interest become passion and passion become commitment? In general the questions are unanswerable, yet the answers are known to every couple ever swept up by romance. But how do people with blood on their work clothes and human suffering as their daily experience ever manage to love? Credit biology or destiny? Possibly. Maybe it was the human spirit or the will to survive refusing to surrender, even when surrounded by death and barbarism. Whatever it was, seeing Millie at the Thanksgiving dinner stirred in Philip a softer side of his personality that recent events had calloused.

A man slathered in mud carrying a dying soldier to a hospital cannot be soft. He must steel his nerves and sensibilities or else his passenger will never have a chance to live. What Philip had seen since joining the Ambulance only reinforced his decision to bury emotionality deeply inside.

But in this short encounter with a charming young woman from Baltimore, Philip was rendered vulnerable again. He wanted to be close to her, to hold hands, to caress. He wanted long walks in the summer grass, and quiet dinners by a fireplace. He wanted intimacy and emotional exchange, he wanted to share ideas and smell perfume, to kiss and to know thoroughly. He wanted the normality of young love.

During the next several months he took whatever opportunity he could find to drive to Juilly. And gradually Millie came to desire his interest as much as he did hers. While her routine had to do with adjusting to the assortment of wounds she faced, Philip was much more in contact with war as it was being fought. From people he met he learned of battles and acts of heroism. These he would take back to Juilly to share with the others, and especially with Millie.

Following one particularly tough slog in December through deep mud and freezing rain, Philip learned of the unofficial Christmas truce that had happened just over the Belgian border. "You'll never believe what happened in Ypres," he explained to Millie. "A few days ago the German and British troops fighting there called an unofficial armistice to celebrate Christmas together! Not the officers, mind you, but the Tommies and the Fritzies, the actual guys in the trenches.

"Can you believe it? In the middle of all this viciousness, the two sides actually met in No Man's Land. They exchanged simple Christmas gifts, sang carols, and a few played music on their harmonicas. They called it their own "Silent Night." Some of them actually played a game of soccer on a muddy makeshift field with a ball fashioned from a bag stuffed with old clothes. I was told the Germans won 4 to 3."

"Maybe this is the beginning of the end of the war," Millie suggested. "What if they gave a war and no one showed up to fight it? What if they decided to sing and kick a ball around instead of kill one another?" she asked rhetorically.

"Well, don't count on it happening again," Philip added. "Hatred is the mother's milk of modern warfare. It's so much easier to kill when you despise. The British officers were irate when they learned of the fraternization. They issued an order that this will never happen again. Such behavior is now outlawed on pain of arrest and court martial. I'll wager the German officers reacted similarly."

"I don't know, Phil," replied Millie. "What are the differences between Tommies and Boches? They speak a different language? They have different forms of government? But are these authentic differences? Are there biological differences? Not really.

"I'm sure some of the German boys vacationed in England and loved it. The same is true for Brits who visited Germany before the war broke out. Politics and military training breed hatred, but beneath that instructed surface, the men all bleed red. We can certainly attest to that."

"Wait a minute, I have something to show you," Philip said. He went out to his truck and returned with a postcard. "I got this from a priest in Soissons yesterday. He took it from the breast pocket of a dead *poilu* after administering the last rites. It's a comical, maybe semi-serious, postcard called The Ten Commandments of the *Poilu!* Just read it."

Millie took the card and read it aloud.

THE TEN COMMANDMENTS OF THE *POILU!*

1. Joffre, alone, will you adore and respect thoroughly.
2. You will love your "Godmother" and your anonymous pen-pal equally.
3. You will think about love only on leave.
4. You will show Courage day and night, as simple as that.
5. You will always be Merry in order to live a long time.
6. Wine and Brandy you will drink in moderation.
7. You will have your Pipe in your mouth constantly.
8. You will Persevere energetically, until the end.
9. Naturally, you will kill as many Boches as possible.
10. In doing all this, you will certainly obtain Victory.

When she finished, Millie paused. "I guess a tourist in a card shop in Paris might find this humorous. But I don't. I've seen the other side of wartime humor, and it's not funny. Too much suffering, too many mangled bodies, too many dead *poilus*."

"I agree," replied Philip. "Let's burn it in the fireplace."

The sharing of moments like this only brought Philip and Millie closer. It was having a partner with whom to share such events that intensified and deepened their budding romance.

The other volunteers at the College recognized what was happening. They actually started a gambling pool to see who could guess the month and day on which Philip would ask for her hand in marriage. To these friends the unfolding love affair also offered a happy drama that was rare in this part of the world.

Helen Judd from Detroit won the pool. She guessed February 14, 1915. And why not, that was Valentine's Day, a time for lovers to abandon reason and declare for *amour*. Indeed, on Valentine's Day Philip asked her to marry and she accepted. Helen collected $55 in winnings.

The engagement was mercurial, however. They were married by the local priest one week after announcing their betrothal. As for a honeymoon, that was out of the question. Renewed fighting in the area around Verdun brought a flood of casualties to the College hospital, and Philip and his staff had a multitude of problems to rectify in villages throughout the region.

Such was love and marriage near the frontlines. But it was life sustaining and emotionally enriching. It gave Philip a renewed enthusiasm for his volunteer work, and Mildred felt honored and special; a lady laboring in muck and blood, but a lady nonetheless.

In honor of the marriage, the newlyweds invited the Juilly medical workers to a wedding feast that they delighted in preparing. Philip gathered the food while on his rounds. In St. Mard he bought goose and several pheasants; in Crépy-en-Valois he found a fresh round of locally-produced brie. Potatoes and other vegetables were already at the College, but he found a glorious array of sweets in a small pâtisserie in Juilly. And in Ermenonville he visited the wine cellar of the Hôtel de la Croix d'Or—the Cross of Gold Hotel—and purchased a dozen bottles of excellent chenin blanc from the harvest of 1910, a perfect accompaniment to a meal based on fowl and wild game.

"Oh, Phil, I love you so much," Millie said as he unloaded his bounty at the hospital. "I am going to prepare an amazing dinner. Our friends will remember this wedding forever." Philip kissed her tenderly then drove off to tend to another vexing village problem. "I'll be back for dinner," he yelled to Millie as he drove down the slippery pathway.

The celebratory meal that evening was memorable. The guests applauded as Millie brought each aromatic dish from the kitchen to the long dining table. No one knew that this dainty nurse was such an accomplished chef. Songs were sung and congratulations flowed. Philip and Millie made the perfect couple: the embodiment of a romantic image that American culture projects as the ideal match. The gathering was an American rite of passage, and no one was more pleased than Mr. and Mrs. Belmont.

But this was also a war zone, and those celebrating the marriage were medical saviors first. Prolonged happiness was not their privilege. Their lot was to administer to the battle-scarred. Soon they were all back at work, even the newlyweds.

8

As crucial as they were in moving the injured to qualified hospitals, many of the American Ambulance volunteers were eager for greater adventure. Working miles behind the frontlines, drivers often expressed discontent with the routine of picking up wounded soldiers from the French Army and delivering them to smaller hospitals or placing them on trains headed for Paris. One of their requests was to be allowed closer to the action.

This was especially true of those operating in Paris. As one driver explained it to Philip, "I didn't come to France just to pick up battered soldiers at a railroad station and drive them to Neuilly. I want to be in the fight—right at the edge of the fighting. I want to smell the artillery smoke, and hear the noise of gun shells being fired. That's why I'm here. I can't legally fight in this war, but I want to know the frontlines first hand."

Monotony was leading some volunteers to excessive use of alcohol, rowdy behavior, curfew violations, inefficiency at work, and a general disdain for taking orders from French military authorities. By early 1915 American Ambulance leadership understood that something had to be done to rekindle the spiritedness and dedication demonstrated by the volunteers in the early months of the war.

In March the head of the Ambulance appointed one of Philip's closest friends in France, Dr. A. Piatt Andrew, to be Inspector of Ambulances. Before being swept into wartime volunteerism, "Doc" Andrew had been a professor of economics at Harvard, and a Treasury Department appointee in the administration of President William Howard Taft. Because they shared a tie to academia, Andrew and Philip had hit it off from the beginning. Whenever Philip was in Paris, he made it a point to call on his friend at the American Military Hospital.

Doc Andrew's new job title was contrived. He was not really expected to drive around northern France inspecting Fords and their drivers. His task was to rejuvenate the organization by bringing management closer to the workers in the field. It was with that charge that he drove to Philip's home on April 1.

Philip and Millie greeted him enthusiastically and brought him into their newly-rented farm house. "What brings you to Juilly?" Philip inquired.

"I can't stay long. I have a thousand places to visit today. But I had to see you about a project I'm working on. I met a few days ago with Captain Aimé Doumenc. He's General Joffre's principal advisor on transportation matters. As an experiment, Doumenc has agreed to let me assemble a small group of Ambulance drivers to be sent close to the frontlines. No more shuttle trucks thirty miles from the conflict, this will be battlefield medical intervention, immediate care and evacuation of the injured. It's what we've wanted for a long time.

"I don't know if it'll work," Doc continued. "Some people in Neuilly think it's too risky. The French are skeptical, too. But our men are restless. We have stallions doing the work of pack horses. Our fellas want to be where they're most needed.

"If we can pull this off, I foresee the French Army redeploying its own drivers to regular service and using us for transporting of all their wounded. We'd be at the front, Phil, dispensing immediate medical attention and ready to rush the injured to medical help. How does that sound to you?"

Philip was intrigued by this bold development. "It sounds overdue. For months I've been hearing gripes from drivers—and always in very blunt English. They're restless. Your project sounds like it might be the answer," he replied.

"Phil has told me stories about disaffected volunteers," added Millie. "There are only a few now, but if you don't correct it soon, this frustration could become corruptive. And keep in mind that each fellow signs on for only six months at a time. If there's no challenge for them here, you'll lose your seasoned drivers when their first six months are up. Who'll sign on for another half-year of monotonous work?"

"And it's not that the French can't use our skills close to the fighting," Philip interjected. "We can do the job as well, if not better than the French medics are performing now. We're at least as good as they are at handling the injured. And when it comes to conquering the mud and ruts and the hills north of here, nothing can outperform our Model T Fords. They're like mountain goats."

"I understand that very well and so do the French," Doc answered. "And that's why I'm here. I want you to join me in this trial run. I'm putting together a special field service unit, the best people I can get. I'm calling it Z Section, and it'll consist of sixteen volunteers and a dozen ambulances. We're going to the front in Alsace to prove our worth to the French commanders. The future of our service depends on these drivers and emergency care providers. I want you to be among us."

Philip was startled by the offer. "Well, I'm flattered by your confidence in me," he replied.

"Look, you've been driving all over France for the past five months or so," Andrew explained. "You know the roads and the terrain. Hell, you probably know northern France better than most Frenchmen. We need you, Phil."

"Normally, I'd jump at the chance, Doc, but I just got married a few weeks ago," said Philip hesitatingly. "And besides, Millie and I are extremely busy right now, she's nursing the wounded here in Juilly, and I'm flitting all over the place managing crises."

Millie interrupted her husband's vacillation. "Phil, if you want to accept this offer, please don't let me stop you," she said. "You know I love you very much, but I don't control you."

"Wait, wait," Doc protested. "You're misinterpreting me. This is not about breaking up a marriage. I want the two of you to operate one of the twelve ambulances in Z Section. I want to use a woman at the front. The British use women drivers to transport their wounded. The French Red Cross uses female drivers. They even have a few American women driving for them. Only the Americans act like Neanderthals in their attitude toward women at the front. Let's show the Frenchies what a man and his wife can do to save lives."

Philip and Mary looked at each other. Their eyes betrayed their excitement at the offer. "I think Philip Belmont will accept your offer, Professor Andrew," declared Millie with exaggerated pomp, "and I know Mildred Belmont accepts it as well."

"Then, let's shake on it," said Doc excitedly. Extended hands soon became a happy embrace. "You take care of all the arrangements here, and I'll stop by with a caravan heading for Alsace in two days. You can leave your old truck here. I'll bring a new Ford for you and Millie with the caravan."

The next days were filled with preparations. Philip informed Neuilly of their intention to joining Z Section. Millie told the hospital that she would be participating alongside her husband in this experiment in military rescue. She also made arrangements for one of the new volunteer doctors to live in their house until they returned. Honeymoon bliss was also put on hold as the Belmonts agreed that saving lives took precedence.

When Doc Andrew and his drivers finally arrived, they came with twelve new ambulances with the words American Ambulance Field Service painted on the side of each. As he remarked to the team, "We're operating as a Foreign Sanitary Section under the control of the Ambulance Service of the French Army. But the words on the side of our Fords tell everyone who we really are."

Doc spoke frankly. He explained the confidential mission on which they were embarking. "As you know, fellas—and gal—this war has bogged down into trench warfare. The northern ten percent of France has been essentially sliced off by a double line of trenches: Germans dug in on one side, French and British Empire forces on the other. The line runs for 420 miles: from the North Sea coast near the Belgian border, downward toward Paris, then northeast to Verdun in Lorraine, then southeast into the Vosges Mountains ending at the Swiss border."

"It's all because the Germans dug in rather than retreat back into their Fatherland," suggested one driver.

"You're partially correct," replied Doc. "The Germans redefined European warfare when they dug their first trenches in northern France and invited Entente soldiers to dislodge them. But if the Boshes hadn't done it, the French or British would have. With all these modern weapons of destruction everyone has to go underground. You can't pitch tents and fight your battles standing in the open anymore. The machine gun alone has made that kind of combat no longer possible.

"Plus, you're relatively safer in a trench," Doc continued. "A French military officer has calculated that to defeat a trench line of enemy riflemen shooting with no obstructions, you need at least twelve charging soldiers for each dug-in enemy. That's at least a twelve to one advantage! What army ever had that numerical superiority? And just think of the number of dead and wounded a battle at those odds would create.

"But Entente military officers—French and British and their Colonials alike—are still trying to attack well-fortified German trenches in the belief that classic offensive tactics still work," said Doc. "All they're doing is killing and wounding hundreds of thousands of their men. And many of those deaths occur because wounded soldiers are not getting medical attention fast enough.

"Look, a French mathematician claims that at the rate General Joffre is moving his troops toward Berlin, he won't get there until 1943! That would mean eighteen more years of this kind of killing and maiming. Hell, we've got to do something to speed up that timetable."

"Now, our job is not to provide war strategy, although I sometimes think anyone of us could do a better job than those mustached old men with all those decorations and braids on their uniforms. Our job is much simpler: to save lives like we never have done before. Z Section will be at the frontlines. We will see gory things, but we cannot be squeamish, and we can't fail. The fate of this macabre war may just depend on how well we perform."

One of the volunteers interrupted Doc Andrew. "Where, specifically, are we headed?" he asked. "You said Alsace, but there are no great battles going on in that region, are there?"

"We're heading for the eastern Champagne area near the resort town of Vittel. It's about 150 miles from here. There's a hospital there and the French want to make sure we're professional enough before they turn us loose. So, try to make a good impression," Doc replied. "Then, hopefully, we'll be sent off to more-explosive battle zones. But I can guarantee that at field dressing stations in Champagne and the Vosges mountains sectors, you'll find plenty of wounded *poilus* and officers. And they'll be more than pleased that we Sammies are rushing them to vital medical attention.

"Remember, this is a trial for us. The French are evaluating our effectiveness. Some in the Army don't like the idea of Americans running any part of their show. So, let's shove off and prove them wrong. And may God help us all."

The caravan headed slowly toward the northeastern frontier. This was the rainy part of the spring and the roads were muddy and sometimes choked with supply trucks, cavalry units, and soldiers walking to and from battle action. In a full day of driving, the group of ambulances might make as many as sixty miles.

The trucks reached the French Ambulance field headquarters in Vittel late on April 6. But before their arrival, Doc Andrew stopped near a river to wash each vehicle. He didn't want mud-splattered ambulances to be Z Section's first impression. "When we get there, I want you all in clean uniforms, standing erectly by your trucks like a team of medical pros," Andrew ordered. "This will impress the French brass hats, I'm sure. A few days of such imagery should help seal the deal for us."

The precision demonstrated by Z Section during those first few days in Vittel even impressed Philip. As he later confessed to Millie, "I never knew we were that professional. If we get much better, they'll be offering us commissions in the French Army."

But it was the effectiveness of the Model T's that was even more convincing. No French or British rescue ambulance could match the American vehicles. As Doc told his drivers when they first arrived, "If our cleanliness and skillfulness don't do the trick, we'll be irresistible once they see how our Fords go up and down the mountains, over narrow roads, and through impassable ruts in order to rescue injured soldiers."

Less than a week after arriving, Doc Andrew was smiling broadly when he ran toward a group of his drivers. "We've passed the test," he shouted. "We've got the go-ahead to work closely with the French military. In fact, they want more of us. I have to rush back to Paris to organize a new Y Section."

The men cheered their own success.

"They loved your workmanlike approach and your spirit, Doc explained to his crew. "But the trucks and the way you handled them, that sealed the deal. I expect when we get enough Sections organized and deployed, we'll completely replace the Army medical drivers.

"This is the biggest compliment that could be paid to us," he added. "By mid-July we could be the ambulance service for the northeastern frontlines. Let me be the first to announce it: the Field Service has arrived."

As the men dispersed and headed for their trucks, Philip approached Doc and offered his congratulations. "I knew they couldn't resist us, and especially our go-anywhere Fords," he said. "But let me ask you a personal question. Don't you think your accomplishments with the French might be upsetting the folks back in Neuilly? The bureaucrats at the American Ambulance might be getting a little jealous of the working relationship you've personally developed with the military."

"Nah, they're fine with it. There's no animosity between us. But, now that you mention it, I have detected some resistance of late—some hesitation, a little testiness in certain quarters," Doc replied. "I think we're still on cooperative terms. But if someday they decide to end our relationship, that's the day when we repaint the trucks and…. Well, let's see what happens before we contemplate alternatives," he added.

The drivers were immediately deployed to dressing stations east and west of Vittel. All along the front, they heard the piercing sounds of German artillery shells—smaller "pips" and larger "whiz-bangs," as the British named them—flying toward French trenches. Then, like a string of punctuation marks, came the detonations of German ordinance exploding near French emplacements.

But the *poilus* were not passive. They unleashed their arsenal against enemy positions across No Man's Land. And the sound was sometimes deafening. If the American drivers had missed the proximity of battle, they were now so close they could smell the sulfur coming from both sides.

Z Section encountered familiar injuries. These were not, however, the most seriously hurt soldiers during the fighting now underway. Most of those near death were still rushed to base hospitals by military operatives. From there, survivors were sent on trains to facilities in Paris or nearby large cities. Still, no American driver complained because his patients weren't one breath from expiring.

For the next week, the American Ambulance Field Service dressed wounds and transported distressed soldiers. Working in shifts allowed the evacuations to go on around the clock. It was a tireless effort as the volunteers wrestled death for the life of each injured soldier.

Millie and Philip were especially involved because Millie's nursing skills made her particularly valuable in working with men whose health was deteriorating due to the long wait to be transported. Although she was not a doctor, in these conditions Millie frequently found herself diagnosing illnesses, ordering injections, and prescribing medicines.

Philip helped to load patients on his truck, both those who were on stretchers, what the drivers called the *couchés*, and those able to sit on the ambulance benches during the trip to the hospital, the *assis*. His fluency in the language, even with the regional and local dialects he often encountered, helped Philip in speeding up the rescue process.

The personnel of Z Section worked well together. Most of the men were seasoned drivers who had already experienced the horrors of war. They toughened their nerves and did what needed to be done. But there were an adventurous few who were new to the brutality of combat. One man, in particular, caught Philip's attention. A rookie volunteer named Leslie Buswell, British-born but now from Boston, had just returned from a hospital delivery with a morose expression on his face. This worried Philip who asked if there was something bothering him.

"Oh, it's nothing I can't get over, Phil," Buswell answered. "It's just that when we were coming back this time a broken-down horse appeared with a cart-load of what looked like old clothes. Instead, I discovered it was a wagon filled with *les Morts*, dead people, or at least pieces of dead people. I'd never seen a dead body until that moment. It was horrible: eight semi-detached, armless, torso-less, and headless bodies—mostly men, but some women—people like us with relatives loving them and waiting for their safe return home. All gone in this horrid way. Because of what? I don't know, Phil, do you?"

Philip had no answer. He patted the young soldier on the back and squeezed his shoulder. It was a comforting gesture, but it didn't answer the question.

Although sporadic fighting continued in the northeast, by the time Z Section arrived in Vittel the French Winter-Spring Offensive was officially over. The results were staggering. At Verdun, for example, following heavy fighting from late December until late March 1915, the French counted 90,000 dead and wounded. Ambulance volunteers speculated that the Germans lost a similar number. The British, Canadian, and Indian troops who also participated suffered sizable losses, too. For this human price there was no ground gained, no ground lost: just an inglorious stalemate.

By the end of April, the drivers of Z Section began hearing rumors of a new advance in militarism, something they never anticipated. From the frontlines at Ypres, a small town in western Belgium near the French border, they learned that the Germans were using deadly chlorine gas to drive French Colonial troops from their trenches and kill horses and other support animals. Apparently, the German Army had moved beyond throwing tear-gas grenades borrowed from city police forces— an annoying weapon the French and British also utilized—and were now disbursing massive clouds of toxic chemicals. The poison gas used at Ypres was released from almost six thousand heavy gas cylinders that the invaders installed near their positions facing the French lines.

The yellowish-green cloud, perhaps fifteen-feet high, emitted from the bank of cylinders wafted into the French emplacements and quickly killed hundreds of unsuspecting soldiers, mostly from Martinique. Men fell dead with a blue coloration in their faces caused by oxygen deprivation, the result of lungs reacting to the toxic chemicals and immediately filling with fluid. Many corpses had hands clenched as if in great pain before death. Those who didn't suffocate were seized by spasms of uncontrollable coughing and vomiting. These troops were then easily shot by the German assault troops that followed safely behind the deadly vapor.

Deployment of poison gas was not foolproof. The Germans had to be aware of potentially unfavorable wind directions. They did not want to risk killing their own soldiers with gas blown back toward their own lines.

But there was hope for human survival. Two days after the original attack the Germans launched another poison gas attack—this time against the 1st Canadian Division fighting alongside the French at Ypres. The results were not as horrific because in the two days between attacks, Paris doctors developed guidelines for resisting the deadly vapor: don't run away; let the poisonous fumes pass by; until effective respirators or masks can be obtained, place a wet handkerchief over the mouth and nose until the gas cloud passes or dissipates; position yourself as high in the trenches as is safely possible because chlorine is heavier than air and will accumulate in low spots.

It remained difficult to protect animals from the gas. If they were turned loose, or if they didn't break away and run in fear, horses, mules, and other livestock died agonizing deaths.

Philip was not stationed near Ypres. Still the horror of gas warfare stiffened his dedication. But this war had already stripped away the aura of civility he had always appreciated about Europe—about humanity, for that matter. He was not surprised that chemists and engineers—scientists who had always worked to improve human existence—were now employed to kill more effectually. The humane was discounted as death-rate productivity increased in importance.

At first it was the machine gun, the modern manifestation of the rapid-fire Gatling gun developed in the United States and first used in the American Civil War. The machine gun by August 1914 was a well-honed instrument employed by all countries to shoot as many people as possible, as fast and efficiently as possible. It exerted a devastating effect on the troops, causing casualty numbers to swell.

Of course, there was the classic use of the machine gun in which positioned artillerymen raked enemy lines and mowed down adversaries indiscriminately. From the first days of battle, automatic firing slaughtered soldiers on all sides. The weapon used by the British, for example, could spray 450 bullets in one minute. It didn't need a replacement barrel until at least 10,000 rounds had been discharged. The French model weighed fifty-seven pounds and could deliver as many as 650 rounds per minute. In response, the Germans had a machine gun that weighed 152 pounds—but it could expel as many as 500 bullets per minute. But because of their pre-war armament program, the Germans possessed 12,000 of these weapons in August 1914.

The killing potential of the machine gun was greatly enhanced by its portability. In times of rapid troop advances, light-weight fixed machine guns could be hand-carried by one or more men and rapidly set up closer to the shifting battle action. But by the first weeks of the war, the British introduced more flexibility to the equation with the motorized machine-gun battery. Here were machine guns on wheels, mobile artillerymen with the automatic weapons mounted on motorcycles, automobiles, and trucks.

When blended with barbed-wire installations, machine guns were even more effective. By erecting elaborate fences and walls of barbed wire in open territory, advancing enemy soldiers could be ensnared or made to trip over the unseen barriers. Strategically-placed machine guns could then strafe the area and kill soldiers trapped on the unforgiving wire.

Another effective deployment of barbed wire was to arrange wire barriers in such a way as to herd the advancing enemy in a certain direction. This effectively funneled enemy soldiers toward an array of machine guns waiting to slaughter them.

There was nothing quixotic or chivalrous in these scenarios. Witness the fate of the horse cavalry. Early popular impressions of the Great War often involved images of mounted soldiers, swords drawn, locked in hand-to-hand combat, while angry, flailing horses reared up on their hind legs. The British, French, and Germans learned as early the first month of the war during the Battle of Mons that machine guns easily killed horses, and exploding artillery shells caused them to panic and scatter in all directions. In just one charge against German emplacements at Mons, the British lost 300 mounts.

There were other reasons to abandon the cavalry fighter. By the time of the Battle of the Marne, one-sixth of all French horses were incapacitated because poorly-trained riders had exhausted or injured their steeds. Lack of proper riding equipment and the scarcity of nutritious feed also worked against the use of horses, as did concerns about rail transportation efficiency since an army could move four soldiers for every cavalryman and his steed.

But it was the science of firepower, augmented by the technology that produced poison gas, which doomed the swashbuckling mounted soldier as the romanticized warrior in this war. An era passed as the horse became increasingly used for pulling cannons and howitzers, supply wagons, and carts filled with corpses and body parts. As war horses faded in importance on the Western Front, the British Army increasingly replaced them with mules—much hardier beasts—as the preferred work animals.

"Phil! Phil! It's terrible!" Millie yelled as she ran breathlessly toward her husband. "The Germans have attacked an ocean liner. They sank the *Lusitania*."

"What do you mean?" Phil replied as he tried to calm his wife.

"A couple of days ago—a German U-boat torpedoed a British passenger liner with American citizens on board," she explained. "I just heard it from a medic from New Zealand. The *Lusitania* was headed from New York to England with almost 2000 passengers—most of them civilians."

"That's terrible news," Philip replied. "How many are dead?"

"They figure about 1200 people died and more than 130 of them were Yanks. Killed in the open waters where everyone expects freedom of the seas to be respected. In fact, the Kiwi medic told me that sea law requires that all civilian passengers be safely removed before such ships are sunk."

"What was the reaction back in the States? Did he say?" Philip inquired.

"No, he didn't know. But I can't imagine the public or the government downplaying it," she said. "The *Lusitania* may have been a British ship, but that's a lot of innocent life lost—a lot of American life."

"I wonder if this will get the U. S. into the war. It's been going for more than nine months now. We have to come in sometime. It's almost inevitable. But when? Maybe this will be the cause for American entry," Philip remarked.

As the other drivers learned the news, speculation about the involvement of the United States increased. Several expected a declaration of war to follow immediately. Philip was more cautious. He pointed out that although the *Lusitania* was a passenger liner, it was not a U. S. ship. Had it been an American vessel, he suggested, the consequences would be greater. Most of the drivers were certain, however, that someday the United States would enter the war if only to break up the defensive stalemate this struggle had already become.

Philip was right. The sinking of the *Lusitania* did not lure the Yanks into the war. In fact there were minimal consequences for the Germans and their campaign of submarine warfare. Still, by mid-May it was clear to Philip that he was committed to the war until the end. He would request a new open-ended contract with Doc Andrews. Research and writing would have to be postponed. Hopefully, his professorship at the University of California could be held in abeyance. But if need be, he was prepared to surrender it. He was not returning to America as originally planned. He wrote as much when he notified the University of his decision to remain on the frontlines.

For Philip the move constituted a major career change from comfortable certainty to an unknown future. Still, he reasoned, it was nothing more than what other drivers were doing. Granted, most volunteered for a single six-month tour of duty, but he could not pull away from this unfinished task. There would always be time for writing a book, he reasoned, but saving the lives of wounded soldiers was immediate and imperative.

When Doc Andrew returned to Vittel in early June Philip asked him to mail his letter of intention when he returned to Neuilly. He also included a few letters for his family in Chicago and his in-laws. As for his request for an open-ended extension with the Ambulance, Doc assured Philip that his request would be honored.

"But I don't think I'll be posting your letters from Neuilly," Doc confessed. "Things are getting a lot worse there. You were right. The American Ambulance wants to rein me in for good. Neuilly is now refusing to give me the funds that American donors send specifically for our work with the French Army. They also interfere with my attempts to get new trucks, even to recruit volunteers. Sometimes when I'm in Paris I feel like they don't even want to talk to me. But I won't give up our work in the field."

"Doesn't that put you in a tough spot?" Philip asked.

"Damn right it does. But I have one option, and I've decided to take it," said Doc. "Since we're practically in the French Army now, I am withdrawing all our drivers from Neuilly's control. We're going independent, Phil. I'm even changing our name. In a few weeks we'll be painting "American Field Service" on our vehicles—no more Ambulance. I sure hope you'll stay with me."

"Stay with you? You're the guy who built this organization. We work well because of what you've made us. Of course, I'm with you—and Millie is, too. In fact, all the drivers are. I'm sure of it," Phil insisted.

"I appreciate the support, I really do. Thank you," Doc replied. "I'm looking for a new place in Paris to be our headquarters. And we'll soon be stepping up our own fund-raising activities back home. We're going to be all right."

Doc thumbed through the stack of letters Phil had just given him. "Here's your letter to Neuilly. Maybe you don't want to send that one," Doc said.

Philip smiled and tore up the letter.

If the battles of 1915 proved anything it was that a well-positioned, entrenched defense was costly to dislodge. On many occasions both sides launched large offensive attacks, advancing in the first days, but inevitably retreating to positions held before the onslaughts began. Battles in and around small towns like Artois, Loos, and Woëvre, and throughout the province of Champagne, killed and injured hundreds of thousands. Neither side, however, could advance and hold ground. It was a style of warfare that kept the new American Field Service busy.

By early 1916 Western Europe was locked in an especially-bitter winter. As a consequence, the French-German front was fairly quiet. Many drivers attributed the battle lull to the fact that soldiers on both sides were exhausted and cold. Of course, there were occasional artillery shells launched in both directions, but most of them had no effect.

By mid-February, Philip began to feel a new anxiety whenever he was near the frontlines. Normally-friendly French officers were now too preoccupied to engage in conversation with the U. S. drivers. Large numbers of troops were being assembled and dispatched on trains and in motorcades, apparently headed as reinforcements all along the Northern Front. Fresh supplies of arms were also arriving from Paris and elsewhere, and then being shipped to outlying destinations. As Philip explained it to Millie, "Something big is going to happen. I don't know if the French are preparing a Spring Offensive or a Spring Defensive. But whatever it is, they're getting ready for something significant."

To compound the problem, the entire area was blanketed for days by heavy snows and gale force winds. This made the roads dangerous and nearly impassable, even for the indomitable Model T Fords. Fortunately, the horrible weather greatly impeded the exchange of artillery fire. It also relieved the pressure on AFS drivers, just in time for Philip and Millie to celebrate their first anniversary on February 21.

The other volunteers organized an elaborate afternoon party for the couple in an empty airplane hangar on base. The itinerary included plenty of wine and cheeses and food purchased from local farmers and merchants. The organizers hired a small band of local musicians to play folk songs and fox trots for the gathering. Even a few high-ranking French Army officers came to honor Phil and his bride, the first female volunteer in the AFS. Not even the lingering snowfall kept the celebrating couple and their guests from the festivities.

The party began in fine fashion with the "Wedding March" played while Philip and Millie walked in to rhythmic applause. The clanging sound of forks striking wine glasses and cries of "Kiss the bride!" soon followed. So, Philip and Millie accommodated—and the revelers again roared their approval.

"This is the first party we've had since we got married," Millie told the happy guests.

"We need to do this more often," Philip said as the crowd applauded. "But as for right now, let's dance."

When the couple began to dance, the attendees again demonstrated their happiness. "Hey, Vernon and Irene Castle have come to Alsace," shouted one of the volunteers. The couple laughed at that suggestion, but continued spinning and enjoying the music, both mouthing the words "I love you" before kissing again.

The joyous celebration came to a sudden halt when a French officer breathlessly entered the hangar and announced an emergency. "Gentlemen, I am very sorry, but I must interrupt your party with urgent news," he announced. The music fell silent as he continued, "This afternoon at 4 o'clock, the Germans launched what appears to be a massive offensive in and around Verdun. There are reports that we have sustained a great number of dead and wounded. All ambulance drivers are now ordered to proceed to the front as soon as possible.

"Verdun is seventy miles from here. The roads will be covered in snow, as you can imagine. But we've already sent heavy trucks ahead to clear the way as much as possible. Be ready to leave in twenty minutes."

"This is a hell of a way to celebrate an anniversary," Philip complained. "And just when I was rediscovering my old dance moves."

"Duty before love," Millie quipped. "We haven't much time to pack and get underway."

They dashed back to the tent in which they had lived for many weeks. They packed their essential items, then raced to their ambulance and joined the other AFS vehicles headed west toward the fighting.

Philip and Millie knew it would be an arduous journey, although bright moonlight illuminated the way. The trucks clearing the road had done a good job of pushing the snow to the side of the road, but icy patches and dangerous holes obscured in the dirt road made driving treacherous. On a few occasions they passed vehicles that had swerved into snow banks. Fortunately, each ambulance was stocked with shovels for such an emergency.

As Philip concentrated on the roadway, swinging his Model T from side to side to avoid crashing, Millie leaned back and surveyed the evening scenery. In any other circumstances the French countryside in the wake of a long snowstorm would have been romantic. The melding of gently rolling hills with flat expanses of farmland and forested areas, all covered in a blanket of pristine snow, offered a beautiful image of serenity and social composure. Punctuating the placid snowscape were many small farm houses with white smoke ascending from tall chimneys. And then there was the animal life, especially the wild deer that stood near the roadway and stared at the passing trucks. Millie understood this snowy panorama as a picture of peaceful domesticity—the way things were supposed to be.

"You know, Phil, when this horrible war is over, I'd like to come back here in the winter," Millie said. "If I didn't have Verdun and the war at the back of my mind, I'd say we're driving though a paradise. Just look at the openness, the order imposed by the way the farms are laid out, the unspoiled views, even the wild animals," she said, her voice trailing off as if silenced by the beauty of the surroundings.

Philip didn't answer. He was too busy negotiating the treacherous road. He knew also that he and the other drivers would have to go all night to reach Verdun as soon as possible. He didn't look forward to traveling in the dark, relying on headlights and the effectiveness of the trucks plowing snow ahead of him. But Philip knew he had no choice because wounded men were dying while the rescue units made their way west.

Not until early in the morning on February 22 did the AFS ambulances arrive at their destination. The rising sun allowed the drivers to see the historic old fort in the distance. As Philip and Millie admired the facility, a young French Army officer approached them. He introduced himself as Lieutenant André Voulland from the coastal city of La Rochelle in Central France. "It may look impregnable," he said to Philip and Millie, "but that big fortress is Fort Douaumont and it's understaffed and unfortified. Months ago we stripped it of manpower and weapons. Everything was redeployed to critical sites along the frontlines. If the Germans get close to it, all they'll have to do is walk in. But they won't find much.

"Fortunately, Verdun is not a single bastion. It's a fortified area," he continued. "Do you know how many forts we have built just for this day?"

Philip and Millie had no idea. All they could see in the distance was the one fortress.

"This area has nineteen different fortified structures, and fourteen of them are reinforced with concrete. There is massive firepower behind some of those walls. Still, we almost lost everything two years ago. The Germans nearly encircled us. But when the *poilus* stopped the Boches on the Marne it disrupted their plans. Now the Boches are back to try it again.

"We must defend these places and we will at all costs. The Germans know that. I predict they will hammer us with artillery and storm-trooper attacks for as long as it takes to conquer the entire area. They'll try to kill everyone until the last man surrenders. This Verdun Offensive could last for months."

"Well, I hope that's not the case," Millie answered. "The war has already become an exercise in mass murder. It gets very discouraging picking up the bloodied bodies of dying soldiers."

"Speaking of that," said Lieutenant Voulland, "your orders are to divide your drivers into two segments. You will be working in conjunction with other ambulance teams—from the Red Cross, from Great Britain, even from the United States. Each of your crews will work a 12-hour shift. Your tent housing has been prepared here on the base—except for the married couple who are assigned a room inside the command building.

"Now, we need the first shift to begin work immediately, no matter how exhausted you are after that long drive through the ice and snow."

As the officer spoke, the noise of large explosions began to fill the morning air. "They're at it again," Voulland explained. "The Germans bombarded us all day yesterday along an eight-mile front. They have long-range howitzers that shoot shells into the air and drop them into our lines, occasionally right into our trenches. They're also using several of their Big Bertha 420mm howitzers which are mounted on railroad cars. Berthas can fire shells from more than six miles away. These are guaranteed to destroy the walls of almost any fortification.

"Unfortunately, we are unable fight back very well. We rely on small 75mm long guns that shoot with a lower trajectory. That means our shells go relatively straight, and we can't drop them into their underground hiding places.

"Yesterday the Germans attacked us in the Bois de Caures and hurt us badly. They used howitzers followed by waves of foot soldiers, many carrying flamethrowers that spewed streams of liquid fire on us. We held them back then, but now we're almost out of ammunition. I suspect they'll move in for the kill this morning. We need you to get there as rapidly as possible and start evacuating the wounded."

Philip was tired and didn't like the order, but the Germans made it necessary. "Where should we take the injured?" he asked.

"We've set up a makeshift medical processing facility a mile from here. You bring the wounded to that site, and we can patch them up and send them south for more extensive care" said Voulland. "Unfortunately, we have to use our small-gauge railway because the German bombardment yesterday knocked out the main rail line."

This was not encouraging news to Philip. While Millie prepared the ambulance for a trip to the frontlines, he gathered the other volunteers and explained the situation. He divided the group into Shift A, the dayshift working from 5 am to 5 pm; and the Shift B, the overnight shift working from 5 pm to 5 am. He and Millie joined Shift A.

The road to the Bois de Caures was in good shape considering the snow and winds that had battered the area for more than a week. In less than a quarter-hour Shift A arrived at the rescue area where the noise from the German guns was intense. It seemed to Philip that hundreds of shells were exploding every minute.

When he saw the men awaiting transportation, however, he forgot the sounds of war. There were the familiar injuries: hanging or missing limbs, heads wrapped in bloody bandages, some soldiers missing parts of their faces; these were the victims of rifle bullets and shrapnel. Those who had been buried alive by collapsing trench walls were usually unconscious or gasping for breath because of broken ribs, internal bleeding, and throats and lungs coated with French soil.

But there was a new type of injury, the melted flesh and exposed bone created by being burned by liquefied fire. For Millie who applied her nursing skills to help all the wounded, flamethrower damage was the most horrific of all. "How can one human being do this to another?" she asked Philip.

As quickly as the Fords were filled, they returned to the medical processing facility and deposited their wards with the medical staff. Then they returned as fast as possible to the frontlines. The American vehicles could pick up and deliver and return in as little as forty-five minutes. But when the ambulance was filled with burn victims, the trip was slower because each bump in the road produced screams of pain from the wounded who rested on stretchers in the back of the truck.

On the final trip of their shift, Philip and Millie arrived expecting to pick up another ambulance-load of maimed *poilus*. Instead, several officers directed their vehicle to a spot away from the main staging area. "We have a special cargo for you," one officer announced. With that a group of soldiers appeared carrying the body of an officer, his corpse wrapped in a large French flag. "This is the body of Colonel Émile Raspail, the commander who withstood the German attack at Bois de Caures for two brutal days," said the officer. "We were outnumbered, outgunned, and we had few reinforcements, but his spirited leadership kept us in the fight to the end. We are now in retreat. Please take this great man to his rest."

"We would be honored," Philip said to the officer. "As a final gesture, maybe we should drive back with only his body?"

"No, don't do that," the soldier replied. "Colonel Raspail was a soldier's soldier. He was shot when he stopped to bandage a wounded infantryman. Please take a full complement of the injured when you drive his remains to Verdun. He would have ordered that."

Philip and Millie proceeded to the main staging area and loaded another six wounded men into their ambulance. Each man saluted the flag-draped corpse of Colonel Raspail. All of them had tears in their eyes. Philip and Millie had never heard of this officer, but the touching way his men respected him was unforgettable.

Philip drove slowly along the short route to the processing facility. He realized that he was carrying an extraordinary cargo. It made him think of the men in 1840 who returned Napoléon's body from Saint Helena for entombment in Paris. Philip remembered, of course, that he was transporting men who were not dead. He was constantly aware that bumps in the road, the accidental loss of control, or any sudden swerve could be excruciating for the wounded in his Model T.

"Quick, look up there," Millie said as she pointed to the sky. "There's a German airplane and it's coming directly toward us."

"It's an Albatross. Those monsters can strafe us with their machine guns. They may even have bombs to drop over the side," Philip replied fearfully. "I better pull over and let the bastard fly by."

But the pilot did not fly over. Instead, he circled the ambulance and positioned himself to soar directly toward Philip and Millie along an open stretch of roadway.

As Philip sat contemplating his response while death headed toward everyone in his vehicle, another aircraft appeared. "Oh, my God," Philip shouted, "It's a Nieuport, a French fighter."

As they watched, the German plane turned immediately and banked upward and toward the right. The French pilot followed, firing his front-mounted machine gun. In less than two minutes the entire incident was finished and the natural order was restored. The quiet sky was now inclining toward darkness and no aircraft was in sight—just a cold, clear February afternoon.

"I sure would like to thank that pilot," remarked Millie. "We'd be dead by now if he hadn't appeared."

"Lord, did you see how beautifully he handled that airplane?" Philip asked. "He saved our lives. But the way he did it. What impressive flying. His combat maneuvering was perfect. And that rapid-fire gun mounted in front of him, what a beauty. Did you see how precisely he used it?"

Philip pulled back on the road and continued toward the medical processing facility and then home base. But his mind was on the aerial incident. His flying skills had grown rusty over the past two years, but he still appreciated expert piloting.

At the medical center he was able to refocus. The wounded *poilus* who never saw how close they came to being murdered from the air were carefully taken by French medics to receive additional medical attention. A few of them thanked him. Most, however, were too injured to speak. But Millie understood what had just happened. "We were lucky this time," she said.

As for Colonel Raspail, his remains were ceremoniously removed from the ambulance and, as Philip later learned, they were sent immediately to Paris for burial in an honored military cemetery.

That evening Philip wrote another letter home to his family. It was difficult to encapsulate the events of the last several weeks. He realized that the full truth would upset his parents but superficiality would not be believed. Nevertheless, he opted for the latter.

His letter was filled with descriptions of injured soldiers; however, he omitted mention of the more horrific wounds. How do you honestly describe a *poilu*—who was, ultimately, only a French peasant boy with a few weeks of training—whose facial features had been melted away by a flamethrower? Another whose legs were blown off by an exploding grenade? Or a young infantryman coughing up pieces of his lungs because he inhaled chlorine gas?

As for the German air attack, in his letter Philip condensed that to a few sentences about the role of airplanes in this war and how he missed flying. It wouldn't have been prudent to explain how close to dying he and Millie had come this afternoon.

9

He was only two days into the Battle of Verdun, but Philip already sensed that there was something different about this German offensive. The massive commitment of men and weaponry by Germany was unlike anything he had witnessed. And the French determination to stop the enemy advancement by standing ground and launching counteroffensives seemed at times almost suicidal. The familiar fixation on killing as many people as possible—a sentiment Philip recognized in both armies—made him worry about the human consequences of prolonged fighting.

Four more months of such fighting and upwards of 100,000 casualties did not change his opinion about the conflict. He and Millie had made countless trips to loading sites along the front, and each time they were struck by the magnitude of the brutality. Troops on both sides were being killed and injured by long-range bombardment, machine guns, pistols and rifles, and airplanes. To these instruments add grenades, flamethrowers, and barbed-wire. In some engagements more than 80,000 rounds might be fired by one side.

Frustrated by the futility of stationary trench warfare, the German assault on Verdun precipitated a conflict that Millie termed "insane." Armies would capture and evacuate, then capture again and evacuate again. Hills and high-points soon became synonymous with victory and defeat. Hill 304 and Hill 344, *Côte de l'Oie* and the appropriately named *Mort-Homme*, or Dead Man, commonplace rural localities became infamous battle sites in and around Verdun. Up and down the hills, into and out of the goose slope, conquer then relinquish then reconquer—but always with the same human result, catastrophic casualties.

The same thing happened with the villages and small communities in the region. Béthincourt, Cumières, Forges, and Fleury were a few of the small communes obliterated by relentless German attacks and unyielding French resistance.

And then there was the French leadership. Within days of the launch of the German offensive, the discredited commander of the area was replaced by General Philippe Pétain who headed the French Second Army.

Pétain was a marked improvement over his predecessor. But, as Philip later discovered, even this change of leadership was less than auspicious because when he was notified of his promotion General Pétain was in Paris sharing a hotel room with his mistress. He had to be awakened at 3 o'clock in the morning and informed of his new assignment. And, while being driven immediately to the Northeast, he developed a bad case of pneumonia. With a high fever the General wrapped himself in a thick blanket and issued orders to his generals by telephone.

General Pétain must have heard the same stories Philip and Millie had been told. Tales of men fighting to their last bullets, men in heavy combat lacking sufficient rations, unfortified positions that were undermanned and in need of immediate reinforcement. One of his early decisions was to order massive supplies and more troops for the defense of Verdun. Although the narrow-gauge railway remained the principal conduit for resupplying the front, the new commander also relied on a 43-mile stretch of country road that ran between Verdun and Bar-le-Duc.

Bar-le-Duc was already famous as the birthplace of President Poincaré and as the source of a popular type of French *confiture*, a delicious jam that blended red and black currants. But in the spring of 1916 the town became known as a vital railroad depot from which battle reinforcements and supplies were dispatched via an undersized rail line; and more so as a terminal for General Pétain's paved road called simply *la route*.

Well-guarded and well-maintained, *la route* also became a strategic evacuation trail for wounded soldiers requiring further medical intervention. When traffic flowed at peak efficiency, it was said that a man standing in a single spot along *la route* would see a motorized vehicle pass him every fourteen seconds.

During the next few months Philip and Millie traveled the roadway many times carrying wounded *poilus* to Bar-le-Duc, and bringing fresh troops back to the battle area. They always felt secure driving this road. Should a vehicle suffer a mechanical breakdown or an accident, there were thirty repair trucks stationed at points along the way. There were few weather-related problems because the road was kept perfectly surfaced in crushed stone, and labor battalions stood ready to repair any impediment to smooth driving. Furthermore, horse-drawn vehicles and foot soldiers were under orders to stay off the road. For protection, French aircraft regularly patrolled the skies to prevent possible German aerial attacks. *La route* may have been crowded, but Philip and Millie were willing to trade speed for security and smooth driving conditions.

On June 22, 1916 the Battle of Verdun entered still another phase of cruel destruction. That evening German forces unleashed a hybrid poison gas against the French defenders. Combining phosgene and chlorine, phosgene-chlorine gas was ten times more toxic than the unadulterated chlorine gas. The new gas had already been tested successfully against British troops near Ypres in December 1915.

Ironically, phosgene was actually a French invention, developed in response to the German use of chlorine gas, and deployed by the French in 1915. It was produced by a team of research scientists headed by Victor Grignard, the French scientist who won the Nobel Prize for Chemistry in 1912.

While both sides rushed to perfect the gas mask as a defense against such assaults, gas warfare continued to terrify, demoralize, wound, and kill people on both sides of the trenches. When it was discharged against French forces at Verdun and its surrounding villages, the Germans had no trouble capturing the deserted community of Fleury from which they could fire shots into nearby Verdun. Only a lack of sufficient reinforcements prevented the Germans from capturing the fortified city in late June.

Philip was repulsed by gas warfare, a tactic expressly forbidden by international treaty. As he expressed it to Millie, "this war is becoming a battle between mad chemists trying to brew the perfect poison gas, and panicked scientists laboring to build the invincible gas mask." Although he and Millie had never been in a chemical attack, they carried masks in their ambulance, and they had known two Field Service drivers who died because of exposure to chlorine. Moreover, they treated many British and French soldiers who were victims of the toxic clouds released by the Germans.

The summer of 1916 was unusually warm along the Northern Front. The heat, however, did not stop either side from fighting and dying. Although the AFS corps continued its tireless work, Philip's world changed that summer. He would never forget the date: August 18th. That's the day the French stopped the great German push toward Verdun. It had been a long battle, and it ended in tiny Fleury when French colonial troops from Morocco captured the village, the sixteenth time Fleury had changed hands in fighting since late June. It was also the day that Millie informed Philip that she was pregnant.

"You mean we're having a child?" Philip asked excitedly. "A baby?"

"Yes, Daddy, we're going to be parents. I've suspected it for a while, but only today was it confirmed by a French doctor," Millie replied, still uncertain of how Philip would receive the news.

"That's wonderful!" he shouted. Running from their room, Philip announced the impending event to all who could hear. "We're having a baby! We're having a baby! Millie's having a baby! I'm going to be a father!" he yelled while running around in broad circles outdoors. Soldiers walking by yelled their congratulations, and ambulance drivers heading to and from the front sounded their horns in approval.

The one-man celebration continued for a few minutes until, exhausted, he walked back to his and Millie's room in the command center. "I forgot to ask when the baby is due," he said.

"Well, the doctor says I'm about three months along. So, that would mean early next year. Late January or maybe February," she explained.

Millie was still uncertain, however. She had primal doubts about how it would affect their volunteer work, how it would impact their marriage, and whether or not this was a proper time to bring any child into existence. "What will we do?" she asked her husband.

Philip had no qualms. He was for parenthood all the way. To each of her queries, he had a fast and definitive answer. "You can't continue AFS work and be pregnant. Sooner or later it's you who'll need medical intervention. And being a new mother in these conditions, with our child, it's out of the question. We can talk to Doc Andrew, but I think he'll tell you to retire."

As for the state of their marriage, Philip's answer was likewise to the point. "Are you crazy? I love you more than ever now. We are having a baby—I mean, you're having a baby—and I am so happy and proud to be the father," he said as he embraced and kissed her.

"Oh, Phil, I'm so glad you're pleased, so pleased," she said with sincerity. "I was worried. I didn't know how you'd react, didn't know if you wanted a child. You know, we haven't had much time to talk about children in this awful war."

"I never thought about it," he replied. "But now that it's here, I love the idea."

"But I still have lingering doubts about bringing a child into such a brutal world," she added. "Not now, with death everywhere, men massacring each other, people being crippled and maimed for life. It's horrific, Phil."

Philip could see that she was deeply worried about her pregnancy. And it was ironic that two people so experienced in handling injury and death were now debating the most fragile form of life.

"Will we raise a boy destined to become cannon-fodder for the next global war? Is that the destiny for our boy child?" she asked. "And if it's a girl, will she be grieving for her lost or disabled husband in another twenty or twenty-five years? What should we do?"

Philip knew that his next answer would have to be a good one. "Sweetheart, our child—only the first of our children, I hope—will become what we raise him or her to be," he replied. "If we are honest and intelligent and loving, he or she will be honest and intelligent and loving. And that's what we are. And our child will inherit our values and our humanity, and armed with these values he or she will become a useful, responsible citizen.

"I guess what I'm saying is that we must have this baby," said Philip. "Maybe our child will be the person who ends war forever, the one who can say 'My parents taught me the horrors of armed combat. We will have no more wars forever.'"

Millie smiled widely, tears welling in her eyes. "Oh, Phil, I love you very much," she said. "You've turned my doubts into happiness, even into pride. I can't wait now to have this baby. And I am so glad that you are the father."

That brought tears to Philip's eyes.

It was a tender and intense moment in their married life. They stood in the center of their room, locked in each other's arms, transcending the reality of where they were, thinking at this moment only of their happy future.

Millie interrupted their reverie. "You know, I was thinking about something else," she said.

"I know," Philip responded. "I know. You were thinking that a war zone is no place to give birth. And I agree."

"How did you read my mind?" she said.

"Oh, that's what happens with old married couples," Philip answered. "They get to know each other so well they sometimes don't need to speak to be understood.

"I think you should go back to the States now, back to be with your folks in Baltimore. They'll be so excited when you tell them you're pregnant, and over-the-moon with happiness when you tell them you're coming home to have the baby."

"I agree," Mille replied. "But what about you? What about us? Aren't you coming with me?"

"I can't go until this bloody mess is over, sweetheart," said Philip. "We both have so much of ourselves invested in the outcome. And there are so many more injured to be saved, some of them are just now joining the French Army, some are still too young to enlist or be conscripted. But all of them will need an ambulance sooner or later. Maybe I'll end up as their driver."

Millie smiled at his answer. "You are a champion, darling. No other word says it better. And I love you for it. Of course, you must stay. Anyway, I think America will be entering this wretched war very soon. You'd join or be drafted eventually."

Philip hugged her again. "Thanks for being so understanding," he said.

Several days later, Doc arrived in Verdun to consult with the Army and to meet with his drivers. There were now five AFS Sections working at the front and Doc and his personnel were more important than ever in the eyes of the French officers. "Hey, Doc," shouted Philip as he spotted him walking across the base camp.

"Hello, Phil," yelled Doc as the two men ran to greet each other. "It's so great to see you. I hear nothing but glowing reports about you and Millie and the work you're doing. There's something very mature about having a man and wife working together. It's not like those single guys who can sometimes get rambunctious."

"Oh, they're great, too," Philip said with amusement in his tone. "Everyone up here is doing useful work—and doing it well, I might add."

"I know that. Just pulling your leg," replied Doc.

"But seriously, Millie and I need to talk to you. In private. Can you come to our room now?" asked Philip.

Doc Andrew followed as Philip led the way. When he saw Millie, Doc picked her up and swung her around in happiness. "It's so wonderful to see you again," he said. "It's been several months."

Millie giggled and kissed Doc on both cheeks in the continental manner. But Philip was more protective. "Ah, Doc," he warned, "it's not a good thing to swing Millie around like that, not a good thing at all."

Andrew was not slow to catch the drift. "You mean?" he said as he turned back to face Millie. "You mean? Pregnant?"

Millie grinned as she confirmed his suspicions. "Yup. We're going to be parents. I know it sounds foolish when you look at where we are.

But the world must be repopulated with civil people who want to live productive lives in peace. It has to begin somewhere, so we Belmonts plan to be the starting point."

Philip interrupted in a more serious tone. "Because of her condition, we've decided that Millie has to leave the American Field Service, Doc, and return to Baltimore where her parents live," he said. "We're hoping that with all your contacts, you can facilitate that as soon as possible. The boat trip back to the States is a long one, and it can be rough. So the sooner she can leave while the weather is decent, the better it will be for enduring the ocean trip."

Doc was reassuring. "That won't be a problem," he said. "I'm leaving here tomorrow morning. I can take Millie to the railroad station in Bar-le-Duc and she can catch the train to AFS headquarters in Paris. We'll get her on the next neutral passenger liner sailing for New York. And if I can't arrange it, I'm sure Bill Sharp at our embassy can. You guys just leave it to ol' Professor Andrew."

Philip hadn't counted on such a rapid and reassuring response. He was grateful to Doc, but it meant that Millie would be leaving tomorrow and he would be left alone for an unknown length of time. Still, he was now preoccupied with the safety of his wife and child. And from that perspective, Doc's assurances were tremendously gratifying.

"I'll be ready," Millie announced. "I don't have much to pack. And I'm leaving my most prized possession here to continue the fight."

In the morning Doc arrived at the command center about 7 o'clock. Millie was packed and ready to go. Philip carried his wife's suitcases to Doc's Model T, dreading her departure, yet happy that she would soon be in a safe environment. After a few more kisses and promises to write weekly, Doc pulled away and headed for *la route* and Bar-le-Duc. Only then did the full reality of the loss hit Philip, and it hurt.

Several hours later an impatient voice rang out from the entrance to Philip's room. "Hello! Hello! I'm looking for Phil Belmont," said a French military officer. "Is Phil Belmont here?"

Philip greeted his visitor, a young man who introduced himself as Lieutenant Antoine Mercier. "I come with unfortunate news," the officer said. "Since your wife is no longer staying here, the base commander has asked that you vacate this room. As you know, it is reserved for married couples. You are being transferred to one of the bachelor tents outside. You will share it with another American Field Service volunteer, a Mr. Allen Pryce from an American city called Omaha.

"Follow me, and I will show you to your tent. Then you can move your clothing. Just leave the room key on the kitchen table when you have finished."

It lacked ceremony, but the order was crystal clear. Philip carried most of his belongings as he followed Lieutenant Mercier to his new quarters. He deposited his valises and returned for the remainder of his gear.

Leaving the room key on the table was not easy for Philip. He and Millie had shared many happy meals at this modest table. Every morning and evening they dined together her presence had transferred it into a banquet table. Still, he left the key and walked away from the sweetest part of his past.

Philip was completing the task of storing his clothes when a blond head peered into the tent and announced, "I'm your new ambulance assistant. Doc Andrew told me to report to you. You're my first assignment in the AFS."

Philip was cordial to Allen Pryce. But the young man's presence only intensified the loneliness he was feeling. Still, he took Pryce under his wing and began to show him what was expected of a volunteer. In many ways, it was like restarting his own career in medical rescue work.

"Well, let's get going, Allen," he said. "There are soldiers waiting to be saved." Together the two men drove to the frontline to do the best they could with the backlog of injured *poilus*. Back and forth all day they picked up wounded and brought them to the base hospital.

In the following two weeks matters changed dramatically. As well as feeling the pain of separation from his wife, Philip noted important political changes around him. First, although Italy had been at war with Austria-Hungary since mid-1915, Italy finally declared war on Germany on August 28, 1916, the same day Rumania also joined the Allies against Germany.

He also heard constant whispers of personality conflicts and rivalries within the French military leadership that involved General Joffre, General Pétain, and other top officers. The junior officers at the base were calling it a Clash of the Titans. But it was producing a tense, divisive situation that had the potential to undermine troop morale.

Since early July Philip had also been hearing rumors of another British and French offensive recently launched along the Somme River in northwestern France. According to the accounts, this Battle of the Somme was already another bloodbath, a smaller version of Verdun. In a single day, according to one ambulance driver, the British suffered 60,000 casualties. Then there was the record of the 1st Royal Newfoundland Regiment at Beaumont Hamel along the Somme. According to men coming from the battlefield, this unit of 801 officers and volunteers from the British colony of Newfoundland was literally annihilated when it charged across No Man's Land toward German trenches. The Regiment suffered 733 dead and wounded in twenty minutes of exposed battle.

For the next several weeks, Philip and his new protégé carried out their ambulance duties. But something was missing in Philip's approach. He was lonely and he began to find his work boring. After all, when the average AFS hitch was for six months, Philip had already completed two full years of service. Maybe that's why his encounter with a French Colonel named Henri Desmoulins was so transformative.

In late September while walking to the base café for dinner he was approached by the Colonel. "Excuse me, but I believe you are Philip Belmont, no?" he inquired.

"Yes, I am. How can I help you, sir," replied Philip.

"I'd like to talk with you. Can you join me in the Officers' Club?" Desmoulins asked. "We could talk over drinks and then have supper. What I have to say is very important."

"Wonderful. I'd love to join you," Philip answered.

At the club the Colonel introduced himself as an officer in the French Air Service. "I understand from reports I've read that you were an accomplished pilot before coming to France. Is that right?" he said.

"Well, I've been known to fly quite a few different planes. I even have my license from the Aero Club of America. My Aero Club registration number places me among the first 200 registered pilots in the United States," he said as he pulled a card from his billfold. "See, here it is: licensed for bi-wing and single-wing aircraft. I flew for years before I came to France in 1914. I'm a bit out of shape now, but a pilot doesn't forget how to fly."

"*Formidable*," Colonel Desmoulins exclaimed. "That's precisely what I wanted to hear, Mr. Belmont. Let's order and I'll tell you what's on my mind."

Over *coq au vin* and a bottle of rosé from Provence, the Colonel explained that he was a recruiter for the *Service Aéronautique*. "France needs flyers, Mr. Belmont. We truly appreciate the wonderful men and women in the American Field Service and other ambulance groups, but we need airmen more than we need medics. And you, sir, are said to be a very good pilot. So, I'm asking you to consider leaving the AFS and joining our Air Service."

The Colonel continued, "Of course, because you are a U. S. citizen and your country is neutral in this war, you cannot join the French military directly. Have you ever heard of the *Escadrille Américaine*, the American Squadron?

"It's a small group of mostly American volunteers who are flying for France. They are fighter pilots who wear French uniforms and are under the command of French officers. Actually, they are part of the French Army. With a little combat training you could become a member."

"This is a bolt out of the blue," Philip replied. "I've heard a little about the American Squadron, all of it good. But I never thought of joining it. It was only formed a few months ago, right?"

"Actually, there have been Yank pilots in our Air Service from the earliest weeks of the war," Desmoulins noted, "but a group of U. S. flyers pushed for their own elite fighting squadron. Paris finally relented last April and allowed the *Escadrille Américaine* to come into existence. Membership is very small. The roster fluctuates between twelve and nineteen members. And, Belmont, we want you among us.

"Before you turn down the offer, however, let me take you to the Squadron's base tomorrow morning. It's at Luxeuil-les-Bain, close to where you were stationed in Vittel. We can drive to the Squadron's old airfield at Behonne, not far from here. I'll arrange for a plane to rendezvous with us and fly you Luxeuil. There you can meet some of the guys and get a fuller picture than I can give you," the Colonel remarked.

"When you're done, one of the *Escadrille* pilots will return you to Behonne. I'll pick up and we'll drive back here. I'll also arrange it with the AFS to get you out of your duties tomorrow," he suggested.

"OK, I can do that," Philip replied. "A little day-trip never hurt anyone."

"Fine. Let's finish eating and I'll pick you up at your tent at 6 am tomorrow," Colonel Desmoulins said.

As he walked back to his residence after dinner, Philip's mind reeled at the thought of becoming a combat pilot. He loved flying. But battling in the air against hostile German aircraft? Avoiding deadly anti-aircraft fire? Dropping bombs on enemy emplacements? Flying into Germany? This was something he wanted to discuss with Millie. But that, of course, was impossible.

As he entered his tent Philip noticed the letters placed on the floor by the mail service deliveryman. He was excited. One was from his parents in Chicago. He had written to tell them about Millie's pregnancy, so he was eager to read their reactions to becoming grandparents. The other was from Millie, her first communication since she sailed from Le Havre in mid-August.

He poured himself a small glass of port and settled into his easy chair beneath a kerosene lamp. Millie's stationary even smelled of her favorite perfume. It brought a wave of sentimentality to Philip as he read of her safe and eventless trip to New York City. Her parents had come up from Baltimore and together the three returned safely to Maryland. Philip couldn't have been happier that nothing adverse had happened and that her family was so supportive.

The note from Chicago expressed his own parents' pleasure at the news. They promised to make contact with Millie and her folks and arrange a visit later in the fall. It was exactly what he wanted to hear.

He went to bed that evening pleased that everything worked out so well at home. But he remained intrigued, but decidedly undecided about the Colonel's overture.

The trip to Behonne the next morning took an hour. Philip attributed the light traffic they encountered to a lull in the fighting in and around the area. He figured the Germans must be hurting because Berlin had recently placed new commanders in charge of the Verdun offensive. Furthermore, intense fighting along the Somme and against the Russians in Eastern Europe probably compelled the General Staff to transfer large numbers of troops and supplies to the northwest and east.

Philip was curious about his upcoming visit. He had seen French planes in the air along *la route,* but he never knew about this sheltered airfield inconspicuously situated on the way to Bar-le-Duc. He was surprised when the Colonel pulled into the base and parked near a long runway where a two-seater French military airplane sat idling.

"I'm going to spend the day on business in Bar-le-Duc," said Desmoulins. "I'll be back here about 6 o'clock tonight to pick up."

As he exited the car, Philip agreed to the timetable then crossed the runway and climbed into the observer seat at the rear of the aircraft. The pilot, Paul "Skipper" Pavelka, introduced himself. Before he took off, however, he pointed a camera at Philip. "I got this camera for Christmas last year," Pavelka explained. "So, I'm now the Squadron photographer. You don't mind if I take a snap for posterity, do you?"

Philip smiled and said "Cheese." Skipper shot the picture then gunned his engine, rolled down the airfield, and the two men sailed into the morning sky.

The flight to Luxeuil was without incident, but it was exciting for Philip. It was the first time he had been in an aircraft since he left the United States. Immediately, everything he loved about aviation came rushing back.

After landing, Pavelka escorted him to a barrack where the pilots, all wearing uniforms of the *Service Aéronautique,* were relaxing. Oddly enough, Philip immediately recognized one of them. Norman Prince was a Chicago pilot he had met several times at the city air strip along Lake Michigan.

"Hey, Phil Belmont, what are you doing over here, fella?" Prince exclaimed as he walked over to Philip, wrapped his arms around him, and patted him on the back. "I haven't seen you since Chicago three or four years ago. You're looking great."

"Nimmie, wonderful to see you," Philip said as he greeted his old friend and addressed him by his nickname. "It's been a long time. I never expected to find you here. I thought you'd be practicing law for some swanky firm on Michigan Avenue by now."

"Nah, that stuff's too dull for me. I like it much better up there," he said, pointing to the heavens. "Forget the law offices; give me the open skies and a slow-moving German bomber.

"Say, you just missed Jimmy McConnell by a few weeks," Prince continued. "He hurt his back in a crash, so he's gone to Paris to recuperate. But Jimmy's another tough guy from Chicago; he'll get better soon enough."

It was an unexpected reunion. And it certainly made the Colonel's recruitment job easier. Nimmie seemed only too happy to show his friend around the Squadron's facility.

For the next few hours the two Chicagoans walked through the air base and talked aviation. Prince introduced Philip to many of the other American pilots. Among them, he met Charles Chouteau Johnson—"Chute," as they called him—from St. Louis. Chute had been with the *Escadrille* since May. He was also an alumnus of the University of Virginia. Another pilot, Larry Rumsey from Buffalo, New York, was a Harvard grad and a professional polo player. He came to France as a volunteer driver in the American Ambulance Field Service, but moved into flying because it offered more excitement.

Bill Thaw was from high-society in Pittsburgh, Pennsylvania. Wealthy and privileged, he ended his studies at Yale prematurely because he fell madly in love with aircraft. Robert Rockwell, a cousin of another *Escadrille* pilot who had been killed in action a week ago, was the latest addition to the Squadron. He had been studying medicine at New York University when he dropped out and came to France to join the French Foreign Legion. From there he transferred out and trained for the *Service Aéronautique*.

Skipper Pavelka, the man who flew him here, was the son of Hungarian immigrants to the United States. No pedigree here, Skipper was from the streets of New York City. As he explained to Philip on the flight over, his education came from experiences: Bronx public school, farm and lumber-camp work, cross-country travel in railroad box cars, sheering sheep on ranches in North Dakota and Montana, migrant work in California, odd jobs in the Canal Zone in Panama, work on freighters that took him everywhere, enlistment in the U. S. Navy. Finally, in November 1914 he joined the French Foreign Legion and soon transferred to aviation.

Didier Masson was similarly different. He was French by birth, but before the war he traveled as a mechanic for one of the early celebrities of French flying, Louis Paulhan. In his wanderings he lived and worked in places from England to California. As well as a mechanic, Masson worked as a flying instructor, a jeweler, and a dealer in animal skins.

Masson's most interesting employment, however, was as a revolutionary in the Mexican civil war. In the spring of 1913 he was hired as a bomber pilot by General Álvaro Obregón whose troops supported Venustiano Carranza in his revolt against the dictatorial President Victoriano Huerta. In this capacity Masson conducted the first bombing raids on armed ships in aviation history. Heroic? Yes. But the fact that not one of his hand-delivered pipe bombs ever hit a targeted gunship continued to make him the butt of good-natured jokes among the *Escadrille* members.

They were all courageous young men because military aviation was a dangerous pursuit. As Nimmie fatalistically explained it, "In this branch you either win the *Croix de Guerre* or the *Croix de Bois*—the War Cross, the highest French military decoration, or the wooden cross they plant on top of your grave."

"What brings you guys up here," Philip asked. "I've been working in Verdun with the American Field Service for months—and before that I was in Vittel—but I never knew about this base."

"We just got here. This is our new home base," Prince noted. "Until a few days ago we were assigned to support the French Second Army and General Neville around Verdun. For that assignment we were housed in a chateau in Behonne. We flew around and did lots of airplane things. This is much better than being stuck in a putrid trench."

Philip smiled. "Then it must have been someone in your Squadron who saved my hide several weeks ago when an Albatross was getting ready to attack my wife and I, as well as an ambulance truck filled with injured *poilus*. Out of nowhere came this Nieuport with machine gun blazing. The German got away, but so did we, thanks to the Nieuport."

Oh, that must have been Luf—I mean Major Gervais Raoul Lufbery. He's our Ace pilot. He has been talking quite a bit about how he rescued a French ambulance in distress. To him, I'm afraid, it was just another day at the office. In fact, we all do that stuff regularly," remarked Prince. "But, come with me. Let me show you more of our tiny American air force."

He led Philip to the area where fighter aircraft were parked. Most of the planes were Nieuports. "This little beauty here is the Nieuport 11. We call her the Nieuport *Bébé*, and she's quite a Baby. She used to be our workhorse. And for a while we loved only our Babies.

"Over there is the Nieuport 16, the one painted in brown and green camouflage with that sky-blue underbelly. This plane is faster and heavier than the 11. She has that deadly Lewis machine gun mounted on her top wing the same as the *Bébé*. But when we're hunting German Zeppelins and other balloons, she carries some God-awful rockets that can blow them out of the air.

"Now, we all love the 11 and the 16. But when they introduced the upgraded Nieuport 17, most of us made the switch posthaste. That's a 17 sitting over there," he said pointing to a silver-colored aircraft sporting a painted profile of an American Indian wearing a war bonnet. "We call her the *Superbébé*. That's because she is a lot like the original 11—except she goes faster and can climb twice as high. Plus, *Superbébé* has a Vickers machine gun that's synchronized so we can shoot between the spinning propeller blades. And that Vickers can fire more bullets than the outdated Lewis that's on the Nieuport 11 and 16.

"Most of us have been flying Nieuport 17s for about six months. They can reach 100 miles an hour and last two hours before refueling. They've made aerial combat a whole lot easier for us.

THE HEADLONG FURY

"We're supposed to get a few more of these by the end of the month. And as for that Indian on the side of the fuselage, we copied it from a crate of ammunition manufactured by the Savage Arms Company. It's supposed to be a Seminole chieftain in full war regalia. It's now our Squadron logo."

Philip was impressed with what he was seeing. "All these Nieuports are double-winged fighters, so, what's that monoplane over there?" he asked.

"That's a Morane Saulnier P. It has one wing and two-seats—a great reconnaissance plane," Nimmie said. "She's used mostly for spotting enemy troop movements beyond the trenches—or for flying spies into Germany to gather information or blow up Boche installations. Front seat for the pilot, rear seat for the observer or the spy. In fact, Skipper picked you up in an MS-P.

"And here's another winner. It's the SPAD VII. It's a brand-new type of plane, different manufacturer with different capabilities. We just received a preview copy. It belongs to our second in command, Lieutenant De Laage. Most of us haven't flown in it yet. The few who have think she's better than the Nieuports. If it's truly a better plane, I expect it'll become the next standard.

"But, talk like that is grounds for divorce. Remember, technically we're Squadron N124 in the French Air Service. The letter N means we fly Nieuports. We're mad about them. But if we learn to love the SPADs better, we'll have to become Squadron SPA124. I don't know if we can be married to two aircraft manufacturers at the same time," Nimmie jested. "I think they call that aeronautical bigamy."

As they walked back to the barrack reminiscing, Philip asked serious questions about the American Squadron. "How did you fellas get here?" he wondered. "And why are you flying for France? I'm amazed that there are so few of you. What do you hope to accomplish?" he said to his friend.

"Look, we're not a big unit. Don't want to be. But we're understaffed right now," Prince responded. "We started in April with just seven Americans and two French officers. Since then we've added eleven more Americans, but we have a large attrition rate. Vic Chapman and Kiffen

Rockwell were killed in action; Horace Balsley was so badly wounded he had to leave; Charlie Nungesser was posted here for only a month then assigned to another flying unit.

"As for Elliot Cowdin, he was so disruptive we asked him to leave the Squadron. And between you and me, Bert Hall—card cheat, forger, blowhard, and all around troublemaker—will be told soon enough to do the same thing.

"How did we get here? Many ways. Some of us joined the French Foreign Legion just after the war began. That's because the Legion is the only French unit that can legally accept foreign volunteers. Most who came through the Legion were involved in ground warfare before transferring into the Air Service. Others came to aviation after working in the Ambulance Service, as you are considering doing now. And a few went straight from the recruitment office to the training aerodrome in Pau, and then to Tours or Ambérieu-en-Bugey for combat training in Nieuports.

"Just a handful of us had backgrounds or connections in aviation, so we were accepted directly into the Air Service, given training, won our *brevet militaire*, our flying license, and were assigned to various French air combat squadrons, not just N124.

"We have guys here with college degrees from Ivy League universities. Many just dropped out before graduating and came to France. And some of us came from the trades and working class backgrounds. Bert Hall, for example, says he used to be a human cannonball in a Midwest circus. There are people like Raoul Lufbery: born in France, educated in Austria, lived in Connecticut, and roamed the planet. He was a candle maker in Connecticut, a baker in New Orleans, a ticket-taker in Bombay, and a member of the U. S. Army in the Philippines where he became an American citizen. And then he found aviation.

"As for motives, take your pick: glory, adventure, running away from a bad situation at home, love of France, hatred of Germany, a chance to restore a tarnished reputation, a love affair gone wrong. Probably another dozen explanations could be added to the list. We're from everywhere, and we got here for every reason."

Philip listened carefully. He could see himself fitting into such a gloriously oddball organization. "But why fly for France?" he wondered.

"I think the better question is why the French allow us to fly for their country," explained Nimmie. "God knows, there are enough capable French citizens trying to get into the Air Service. And when they're fully trained, those Frenchies make excellent fighter pilots.

"France doesn't really need Americans to pilot their airplanes—at least France doesn't need us *militarily*. But, as propaganda we work wonders in the States. Believe it or not, we've become folk heroes back home. They're writing books about us. I hear that while he's in Paris recuperating from that wrenched back, Jimmy McConnell is writing about his air combat experiences fighting for France. Needless to say, we'll be in that volume.

"They can't get enough of us in America. We're fascinating rogues, romantic throwbacks to Kit Carson-types who pioneered the Wild West. Newspapers report all of our victories, and unfortunately, all of our deaths. They write magazine articles that flatter us. I'll bet they'll be making flickers about us pretty soon. And while all this is going on, we make France and the Allies look real good and Germany look fiendish.

"Someday America will be getting into this war. Because of us, there's no way the Yanks will be joining the German side. We flying Americans are part of the reason why public opinion at home will demand that our leaders side with France and Britain and Italy in crushing the Boches.

"So, when you join the *Escadrille Américaine* you become a French propaganda tool. But you get to fight Germans. And it still beats researching in a law library in Chicago for Winston, Payne, Strawn and Shaw," he concluded.

As they reentered the flyers' barrack, Philip was startled by a loud growling sound. He knew it hadn't come from any aircraft, but it sounded familiar. When he heard the noise again, only louder, a laughing Prince explained that the Squadron had its own pet, a young lion. The cub lived in the building with the pilots.

"Dud Hill and a few of the flyers bought the animal from a Brazilian dentist in Paris for 500 francs," Prince explained. "The dentist had it as a waiting-room attraction. But, apparently, his patients didn't like the idea of mixing exotic wildlife with toothaches. So our guys purchased the cub and shipped him here on the train. Bill Thaw wanted to ride with the beast in a passenger car. He put him in a box and labeled it 'African dog.' The railroad people weren't fooled. They made Whiskey—that's his name—ride in a wooden crate in the baggage car."

"Sounds reasonable to me—I guess," Philip replied incredulously.

"Don't tell that to Whiskey. He was very upset that his travel plans were so rudely changed by those French railroad inspectors," Norm whispered to Philip.

He then led Philip to the young lion. "Here, you play with Whiskey while I arrange to get you back to Behonne," he said.

"Does joining the Squadron mean I'd be sleeping next to the lion, especially when he grows to man-eater size?" Philip asked.

"Oh, he's nothing but an inflated pussy cat. Whiskey would never eat a nice American pilot," said Chute Johnson.

"Nah. As long as you're carrying a slab of raw steak or a dead chicken, Whiskey will never eat you. He's well-trained, as a gourmet. And as a man-eater, he only devours Germans," Skipper Pavelka chimed in.

"Besides, how do you expect to stop Germany's Ace of Aces, Baron Manfred von Richthofen, if you can't handle a cuddly house cat like Whiskey?" Bob Rockwell inquired.

"Yeah, the Red Baron is a lot scarier than poor wee Whiskey," Johnson added.

The entire barrack broke into laughter at the wisecracks made at Philip's expense. Philip laughed with the flyers, but uneasily. Try as he might, he didn't care for lions unless they were in picture books or behind thick metal bars in a zoo.

"Hey, Belmont," yelled Dud Hill from the rear of the barrack. "Did you hear the one about the Professor who asked his student 'What has been the dominant character of America's military program up to the last three years?' And the student, who'd been at a party the night before, yawned and said, 'Not prepared, sir.' 'Correct,' said the Professor.

THE HEADLONG FURY

Laughter and groaning followed. "Oh, that's Dud the Witty. Always telling those unfunny stories," remarked Nimmie. "He's got too many of 'em. If he weren't such a damned good fighter pilot, I don't think the fellas could stand those cornball jokes."

"Did you hear about the Kaiser's telephone call to Heaven," Hill continued. "Seems Wilhelm telephoned Heaven, but got no answer. 'God's not answering,' said the German leader. 'Nuts! I'm afraid He's gone over to the Allies.'"

Again, mixed reactions followed. "Hey, Dud, don't you know anything but those lame political jokes," Chute Johnson interjected.

"Yah, sure," Hill answered. How about something nonpolitical? Have you heard about the woman who switched icemen. The new guy promised to deliver her colder ice for the same price."

This one received more approval from the flyers, but not so much as to encourage further joking. "Have mercy on us," Nimmie yelled out.

"Ah, does that mean you want more political funnies," Hall responded. "How about an anti-German poem. It's one of my best.

> "Give us our place in the sun," they cried.
> "A place that matches our worth."
> "Take *all* the sun," mankind replied.
> "But please get off the earth."

Philip and many of the American pilots were eager to change the mood. "Tell me, what it's like fighting the Germans in the sky?" Philip asked.

"Well, it's not easy," offered Nimmie. "They're tough pilots, and they know every trick. But we hold our own in dogfights despite the recent deaths we've had in our ranks. We've lost some good friends. Lord only knows who'll be next."

"But isn't your armament improving?" Philip inquired. "Aren't you better prepared now for aerial combat?" Philip asked.

"That's right; but Boche armament is improving, too. And that makes them better prepared for us," Larry Rumsey interjected. "And those Boches sure know how to use those improvements, especially those through-the-propellers machine guns. They're mean weapons."

"Makes me long for the old days," added Lufbery. "I'm talking 1914, maybe 1915. In those days we sometimes used pistols to shoot enemy pilots. Just flew up next to them and shot 'em dead in mid-air."

"And don't forget the bricks," Chute Johnson reminded Luf.

"That's right. In the early days we'd take a load of bricks up with us and throw them into the propellers of German planes," Lufbery continued. "Believe it or not, we actually downed a few enemy planes—a very few—using that rather primitive weapons system."

The men laughed loudly at this reminder of the primeval days of aerial combat.

"Do you remember those Lewis machine guns we had on the early Nieuports?" recalled Norman Prince, who had rejoined the conversation. "They were mounted on the top wing and you had to fly with one hand and fire with the other extended upward. After shooting off forty-seven bullets, you had to replace the spent drum with a fresh one to get another forty-seven bullets—that's if you remembered to bring extra drums with you."

"Not much fire power there," he continued. "I could empty a full drum in five seconds. And those drums added up: each one weighed about five pounds. Ten extra drums got you fifty seconds of rapidly-fired bullets—but it added fifty pounds to your flight load."

"And what great fun reloading was," added Lufbery. "You had to hold the joystick with your knees while you stood up and to change the drum. But sometimes you couldn't open the chamber to insert a new drum. Or the empty drum got stuck in the gun."

"Meanwhile, the wind was blowing a hundred miles an hour right into your face," recalled Didier Masson. "I'll bet lots of guys got shot in the ass trying to reload."

The pilots burst out laughing at the absurd images conjured up by this lesson in aviation history. The fact that Didier's quip was based on truth made the imagery all the more hilarious.

"Now that we're down in the mud, there's one thing you must always guard against when you're flying for France," noted Skipper Pavelka in a mocking tone. "Never get caught in the situation where you need a toilet when you're flying. You can piss your pants with impunity—well, maybe a little embarrassment. But anything else in the air is impossible. If you feel that call of nature while you're flying, land as fast as you can, even if you're ready to finish off a Boche fighter pilot. Land immediately! They'll never give you a medal if your pants are full."

This scatological warning resulted in uncontrolled amusement that lasted more than two minutes. "Stop giving away our trade secrets," yelled Bob Rockwell, feeding the comic frenzy.

"Yeah, we're supposed to be the swashbuckling heroes of this damn war. But if you keep talking like that no one will even want to be around us," Prince injected. "Especially if we're late making that emergency landing."

The flyers were still snickering when Philip and Skipper walked toward the door. "Take it easy, fellas, but take it," Philip said as he waved farewell.

He was glad to be heading back to his rendezvous with Colonel Desmoulins. Philip knew he would be questioned about the visit, but he remained uncertain about accepting the invitation to join the *Escadrille Américaine*. He had no answer yet. He needed time to think over such a major decision.

10

Philip was growing distressed. While he was still weighing the offer to join the French air force, the love of flying that had captured him before he came to France was again stirring in his soul. But he was lonely for his wife who was expecting their first child in Baltimore in a few months, and flying as a fighter pilot meant risking his life.

The war was also dragging him down. While his AFS work remained valuable to the French Army, after two years of battered *poilus*, he was becoming emotionally drained. The inexhaustible supply of the injured, the grievous nature of their wounds, the many dreams he saw shattered, the fear that filled every moment for those operating at the front: it was all very stressful. Increasingly, Philip was coming to understand the conflict as an interminable demonstration of human cruelty.

Fortunately, by early October there was a lull in fighting in and around Verdun. But that was only because for several months German forces were being deployed westward to sites along the Somme. In ferocious fighting there both sides endured massive losses. The brunt of the Allied effort on the Somme was being borne by Great Britain and its Dominion troops. French soldiers, nevertheless, were a sizable component in the bloody engagement. Already estimates of dead and wounded ran into the hundreds of thousands.

That's why Philip was not surprised when Doc Andrew drove up from Paris to inform his drivers that several sections of AFS ambulances were being sent to assist the rescue crews already working on the Somme. "I'm told it won't be a lengthy assignment," Doc told the assembled drivers, "but we are hemorrhaging in that area. So, we go where we're needed and ordered. And that means we'll be leaving here in one hour."

There was not much time for forty to fifty ambulance drivers to prepare for reassignment. But Philip and Allen Pryce and the other volunteers swiftly gathered their belongings and pulled out on a 140 mile road trip across the top of France. The roadways were dry and unimpeded in the early autumn, so the drive took less than seven hours. By late afternoon the American ambulance workers were already transporting wounded soldiers from dressing stations to field hospitals and railroad depots. There was a difference, however. Now most of the injured were Tommies, not *poilus*. That was because the British together with troops from Canada, South Africa, India, New Zealand, Australia, and other imperial holdings were the driving force of this tremendous battle.

Conversing with English-speaking soldiers with accents from Scotland, Wales, Ireland, and even some regions of rural England, made Philip wish he were back dealing with French troops, even those with regional accents. On more than one occasion he had to communicate in French to overcome the strange way some of the U.K. troops spoke. One of his first rescues was a talkative Scottish sergeant whose neck had been pierced by a German bayonet. When he learned that Philip's wife was anticipating the birth of their first child, the Scot said that he hoped it would be "a bra bairn." Luckily the sergeant spoke a little French so he translated his wish that the child would be *une belle bébé*—a beautiful baby.

It was the only thing amusing about his first day on the Somme. Otherwise it was all too familiar. British troops bled exactly the way French soldiers did. The wounds were the same. As for the Tommies who died, they died just like *poilus*.

While driving to the field hospital with a load of injured Welch soldiers, Philip and Allen encountered something neither had ever seen before. It appeared to be an amazing war weapon with a gun turret on top. The sides of the massive contraption consisted of riveted sheets of thick steel. It was powered by two caterpillar-like bands of revolving metal plates. In many ways, it reminded both men of a small ironclad boat operating on dry land. "What in blazes is that?" Allen exclaimed. "It looks like something Jules Verne might have dreamed up in a fantasy novel."

At the hospital Philip learned that it was a new British weapon of destruction called a tank. It got that name because when this secret weapon was imported from England a few months ago it was listed on shipping manifests as a water tank in order to mislead possible German spies.

"We've got about fifty of those Big Willies around here," a British sergeant-major boasted to Philip. "They've been used in combat for the past two or three weeks, but they've got a lot of problems. They get stuck in the mud too easily, even in the large craters made by the Jack Johnsons. That's what we call 150mm German artillery shells that explode in black smoke with the awesome power of your former boxing champion, Jack Johnson. They make quite a large hole in the ground, they do.

"But that's not all. Tanks aren't agile," he added. "They're too awkward to turn quickly. With a top speed of four miles per hour, they can't even keep up with the infantry on foot. And working conditions are wretched for the eight unlucky blokes pulling levers and firing machine guns from inside each of these coffins on caterpillar tracks. Other than that, these land ships are great.

"Oh, I forgot, they have one advantage: they scare the Dickens out of the Germans—for now, at least."

To Philip this mechanical monster represented one more step in the advance of indifferent war technology over human life. To the list that included poison gas and aerial bombardment now add the tank. All delivered death efficiently, relentlessly, and anonymously.

The AFS ambulance sections had arrived in Arras on October 4. Most of the volunteers figured they would stay there until the end of the year. Within two weeks, however, they were ordered back to Verdun. "Something must be happening in Lorraine," Allen responded when told of the sudden turnaround.

"I'm betting on some sort of a French Fall or Winter Offensive very soon," Philip said. "They're dragging us back because Joffre and General Mangin are going to be attacking something very soon."

To a man, the volunteers were upset about the order to return. There were so many soldiers in need of assistance right here. But, orders being orders, on October 18 they packed their kit bags, filled the gas tanks, and drove back.

Everyone was exhausted when the ambulances finally reached Verdun. Two straight weeks of twelve-hour workdays was fatiguing. Philip was heartened, however, when he found mail waiting for him in his tent on base. He reverted to his ritual: he carefully opened a bottle of wine, increased the brightness of his gas lamp, and plopped himself on a comfortable chair and began to read.

A note from Chicago reassured him that his parents were leaving soon for Baltimore to meet Millie's folks. They were planning to take the train at the end of October.

A letter from Millie answered the question that had been agonizing him for several weeks: yes, she was doing well; yes, she felt she could handle the birth with the assistance of her parents; no, she didn't think it would be necessary for Philip to return for the birth, given the life-and-death seriousness of what he was doing; and yes, she agreed that leaving the AFS and joining the *Escadrille Américaine* would be good for his sanity—and it just might help bring an end to the war sooner.

Millie's encouragement made him feel wonderful. It convinced him to tell Colonel Desmoulins tomorrow morning that he was ready to join the Air Service. But, it would have to be with one important proviso: he would never strafe or drop bombs on innocent civilians. He always hated the Germans aviators who seemed to have no misgivings about dropping explosives on townspeople and turning their machine guns on non-combatant targets. And as much as he detested the victory of mechanical technology over life, he was willing to join the highly mechanized American Squadron because he felt the only way to stop the inhumanity of this war was to win it as speedily as possible and then take steps to prevent another one.

The first two letters made Philip feel good, but the third letter stunned him. It was a note from Colonel Desmoulins informing him that Norman Prince died on October 15 as a result of injuries sustained in a forced landing near the frontlines. Accompanying the notification was a newspaper clipping announcing the death of the war ace and co-founder of the American Squadron. Prince was only thirty years of age when he passed away.

But to Philip it was more. Prince was a friend from prewar days in Chicago. Meeting him so unexpectedly in Luxeuil was the highlight of his visit last month. The chance to work alongside Norman Prince was one of the reasons Philip decided to join the Squadron.

According to the newspaper clipping, on October 12 Sergeant-Major Prince was making a night landing at an emergency airfield and failed to see the high tension wires that stretched across the tree tops. His landing gear hooked one of the cables, flipping his Nieuport forward and into the ground. He was thrown from the plane and suffered two broken legs. The following day a blood clot caused by the crash lodged in his brain and he lapsed into a coma. He never regained consciousness.

Solemnly, Philip refilled his wine glass then raised it in tribute to his hero and friend. "To you, Norman Prince, for all the good you have done to help end the war. I raise a toast to you and your courageous commitment. I salute my friend and colleague. Here's to you, Nimmie, long may your soul fly in clear and peaceful skies." With that he sipped the wine and brushed tears from his eyes.

The following morning he knew exactly what to say when he entered Colonel Desmoulins' office. "Colonel, I'm here to replace my friend, Norman Prince. I accept your offer to join the *Escadrille Américaine*."

With a sad smile, the Colonel embraced Philip and kissed him on each cheek. "It was truly tragic news," he said. "France lost a champion. America lost a citizen of great courage and integrity. He was your friend, was he not?"

"Yes, I knew him in Chicago years ago. I was a few years older, but we became good acquaintances because we both loved to fly," responded Philip sadly.

"Well, I'm sure he is looking down right now and is proud of what you are doing to honor his memory," Desmoulins said. "I am very pleased that you wish to join us. Thank you.

"Now, let me see," he continued, "there are a few technicalities. First we have to swear you into the French Army. The easiest way is to induct you into our Foreign Legion, then transfer you immediately to the Army, specifically to its aviation branch, the *Service Aéronautique*.

"Because you are a seasoned pilot, your training period should go smoothly and fast. We'll send you to the School of Combat in Pau for training in Nieuports, and maybe even in the new SPAD aircraft we are getting soon. Once you're brevetted you'll be transferred back to Luxeuil as a member of the American Squadron."

"That sounds great to me," Philip responded.

"Actually, I anticipated your agreement. So, weeks ago I prepared the necessary paperwork. All I need to set the process in motion is your signature on this document," Desmoulins said as he handed Philip an enlistment contract.

"What about Doc Andrew? Will you notify him that I've left the American Field Service? Or should I do that?" Philip asked while perusing the document.

"Don't worry about anything, Private Belmont. You like that new name, eh?" Desmoulins said with a glint in his eye. "Doc and I have been collaborating on this aspect of your recruitment, too. He's in agreement that it's time you had a change. He is so proud of you. You were one of his first ambulance volunteers. But he knows that you can do much more for our cause as a fighter pilot."

"Thank you for the encouragement. When I see Doc again, I'll tell him just how much those AFS years mean to me," said Philip. "I wouldn't be married and awaiting the birth of a child had it not been for Doc and his medical volunteers," Philip conceded.

"And France would not have saved so many lives had it not been for you and your lovely wife," Desmoulins added.

"Well, before I start crying at this love fest, let me sign the paper; then take me to Pau," Philip said with amusement. He signed the document and was immediately sworn into the French Foreign Legion. Just as speedily was transferred out of the Legion and assigned to the Air Service. He was now in training to fly for France.

"We'll send you by train to Paris where you will have a week to relax and prepare yourself for aviation training. You will report to Pau on October 27 by noon," the smiling Colonel announced.

"Oh, by the way, when you see the men of the American Squadron, tell them there's been another change of name. Seems like the German government protested the word *Américaine* in their official squadron name. They asked Washington why, if the United States was officially neutral in the war, France had a combat unit named after the United States of America.

"We didn't care much about the German complaint, but when your Secretary of State asked Paris to change the name, we had no choice. In a few weeks Squadron N124 will be renamed as the *Escadrille de Volontaires*, the Volunteers Squadron."

"That's a terrible name," Philip responded frankly. "It sounds so dry and technical. Nobody in the Squadron will like that one. You need something more thrilling or the Yank flyers will keep calling themselves the *Escadrille Américaine*."

"I know, I know," said Desmoulins. "We figured the American pilots would despise the new name. None of us likes it either—even Paris hates the name. But France was under pressure and we had to come up with a quick alternative.

"And remember," he continued, "we have almost 200 Americans flying in other French squadrons. They're not going to like the name either."

Philip interrupted the Colonel. "Do you mean the comprehensive Franco-American Flying Corps is now the Volunteer Flying Corps?" he asked.

"Ugly name, I know, said the Colonel. "But there's good news. Be patient. Off the record, I've heard that next month your Squadron will be renamed again. This time you'll be called the *Escadrille Lafayette*, the Lafayette Escadrille. That's in honor the French officer who helped General Washington in your War of Independence—and to salute your wonderful nation.

"In fact, since June all Americans flying for France in any squadron have been considered part of the inclusive Franco-American Flying Corps. And I wouldn't be surprised if that name is eventually changed to the Lafayette Flying Corps. Then everyone can be happy: you Yanks, we French, and those legalistic Boches," Desmoulins concluded wryly.

"Great names! I love them," replied Philip. "But it sounds like France needs lawyers as much as it needs fighter pilots."

Leaving his meeting with the Colonel, Philip was filled with a feeling of accomplishment and anticipation. He felt good about his work in the ambulance service. He had dedicated years to the job, working long hours with little time off. He had even suspended his academic career and his historical research in order to help France survive.

He was actually excited about moving into the *Service Aéronautique*. It was something refreshing, a new perspective. And the thought of getting back in a cockpit and waging war in the skies also exhilarated him.

Philip looked forward to the week-long respite in Paris. Until it was offered, however, he never knew he needed time away from the battlefields to renew his spirits. He hadn't been in Paris since joining the American Ambulance two years ago. He was eager to compare the contemporary situation with his memories of prewar life in the French capital.

His first point of comparison was with his accommodations in Paris. While Colonel Desmoulins had provided him a list of inexpensive lodgings where he might stay, Philip wondered if he was still listed at the Hôtel de Crillon as a guest of the French state. It was worth an inquiry. He suspected that the Crillon was still the plushest facility in the city, and none of the cut-rate hotels on the Colonel's list could compare.

Arriving late that afternoon at the Gare de l'Est, he took a short trip on the Métro to arrive at the Place de la Concorde. Everything appeared so familiar. The subway was filled with passengers; musicians in the station passageways, especially at Châtelet, performed with instrument cases and hats strategically placed to accept donations of sous and centimes—even francs, were a wealthy passerby so inclined.

Inside and even waiting outside the subway cars he spotted the familiar signs of young love in Paris: romantic couples standing while embracing and quietly sharing short and frequent kisses. Even as he wedged himself and his suitcase into an overly crowded passenger car, he sensed that Paris was getting back to normal.

Emerging from the subway, Philip recognized another customary Parisian pattern: automobiles and pedestrians, electric tramways and taxis flowing in and out of the expansive traffic circle that was the Place de la Concorde. But it seemed to have changed substantially since he was last in the city.

Paris was now militarized. Convoys of Army trucks filled with soldiers wove through the civilian traffic. Military men in the uniforms of many nations drove or walked in all directions headed for varied destinations. Countless nurses scurried along the boulevards and avenues headed to and from their life-saving work.

As for the shops of Paris, many displayed patriotic red, white and blue bunting. Some prominently placed posters in their windows urging citizens to subscribe to the support of soldiers and sailors fighting the hated Germans. This was no longer a city fearful of enemy dirigibles and imminent surrender, it was a unified people locked into victory and laboring diligently to defeat the savage invaders.

Philip was pleasantly surprised when the Crillon receptionist verified that the French government still maintained an open account in his name. "Thank you, Mr. Delcassé," he whispered under his breath as he registered for a week's stay. As he unpacked in his suite, he was overjoyed that he would be staying here instead of in a cheap room selected from Desmoulins' recommendations.

He explained his good fortune in letters he immediately dashed off to Millie and to his family. With directions from the concierge, Philip headed for the nearest post office to mail them. It had been a long time since he had been in a real post office. "How underappreciated is a post office," he thought as he walked. "What a glorious embodiment of social achievement and civilized arrangement! Be without one for a few years, and you learn just how wonderful a post office is."

THE HEADLONG FURY

After mailing his correspondence, Philip decided to continue walking, a favorite pastime for visitors and Parisians alike, and especially on a beautiful afternoon such as this one. Each street he traveled offered an array of small shops selling everything from foodstuffs to clothing to personal services.

One storefront that grabbed his attention along a short street in the 2nd arrondissement was that of an extermination company, *Vartanian et Fils*. This company specialized in purging Paris of *chats sauvages*—feral cats. Of course Vartanian and Sons also exterminated rats, moles, and other vermin. But wild cats seemed to be the principal target of their eradication efforts.

To underscore their dominance over these fierce urban beasts, the owners had arrayed stuffed skins and pelts of ferocious felines they had trapped and killed. Snarling dead cats hung in space, their limbs fully extended as if waiting to be drawn and quartered. The dead cats were grotesque trophies in the war between man and nature. Even after his brutal experiences on the frontlines, Philip was still unnerved by this tableau glorifying feline execution. He walked quickly by.

As he meandered through the streets, he was heartened to see them brimming with foot traffic, even away from the principal boulevards. People of all types were on their way from and to their destinations.

Peering ahead Philip saw something unusual. A young girl, perhaps eight years old, was approaching the pedestrians and offering each one a small piece of paper. Some accepted, others walked by as if the child wasn't there. When he approached the little girl smiled and extended a piece of paper to him. He took it and walked on. The message written on it was at once startlingly and simple: "France will survive. Keep faith with our leaders and our military. *Vive la France.*"

Philip turned and hurried back to the youngster. "Did you write this note?" he asked her.

"On, no, monsieur," she replied. "My mother spends hours every day writing the same message on scraps of paper. She hopes to spread her optimism among the people of Paris. She's sure that France will be victorious, and she wants the people of the city to know and share her feelings. So, she composes the notes, and I pass them out to people strolling along the sidewalks."

Philip was stunned. "What a beautiful thing to do," he said to the child. "Tell your mother that I share her attitude totally. And tell her she is raising a remarkable daughter who is bringing joy to a sad Paris."

As he spoke, he reached into his pocket and found a ten franc note. "Please give this to you mother from an appreciative pedestrian."

"On, no, sir, I'm not supposed to accept any money for this," the girl replied. "Mama and I are not working for a profit; we are working for love—love of France, love of Paris, love of other people. To accept money would misrepresent our goal. Please accept the message, and perhaps give your money to a poor person begging on the sidewalk."

Philip smiled and walked away, amazed but better for the experience. When he finally passed an authentic beggar—an elderly blind man with a guide dog sitting on his lap—he placed the ten franc note is the man's inverted chapeau and wished him well.

After thirty minutes or more of aimless promenading through the rich and poor sections of the city, Philip found himself in the Marais, the colorful old section of central Paris near the great market of Les Halles. Occasional chateaux illustrated that the Marais was once an aristocratic section, while synagogues and storefronts bearing Hebrew words showed that it was now the Jewish section of Paris. The cheap *bouillons* and *brasseries* and inexpensive restaurants also suggested that this was a working-class neighborhood.

Above all, Philip saw the Marais as vibrating with cultural diversity as people, many dressed in Asian and African clothing, mingled in the streets and stores. He figured that they were from various French colonies which made them citizens of France according to the Republican constitution. For Philip the area was fascinating admixture of peoples, a global swatch illustrative of what made French society so beguiling. His Russian mother would love to be here walking with him, he concluded.

As he passed a small tavern called *La Rendezvous des Routières*, Philip heard the loud crashing noise of wooden chairs being smashed and glass breaking. It came from inside the bar. When he peeked in the doorway he saw a fistfight underway. A large older man and a smaller, athletic black man were engaged in a strenuous fistfight. Although outweighed, the black man in his late twenties was clearly winning. He punched with precisely-placed blows administered in combinations of jabs, hooks, and occasional uppercuts. He moved like a professional boxer, ducking wild punches and tiring his opponent to the point of collapse. Interestingly, the black man was wearing a French military uniform.

Instinctively, Philip intervened to break the two men apart. He was especially worried that the French soldier might seriously injure his opponent. "OK! OK! Stop before you kill someone," he shouted reflexively in English as he dragged the younger man away from his bleeding opponent. With reluctance, the black man heeded Philip's command and pulled back. The other man was too exhausted to resist the order to stop. After a few seconds spent catching his breath and wiping blood from his face, the beaten fighter staggered toward the door and left the tavern.

"Thanks, buddy, I'm glad you broke us up before I did kill that big fool," the French soldier said in English with a U. S. accent that was distinctly southern.

Once he had pacified the situation, Philip turned to the American. "You're from the States. Where from?" he inquired.

"Me? I'm from Columbus, Georgia—but more recently from Glasgow, Scotland. The name is Bullard, Eugene Bullard," said the man as he dried the sweat that glistened on his forehead. "But you can call me Gene. And you are?"

Philip introduced himself. "What was the fight about?" he asked.

"Oh, he's just a bigoted old Dutchman. He came up with some pretty offensive names for me. Called me a *boule-de-niege*, and you know it means more than snowball in French. That's equivalent to calling me a nigger. He also called me a kaffir. Told me that I was a disgrace to the French uniform and ordered me to go back to the Congo where I belonged.

I don't take that racist baloney from anyone. That's why I left the States. I hated it there, and I'm not going to tolerate it over here," Gene explained.

"Well, you handled yourself pretty well in that bout you just had," noted Philip.

"Oh, you noticed. When I lived in Scotland I did a little prize fighting—fought a few rounds of bare-knuckle around Europe," Gene replied. "But when the war broke out I came to Paris and joined up. We *poilus* don't get to fight with our fists very often. I'm a bit slow now, but it felt good."

After signaling the bartender to bring over two beers, Philip mentioned that he had joined the French Army yesterday after two years in the American Field Service ambulance corps. "I'm off to aviation training in a week. Gonna fly airplanes for Uncle France," he remarked.

"I think it was an AFS ambulance that took me to the hospital when I got shot at Verdun back in March," Gene explained. "Got a bullet lodged in my thigh, and most of my teeth were knocked out. It took me out of commission for a while. But six months of doctoring fixed me up."

"By the look of that guy who just left, you're fully recovered," Philip replied.

The two men laughed heartily.

"Say, what's all that metal and satin pinned to your tunic," Philip asked. "Either you're a war hero or you picked that up in the Paris flea market."

Gene smiled. "A few trifles I acquired in the last couple of months," he said modestly.

"Trifles?" Philip responded. "One of those is the Croix de Guerre. That's the highest award the French give for bravery on the battlefield."

"Ah, they're all mere trivialities," Gene replied. "Everything pinned to my tunic happened in the past. I'm concentrating on the present and the future. Right now, I'm on leave from aerial gunnery school. But I want to hear more about this piloting stuff," demanded Gene.

He continued, "I've actually given thought to becoming a pilot instead of a gunner. Why did you join the French Air Service?"

For the next two hours and several more beers, the two men discussed the new world of military aviation. Philip's enthusiasm for flying was evident as he explained his situation. Gene's curiosity was raised. He listened intently and asked lots of questions about piloting aircraft.

"You know, I'm gonna check into this flyboy business as soon as I can. Maybe tomorrow," he said. "Do you think they'd accept a black man for training as a fighter pilot?"

"The French? Sure they would," Philip responded. "Even the Turks have an African man, a Somali from Iraq, who's a combat pilot. Yeah, I think the French would give you a shot at training.

"Hell, you'd have a secret weapon with that uppercut of yours. You could stand on the top wing of a Nieuport and bring down German planes with your bare fists. Air boxing! It could shorten the war by months," Philip joked.

In a serious vein he added, "But the Americans? That's a different kettle of fish. I'm afraid the Yanks are too bigoted. Back home our army doesn't allow Negroes in its new Air Corps. You'd be more likely to be shot down by one of your own guys than by a German pilot."

"But I'm not even half Negro. My daddy was one-quarter Creek Indian, and my mama was more Creek than that," Gene protested.

"Ha. The white Americans don't like Indians either. They serve with the white soldiers, but it's an uneasy relationship. Same is true for Americans of Mexican ancestry," said Philip. "So, check and checkmate! But with the French you'd be the first black pilot fighting for democracy—and the first American Indian combat pilot, too. They'd get two for the price of one! They would like that. *Quelle distinction!*"

Gene laughed at the absurdity of his situation. "You're right. I'd be making history twice, wouldn't I? I like that. Tomorrow, I'm gonna check into becoming a French fighter pilot instead a gunner," he declared. "Hey, Belmont, I'm glad I met you."

Philip and his new friend enjoyed small talk for another half hour before saying goodbye. It was nighttime when Philip finally returned to his room. He was amused that he might make a better recruiter than an aviator.

For the next five days he played the tourist and visited the city. One of his first visits was to Notre Dame Cathedral, something he never got around to doing when he was researching at the Quai d'Orsay. He also took short day trips to Versailles to see the amazing palace made famous by Louis XIV—and to Chartres where one of the most beautiful medieval cathedrals was located. Fortunately, none of these historical sites had suffered battle damage.

Although Paris itself seemed familiar, the longer he stayed the more he detected a well-disguised tension among the people he observed. The street promenade, that leisurely stroll of the *boulevardiers* and *flâneurs*, was dramatically curtailed. Pedestrians may have been plentiful and confident, but, he realized, they walked purposefully and directly to their destinations. On more than one occasion he saw walkers rush for cover when they heard an airplane or spotted a military balloon floating over the city. Loud noises also caused many to seek safety inside nearby *Métro* stations in case the sound was caused by long-range German artillery shells or even bombs falling again on the city. The lessons from the summer of 1914 were not forgotten.

Following dinner in his final full night in Paris, Philip returned to his hotel room where in a lengthy letter to Baltimore he described the highlights of his week of excursions. Describing what he saw gave Philip the feeling that Millie was somehow traveling with him. It was self-deluding, but he enjoyed vicariously sharing with his wife. It eased his loneliness, if only temporarily.

11

In the morning of October 26 it was time to leave the Crillon and catch the train to the training base. Philip was ready for this next challenge. But the journey from the Gare St. Lazare to southwestern France was long and exhausting. Located near the Spanish border and the French religious shrine at Lourdes, Pau was geographically isolated. But it was ideal as an aerial training site. The area was flat and expansive. Warm relations with Spain plus the nearby Pyrenees Mountains protected the southern flank of the base from air attacks launched from a foreign country.

But for Philip now, Pau lay at the end of an arduous train ride that would take almost a full day. He approached the trip with a sense of patriotic resignation. *"C'est la guerre,"* he quipped to himself.

When he did arrive at his destination, he was stiff after twenty-six hours on a slow, cramped train that seemed to stop at every railroad station in France. Still, he was glad he arrived in time to meet the deadline established by Colonel Desmoulins.

Together with twenty other trainees who came down from Paris, Philip poured himself into an Army truck waiting to take the would-be pilots to the School of Combat. "Some of you have experience with airplanes and are being transferred to Pau from other bases. Many of you are brand new when it comes to flying," said the driver, a husky

Sergeant with a decidedly unfriendly demeanor. "If you are new and don't have a uniform, you will be issued one at the airfield. But you will have to buy your own boots. They're for sale at the base. Those of you already in uniform, tuck in those shirts, straighten your trousers, and button up those tunics. Make yourselves look like soldiers, not *clochards*—a bunch of Parisian tramps living on the streets.

"You're in for some rough training. A few of you will fly through training, forgive the pun. Others will require months. Still others will wash out. So turn to the man on your right, then turn to the person on your left: one of you three won't make it, another will have a tough time, but he will make it through. For the third person, it should be challenging, but a lot easier. Welcome to the future of warfare—welcome to military aviation," the sergeant barked over the noise of the truck's engine.

Philip was among the group for whom training would easy. He needed only two weeks of training in Blériot airplanes to demonstrate his proficiency. Piloting one of these aircraft reminded him of the old bi-planes he used to pilot in Chicago. He had little problem handling these slow-moving, flightless trainers—the non-flying, pseudo-airplanes derisively nicknamed, Penguins. They were used to acquaint trainees with landing and take-off procedures without the danger of leaving the ground.

When he was moved up to a standard Blériot that could fly at a top speed of sixty miles per hour, Philip continued to impress the instructors. Where several of his colleagues actually crashed their planes while attempting to land—and one trainee regrettably closed down his engine too early and glided to a stop on top of a large oak tree—Philip impressively displayed his aerial acumen.

By mid-November, he was deemed fit to attempt the final requirement: completion of three separate routes of about 180 miles to be completed solo using only a map and a compass, the navigational essence of modern French aviation.

The route was triangular, flying from point A, to point B, to point C, then back to point A. At the end of each leg, a trainee had to land and sign a document authenticating completion of the route. It was a test of a pilot's navigational abilities as well as his piloting skills.

It was uncommon for the three legs of the test to be completed without incident, but Philip was already a very good airman. He had no mechanical problems and no fuel problems. He took his exam in a standard Blériot.

When he landed back at Pau after finishing the third leg, the small group of onlookers actually applauded his unusual performance. "I think we have an Ace in the making," said one French officer. "I've never seen a trainee pass these test courses so easily," added another.

Completion of the triangular solo-flight meant that Philip had earned his French Army *brevet*, the coveted combat pilot license issued by the International Aeronautical Federation. He was also promoted to the rank of Corporal. He had won his wings.

At this point he should have been given a four-day leave as a reward, but the commandant at Pau had other plans. As he explained to Philip, "You've done so well, we're shifting you to combat training at our flight school in Tours. Normally, we would send you to gunnery training in Cazeaux. But I don't think you need that.

"We are condensing training for you. Instead, at Tours they will teach you the fundamentals of machine gunnery, but more importantly you will learn to fly the new SPAD VII, our best attack airplane. No more Nieuports, we're already phasing out that old workhorse. I think you will love this new and improved pursuit aircraft."

Philip wasn't excited about packing and moving to another base 300 miles away. Further training meant extending the time before he could join his squadron. More importantly, however, Millie was getting closer to delivering the baby and Philip was consumed with worry. He checked his mail daily, but relocating to Tours meant rearranging the delivery of his letters. He feared a note from Millie might get lost in the postal system of the French Army.

Nonetheless, he was resigned to "the needs of the Army" controlling his life. Besides, he would be learning to fly the latest in French military planes, as the Volunteers Squadron evolved toward becoming Squadron SPA124.

He had been reading about the SPAD VII in training manuals available on the base in Pau. The plane was manufactured by the *Société pour Aviation et des Derivées*, the initials of which gave the aircraft its name. Compared to Nieuports, SPADs were faster, larger, better built, and safer to fly and land.

As for performance in combat, the plane could fire more rounds at a faster speed than any model of Nieuport. Nieuport pilots claimed the plane was heavy on the controls, but those flying the newer aircraft never complained. Whatever the differences, the French Air Service seemed committed to this latest fighter.

Fortunately, Philip was able to find a pilot flying to Tours in a two-seat Morane Sualnier P. The pilot was happy to have his observer seat filled. And Philip didn't have to suffer another long and uncomfortable train ride. By air he was in Tours in less than four hours.

Arriving at the base, Philip anticipated this next training assignment as the final hurdle before he could join his unit. He parked his luggage under an open cot in the base dormitory and headed for the mess hall. It was noon and he was hungry.

As he sat alone eating, he recognized a young trainee approaching the food line. "Gene, Gene Bullard!" he yelled to the man. "Over here. It's Phil Belmont."

Bullard looked around to discover who was calling his name. When he spotted Philip, he smiled broadly and rushed toward his friend. "Belmont, how are you, old man?" he said as he vigorously shook Philip's hand. "It's been a while since you broke up my boxing exhibition in the Marais."

Bullard stepped back, as if admiring Philip's uniform. "But look at you. You've gotten a change of clothes since we last met. And I see that you're a Corporal now. And you've won your wings. Congratulations are in order."

"Yeah, I've been working hard. But, hey, what about you? What are you doing down here? More machine-gun training?" Philip asked.

"Oh, no! I'm on my way to becoming a fighter pilot, too. I took your advice and ditched gunnery school in favor pilot training," Gene remarked. "And you were right. The French Air Service had no problem when I told them I wanted to change directions."

Philip smiled. "Then, I'm happy for you. We may even end up in the same *Escadrille*," he added. "But, go grab your food and join me for lunch."

"I'll do that," said Gene.

Bullard returned shortly with a typical trainee's lunch: a bowl of thick soup, a small baguette, and a cup of strong coffee. For the next hour the two men ate and discussed the ordeals that lay ahead of them. There was a big difference between them, however. Philip already was an accomplished aviator while Gene Bullard knew nothing about flying airplanes.

"I guess you'll be out of here and dropping German planes long before I get my *brevet*," Gene said enviously.

"Don't worry," Philip replied, "I'll leave a few so you can get a kill or two. There'll be plenty of Boche fighters and bombers for you to feast on. I may even leave some blimps and Zeppelins for you to blow apart to see what's inside."

"Damn well better or I'll be spending all this time training for no good reason," Gene quipped.

"Any idea where they'll assign you?" asked Philip.

"No idea. I have a few months before that issue comes up. But I don't think it'll be with your *Escadrille de Volontaires*. There's an American doctor in Paris who is very influential with the French Air Service. He's got it in his head that I'm a malcontent. I think he's a racist who doesn't want someone like me debasing the purity of his pet white Squadron.

"But there are dozens of other *Escadrilles* that have American combat pilots in their ranks. I'll probably end up in one of them. I don't care. Let me do something for my country and my peoples. I have to show those Yanks what they're missing in me and every other black man and American Indian. Every kill I get will be a blow against Jim Crow.

"I even have a name for my airplane when I earn it. I'm planning to call it 'The Black Swallow of Death.' Great name, no?" Bullard announced.

"Well, it is unique," Philip conceded. "How did you ever come up with that moniker?"

"You see, when I was a *poilu* I was in the 170th Infantry, a fierce regiment the Germans admiringly called 'The Swallows of Death.' So, I started conceiving of myself as the Black Swallow of Death. So, that'll be the name of my airplane when I earn the right to fly for France."

"Well, if you can't do it, Gene, no one can," said Philip respectfully. "You're an Ace in the making. I wish you the best of luck. You're an unforgettable guy."

Philip and Gene ate and laughed a little longer. They then said goodbye and returned to their training groups.

By the beginning of December Corporal Philip Belmont had completed all his requirements: a licensed pilot and trained in aerial gunnery, he was a fully-certified fighter pilot. As planned, he was assigned to the *Escadrille de Volontaires*.

As part of his reward for doing so well in training, the French government presented him with his own new SPAD VII. It was a beige-colored beauty complete with the Squadron's own Seminole chieftain stenciled on the side of the fuselage.

His first assignment was not an easy one. Philip was ordered to join the Squadron in Cachy Wood near Amiens on the Somme. Only this time he was expected to fly himself to join the outfit. He knew that this would not be an easy assignment.

Flying in the winter months of 1916-17 was a daunting task. The weather was exceptionally cold in northern France this winter, so miserable that combat statistics were depressed because fewer pilots on both sides were taking to the air. Open cockpits in the Nieuports and SPADs rendered every pilot vulnerable to snow, sleet, rain, and fog, icy winds, and cloudy conditions. And the construction of the aircraft—metal internal framing enclosed by light-weight sheet steel—provided little protection against the punishing temperatures.

Moreover, Philip's flight had to be accomplished in daylight which rendered him open to attack by German fighters. He well understood that flying at night was out of the question. Spotting on-coming enemy aircraft was difficult in dark skies. Finding a specific place to land was extremely dangerous in the darkness because once a pilot was airborne there was little chance of survival if he couldn't spot a smooth meadow or field to accept his plane. With no field lights or bonfires illuminating a landing space, a flyer took his life in his hands attempting a night landing.

Although the Germans had developed parachutes—for men assigned to tethered observation balloons and for some pilots of fixed-wing aircraft—the Entente air forces had yet to distribute such escape devices. There were also complaints about enclosing cockpits with glass canopies. Many pilots, Philip among them, argued that a covered cockpit would inhibit his ability to see and hear approaching aircraft. As for adding lights to fighter planes for night combat and landing, most pilots considered that to be an invitation to be shot down by anti-aircraft ground fire.

All these ideas flashed through Philip's mind as he flew toward Amiens. He was clothed in the thickest uniform available, and wrapped in thick woolen blankets, his capped head covered by several supplementary neck scarves. And he was still cold, particularly his unprotected face that nakedly confronted the freezing wind.

To fight the bitter temperatures, Philip thought warm thoughts about Millie and the new baby that was due soon. He also was still excited about having his own airplane. He planned to name his aircraft after the baby by writing the name Elizabeth for a daughter or Johnny for a son on the side of the plane.

It took almost five hours that included two refueling stops to reach the Somme. The *Service Aéronautique* did not provide much in the way of navigational aids. A compass, a clock and a map; plus a tachometer to measure engine rotation, an oil pulsator to gauge oil flow, and an altimeter; that was the extent of Philip's navigational equipment. But, the sky was clear at lower altitudes so he could see where he was going.

Philip hoped, too, that no German planes were in the air when he arrived. He wasn't emotionally prepared for a dogfight after flying such a distance in foul weather.

Fortunately, his map helped him find the base. The sleet he experienced during the last half-hour of the flight may have discouraged enemy pilots because he spotted no aircraft of any sort as he approached Cachy. Despite a frozen field filled with crevices that challenged his pneumatic tires, the landing went without incident. He maneuvered "Elizabeth/Johnny" to a dry spot in a nearby hangar. Philip was ready to meet his new comrades in arms.

When he opened the door to the Squadron barrack, the first to greet him was a growling and growing male lion. Philip froze in his tracks. He had forgotten that the Squadron had a pet lion and that Whiskey would be larger in December than he was in September.

"Whiskey! Get away from the nice young aviator. You've already had your dinner. Besides, he's one of us now." It was Chute Johnson and he playfully coaxed the pet lion away from the frightened newcomer.

"Hi ya, Phil. Chute Johnson. Remember me?" the lion tamer asked.

"Of course, I do," Philip replied. "It was only a few months ago that I visited you guys. You had a bigger facility back then."

"Yeah, we were at our luxurious retreat in the Vosges mountains," Chute responded. "The Frenchies wanted us to bond like brothers. This winter they've sent us on another brotherly vacation, but this time to Hell fighting the Boche along the Somme and trying to save Tommy Atkins from being annihilated.

"But the Somme campaign seems to be over. Too much muck and lousy weather. Too many dead on all sides. And for what? To gain a few square miles of territory? Because that's all we won for all that spilled blood.

"But, come in, laddie" said Chute changing his tone of voice. "They told us you would be joining our little party. And don't mind Whiskey. He still won't hurt you. I'd be more careful with the two-legged carnivores around here," he jested.

For the next few hours Philip greeted his new colleagues: men he visited in September, new recruits who recently joined the Squadron, and the now-repaired and still-garrulous Jimmy McConnell.

"Jimmy, how are you?" Philip said as he embraced his friend from Chicago. "You were in a hospital in Paris when I was here earlier this year. It's terrific to see you again. Are you OK?"

"Great to see you, Phil," responded McConnell. "It's been a long while since we flew out of that little air strip along Lake Michigan. Who'd have guessed we'd end up in France fighting for a foreign country in a quasi-American fighter unit? As for my health, I feel great. A little stiffness in the back now and then, but otherwise I'm in top-notch condition."

"That was terrible news about Nimmie," Philip said, shifting the tone of the conversation. "I got to see him and talk with him only a few weeks before he died."

"Tore me up, too," McConnell admitted. "Norm Prince and I were in this game together for a long time. We were both Founding Fathers of the Squadron. He was a great man who should not be forgotten.

"In fact, his older brother has joined the *Escadrille*. Have you met Fred Prince yet?" he asked Philip.

"No, but I'd love to. I never knew him in Chicago. I guess he stayed back east," Philip said.

"Come on, then, I'll introduce you two," McConnell replied. "He's another Harvard man, like his brother. And he's a lot like Nimmie in the air, too. He's going to be a great fighter pilot.

"Hey, Fred, come over here. There's someone I want you to meet," Jimmie yelled to one of the pilots.

"Fred Prince, this is Phil Belmont. He was a pal of Norm's from his lawyering days in Chicago. He's come up from training in Pau and Tours to help us win the war for your brother."

The two men shook hands.

"How are things in Pau?" Prince inquired.

"Ah, what a beautiful training site," said Philip. "Flat green fields, isolated, gorgeous scenery."

"I'm glad to hear that since my family owns an estate there. I used to vacation in Pau as a kid. In fact, my dad gave the French government the land on which the flying school is built," Prince explained.

"That's strange. Every time I took off I would see this beautiful chateau with elaborate gardens. That might have been your family's residence. It always appeared so peaceful. Such a contrast with what I was doing then, and what we're all doing now.

"As for the training facility, it's excellent. Quiet, smooth, spacious, protected, and demanding instructors: perfect for learning; but not very good for nightlife," answered Philip.

"Unfortunately, my dad didn't own land in Paris to donate," Fred added. "That would have been a great place to build a training site."

"Excuse me, Fred, but I need to introduce Phil to the other new flyers," Jimmy said as he guided Philip toward another part of the barrack. "See these monkeys here?" he said in jest, "these guys weren't here three months ago. Ron Hoskier, Willis Haviland, Bobby Soubiran, say hello to Phil Belmont."

The three young men welcomed Philip to the Squadron.

"Don't let that water behind their ears fool you. These guys are first-class combat flyers," Jimmy joked good-naturedly.

As Philip continued to talk with old and new acquaintances, a French officer approached him. "Excuse me, gentlemen," he said as he entered the conversation, "but I haven't had the pleasure of meeting our newest member."

Turning to Philip he extended his hand in greeting. "Hello, Corporal, I'm Captain George Thénault. I'm the officer in charge of the *Escadrille*."

Startled, Philip snapped to attention and saluted the Captain. "Excuse me, sir, for my lack of formality. I am Corporal Philip Michael Belmont. I've been assigned here by the commandant at Tours. Here are my official papers."

The Captain stared at Philip, then perused the documents and stared again at the newcomer. Then with a broad smile on his face, he declared, "Welcome, Yank. Welcome to the Squadron." The men watching this little drama all cheered and began slapping Philip on the back and shaking his hand.

"The Captain is a great guy," remarked Bill Thaw, himself a lieutenant and the highest-ranking American flyer in the group. "He knows we're aerial artists; we need space and freedom—not military rigmarole—to do our jobs. He's in command, but he lets us do what we do best: fight the Boche and stay loose for the next battle."

As he turned to leave, Captain Thénault asked Philip to meet him the following morning for an informal conversation. "I'll be in my office by 10 o'clock. I'll see you around that time," he said.

The rest of the night was spent with plenty of good food from the group's private kitchen, and those favorite friends of idle time, gambling and booze. As Philip recognized, this was no specially-staged evening to welcome a new recruit. These fliers seemed quite familiar with this kind of activity.

A highlight of the festivities occurred when Philip shared his inside information that any day now—perhaps in less than a week—the Squadron was going to be renamed the *Escadrille Lafayette*. "No more *Volontaires*," he announced with pride. "From now on—in English— we'll be known as the Lafayette Escadrille."

A loud round of applause followed Philip's announcement.

The festivities ended about 2 o'clock in the morning when the final hand of poker was won and the last bottle of Burgundy was emptied. Philip had already retired, exhausted from his long flight and socializing through much of the evening. Besides, he had an important meeting at 10 o'clock.

Entering the Captain's office that morning, Philip was unsure about what was happening. Captain Thénault came immediately to the point.

"I enjoyed meeting you last night, Corporal Belmont," he said. "I invited you this morning to answer any questions you may have, and to welcome you more formally."

"Well, sir, I am wondering about battle action—when it might come, what form it might take," Philip replied.

"You will see action," the Captain replied. "But it depends on the elements. Not even the Germans like to fly in this weather, and this has been another rough winter. A few times when conditions moderated, the Boche sent over a Gotha with fighter escorts to bomb British emplacements along the Somme. We responded with our Nieuports and drove them away. But the weather has to change before we can challenge the enemy with any regularity.

"Of course, these conditions also discourage our own pilots. No fighters accompanying bombing runs across enemy trenches. No raids into German territory. But, it can't last. Officially, it's still winter. But unless this is the beginning of a new Ice Age, things will heat up, weather-wise and military-wise."

The Captain switched his tone as he continued. "I have a short speech I like to deliver to groups of new flyers who have made it into the *Service Aéronautique*. But since you are alone, I'm not going to stand before you and deliver a formal oration. Instead, I'll share my thoughts more informally.

"Let me impart a few words of appreciation and admonition. Fighting in the air requires the highest qualities of combat because you, the aviator, fight alone. You are not in touch with your commander or your comrades. You won't have the close contact, the shoulder-to-shoulder morale that exists among those fighting on the ground.

"You fly in the deafening clamor of your motor—no word of warning or command can reach you. You can't stand still because you are ever in motion at great speed. You must depend upon yourself and above all upon your aircraft which is a delicate instrument and of limited flight.

"Aviation combat is a new science, a development of this terrible war. There is no class of experienced men from which to draw. France has taught you the theory of aerial battle, but you can only learn the art by being under enemy fire.

"So, Corporal Belmont, I welcome you to the *Escadrille Lafayette*. We who have survived thus far salute you who are about to join our profession. *Bienvenue*, my new comrade in arms. Welcome to the struggle."

"Thank you, Captain," said Philip with humility. "I'll remember your wisdom." With that, the men parted and Philip returned to the dorm where the flyers sat waiting for the skies to clear and the ice and snow to melt."

Four days after Philip's arrival, the telephone rang in the Squadron office. Enemy aircraft—a Gotha bomber and an unknown number of Fokker and Albatross fighter escorts—had been seen heading for Amiens. "Finally! Here, we go fellas," yelled Raoul Lufbery as six pilots raced to their aircraft. Philip was one of those volunteering to intercept the Germans.

Wrapped in woolen coats and scarves as well as caps and wool-lined gloves, the men rushed to the hangars and quickly jumped into two SPAD VIIs and four older Nieuport 11s. Each took off and rose to about 400 feet, slightly below the layer of low clouds that blanketed the area.

There was no formation involved, only a half dozen scattered French aircraft heading toward Amiens in an effort to intercept a German raiding party. Philip was located in the middle of the pack. Off to the right was Lufbery and to Philip's left was Jimmy McConnell. When Luf gestured from his cockpit for a strategic turn, Philip and McConnell followed. The other flyers—Skipper Pavelka, Dud Hill, and Fred Prince—who continually turned their heads watching in all directions—spotted the shift and joined the maneuver.

A few minutes later the American pilots found themselves approaching the enemy raiding party from the rear. Clearly, the Germans had not yet reached their target. Coming up from behind gave the Lafayettes an advantage. Instinctively, they rose another hundred feet and vanished into a cloud bank. All pilots had been trained to exploit the clouds as hiding places, then swoop down for actual engagement.

Philip checked his watch when he entered the cover. He calculated that three minutes in the thick mist would be sufficient to put him within striking distance of the Germans. At that exact moment he dropped down and rapidly reconnoitered his position. Luf, Jimmy, and Fred had already exposed themselves. Soon the entire contingent of Squadron fliers was in the open and bearing down on the German raiders who were about fifty yards ahead. It was a perfect match: six enemy aircraft and six *Escadrille* fighters.

The rear gunner in the Gotha was first to fire at the approaching planes. When he did, three Fokker pilots and two Albatross flyers turned to assume defensive positions. Within a few seconds, machine-gun fire flared from both sides.

Philip remained calm as he maneuvered his SPAD to confront one of the escorts. He kept repeating a passage from the combat guide he had memorized while training in Pau: "Pursuit flying is continual acrobatics. In order to protect one's self on all sides, one must never fly in a straight line. One banks gently on one wing, then the other, in such a manner as to clearly observe what is happening on all sides. Sudden reversals of flight course and abrupt climbing turns are good in order to avoid surprises coming from the rear. One must surprise and avoid being surprised."

Philip darted above the enemy then zigzagged his way toward the tail section of an Albatross that had drifted from the others. He sent bursts of heavy gunfire toward the plane. Most went harmlessly into the sky, but he could see that some bullets found their target and actually tore into the fuselage of the German plane.

Meanwhile, Jimmy was intent at getting to that menacing Gotha bomber. He knew that German aerial gunners were deadly, so he stayed out of range until he was prepared to make his move. A sudden barrel roll put him closer to his quarry. As the gunners fired at him, McConnell's Nieuport took some hits. But nothing structural was damaged; and Jimmy remained in control of his plane. He bobbed from left to right, then suddenly dropped below the big bomber. Just as rapidly he swerved upward toward the belly of his target. He positioned his gun in an upward angle and began firing as he passed under the bomber.

It was a bold move, and it inflicted damage. As well as sustaining bullet holes to the underside, one of the Gotha guns fell silent. The machine gunner was apparently hit. McConnell sensed a kill as he turned and readied his Nieuport for another pass.

Jimmy figured that his ability to come so close to the bomber must have intimidated the Gotha crew because these immense planes usually carried fourteen bombs each weighing sixty pounds. If hit by gunfire, a bomb load could explode and destroy everyone on board. The bomber pilot immediately recognized his vulnerability. Before Jimmy could reorient his plane and move in, the German pulled back his control stick and moved into the clouds. Unable to defend his compromised aircraft and crew members, the pilot was on his way back to Germany.

Several hundred yards away, Fred Prince and Dud Hill fought an intense cat-and-mouse duel with an Albatross. Blazing weapons fired by everyone inflicted damage to all three planes, but nothing vital was struck. It was a standoff, but with the Gotha peeling away and headed back to German air space, the Albatross pilot lacked the will to play the hero against the Lafayette flyers. After all, the task was to protect the Gotha on its bombing run. And with the bomber departed, there was no reason to continue the mission. The Albatross pilot turned upwards and into in the thick clouds.

Skipper Pavelka went after one of the Fokkers. But the enemy pilot seemed hesitant to commit himself to a dog fight. The German pulled away from his colleagues and headed north to the Fatherland. Skipper stayed on his tail for a while, but he dared not fly over hostile territory where anti-aircraft fire could prove fatal.

Instead, Pavelka banked left and flew back toward a second Fokker. It was preparing for a run at Jimmy McConnell, but Jimmy was too preoccupied with flying to the assistance of Phil Belmont to notice his unwanted guest. A few bursts from Pavelka's machine gun convinced the German that he didn't want to confront several Lafayettes simultaneously. He too darted into the clouds and vanished. Although Skipper tried to follow him, the pilot was apparently done for the day and well on his way home. What began as a battle of six versus six was now six versus two.

Lufbery had been the first *Escadrille* pilot to shoot at the enemy airplanes, and he was the only flyer to get a kill that day. When the German flyers first turned to face the oncoming Americans, Luf fired several bursts from his machine gun, but then slid upward and out of sight. He used this invisibility to fly beyond the enemy planes, then then rolled his SPAD out of the cloud cover and positioned himself in front and below the enemy fighters.

Luf selected the final Fokker and closed in for the *coup de grace*. Flying upward toward the underside of the German plane, he unloaded a full magazine of bullets at his target. The shots tore multiple holes in the tail section and the left wing of the enemy craft. This rendered it impossible for the pilot to turn his aircraft to face the American threat. Luf deftly placed a new magazine in his rapid-fire weapon and resumed his attack.

The Fokker began to sputter and burn. Luf had severed the German's fuel line and started a major fire. A few hundred yards later, the Bosch plane turned downward and began spiraling toward the ground with black smoke trailing its descent. Luf watched the fiery explosion when the enemy airplane crashed into an open field. Ten minutes into the air battle and one Fokker had been shot down, another clean kill for Raoul Lufbery.

Philip in his new SPAD faced off against the second Albatross. Most of this confrontation involved jousting for the best positions from which to shoot down one another. Both pilots had fired, but no major damage was yet inflicted. But with the other enemy aircraft now gone, the five other American flyers converged in support of Philip. The Albatross pilot instantly recognized that he was alone against the entire Lafayette team. He banked upwards and pulled away from the Americans and headed for the safety of German-controlled air space.

The merriment at Cachy that evening was as much cathartic and it was celebratory. "Our drought is over," yelled Pavelka. "Let's have a party!" yelled Bobby Soubiran. Throughout the night the men swapped tales about what they were already calling the "First Battle of Gotha." And with ample libation flowing into the early morning, the stories grew in number and in self-flattering detail.

The entire Squadron was pleased about three things: no one had been injured; Luf was still the greatest pilot in the Air Service; and Phil Belmont had performed masterfully in his first combat engagement.

"But I didn't get my opponent," Philip protested. "He got away!"

"Kills are great. But they're not very common," explained Jimmy. "What's important is that the ugly monster bomber didn't get to its destination. Men are alive tonight because we turned that black menace back to the Fatherland. You, my friend and colleague, were crucial to driving it out of France. The Albatross pilot you engaged and fought to a draw might have killed two or three of us if you hadn't stopped him."

Philip was flattered and gratified.

"Wait a minute, fellas," Lufbery said as he motioned for attention. "You all know our tradition: a kill gets the victorious pilot one mouthful of the ancient whiskey we've been saving. But for tonight only, I propose that the mouthful I earned today be given to Phil Belmont. I might not even be alive had he not kept that Boche pilot away from the rest of us."

"Here! Here!" said a few voices at first, then everyone joined in approving Luf's suggestion.

Philip was speechless. He knew that the bottle of vintage whiskey was sacred to members of the *Escadrille*. One mouthful per kill had become a revered ritual among the American pilots. And to have an Ace of Aces invite Philip to drink in his place was as close to a *Croix de Guerre* as the flyers could bestow on one of their own. When Philip gripped the bottle and raised it to his lips, it was clear to his flying brothers that he took only a small sip.

"Maybe someday I'll earn the right to take a full mouthful," he said to the crowd. "But tonight is Luf's night. I thank him for his generosity. I'll be happy to fly with Raoul Lufbery alongside me anytime and under any circumstances."

The pilots cheered loudly and returned to retelling stories about today's air action.

12

Bad weather dominated the next several weeks. A new year may have been celebrated on January 1, but 1917 offered the same terrible flying conditions as its predecessor. And when the icy winter softened, the cold rains of a premature spring became a new impediment to aerial activity.

Of course, there were occasional days when the skies were clear enough to go up in search of enemy aircraft, but these were generally fruitless adventures.

Also, with combat ceased along the Somme, troops on both sides huddled in their cold, damp trenches trying to keep warm. Changes in leadership in the French and German commands—General Robert Nivelle replacing General Joffre, and Generals Paul von Hindenburg and Erich Ludendorff superseding General Erich von Falkenhayn—also stalled battle movement.

"Everyone's thinking Spring Offensive," Ron Hoskier explained. "The French love seasonal offensives. So do the Germans. New military leaders always need time to reevaluate old plans or make fresh ones.

"Hang on boys," said Hoskier, "and we'll get our war back in March or April."

In the interim the Squadron faced internal challenges. Several members were reassigned. Fred Prince, for example, was transferred to Pau to become an instructor. Some speculated that his influential father forced the change because he didn't want to lose another son and heir.

Paul Pavelka always said he hoped to see the war on all its fronts. He was also depressed over the deaths of several of his close friends. So, he asked for and received a transfer to Salonika on the Macedonian Front where he joined Squadron N391, an aerial contingent of the fabled international *Armée de l'Orient*, the Army of the Orient—a Balkan force made up of French, British, Serbian, Italian, Greek, and Russian contingents.

Then there was another change of venue. The *Escadrille* was sent in late January from Cachy to the Ravenal airfield in the vicinity of St. Juste-en-Chaussée. It represented a move of less than fifty miles south. But it meant no relief from the miserable weather that enveloped northern France.

While their enthusiasm for combat was frustrated, the men continued nevertheless to cavort at night and enjoy fine dinners, often shared with visiting French and British officers. Tobacco and liquor also remained plentiful in the Squadron's facility.

And the flyers continued to make money. On top of their modest salaries as members of the French Army, each was paid 200 francs per month by a committee of wealthy U. S. businessmen whose donations were used to cover not only these monthly stipends, but financial bonuses for acts of exceptional valor and enemy kills. To this money, add fees that individual pilots pocketed for giving press interviews and endorsements of commercial products.

Still, the American pilots were eager to return to a regular combat schedule. Out of general restlessness, however, they sometimes went up alone. Although that meant enduring adverse weather, they took off "just in case a German happened to fly by," as Chute Johnson phrased it. Philip was among those who occasionally went solo scouting for enemy aircraft.

On the morning of March 3, he was ready to try again. He explained that he would fly along the border and maybe near the German trenches, "just in case." But, Philip noted, he would stay high enough to discourage anti-aircraft fire from ground artillery.

It was a thickly overcast day, so he climbed above the low clouds and headed northeast toward the German border. To Philip the clouds below seemed to form an ethereal scenario of ice and snow that approximated photographs he had seen of the wilderness in northern Alaska and Greenland. What he saw in the sky was a panorama of imaginary valleys, mountains, and plains, all created by massive accumulations of billowy clouds. He fashioned himself as a pilot passing between earthly reality and a romantic, cotton-white fantasy world. Eerily silent, save for the monotone of his SPAD engine, to Philip the view appeared to be a glide path straight into Heaven. If only he could fly for hours in this magical kingdom built in the clouds.

As he mused to himself about the fantastic imagery before him, he suddenly became aware that another aircraft was approaching from the rear. Convinced that it was a German about to attack, Philip prepared to take defensive action. But as his pursuer came closer, Philip could see more clearly. He realized that it was not hostile. It was a French aircraft, a reconnaissance plane—the Morane Sualnier P. that was so important to intelligence gathering.

Philip slowed his air speed to allow the plane to come along side. He couldn't speak to the pilot, but he figured there might be an important message waiting for him. He hoped that the pursuing airman could communicate through hand gestures or even hold up a note if the words were written large enough.

When the MS-P reached within fifteen yards from his right wing, Philip recognized the pilot as Captain Thénault who began waving dramatically and pointing downward. Philip immediately understood that the Captain wanted him to land as soon as possible.

While he dove through clouds and into low-level open skies, the Captain continued to stay close. Philip began to look for a landing spot that was long and flat enough to be an advantageous place from which to takeoff. Spotting an open field that seemed to meet these requirements, he touched down and rolled to a halt. He was perilously close to German-held territory, but a small forest on the north side of the field provided sufficient cover.

A few minutes later Captain Thénault landed and taxied to a halt nearby. "Phil, get in the observer seat I need to talk to you, now," ordered his commanding officer.

Philip deplaned and entered the rear seat of the Morane. "What's wrong?" he asked with a tinge of anticipated terror in his voice.

"I have two messages for you. The first is a letter from your wife. It arrived after you took off," said Captain Thénault as he handed Philip an envelope. "You can read it now if you like," he added.

This was the letter Philip had been awaiting for weeks. He tore open the envelope and began reading. "I'm a father!" he yelled to his Captain sitting only five feet away. "And it's a baby girl weighing 6 pounds, 3 ounces. Born February 10. This is wonderful news. Sure took a long time for this letter to get to me. But it's here now, and I'm ecstatic. If I had some cigars with me, Captain, I'd offer you one right now."

"I'm happy for you," said Thénault. "What's her name?"

"We decided to name her Elizabeth! The same name I'm going to stencil on my SPAD," answered Philip. "That way I can announce to the Germans that baby Elizabeth Belmont is a gal to be reckoned with."

"Well, congratulations, Papa," the Captain responded. "I wish you had those cigars, I could use one right now. It might calm my nerves. That's because I have a second message for you. I received orders from Paris that today you are going to die," he announced. "This is the end of Corporal Philip Belmont."

Philip gasped.

"No, no, sorry. You're going to die *officially*, not *literally*," the Captain responded. "The orders for your death came in a Top Secret memo from the Ministry of War. Authorities at the highest level—and I mean the highest level—have agreed to a request from Washington that you be returned to the United States immediately. That's why we are going to make your removal appear as though the Germans captured or killed you.

"So, here's what we are going to do. Taxi your SPA to the edge of that little clump of trees. We'll drain the rest of your fuel. That will make it seem like you ran out of gas. I'll shoot bullet holes in the plane to give the appearance that a firefight occurred and that you're either dead or captured. We want to make it look like Philip Belmont was either killed here, or taken prisoner and locked up somewhere in Germany. And don't worry about the Boches capturing a SPAD VII—they already have four of five of them."

"I don't get it," Philip said questioningly. "The French spent all this time and money to train me, and now I'm a casualty and out of the war? For all practical purposes I no longer exist?"

"Don't ask me, Phil. I'm simply following orders—and these are highly-confidential orders," the Captain explained. "It's a priority project; that's all I know. I'm commanded to fly you to an airstrip along the British coast. There, I'm to introduce you by a new name. For now at least, you are Lieutenant Josef van Weeden of the Belgian Air Service. Not only are you dying, Phil, but you're being resurrected as a Belgian officer. And with a name like this new one, it means you're now Flemish.

"So, let's get to it. We'll tend to your aircraft, then I'll fly you out of here. I wonder how I am going to keep up the pretense when the Lafayettes start looking for you. I can't tell them the truth. I am under orders to speak to no one about this little rendezvous. I will find an answer, I hope."

It took the two men about thirty minutes to position Philip's plane and drain the fuel. They fired bullets from Philip's mounted machine-gun to make appear that he resisted the enemy attack. Then the two men then riddled the fuselage with bullets. "I hate to waste a beautiful new SPAD, but that's what they told me to do," the Captain lamented as he emptied his two handguns into the body of the SPAD VII.

Soon Philip and his commanding officer were flying to an air facility along the southeastern coast of England. Before taking off, however, Captain Thénault handed Philip a sealed dossier. "The courier from Paris told me to give you this packet. It contains your life story—I mean van Weeden's life story. Study it as if your life depended on. It probably does.

"And here is a complete change of clothing, everything from a pair of worn shoes to a thick woolen topcoat—all civilian clothes, all made in Belgium. Paris wants you dressed like a Belgian civilian when I deliver you. Don't ask me why, change your clothes and remove everything that can link your uniform to the Lafayette Escadrille. No pins, name tags, decorations, or shoulder patches. Get rid of those Corporal stripes, too. Long underwear, socks, any French currency and coins, your comb and billfold. Even that letter from your wife. There can be nothing linking you to France. I'll be dropping everything out of the plane periodically as we fly toward England."

"One more thing. You're ordered to speak only French to the Brits and anyone else who speaks English. Just forget that you speak the language.

Changing clothes in the backseat of an airplane in freezing temperatures was a singular experience. Changing underwear was especially difficult. But Philip fought through the difficulty and passed everything to the Captain who methodically discarded the articles along the route. Out of his sense of appropriateness, the Captain allowed Philip to drop his own underwear over the French countryside.

The flight to the British airfield took about ninety minutes. When the men landed, they went immediately to the office of the general in charge. Thénault introduced Philip as Lieutenant van Weeden.

It was a bang-bang operation after that, with no time even to thank Thénault for his help. Philip was marched back to the airfield and placed in a two-seater aircraft. It departed immediately for Southhampton.

No sightseeing allowed: Philip never left the Southhampton military site in southern Britain. Instead, he was transferred to a waiting seaplane equipped with pontoons. "We are taking you to a spot off the coast of Cornwall, near the Isles of Scilly. Here you will rendezvous with an American warship for transport to the United States," explained a British General in broken French. "Here's a sandwich and a cup of tea. You can eat during the flight."

The sun had not yet set and Philip was in the air being flown to a splash landing in the Atlantic Ocean. He had never been around seaplanes, but he had been fascinated with their physics since they were introduced a few years ago. When the pontoons hit the choppy Atlantic water and slid to a stop about thirty yards from an American battleship, he made a mental note to learn to fly such an aircraft.

Five minutes later a U. S. Navy motorboat tied up alongside the amphibious plane. "OK, Lieutenant van Weeden, here's where you get out," said the pilot. "Pull the door open and the Yanks will help you into their boat. And the best of luck, sir."

The entire operation went smoothly. Within a few minutes Philip was aboard the USS *Georgia* and heading northwest. He still had no idea what was unfolding. He didn't even know where the ship was going. But Philip was a trained soldier who knew when to shut up and follow orders.

He knew little about the U. S. Navy, but during his stay aboard the *Georgia* he learned that she was once a mighty battleship of the line. She was less than two years old when she traversed the oceans as part of the Great White Fleet that, on the orders of President Theodore Roosevelt, spent all of 1908 demonstrating American naval prowess in Atlantic, Pacific, and Mediterranean ports. For Philip this was classic T. R. boastfulness: a bold and brassy announcement to the international community that the United States was now a formidable oceanic power. The *Georgia* helped deliver that message.

But too many trips to the repair yards plagued the vessel, and in early 1916 she was decommissioned. Now she was a receiving ship usually docked in Boston: a housing facility where sailors resided until their final assignments came through. Philip discovered from conversations with crew members who spoke French that the ship was returning home following a special assignment in the western Mediterranean. She was anchored off Falmouth in Cornwall when a communication sent via trans-Atlantic cable ordered the Captain to pick up a priority passenger who was coming aboard at sea, and to transport him to Boston immediately.

The seas were much calmer than the first time Philip crossed the Atlantic. The result was that the *Georgia* reached U. S. waters in five days. But instead of docking in Boston, the Statue of Liberty and the skyline of New York City made it obvious that the ship was anchoring off New York harbor.

"Lieutenant van Weeden, it's time for you to depart," said a junior officer who knocked on his cabin door. "A government boat is coming to take you into the city. Please be ready to disembark in five minutes, sir."

Philip was excited. He had no idea what American authorities wanted from him that would require such secrecy and speed. But, he was home now, and he hoped to be allowed to squeeze in a visit to Millie and baby Elizabeth in Baltimore before he was finished.

Exactly as planned, Philip was soon climbing down a rope ladder toward a government motorboat that had tied up next to the *Georgia*. As he entered the bobbing craft, an agent in a dark suit reached out to shake his hand. "How do you do, Lieutenant van Weeden? Welcome to the United States," he said in French. "I'm Federal Agent Roger Macray."

Philip answered bluntly in character. "It's a pleasure to meet you, monsieur. I am very tired from the events of the past week. And I am exasperated by trying to understand what's going on. For heaven's sake, can you tell me what's going on?"

"I am not privy to such information," Macray said. "I was told to meet you here and accompany you to Washington, D.C. I assume you're here for meetings. The people in Washington love to hold meetings. But I can't be certain.

"My orders are to get you to Hazelhurst Field on Long Island as quickly as possible. We're scheduled to fly to D.C. from Hazelhurst."

"Say, Macray," asked Philip in English, "is there any chance I can take a side trip to Baltimore? There are some important friends in that city I would love to meet."

"That's outside my purview," the agent replied, betraying no surprise at the sudden change of languages. "You'll have to take that up with the folks in Washington. All I know is that you are going to the New Willard Hotel. There's a room reserved for you there. You must be someone pretty important. The Willard is the capital's finest hotel."

What happened next was a blur to Philip. A short boat ride and car trip to the airstrip, a flight to Washington, D.C., and then a limousine ride to the Willard. After he checked into his room, the last thing he remembered was Agent Macray telling him to be ready for a meeting at 10:00 am. Exhausted, Philip collapsed on the bed. He slept deeply until the sun was bright in the morning sky.

Philip jumped from his slumber and hurried to prepare for whatever lay ahead. A comfortable shave, a quick shower: Philip felt wonderful as he readied himself. When he opened the door to go to breakfast, however, an armed guard urged him back into his room. "I'm sorry, monsieur, but you'll have to stay here until it's time for your meeting. Please return to your room. If you're hungry, I can order whatever you wish from room service. But I can't allow you to leave right now."

Philip returned to the room, but not before ordering an ample breakfast that included a large glass of orange juice, something he had not seen or drunk for almost three years.

At exactly 10 o'clock someone rapped on Philip's door. It was Agent Macray.

"Time to go, Lieutenant," he commanded.

The two men walked down a flight of stairs to the first floor, through the ballrooms and toward a room at the rear of the hotel.

"We maintain a private conference suite here," Macray explained. "It's comfortable and private. And it's discreetly accessible from the rear of the place. Please wait in the room. Your meeting should begin in a few minutes."

The suspense was building inside Philip's imagination. "Maybe they're bringing Millie here to meet me. Wouldn't that be perfect?" he mused aloud. "Or, maybe the Secretary of War wants my autograph," he thought, more cynically.

At that moment the door opened. When Philip saw who entered, he rose swiftly to his feet, stood erect and delivered a crisp salute. No doubt about it: he was face to face with the President of the United States, Woodrow Wilson.

The President returned the salute then urged Philip to sit down and relax.

"Corporal Belmont—or should I say Professor Belmont—I am very pleased to meet you. I've heard much about your exploits in France and Italy, and I'm proud that you're an American," said the President.

"Thank you, sir," Philip replied.

"Now, you might be wondering why the government has gone to such extraordinary efforts to get you here so speedily and anonymously. We've done that because the time is urgent and we need you right now," Wilson elaborated.

"I was reelected last November, but it was close. I won by only twenty-three electoral votes. That's a very narrow victory. And what got me reelected was the fact that I kept the United States out of the Great War for almost three years.

"Don't get me wrong. I was sincere. I am committed to peace, and most Americans want peace, too. In my second term I will try hard to keep the United States out of the war. I will also continue to seek a resolution by bringing the combatants together to negotiate a peace treaty. But since the Germans at the beginning of January 1917 announced that they will wage unrestricted submarine warfare, they have sunk three of our unarmed neutral freighters—and since they schemed to lure Mexico and Japan into a secret alliance against us, as we learned in an intercepted telegram to the Mexican government from German foreign secretary Arthur Zimmerman—it has become extremely difficult to avoid a military response.

"Something has got to be done to end this bloodbath in Europe. It's frightful. But if it continues this way, I'm afraid we will have to join the battle to bring it forcefully to an end.

"You know this war, Professor. You've been in it from the beginning. That's one reason why we brought you here. You know the human cost, the deaths, the terrible wounds, the futility of it all.

"My advisors and I know the war only statistically. You've actually been involved in many of these horrific campaigns. Take the Battle of the Somme. Do you know how many people were killed or wounded in that fourteen-week battle that ended about the time I was reelected?"

"No, sir, somehow those figures never make it into the public discourse in France," answered Philip.

"I'll tell you, young man," President Wilson continued. "More than a million were killed, wounded, or disappeared. The British lost more than 400,000; the French approximately 200,000; the Germans could have lost as many as half a million. And what did the victorious Entente armies gain? About 125 square miles of territory.

"That absurdity was at the Somme. Remember Verdun? Somewhere between 700,000 and a million young French and German men were casualties in that bloody campaign in 1916.

"You were involved with the French stand at the Marne in 1914. If I remember correctly, about a quarter-million French and another quarter-million Germans were casualties there. That's half a million human beings dead or wounded or missing."

"It's so absurd, President Wilson," Philip interjected. "I know when my wife and I worked with the American Field Service those injuries were not skinned knees and superficial gunshot wounds. We saw limbs amputated; mangled stomachs; men spitting up their insides. And these wounds didn't come from handguns and rifles. Tanks, flamethrowers, poison gas, aerial bombs, grenades, machine guns—the new technology of mass death—were to blame."

"How long can this bleeding continue?" President Wilson asked. "Four years? Seven years? Ten years? A century? How many more millions of citizens can these nations afford to lose before they realize that this is not war, it's mass insanity?

"But there's another aspect of the quandary, Professor Belmont. Many of our wealthiest companies and individuals have investments in Europe. Many warring nations have borrowed huge amounts of money from the United States Treasury, too. We are economically tied to this carnage because we are owed millions of dollars.

"So, what happens to the U. S. economy if the fighting continues indefinitely? There's nothing but war material being made in Europe these days. Each year the belligerent nations are falling further behind. Their economies are stagnant or collapsing; their debts soar while their people grow hungrier. The ability of their workforces to compete is in decline, and everywhere international trade is atrophying.

"Now, add German submarine warfare. It's crippling the industrial world. German U-boats can't defeat destroyers and aircraft, but they can devour unarmed freighters and ocean liners. With freighters, they seem to be sunk as rapidly as they're launched; even faster than new ones can be built. The result is that we can't move supplies and manpower safely for fear of submarine attacks. We are hamstrung in bringing petroleum from Russia to Western Europe and the United States because tankers are being torpedoed. But the Allies absolutely must have imported oil to run their modern economies. The same is true for the shipping of foodstuffs and even war supplies.

"If the mayhem continues Europe will crash and the entire capitalist system, that intricate economic arrangement that allows this planet to thrive, will implode and cease to function.

"Did you ever contemplate the consequences of the collapse of our system of interconnected economies, Professor Belmont? I have, and it's my conclusion that the end of capitalism means the end of civilization in its present manifestation.

"If capitalism is destroyed, then everyone goes back to the eleventh century and we start all over searching for an economic model to bind the nations constructively. Do you realize, Professor, that if this war is allowed to continue indefinitely we are inviting the destruction of contemporary global organization?" Wilson asked.

"Simply put," he added, "I cannot—no, I will not—allow this to happen."

"With all respect, Mr. President," suggested Philip, "I think the reorganizing of global politics is already underway. The overarching theme of this mad conflict is the birth of new social arrangements that are at once liberal and democratic, nationalistic and self-determinative. But such development was not born of this war. It began with our own struggle for independence and accelerated considerably with the French Revolution and the Napoléonic Wars. The popular aspirations of 1789 may have been quashed by 1815, but only organized repression kept those ambitions under control throughout the 19th century.

"In my opinion, we are now moving to a time when nationality and affiliated citizenship within the democratic state cannot be denied. Ethnic groups have become nationalistic forces demanding independent statehood; they fight for a decisive role in fashioning their own government and place in the sun. The French Revolution has been reborn and its legacy is affecting contemporary political life.

"Look at the Austro-Hungarian Empire," Philip continued. "The flood waters of nationalism are drowning that medieval monarchy. I have no doubt that someday there'll be a Czech state, a Slovak state, a Slav state or two for the peoples of the Balkans. There will even be democratic republics in Hungary and Austria.

"Monarchy cannot cage the dynamism of the masses. They may not even realize it, but the masses are on the way to power—for good or for evil. Social control will have to be reorganized. The old models will no longer work. Mass man with all his strengths and all his prejudices and failures can no longer be taken for granted because he is now determining his future and ours.

"That's who's fighting this war, Mr. President. It's the Tommy, the *poilu*, even Fritzy boy from Berlin. They're the little men, the average men, the regular guys who stop bullets for vainglorious Emperors who parade around in outlandish costumes with cockades and shakos stuck on their hats, and absurd notions of reincarnating ancient Rome stuck in their thick heads.

"Meanwhile, at home wives and families of these fighter-commoners suffer in silence. Their sacrifice has become a national rite, a pained ritual of self-denial that should entitle them to new consideration when this slaughter has ended. Believe me, sir, their understanding and tolerance will never be the same.

"And lest we grow complacent and think this disorder is found only in Central and Eastern Europe, let's not forget what happened in Dublin last Easter when Fenian nationalists led an armed rebellion against their British overlords. They're at war right now, and they've declared Ireland to be an independent and democratic republic. How long that revolt will last is anyone's guess. But one thing is for certain: the Irish will never go back to the old ways.

"It's happening everywhere, Mr. President."

Philip and President Wilson continued to talk. Two university professors: one a young scholar still seeking to make his mark, the other a former Governor of New Jersey and President of Princeton University who published several important treatises on modern government.

It was an especially edifying experience for the President. "I'm impressed with your insights, Professor," he remarked. "I have lots of excellent advisors with intellectual insight, but I lack advisors whose conclusions are drawn from involvement on the ground with this war. I need that experiential perspective to inform my decisions.

"That's why I am asking you to come to work for me. I want you to become my special advisor on wartime matters. Specifically, I need you to visit and examine certain battle zones. I need you to report from the ground up. Send me accounts that are informed by research among the people, drawn from citizens and soldiers, every social class, and politicians on all sides. I need observations that are insightful, suggestive of policy directions, and communicated to me in a highly confidential manner."

"That sounds most flattering, Mr. President, but I'm a member of the *Service Aéronautique* of France," Philip answered. "I don't know if I can simply up and leave. Wouldn't that be desertion?"

"You have already left the French military, Corporal Belmont. Remember that little scene where you died? We arranged your death with the cooperation of French political and military leadership, and it appears to have worked. The Lafayette Escadrille considers you dead. The French have officially listed you as missing in action with the presumption of death. To the world Philip Belmont perished in the line of duty. That's why we brought you here under a false Belgian name."

"But, there's the matter of my wife," Philip said in interrupting the President. "I can't let her spend years believing that I died in a plane crash. I really need to see her to explain," Philip pleaded.

"That's already taken care of," said President Wilson. "When you return to your room after this meeting your wife and infant child will be waiting for you. You can spend the next forty-eight hours together before you undertake your first assignment. But for your own safety, you cannot tell her the details of where you are going, what you are doing, and for whom you are doing it. Ours is to remain a highly secret arrangement.

"One immediate benefit, Professor, is that your salary as my special advisor will jump considerably when compared to that of a member of the *Escadrille*. We've arranged for that salary to be sent directly to your wife's bank account on a monthly basis. So, you don't have to worry about the well-being of your family. And as long as that money continues to be paid, your wife will know that you are alive somewhere."

"I always heard stories about confusion and lethargy in Washington," Philip remarked, "but you've changed my mind, Mr. President. Everything has been so zip-zip and accurate. You've answered my questions, some of them before I even asked. I'd be happy to sign on with a team such as this."

"Excellent!" exclaimed the President. "But I am not asking you to become a team player. You'll be working as an independent operative. You're my researcher, my observer, my personal spy, if you will. You'll be telling me about the real scene in selected trouble spots. I have embassy and consular types who can do the detached research. From you I expect a unique perspective, a point of view drawn from being among average people.

"It may be to your advantage to make up a new name for each project. Agent Roger Macray will be your contact in the United States. Overseas, your contact will approach you with a code phrase. Macray will fill in the details. He's the only person with whom you can be candid; he knows all about your assignment. But tell no one else, not even your wife and parents. Their safety is at stake as well as yours.

"By the way," the President added. "Your acceptance means that you will be sworn into the United States Army at the rank of Major. Think of it as a battlefield commission. In fact, if you raise your right arm I'll administer the oath to you, personally."

Philip accepted the offer. He figured that with such a meteoric rise in rank and an oath administered by the President of the United States, this must be a special assignment of overwhelming significance.

"One more thing, Major Belmont, your first project will be to go to Petrograd and report to me on popular Russian attitudes about recent developments there. This is most urgent. Our diplomats report that Russia could be in the beginning stages of social revolution. It began only hours ago. It could be a simple political coup d'état. Or, it could be much more profound. Maybe an uprising that will affect Russia's war effort—or perhaps a revolution with even broader implications for the future. I look forward to your observations and recommendations in about a month.

"Meanwhile, I have to prepare for my inauguration in less than two weeks, and for my decision about the future role of the United States in this world war."

Their meeting concluded, President Wilson exited while Philip stood at attention, his right arm and hand locked in a rigid salute. However, Philip was still confused about the details of his new position, and thunderstruck about his assignment to Tsarist Russia. What he had told President Wilson about the Austro-Hungarian Empire was equally true for the Russian Empire. He would soon have a chance to verify his political insights.

The President departed. Agent Macray quickly returned to elaborate on Wilson's explanation..

"O. K., here's what we plan to do. Because of developments rapidly unfolding in the Russia, we've had to reschedule your departure," Macray announced. "You will be leaving immediately. Specifically, you'll shove off tomorrow morning at 9 o'clock from the Naval base in Norfolk, Virginia. You will be aboard the USS *Fanning*, a destroyer we just scheduled for an official visit to Helsinki in the Grand Duchy of Finland.

"From there you will go by railroad to the Finland Station, the main rail depot in Petrograd, or as many still call the city, Saint Petersburg. You'll be staying at the Hôtel de l'Europe. We've booked a room for you under the name of Jean-Luc Corbière. You're now a Swiss businessman, a petroleum broker, who has come to Russia seeking crude oil contracts for clients in South America.

"On the voyage to Helsinki you will have plenty of time to read the background materials we've accumulated for you.

"Finally, we know you're fluent in the Russian language because of you mother's ancestry. And, of course, you speak French like a native. So, you should do well. Try to avoid English.

"You will be met at the Finland Station by a contact with further instructions. But to be certain, there is a coded exchange that must occur when you meet. The agent will speak to you in Russian saying, "I can't wait for the spring weather to arrive." You will counter with, "It's the same all over Europe." And he must reply, "Yes, but I don't live in Europe; I live in Russia. And it's too damned cold here."

Philip listened attentively, taking mental notes on the details.

"All this secrecy and name-changing may not be necessary," Agent Macray continued, "but we want to protect you as much as possible. A U. S. citizen snooping around Russia in this explosive atmosphere could raise questions or dangerous reactions from enemies of our country. It could also compromise the official neutrality of the United States.

"So, Jean-Luc Corbière from Geneva, Switzerland, think of all this secrecy as battle equipment for an otherwise unarmed soldier, something you have to wear because it's the only protection we can provide you. It might save your life, or it might be unnecessary. We'll never know. So, let's err on the side of caution," Macray explained.

"Then, there's the case of my wife," interrupted Philip. "If she's upstairs as you promised, what do I tell her? How do I explain that after a year of separation, the anxiety she experienced daily while I was flying for France, the arrival of our first baby whom I have still not held in my arms—after all this depravation, how do I explain that we can only be together for a few hours because I have a ship to catch?"

Agent Macray was a bit embarrassed. "I'm truly sorry your meeting can't last beyond tomorrow morning. We had originally planned for you and your family to be together for two days. But the Russian situation has to take precedence. It began with waves of industrial strikes on March 8, and yesterday, March 10, Army troops loyal to the Tsar were firing on strikers in Petrograd. That's the latest news we have.

"Remember, sir, you're not alone in sacrificing to win this war. There are millions of families around the world with anxious or grieving wives, babies with absent or dead fathers, families torn apart by the events of this war. Yours is one of the first such American families. But if and when the U. S. enters this war, countless people right here in America will find themselves in similarly painful predicaments.

"And besides, what are you doing in this battle? Why are you sacrificing your time, your energy, your personal happiness, maybe your life? You want this conflict to end. You want families everywhere to be free of war, free of having to make decisions as agonizing as the one facing you.

"You can't quit now, Major. Even before your induction into the Army, you were an American soldier, one of the first in a ferocious struggle that's still not fully understood by our citizens. But like any soldier or sailor, you're involved until either you end or it ends."

Philip was reluctantly persuaded. He knew what he was doing when he joined the French military last year. This new assignment was simply another posture from which to struggle for democracy and the new international order he knew was emerging. "Oh, I almost forgot," Agent Macray cautioned. "If you should get into an impossible situation where you need direct U. S. government assistance to rescue your mission, contact any American diplomatic office anywhere and communicate the identifying code that I'll give you. Transmit this code—then send your message. The transmitter will automatically encipher your message. But only trust the State Department's secure trans-Atlantic cable, none other. That's only available at our embassies, consulates, or legations. Now, please memorize the code because no one else can know this.

With that the agent showed Philip a paper on which was written a sequence of numbers and letters. "But don't use it unless your conditions are dire," he emphasized.

"Now, go to your room and be with you wife and child," Macray ordered. "Stay in, or go out on the town, whatever you want. And if you need a babysitter for the evening, ask the person guarding your door. He'll make the arrangements.

"Meanwhile, I'll see you downstairs first thing in the morning, at least two hours before the *Fanning* shoves off."

Racing upstairs to his room, Philip was filled with joy. He hadn't seen Millie in a year, and now she was waiting for him. He flung open the door and rushed into her arms, kissing and holding her tightly. The softness of her body and the fragrance of her perfume brought wonderful memories of how things used to be.

The terrors of war have a way of scarring a man's emotional mechanisms, hardening them against exposure while hiding them behind a façade of cynicism and toughness. This moment with Millie, however, completely melted Philip's self-protectiveness. He was transported to a softer reality where he willingly surrendered to the tenderness of the moment. No longer was he the jaded warrior. Instead, he was provider and protector, lover and best friend, and most of all, husband.

Crying from the bedroom instantly reminded him that he was also father.

"Where is she? I want to see her? Where is she?" he asked with happy impatience.

"She's in the bedroom waiting to welcome her daddy home," said Millie. "Follow me."

Elizabeth was even more beautiful than Philip expected. Her tiny feet and hands, her wavy hair, the way she was wrapped in a bright yellow blanket, the aroma of her talcum powder—here was his little girl, and he loved her instantly. It was a magical moment for Philip. He held Elizabeth in his arms and reveled in the euphoria of parenthood; he then reached out to enfold Millie in an unspoken communion of family. These were emotions he dared not expose on the battlefield.

For several hours Philip and Millie talked and loved. On one level, he wished to spend the entire time alone with his family in that hotel room. But he also needed to do things that married couples do in peaceful societies. Dinner together at a nice restaurant—a leisurely promenade along the boulevard arm in arm—nodding to people passing by—staring into store windows—feeling accomplished and civil and at peace.

"Let's go out for a walk," Philip announced. "I'll get a babysitter and we'll spend a few hours being social folks."

Millie agreed, and after summoning a hotel nurse to stay with their child, Mr. and Mrs. Belmont left for the evening. Somehow, Philip loved being a married man. It renewed his spirits.

Following supper at a local restaurant, the couple strolled about the city and spoke of matters mundane as well as serious. Millie was careful not to poke too deeply into her husband's assignment, but she was extremely curious.

"Does it have anything to do with the war?" she asked. "I'll bet America is preparing to enter the war as soon as Wilson is inaugurated."

"You know I can't speak about my work," Philip replied. "It's too risky for all of us. So, it's best to say nothing."

Millie continued her talk of impending war. "If the President and Congress were to declare war, there could be a significant public backlash. Americans voted for Wilson because he kept us out of the war. To betray that commitment so soon after being reelected could be publically disastrous.

"Do you know what song has dominated the public for the past two years?" she asked rhetorically. "I know you've never heard *I Didn't Raise My Boy to Be a Soldier*. But it's everywhere from phonograph records and sheet music, to performances in movie theaters and around living room pianos. It's very popular because it connects with public opinion. I've heard it so often I know the lyrics by heart." Millie proceeded to sing the song to Philip,

> I didn't raise my boy to be a soldier,
> I brought him up to be my pride and joy,
> Who dares to put a musket on his shoulder,
> To shoot some other mother's darling boy?
> Let nations arbitrate their future troubles,
> It's time to lay the sword and gun away,
> There'd be no war today,
> If mothers all would say,
> I didn't raise my boy to be a soldier.

"That's powerful propaganda," Philip remarked. "But if America ever did go to war, wouldn't public attitudes shift profoundly? Wouldn't some songwriter soon come up with a pro-war song with lyrics as effective as your anti-war tune?"

"Oh, you're so cynical," Millie said.

"No, not at all. If I were a Tin Pan Alley composer I'd be writing pro-war songs right now. Why wait?" Philip responded. "I'd call them something like "Hang on France, the Yanks Are on Their Way" or "America, Here's My Son" or perhaps "Democracy, We're for You." Something heroic, self-sacrificing, and filled with moral boasting."

As they walked Philip and Millie passed dozens of other couples on similar sidewalk rambles. When they approached the Rialto motion picture theater, Philip stopped as if transfixed. "I haven't been in a motion picture theater since I went to France. There are photoplays showing in the Paris cinemas, but I never went once. And, needless to say, there are no theaters in Verdun or Pau.

"But look as how sophisticated the industry has become since 1914," he said as he gazed at the colorful lobby cards and a brightly-lighted marquee announcing that the Rialto was screening two Douglas Fairbanks features, plus a serialized adventure called *The Liberty Boys of '76*.

"I know the Liberty Boys of '76," Philip said. "When I was a kid I read their adventures in dime novels. They were always fighting Redcoats and Indians for America's freedom during the Revolutionary War. I really enjoyed their stories, at least when I was young."

As they walked beyond the Rialto, a young man distributing handbills stopped them. "Want to know what's really going on in the European war?" he inquired. "Come tonight and find out. The Liberty Boys of '76 Club is gathering tonight at 9:00. We're meeting a few blocks from here. Come and join us. Learn the truth about the British plot to draw America into war against Germany."

In an instant, Philip understood. "I'll bet there's German money behind this movie serial and this political club. Don't you see, Millie, it's a German scheme to stir up anti-British feelings? Remind the American people of Revolutionary War hatred. That way you turn public attitudes against the English. At best the Americans would join Germany in a new war against British dominance; at least, the Yanks would stay out of the war because, as the Liberty Boys remind us, England fought to prevent our independence."

"Sounds incredible, but you may be right," replied Millie. "I've seen advertisements for Liberty Boys of '76 Clubs all over Baltimore. They've been operating for about a year. It would be interesting to attend one of their get-togethers to test your theory. Ask them flat out if they're secretly working for German interests in this war."

"Yeah, but not tonight. This is our first and last evening together for a while. No Boche propagandist is going to disrupt us," Philip asserted.

Millie smiled and the couple moved on. While passing an open stationery store, however, she stopped suddenly. Let's go inside right now," she insisted. "Come on. There's a new product on the market and I want to buy it."

They entered the store and Millie immediately dragged Philip toward the section selling writing supplies. "Now I know you have a beautiful fountain pen, so I figure your unreliability as a letter-writer must be caused by your fear of carrying around a messy bottle of ink. It's very inconvenient, I know. You might spill it or accidentally break the bottle and stain everything. So here's the product for you: Parker Ink Tablets, a product of the Parker Pen Company. All you do is drop one tablet in a little water and, *voilà*, you have ink to write letters home to your wife. No excuses tolerated. Ink Tablets are definitely for the warrior on the go."

Philip laughed. "Great invention," he exclaimed. "If we had any extra money, we could invest in Ink Tablets and make a fortune. They'll never go out of style."

It was after 9 o'clock when Philip and Millie returned to the Willard. It had been a thoroughly delightful evening. Although the nurse was reluctant to accept anything, they paid her for her time and went to the bedroom to admire their child who was soundly asleep. While Millie adjusted Elizabeth's sleeping position, Philip slipped into the bathroom and dropped an ink tablet into a small glass of water. He emptied his fountain pen, then refilled it with freshly-made ink and tested it on a plain piece of paper.

"They work," he said in exaggerated excitement. "The Ink Tablets work."

"Let me see. Show me," said Millie as she came to witness this miracle of stationery science. Staring at the sample Philip handed her, she turned back to him with tears in her eyes. The words "I love you" were never more honestly shared in dark blue indelible ink.

13

Even before he arrived in Russia, Philip learned much about the social and political condition of the Tsarist Empire. His cabin on the USS *Fanning* had been stocked with a library of books touching on Russian history, politics, economics, culture, and social life. The State Department also provided two dozen recent accounts filed by the U. S. Embassy in Petrograd. There was even a street map of Geneva for him to study in case someone in the capital knew the Swiss city and questioned his authenticity.

These reading materials helped Philip cope with the length and arduousness of the voyage. They also provided a firm foundation for understanding present-day events. Above all, they confirmed what the international press was reporting daily: Russia was in crisis.

It was a long, cold voyage to Helsinki. This was, after all, early March and Europe was still gripped by the same foul weather that had chilled northern France. As a destroyer, a lighter ship than an ocean liner or a battleship, the *Fanning* reacted severely to high waves and winds. And Philip soon discovered that when crossing the Atlantic Ocean and the Baltic Sea at this time of the year a passenger should expect rough seas.

One aspect of the voyage, however, particularly fascinated Philip. He had wondered where the *Fanning* would refuel. Where older coal-burning vessels had a range of 1800 miles before a collier or a friendly port was required to replenish their coal supplies, newer ships like the *Fanning* burned oil and had a capability of 3000 miles. Still, Helsinki was far away and his destroyer would need oiling again before reaching port.

But Philip did not know about the USS *Maumee*, a modern refueling craft stationed in Iceland and designed for what the Navy called "underway replenishment" for oil-burning warships crossing vast distances. Halfway through the run to Finland he watched in amazement as the *Maumee* rendezvoused with the *Fanning*. In a clever maneuver, both ships cut their engines allowing the *Maumee* to come alongside and send over a large oil hose. Several hours later, and with minimal manual labor from either crew, the two vessels uncoupled and the *Fanning* had enough fuel to reach its Finnish destination.

Philip was impressed by this innovation in international shipping. Watching the operation unfold, he wondered how long it would be until an oil-burner could travel around the globe without needing to dock.

By the time he reached Helsinki, Philip was well-acquainted with the Russian situation—as seen through professorial scholarship and government reports. Lacking was the common person's viewpoint, the so-called man-on-the-street perspective that President Wilson had specifically requested.

But he had unanswered questions. What about Russian nationalism? Where did the average Russian stand on loyalty to the state, to the Tsar and the Romanov dynasty? Did the notion of revolution scare or encourage the average Russian? What differences of opinion existed between industrial workers and peasants who worked the land, between the bourgeois class and the urban working class? Did loyalty to a particular political party play a role in the divisiveness existing within Russia? How ready was Russia to follow a new, even radical course into the future? What was the role of Germany in fomenting and encouraging the revolution? Could the revolution be crushed? Would civil conflict knock Russia out of the war?

But what most concerned Washington: would popular opinion prefer withdrawal from the war or continuation of the struggle against Germany? Was participation in the Triple Entente a liability or an asset for Russian leadership in this time of unrest?

Even before reaching Russia, Philip learned of the intense animosity underlying Russia's dilemma. It manifest itself when he was on the final leg of his journey, the railroad trip from Helsinki to Petrograd.

Walking from his coach seat to the dining car, he saw two young men arguing loudly in Finnish. Philip understood nothing either man was saying, but neither appeared to be winning the shouting match. They were, moreover, close to trading blows. When Philip tried to placate the men, he met with resistance from some of the onlookers. He pulled back to let the argument continue. But one man used the confusion as an opportunity to punch the other.

What had been a verbal standoff rapidly devolved into a bloody fight in which fists, feet, and knees were weapons. It lasted several minutes. Eventually, the man who threw the first punch fell and was unable to get up. But victory was not glorious. The winner was exhausted and considerably bruised. It pained him simply to walk.

Speaking in Russian, Philip apologized to the victor for his feeble attempt to stop the argument. He invited the man to join him for lunch once he had treated his wounds.

A half-hour later Philip was conversing with his luncheon guest about the fight. The man was Kimmo Harju, a Finnish fishing boat operator out of Turku, who explained that he was a nationalist who advocated self-determination and political independence for Finland. The fact that Philip's alter ego, Jean-Luc Corbière, was Swiss and neutral in the war seemed to relax the fisherman. He spoke freely and passionately about his motivations and his disdain for the Russian man he had battered.

"That foreign swine riding on a train in my country. He called me Finnish scum and spit at me. When he threw a punch, I lost my head and reacted," Harju confessed.

"Sounds like a justifiable response to me," Philip said.

"Do you know how long we've had to suffer those Russian louts? We've been under Russian control for a century—ever since Tsar Alexander I stole Finland from Sweden and declared it a Grand Duchy and a Russian possession. Of course, he installed himself as our Grand Prince.

"Just like that: one day we were Swedes, the next day we were Russians.

"But we were neither. We were then, and we remain today, Finnish. We don't speak a Germanic language like the Swedes. We don't speak a Slavic language like the Russians. Our ancestors came from a different place. If you want to get technical, in Europe our linguistic cousins are the Estonians and Hungarians.

"That means we have an obscure language, a different history, a unique culture. We are Finns. And it's time for us to be an independent nation state. Right now thousands of Finnish nationalists are receiving military training in Germany. Civil war against Russia and her supporters is coming, and when it arrives we'll be ready to fight. It's time for a free Suomi, a free Finland."

Philip was taken aback. Few of the materials he studied on the voyage had delved deeply into the nationalities situation in Russia. But there were numerous ethnic and language groups of great size in the Tsarist Empire. If the situation in Finland suggested broad ethnic discontent, then from Poland to Siberia politicized nationalities demanding autonomy and independence could tear Russia apart.

"What did you not like about Russian control?" Philip asked in hopes that Harju would embellish his thinking.

"You're talking about a century of suppression by the most backward and brutal government in Europe," he answered. "Sometimes we had a degree of autonomy, but we were never independent and always subject to the political whims of the Tsar. And the present Tsar has been the most tyrannical of all. Damn this Nicholas II and his elected Duma of dynastic toadies.

"But history is with us. Look at Europe and you see a maze of nation-states. Do you know what that means, sir? It means political states formed by the various nations: France for the French, Italy for the Italians, Germany for the Germans—even Norway for the Norwegians.

"In some instances there is a balance of nationalities living together: the Walloons and the Flemish in Belgium; the Scottish, British, Welsh, and Irish in the United Kingdom. And your own country, Switzerland, has this balance among various cantons where the French or German or Italian language predominates. Even the small number of Swiss who speak Romansh is treated with respect.

"In Russia no one has liberty, and few have rights. And there sits the Tsar like an enormous weight crushing nationalities that want their freedom. His victims include Poles, Ukrainians, Armenians, Moldavians, Georgians, and farther to the east, Turkmen, Kazaks, Mongolians, among others. So, we Finns are not alone on this vast Romanov ranch."

"It sounds like the same problem facing Austria-Hungary," Philip replied.

"It is, indeed," the fisherman said. "But our new century will be an age of change. I predict it. Unleashed nationalities will gain their independence, either peacefully or through bloody combat. We are building a new Europe. The old empires with pretentions drawn from ancient Rome are now crumbling and will soon be gone.

"Do you know the root of the words Tsar and Kaiser?" Harju continued. "It's the Latin word meaning Caesar. These crazy old monarchs pretend to be reincarnations of the Caesars of Rome. That's absurd. Unfortunately, they oppress and exploit millions of diverse peoples while playing out their antique fantasy.

"They're anachronisms. In a modern world of capitalism and electricity, motorcars and democracy, these decrepit empires can't survive. The question is how many people must die before the transition is complete."

As the two men conversed, a conductor came through the restaurant car ringing his chimes and reminding people to get out their passports because they were less than ten minutes from Petrograd.

This announcement ended conservation. Philip and Kimmo Harju returned to their seats. Philip rummaged through his pockets until he found the Swiss passport prepared for him by the State Department. It didn't appear counterfeit, and when he left the train at the Finland Station a Russian policeman checked the document carefully then stamped it without question.

Walking from the train station he felt a sense of historical regression, as if in entering Imperial Russia he were moving back in time. There was something regressive about the Empire. Proof of that confronted him immediately because the Russian calendar was literally behind the times. Although around the word today was March 23, 1917, in Russia it was only March 10. This was because, at the insistence of the Russian Orthodox Church, the Tsars for centuries clung to the faulty calendar established in 45 BC by Julius Caesar.

Centuries ago astronomers proved that the Julian calendar annually made the year ten minutes and forty-eight seconds longer than it really was. With this miscalculation, the "slower" Julian calendar lost three full days every four centuries. This was significant, especially for Christians, because precision was necessary in astronomically determining the arrival of Easter Sunday.

In 1582 a revised calendar was introduced by Pope Gregory XIII. By 1917 this Gregorian calendar was accepted by all countries except two Orthodox nations, Russia and Greece. By that date, moreover, the discrepancy between the rival calendars had grown to thirteen days.

Philip came to Russia with no agenda except to watch and listen and report his observations to President Wilson. Yet, all he knew for certain was that he had a reservation at the Hôtel de l'Europe. He was entering Russia with no preconceived notions. But, it was not reassuring when he approached the station exit and accidentally collided with a foolhardy stranger running toward the opposite end of the building. The collision knocked Philip to the ground, and sent his suitcase skidding across the station floor. Fortunately, he was not injured, but he was perturbed.

At least the clumsy runner was courteous. He stopped and helped Philip to his feet. He also retrieved the valise, and apologized as he returned it. Philip appreciated the gesture. As Philip brushed dirt from his topcoat, the stranger casually remarked, "I can't wait for the spring weather to arrive."

Philip was startled, but he recognized the phrase. "It's the same all over Europe," he quickly responded.

"Yes, but I don't live in Europe; I live in Russia. And it's too damned cold here," the stranger said. With that he stuffed a small envelope into the Philip's coat pocket and walked into the crowd.

The choreography of the exchange was artful in its execution. It was all the more impressive because Philip had no idea such a transfer was going to happen. He had only been told by Agent Macray that a representative would meet him in Petrograd. Details of that meeting were never revealed.

Standing in line to engage a droshky—a horse and carriage that served as a public taxi in Russia—Philip carefully opened the envelope. It held Russian currency for which he was grateful. It also contained the key to a safe-deposit box at the Russian State Bank. Instructions inside told him to use it when he was ready to file his observations. He would then receive further instructions.

He was also ordered to throw the key into the Neva River once he locked away that final report, and to destroy all written instructions as soon as he read them. Until his assignment was complete, however, he was to guard the key with his life.

Operatives in Washington had booked him into the lavish Hôtel de l'Europe located on the city's principal boulevard, the Nevsky Prospect. The facility was near the Alexander III Museum and a picturesque memorial church erected on the site where nihilists in 1881 assassinated the reformist Tsar Alexander II. This was no insignificant lodging. It was considered one of St. Petersburg's finest residences, a home to diplomats, foreign businessmen, celebrities, and Russians of social importance. That's why Philip felt slightly embarrassed when he directed his droshky driver to take an alternate route that would show him the damage left by weeks of upheaval.

Obligingly, the coachman took him past buildings damaged by fire and pocked by bullets. Philip saw many burned automobiles sitting along the streets, mute testimonials to recent violence. Shattered glass from broken store windows remained on some sidewalks, and cobblestones and pavement bricks torn from the roadway still awaited replacement.

"This is the physical evidence, but the real story is in the politics," said the driver. "In the last week or so we've experience a mutiny by the troops stationed in Petrograd, the establishment of a Provisional Government, the forced abdication of the Tsar, and the renunciation of all imperial claims by Nicholas and the Tsarevich, his eleven-year-old son Alexei Nikolaevich. Then Nicholas' brother Michael was named Tsar, but he resigned the next day. So, forgive my excitement, but it's still sinking in: for the first time 300 years we are free of the decadent Romanovs! Russia is liberated! Long live freedom!

"The times are promising, monsieur. However, because I am Russian I naturally fear there will be big trouble," he continued. "A few days ago, the new government announced that Russia would continue the war against Germany and Austria until victory was won. That was a very bad decision. In my opinion, it means the eventual destruction of the Provisional Government. It will never conduct elections for a constituent assembly, and that's why it was it was created. It won't survive long enough to organize such elections.

"Nobody wants that horrible war except the elites. Continuation of the war is unacceptable to the average Russian. The soldiers want the blood-letting to end immediately. So do most peasants and city dwellers. The socialist revolutionaries want to quit the battle immediately. No one except those in power wishes to continue this endless war."

Philip was intrigued by the driver's forthrightness. Clearly, this was not the Russia of oppressive secret police he had read about. This man was speaking openly and bluntly. "What's wrong with the war?" Philip inquired innocently.

"What's *right* about this war?" the driver snapped back. "Russia has won nothing except death, debt, and defeat. You may know a lot about French and British successes on Germany's Western Front, but we Russians know only destruction on Germany's Eastern Front.

"Take our first great battle, Tannenberg in 1914. Of the 150,000 Russian troops who fought the Germans for six days, only 10,000 escaped. The rest were captured or wounded or killed. Then came the battle of the Masurian Lakes: another 125,000 Russian casualties. Do you know how many Russians in our cities and villages still mourn these losses of life and health? It's incalculable. Can you understand how badly these early blows crushed our morale and devastated the people?"

"Then there was General Alexei Brusilov and his great Spring Offensive of 1916. Oh, the great Brusilov Offensive! We were told that this was the campaign that would get us even. And, indeed, it resulted in decisive Russian victories over the Austrians. Some say we were on the verge of breaking their army for good. But, against the Germans who were quickly transferred from northern France it was a different story. They pushed us back and conquered all of Poland, Lithuania, and Courland, the most strategic part of Latvia. Oh, I forget to add: this Brusilov Offensive inflicted another million casualties on our military. Hundreds of thousands of brave Russian soldiers actually deserted rather than fight this pitiless adventure in mass murder.

"Russia's greatest weapon seems to be the ordinary foot soldier who uses his underfed body to stop enemy bullets. We don't have modern weapons; we don't have enough rifles; we need more ammunition; we lack proper training. But if the Germans and Austrians run out of ammunition from shooting so many of us, maybe we can beat them with our fists and win that way," he said sullenly.

"To add insult to injury, after General Brusilov's glorious failure, our army got a new chief strategist. Tsar Nicholas placed himself in charge of Russia's military planning. Our own little Nicky, a general? What a joke that was," the driver sarcastically remarked.

"You have little respect for the Tsar of All the Russias?" inquired Philip.

"Nicholas is a stupid, spineless man whose family life and even his political policies were influenced for years by a dominating English wife and her crazy advisor, a mad monk named Rasputin. And he may have been more than the Tsarina's advisor, if you get my drift. At least that's what I've heard. Fortunately, Rasputin was killed three months ago by a group of noblemen who said they were trying to save Russia. It took poison, several bullets, and one-way trip to the bottom of a river to bring down that monster from Siberia.

"But until last week our other monster, Nicky, was still there, eating his adored cream puffs for breakfast while designing strategy for a hollow army of unfortunate peasants boys marching off to meet certain death. It was criminal."

Philip was beginning to appreciate the opinions offered by the taxi driver. "How do you know these things?" he inquired. "Do your newspapers publish these stories and these statistics?"

"No, don't be silly. Our newspapers are puppets of the old regime. But men of importance travel in my carriage. I've heard them talking in their various languages. They don't know that I also speak French, Polish, and German, even a little English.

"I understand their conversations. They joke about the simple-minded Tsar. They speak of the devastation inflicted on us by the Central Powers. They always mention that Russian troops are poorly-trained and poorly-equipped and lacking in motivation. Sometimes they say this with sadness in their voices, other times they speak as if this is just one big farce. It's all I can do to hold my tongue when I hear such criticisms."

"We can go to the hotel now," Philip said.

As they drove toward his destination, Philip changed the subject. "Where can I go in Petrograd to drink with average people? Don't let the Nevsky Prospect address mislead you, I want to meet the average people of Petrograd. I'm from Switzerland. I'm in the petroleum business, a broker. To represent my clients properly, I need to know everyone's opinions on Russian matters."

The driver hesitated. "There's a problem with your request. Alcohol is now prohibited in the Empire. When the war broke out the government imposed anti-alcohol laws on us. Lots of other countries did so, too," he explained. "Today you can be arrested for drinking a simple glass of vodka."

Philip wasn't buying that line. "Oh, come on," he said as he passed a gratuity to the driver. "In a city this size there must be places that sell liquor to discriminating customers, places where people gather to pass the time with friends and swallow a little.

"Your police are human, are they not? They must accept financial rewards to look the other way. They do it in every city around the globe. Petrograd can't be different. Where can I go to share an evening of social drinking?"

"Well, I do know of one place along the waterfront," the driver admitted. "It's a shabby bar called the Baltic Sailor. They may have vodka and schnapps; maybe some whiskey, too. But you can't get in unless you tell them who sent you. I'm Ivan Rostokovsky. Remember that name if you want to get past the guards.

"But let me tell you, if you want to hear the voices of anger and frustration don't go to the saloons, go to an open session of the Petrograd Soviet. They're meeting right now to plan a manifestation set for tomorrow. In my opinion, the future of Russia lies in the soviets—not the Provisional Government."

Philip knew of the soviet movement, but was anxious to hear his driver's definition. "What is a soviet?" he asked, "and what's special about the one here in Petrograd?"

"Soviets are self-organized local political councils. They are created locally by the Socialist Parties to represent the interests of workers, people in the military, and those who are exploited in general. When the Revolution began a month ago, soviets popped up in many Russian cities and towns.

"But the socialists are not unified. There are moderates like Alexander Kerensky. He collaborates with the Provisional Government. In fact, he's the Minister of Justice in the present government. On the other hand, Vladimir Lenin is a radical Bolshevik Socialist; he calls for social upheaval and the creation of a new society. Lenin shares his ideas through magazine essays and propaganda publications because he lives in exile in Switzerland. But I've heard people say that he will return home if matters in Russia continue to deteriorate.

"As for the Petrograd Soviet, it's dominated by radical voices that condemn the Tsar and his court, favor land reform, and demand an end to Russian participation in the slaughter that is this war.

"Urban laborers, angry sailors from the Russian Navy, even peasants from the countryside belong to the Petrograd Soviet. They joined to express disgust with our economic and social collapse. They blame all our problems on the war. They joined also because there is hoarding by greedy landowners wanting greater profits; there is corruption everywhere; there are unrepaired roads and bridges that affect the delivery of food supplies to the cities, so people here are very hungry. Everyone is weary. Our Empire is grinding to a halt.

"Go visit one of their meetings. Go! You will hear the authentic voice of Russia. If you really want to hear it, you'll find it in the soviets. And don't waste your time and money in illegal bars where most of the clients are foreigners anyway."

By this time the droshky had reached the hotel. Philip gave the driver a large tip. He had learned much. He hadn't officially started his research, but between the train trip from Helsinki and the arrival at the hotel, he had already heard compelling interpretations that he would include in his comments to President Wilson.

Once he checked in to his hotel room, Philip went to bed and slept soundly until morning.

For the traveler in need of morning replenishment, the Hôtel de l'Europe presented a delicious selection of food at its buffet. It was difficult for Philip to believe that anyone in the Empire could be hungry when hotel guests were offered such delicacies as Caspian caviar, pheasant sausages, and French champagne as breakfast choices.

He made his selections and moved to the dining area where about two dozen other guests were busy eating and conversing. He chose a seat near an overweight elderly man with a massive moustache and thick sideburns. Philip introduced himself as businessman Jean-Luc Corbière from Geneva. In a friendly manner, the man explained that he was the Grand Duke Ivan Ivanovich, a retired Russian military officer and a distant cousin of Tsar Nicholas.

"How do you like our Russia, Monsieur Corbière?" the Grand Duke asked with a happy smile on his face. "Except for this cursed winter weather, I trust you will find Petrograd to your liking."

Not wishing to argue, Philip politely nodded and added, "And when the heat melts the ice in the harbor, it will be even nicer in Petrograd."

The Grand Duke sat motionless for a few seconds then erupted in booming laughter. "Oh, I do love clever repartee," he said as he relished the younger man's quip. "Tell me, sir, what brings you to this city of igloos and burning automobiles?"

Philip smiled and explained that he was here from Switzerland as a broker for South American clients seeking long-term arrangements for the purchase of oil. "When I booked my reservations, however, I didn't realize I was reserving a front row seat at a civil uprising."

"Now, now, my boy, don't let the current political predicament dissuade you from your business," responded Ivan Ivanovich. "Mother Russia will persevere.

"Whichever side wins the struggle—and it will be mine—oil will always be for sale here. I dabbled in the industry for years, so I know we always have more than we need. That's to your advantage. It means low prices for both crude and refined.

"Things are changing, however," he continued. "Better move fast. I hear the Germans are searching for sources of oil. They would have a difficult time taking our fields in Baku, but there's a good chance they could steal the oil deposits in Rumania. In less than five months Germany and Austria-Hungary have battered the Rumanian Army. They now occupy Bucharest and most of the petroleum properties in Polesti.

"There are unlimited pools of petroleum beneath Rumania. You just need the wells to pump it out. If the Germans manage to knock the Rumanians out of the war, as they appear close to accomplishing, Berlin would become oil-rich overnight. What that would do to the world price of petroleum is anyone's guess. My advice, monsieur, is to make your deals now; lock in a good price while it's still low."

Philip didn't like the course this conversation was taking. His expertise in the oil business was fictional, something dreamed up by the State Department as a guise. He never expected anyone to approach him as an actual oil agent. He used gasoline when flying in Chicago, and at Berkeley he visited the massive Standard Oil refinery in Richmond, a few miles north of the university. But that was the extent of his relationship with the petroleum industry.

"This is my first morning in Petrograd, so I've not had an opportunity to make the proper arrangements for meetings and sales pitches," he told the Grand Duke in Russian. "When I do, I trust matters will proceed expeditiously."

"Oh, I'm certain they will," the old military officer added. "In fact, I would be pleased to make some calls for you. I have strategic friends in Baku down in the province of Azerbaijan. And here and in Moscow I have important contacts at the Ministry of State Properties."

"That would be wonderful," said Philip with as much sincerity as he could fake. "But my clients provided a list of people they want me to see. I don't think I should go against their wishes—at least not right now."

"Nonsense. The names are probably the same as those I was going to suggest anyway," the Russian nobleman replied excitedly. "Give me your business card. Here, give me one," he insisted.

Philip surrendered one of the fake business cards the State Department had printed for him.

"I'll have several appointments for you by this afternoon," Ivan Ivanovich boasted. "Which oil company do you want to see today? Branobel? The Russian General Oil Corporation? Anglo-Russian Maximov? Royal Dutch Shell? Volga-Baku?

"I can get you into any of them. Just give me until 11:00 o'clock. I'll meet you here for coffee with at least two meetings arranged for later today."

Philip faced a dilemma. He couldn't back down, but neither could he negotiate an oil deal for non-existent clients. When the Grand Duke departed, Philip sat for a moment trying to calculate his next move. Still baffled, he bundled himself warmly and went for a morning hike to clear his thinking. He walked for about a half-hour but still had no idea of what he would do.

Finally, he decided to bluff his way through whatever appointments the old man made for him. Resigned to continuing his charade, he turned back toward the hotel.

Curiously, in the distance Philip heard the sound of a crowd chanting. He could also hear boots hitting the pavement in unison. As he retraced his way back to the hotel, the distant noise increased in intensity. And it continued to grow louder. Suddenly, he identified the source of the crescendo. This was a manifestation, and a mass of spirited demonstrators was on the march. It reminded him of the *manif* in which he participated several years ago in Paris.

A virtual army of protestors turned the corner and walked defiantly in his direction. The dissidents carried banners and posters denouncing the deposed Tsar and his successors. Other signs demanded dissolution of the Provisional Government and proclaimed "All Power to the Soviets." The abundance of red banners gave the protest a festive appearance, magnified by the marchers who sang political songs apparently to maintain their morale. Philip recognized *The Internationale*, a socialist anthem from an era when the young Marxist movement tried to organize labor through the rhetoric of working-class solidarity.

The closer the crowd came to Philip, the more intimidating it became. The street was now completely spanned by protesters many blocks deep. Shoulder to shoulder they tramped. Thousands of discontented people, unified and hostile to the old order.

The size and intensity of the *manif* forced Philip to turn around. Soon he was marching with them simply to avoid being crushed. And there was no chance to dart down a side street because large contingents of mounted Cossacks controlled the marchers by blocking access to any escape route.

There may have been ice and snow on the streets, but the dynamism of the event seemed to warm everyone. As Philip saw it, these were dedicated opponents of the *ancien régime* who were unshackled now from chronic despotism and optimistic that they owned the future. This was idealism in full political stride.

After marching for another ten minutes the group reached its goal, a large city park. Massive red flags bordered the gathering place, and platforms were erected apparently in anticipation of public speeches.

Soon the demonstrators were applauding the words of a long list of revolutionaries who preached a gospel of forceful change. This was especially the case with the Bolshevik speakers whose ideological bombast particularly enthralled the listeners. The Bolsheviks promised land reform and food and immediate withdrawal from the war. They assured the crowd that history was on the side of the people, and consequently even in this wretched land it was possible to build a new and perfect civilization. Each speaker who touched on these themes received thunderous cheers.

Eventually, the crowd began a steady chant of "Bread, Land, Peace," the Bolshevik themes condensed to three words. It grew in loudness until a spokeswoman for the radical Social Democrats invoked the word Lenin in her fiery speech. At the mention of that name, the crowd exploded, applauding and chanting "Lenin, Lenin, Lenin."

Philip was amazed. He had come to Petrograd thinking the so-called revolution might be over. When he learned that Nicholas II and his rightful heir had been deposed, he was convinced that ending the Romanov dynasty would settle matters and allow the liberal Provisional Government to steady the nation. But events today convinced him that this rebellion had a long way to go before it would be resolved.

THE HEADLONG FURY

The protest continued for much of the day fluctuating in enthusiasm depending on who was speaking. The leftist agitators met with widespread approval. The few people who defended the Provisional Government, however, were actually hissed off the platform, their ideas generating only disdain among those in the park.

When members of the Petrograd Soviet were introduced, the crowd stomped its feet and hooted approvingly. Chants of "All Power to the Soviets" rising from the sea of protesters seemed to make the earth shake.

Philip became so enraptured by the events that he hardly noticed that 11 o'clock came and went, as did a good part of the afternoon. He had thought about leaving to meet the Grand Duke, but each time dismissed the idea. This was historical, perhaps a pivotal event in the Russian Revolution. How would state and city authorities deal with such defiance? Conversely, how could such intense disaffection with the state be contained by any governmental agency when Russia's civic structure was eroding and social protest was unrelenting? Most importantly, what would be the consequences when the peaceful protesters eventually confronted the government with weapons in their hands?

It was dinner time before hunger finally forced Philip to leave the *manif* and return to the hotel. But the revolutionary comrades stayed, still reacting noisily to the speakers who continued to insist that Russia belonged to the people united.

When Philip entered the ornate lobby, the Grand Duke was waiting for him, and he did not appear pleased. "Well, Monsieur Corbière, you missed our meeting at 11 o'clock. And I had an appointment for you to meet the head of contracts at Branobel. That's a massive oil company, you must know, that was founded by the brothers of the famous Alfred Nobel. You have heard of the Nobel Prize, have you not? It's only been awarded for the last sixteen years."

"I am truly sorry, Imperial Highness. I went for a quick stroll, but I was swept into the largest protest march I have ever seen," Philip said with conviction. "There were tens of thousands of leftists parading, chanting, and demanding political power. For hours Cossack cavalrymen confined the demonstrators to a public park several miles from here. I couldn't get away.

"I know you went to a lot of trouble for me, and I am deeply grateful for that. But I was trapped. I apologize profusely."

"Those damned anarchists and Bolshies—and all the other socialists," the Russian angrily replied. "They're destroying all we've worked for, all that's held us together for centuries."

The nobleman quickly changed his demeanor. "I'm sorry you were trapped by the riff-raff," he said sympathetically, "but I'll get you some appointments for tomorrow."

The two men parted on friendly terms, although that was not especially encouraging for Philip. It only postponed the inevitable showdown with the oil executives.

That evening Philip spent hours at his desk composing a summary of the events of the day. It occurred to him, however, that he was only meeting people hostile to the revolutionaries. Ivan Ivanovich was obviously against the revolution, but that was to be expected: he was a Romanov, and his cousin and the imperial family had just been booted from power. Philip made a mental note to seek out counter-revolutionary opinions, if he could find them.

By breakfast the following morning he had developed an excuse he felt certain would stop the interfering Grand Duke. When Philip greeted him, he began his contrived tale of woe. "I don't think you should make any appointments for a while," he suggested. "I heard this morning from my clients. They are extremely worried about the viability of your Empire and therefore the trustworthiness of any contracts I might send them. They have ordered me to postpone my efforts in Russia until further notice."

"You mean they're scared off by those protesters?" asked the old man. "Didn't you tell them that this is only temporary, that once the warm weather comes people will forget all that reform blather and go back to their normal ways? You watch, by July our Nicholas will be back in control of the Alexander Palace in Tsarskoye Selo, and order will be restored across the land."

"I'm afraid my backers can't accept that conclusion yet," Philip answered. "They've been reading the international press, and the newspapers are reporting deep social instability here, particularly because your government continues to fight against Germany and Austria-Hungary. Maybe when Russia leaves the war my clients will revisit their plans. Right now they seem excited about new oil deposits recently found in Mexico."

"Let me tell you, Corbière, what's happening these days is abominable. It's a crime against God and Order," Ivan asserted. "Men of breeding and education and religion have been running this world for centuries. Sure, we've made mistakes, but we're not adverse to reform. Over the years, small revolts and enlightened monarchs have led Europe to its modern place of greatness. Europe is the very model for global emulation, a continent of achievement under the watchful eye of God and the leadership of born leaders. Everyone, from Peking to Timbuktu wants to be like the Europeans.

"And what are the Europeans doing these days?" rhetorically asked the nobleman. "They're tearing apart this civilization formed by man guided by the Divine. Our accomplishments are disintegrating, and we are causing that to happen. Surely God must be crying."

Philip had come to enjoy the Russian's conversations, so it was painful to watch him, born into great privilege in the 1830s, flailing blindly as he tried to explain contemporary social dysfunction in Russia.

"Certainly, the modern system needs reformation," he continued, "but the blood of millions of soldiers, sailors, and civilians will not purify the Order that has benefitted us all. We Russians have a legislature, the Duma. France and Britain have their parliaments. The Germans and Italians and Austrians have elected parliaments. Even Bulgaria, Serbia, Belgium, and yes, the Ottoman Empire have elected legislative bodies. Everybody nowadays has a form of democratic government. This makes Russia backwards?

"And most have powerful kings and Tsars and Kaisers—even one Sultan—who retain by the Will of God the authority to thwart the outlandishness of unthinking elected officials. If that is a structural strength or a flaw depends on the situation. But we can work it out with patience. We're getting there, just give us a little more time.

"Meanwhile, consider what's happening because of our misfortunes in the war. The bottom is now rising to the top. The uneducated, uncivilized, irrational masses demand full control. They're calling Russia their country! They're turning everything upside down.

"And it will not stop with the disintegration of our old, stable order. If the mob rules, discipline will disappear. If the war ended tomorrow, you would see immediate popular rejoicing; but in a few years the same masses will be back slaughtering new enemies—but with the assistance of a few years of technological improvement in the weaponry of death. If you think we've made mistakes, just wait until you see what mass man will do. Killing will only come more easily and more often if the gutter ever gains control."

"This is no time to discuss politics," Philip interjected. "My stomach is empty. Come, let me buy you breakfast. It's the least I can do for you after all the effort you exerted yesterday on my behalf."

"Ah, you're right," said the old Romanov. "I am hungry, anyway. A little caviar and champagne would go well right now."

Over a lavish morning meal, the Grand Duke lost his passion for political discussion. He seemed more concerned that Philip's clients were abandoning their pursuit of Russian oil. "You know, Corbière, I would have gained a sizable commission from whatever oil company struck a deal with you. Your clients just cost me many thousands of rubles," he admitted.

"You old dog, I never suspected," said Philip. "I figured you were just another of the wonderfully helpful citizens your country is famous for. But as the French would say, *cherchez les rubles*."

Again the Grand Duke thought about it before bursting into laughter. "Still a master of the *bon mot*, the right word," he remarked. "You are clever, my boy, very clever. I wouldn't want to match wits with you in a business deal. You're too bright for me.

"But does that mean your stay here is finished? You've only been here a few days."

Philip's mind raced for a response. "No, they paid me to remain here for a month," he answered. "So, I'll spend the next few weeks as a tourist. I want to see more of your beautiful city. I may also visit Moscow. Despite the snow and ice, I'm now thinking of this as my Russian winter vacation."

"That sounds sensible," the Grand Duke concluded. "I know lots of people in Petrograd and Moscow, in most of Russia for that matter. I can contact them and tell them you're available for appointments."

As he spoke the eager Ivan Ivanovich realized he was unconsciously making decisions for Philip again. His hearty laughter could be heard throughout the hotel as he checked himself. "Well, at least I can point you in the direction of Moscow…if that's where you want to go," he explained with a wide smile.

"Just go east for about 400 miles and the city will be there waiting for you," he said, pointing toward the east.

14

For the next two weeks Philip rode trains throughout western Russia visiting major cities and smaller towns. In each place he encountered interesting people and found new perspectives on the nation's social dilemma. Yet, the additional information only confirmed the general conclusions he had drawn during his first days in Petrograd: wracked by deep social unrest, Russia was on the verge of disaster. The nation's future as a monarchial state ended with the Tsar's abdication; but the form of government the country would take remained unclear. Indeed, here in April, 1917 there was an ongoing battle for the Russian destiny.

He conversed with aristocrats and politicians who supported Nicholas II, but they had few ideas about how to alleviate the abject conditions confronting the Empire. Poverty, land reform, war, state finances, industrial backwardness, primitive agricultural practices, and the necessity of rebuilding national cohesiveness: these were some of the motivating problems behind the revolution. In many cases, however, the aristocratic bloc even refused to admit these were valid concerns.

Instead, most seemed more interested in restoring imperial privileges. Some felt the Tsar's hemophiliac son should assume his father's office, but they would accept a new Tsar drawn from another royal family. A few even suggested Ivan Ivanovich as a potential Tsar. Many others felt that a new dynasty should be established by inviting a foreign prince to accept power and relocating him to Petrograd. That way Russia would have a Tsar free of the legacy of the repression and indifference that centuries of Romanov rule had created. The vast majority, however, wanted Nicholas II released from his Bolshevik captors and returned to full power. And often the reasoning behind these solutions was the desire to have homes and land and other properties returned from revolutionaries who had expropriated their holdings.

Philip found only a small constituency for the reformist agenda of the Provisional Government. It tended to consist of businessmen who liked the liberal policies championed by Prince George Lvov, head of the new government. But the Provisional Government alienated a large conservative constituency when it announced plans to confiscate church and Romanov properties.

When it came to the war, supporters of the Provisional Government insisted that Russia must honor its commitment to the Triple Entente. Some suggested that unilateral withdrawal would undermine the nation's international reputation and its credibility as a business partner. Others felt that Russia would then be isolated: hated by the Germans and Austrians who most likely would demand financial reparation from Petrograd; and spurned by the British, French, and Italians who controlled the global banks and large investment houses upon which Russia depended for long-range economic development.

As for the minorities problem faced by the Empire, little had been accomplished. Finland and Estonia had gained their autonomy, but they were compelled to remain within the Russian Empire. Although committees within many such communities plotted to free themselves from Russian rule, no ethnic or racial group had yet become an independent state.

Dutifully, Philip sketched these and other issues in the small notebook he carried. For protection, he wrote his findings in French in case his notes fell into unfriendly hands.

Philip learned from the people he met. One of the more interesting insights he gained was from a Russian shopkeeper in a small town along the Petrograd-to-Moscow railroad line. The man was elated at the news that President Wilson and the American Congress had declared war on Germany on April 6. "Russia will now win the war," he said excitedly. "This is the death blow to Germany and those traitorous Bolsheviks who speak of building a social paradise in Russia.

"The Americans will be fighting in France very soon. They will draw the Germans away and that will leave our military time to regroup and win in Eastern Europe. We can easily defeat the Austrians. It's perfect. We can't lose now."

Philip knew that the United States Army was miniscule by European wartime standards, totaling less than 100,000 troops when the war began in 1914. By comparison, the Russians in 1914 had six-million men in arms. Similarly, the two-ocean United States Navy in 1914 consisted of 57,000 men while the Germans had 79,000 and the British 209,000.

Philip understood, too, that no sizable units of U. S. soldiers could be enlisted or conscripted, then trained, equipped, and transported to France in less than six months. That would place them in Europe in wintertime with little action planned until the spring of 1918. He didn't want to diminish the shopkeeper's euphoria. In Russia's present circumstances any joy, even if born of delusion, was to be cherished and unchallenged.

On his way now to Moscow, Philip gazed out of the train windows and marveled at the Russian steppes. Vast and empty, with occasional rivers paralleling the tracks, the land was pristine, unspoiled by industrial excess or human architecture. It reminded him of the rich farmlands that extended a thousand miles west from Chicago, the flat green and brown patches that constituted the American agricultural breadbasket. In his mind he speculated about how much could be accomplished in Russia were it properly governed, educated, and inspired.

As he admired the beautiful openness before him, he could envision a national revival based upon agrarian reform and the development of vast farming areas. On such an expanding agricultural base, old production practices could be updated and a new wave of industrialization could be commenced. A few decades of such rational development could turn Russia into a global economic leader.

But Philip was suddenly shaken from his musings about Russian development. For no apparent reason, he felt the speeding train begin to slow down. He had heard no odd noise that would reflect mechanical malfunction. And there were no towns in this area that might require an unscheduled stop. Within a few minutes the train stood totally still in the middle of the open steppes.

It began with the sound of argument and muffled screaming in a passenger car ahead. Suddenly, someone burst through the entrance into Philip's car. One after another a motley assemblage of angry armed men entered his coach and began demanding money, jewelry, and other valuables from the terrified passengers.

It was a forbidding gang of characters. Some wore disheveled military uniforms. Others appeared to be Cossacks wearing large fur hats. One man, who seemed to be the leader, actually sported an oversized sombrero in the fashion of a Mexican warlord. He even had two bandoliers of bullets crisscrossing his chest.

Each robber carried a pistol or a rifle; some had both. And the invaders were not reluctant about shoving their weapons into the stomachs of passengers who hesitated in surrendering their possessions. This intimidating tactic never failed to elicit piercing screams and immediate cooperation.

When two thieves pointed their guns at Philip, he handed them his wallet. Fortunately, the bulk of his Russian currency was hidden in the lining of his valise, but he still lost about a thousand rubles—approximately $500—that were in the billfold.

As the men moved beyond Philip, one of them yelled out, "Hey, wait a minute! I know that man! Hold him!"

The robber moved up the aisle until he was face to face with Philip. "I know you. You're a spy," the man snarled. "I saw you at the soviet demonstration two weeks ago in Petrograd. The way you were dressed, you looked like a bourgeois banker. You said nothing—just watched the speakers and the crowd for hours. Were you taking notes for the police? Did you get the speakers' names?"

Philip stood silently, unsure what he should or should not say. "What are you talking about?" he finally responded directly into the face of his accuser.

He grew increasingly defiant. "Sure, I was at that event. Thousands of people were there. And I was watching the speakers and the reactions of the crowd. Does that make me a spy? When you stage an outdoor demonstration don't you want people to see the event and listen to what's said?

"And if I'm a spy, for whom? Maybe I was spying for the Tsar, trying to rally the crowd to demand a return of the Romanovs. Maybe I was working for the Petrograd Soviet, itself, detecting political deviation in that mob of revolutionary enthusiasts. Maybe I was a secret agent for one of the political factions in between. You're my accuser. You tell me. Who asked me to be a spy?"

Philip's angry boldness took the bandits off guard. Even the rifle barrel poked in his stomach had not diminished his brazen attitude toward the bandits.

"Take that man with us. We'll get the truth from him later," commanded the man in the Mexican hat. "Finish collecting money and valuables from the passengers. Then let's get out of here before the Army comes."

While the thieves continued harassing the travelers, two thugs grabbed Philip and began dragging him from his seat. "Wait a minute! Wait a minute!" he screamed at them. "Let me get my suitcase. Then I'll come."

He reached into the overhead rack and slowly retrieved his luggage. "Now I'll go with you," he said.

The invaders pushed Philip through the aisle until they reached the stairs leading outside. "Climb down," ordered one of them, underscoring his command by pointing his pistol at Philip's head.

In short order he found himself standing in the middle of nowhere surrounded by gleeful thieves admiring their day's work. As the train slowly departed, another bandit asked ominously, "Shouldn't we just kill this guy now?"

"Yes, shoot him here and let's get going," agreed another. More voices expressed agreement. A consensus for instant death was growing fast.

"No. Wait a minute," said the original accuser. "I want to know more about this swine. We need to question him. We need to know everything so it can't happen again. Take him with us.

"I've got it, we'll hold a trial. That's the plan. In the spirit of the new Russia, we'll put him on trial for espionage. Death will be his sentence after we convict him."

That novel solution swayed the crowd. Everyone fell into accord. Philip was terrified, but he knew he had to maintain his composure. His life depended on it.

The men poured their loot into cloth sacks strapped to the sides of several pack horses. They tied Philip's hands then hoisted him up and onto one of the animals. Then they mounted their own steeds and rode toward the afternoon sun.

Fortunately, Philip knew how to ride a horse. Even with his hands bound, he rode well. He may have been born and bred in industrial Chicago, but summer stays at his uncle's ranch in Wisconsin had familiarized him with horseback riding, and at the moment this youthful experience was proving valuable.

Because this gang reminded him of characters from a cowboy movie, Philip expected a campsite similar to those in films featuring William S. Hart or Dustin Farnum. Instead, the Russian desperadoes led him to a large encampment containing upwards of a hundred men wearing a variety of military uniforms and civilian clothing.

"You see, Mr. Spy, we are numerous," the sombreroed robber announced. "We are all deserters from the Tsar's Army who have come together to live in harmony. But every now and then we need cash to replenish our funds—we don't have factory jobs with weekly salaries. And, trains are so easy to rob out here in the wilderness. You were just unlucky to be there when we dropped in for a visit.

"Now, let me see your papers," the leader barked.

Philip was untied so he could show his identification documents. He offered his passport.

"How do I know this is not forged? How do I know you're not a German spy or a French spy? Or an agent of the Tsar's secret police?" the leader asked defiantly. "How long would it take you to notify the authorities of our position so they could come and kill us?

"I am not a spy," Philip asserted as strongly as he could. "Get that straight: I am not a spy. I am a businessman from Switzerland. I speak French and Russian. And I am here to negotiate oil contracts on behalf of clients in South America. No espionage, no contact with the authorities. I'm just a man interested in purchasing Russian crude."

"Wait a minute," interrupted another of the deserters. He then whispered something to the man in the large hat.

The leader turned toward Philip. "Does the name V. I. Lenin mean anything to you, Mr. Bourgeois Businessman?" he asked.

"I've heard of the man," Philip responded cautiously. He sensed a soft spot in the animus against him, but he was not sure what the renegade soldiers thought about Lenin.

"I'll bet you have," said the leader. "What's your relationship to Comrade Lenin?"

"Well, he lives in the same country as I. But I'm a citizen, and he's living in exile from Russia," Philip answered. "Why do you care about Lenin?"

"Care about him? We love the man," said the leader. "We are prepared to die for him. We may be Army deserters, but we are also Bolsheviks, and we will build a new society when our Moses returns."

"You are from Switzerland. Do you know something about his return?" asked one of the train robbers.

Here was the opening Philip had hoped for. He was a dead man otherwise. "Well, between you and me, I have heard rumors that he may be in Russia very soon," Philip announced. It was pure fabrication, but it moved the soldiers who seemed electrified by the "news."

"When will he be here?" "How will he get here?" "Where will he enter Russia?" The questions came fast from men in the group.

Philip embellished his story. "Let me see. Today is April 14, by my calendar. He could be here as early as next week, maybe even sometime this week, but certainly within two or three months."

Knowing that Lenin could only reach Russia safely if he traveled through Germany, Philip continued. "My business contacts in Geneva and Zurich, tell me that the Germans will allow him to travel through their country, probably to Petrograd. They would travel through Germany, then most likely by ferry to Sweden or Finland where he could catch a train to the Finland Station."

For Philip it was pure conjecture. But it was the only course the Germans could follow because of French and British troops on their western borders, and Russian forces along the eastern frontier.

The army of deserters reacted enthusiastically, firing rifles into the air, gulping down vodka, and dancing with abandon. This was what they wanted to hear. It completely changed the gang's attitude to Philip.

"Comrade Corbière, join us. Drink! Dance! Enjoy the moment! Lenin will be home soon! Tonight we celebrate his return and the beginning of the new Russia," the man in the sombrero commanded.

"And return the Comrade's wallet and its belongings. He's one of us now," the leader told one of his subordinates.

Philip joined the revelry. He drank the vodka, danced with merriment, and whooped every time someone yelled out Lenin's name. Privately, however, he was celebrating his own reprieve from a firing squad.

In the morning he was awakened by one of the deserters who ordered him to get up and prepare to move. Five minutes later the group leader approached him. "Are you ready to ride, Comrade Corbière?" he inquired.

"Yes. But I could use a piece of bread and a cup of strong Cossack coffee, then I'll be fully ready," said Philip.

"Good man. You have your coffee and bread, then we ride to Petrograd," the chief desperado declared. "If Lenin is coming this week, I must be there—and you'll want to be there to greet him as an unofficial representative of Switzerland. Am I right?"

"Definitely. I'll be happy to greet Lenin on behalf of my country and notify my contacts in Geneva and Zurich that he has arrived safely," Philip answered.

"Since we now trust each other," said the commander, "let me introduce myself and the others who will accompany us. I am Dmitri Pavlenko, former lieutenant in the Tsar's 4th Don Cossacks cavalry. These two fellows are Feodor Zamiatin and Nickolas Voroshiloff, foot soldiers who once served in the Russian Third Army, the one so ineptly commanded by General Alexei Brusilov.

And this one is Sergeant Vladimir Lubinsky, formerly a sharpshooter attached to a Polish Rifle group. He's the man who recognized you from the demonstration last month.

"Sorry about that, Comrade," Lubinsky said sheepishly extending his hand to shake. "It's just that you looked so out of place at the rally. I thought you were an undercover policeman or something."

As the former Polish soldier offered his hand in reconciliation, Philip could not avoid noticing that a sizable portion of Lubinsky's right hand and forearm were missing. All that remained for Philip to grasp was a mangled stump.

The other men watch closely for Philip's reaction to the proffered handshake.

"Apologies accepted," he declared reaching for the mutilated limb. He shook the deformed hand in friendship. "Seems like we both cheated death," Philip said to the wounded man. "Forgive me for my bluntness, but I've been around wounded men before. But I have never seen an injury such as yours."

"You are observant, comrade," said the rifleman. "This is not from a bullet or shrapnel. This is the result of a wolf attack."

"A wolf attack?" Philip asked incredulously. "Is this the latest German special weapon?"

"Not at all," Lubinsky answered. "Last November when I was stationed somewhere between Minsk and Vilnius, the battlefield became overrun with roaming packs of starving wolves. The beasts were so famished in the freezing winter they began attacking us soldiers, especially when we were alone or in small groups.

"They dined on Russians and Germans equally," he added with a hint of humor. "So they were definitely not one of the Kaiser's new weapons. In fact, the opposing armies had to call a temporary truce so they could exterminate the beasts. Together, we shot more than a hundred man-eating wolves. Then we returned to slaughtering each other.

"But that was the last straw for me. I had the wound cleaned and bandaged then just walked away from the Army. I headed toward Moscow. Six months later, here I am with this rag-tag bunch of Reds. This partial hand is the only award I ever received from the Tsar's army."

"Enough talking. You've finished eating, Comrade Corbière, so let's ride," ordered Pavlenko. "We have a distance to go before we rest tonight; and we have a full day's ride tomorrow. Just be careful not to exhaust your horses. We won't get fresh ones until tomorrow."

The ride to Petrograd was slowed by bouts of rainy weather that made the footing perilous for the horses. Unexpectedly, twice along the way the riders were able to obtain fresh animals from Bolshevik sympathizers. As a result they were able to make up much of the lost time.

Philip and the army deserters arrived at their destination late on the evening of April 16. They dismounted behind a large house in a working-class section of the capital. The men were exhausted and hungry.

"This is where my old friend Mikhail Korotkin lives. He'll be happy to see us. Come on, let's go inside," said Pavlenko. Without bothering to knock, he swung open the unlocked wooden door and walked in, confident that he and his compatriots would be warmly greeted. Instead, they found the house empty.

Eventually, a boy about twelve years of age came downstairs to confront the men. By the way he was rubbing his eyes it was obvious that the noisy visitors had awakened him. "Sasha, it's me, Uncle Dmitri. Ah, we must have awakened you. We are so sorry."

With due propriety, Pavlenko introduced young Aleksandr Korotkin to the men. "My friends and I have come to visit your papa," he explained. "Is he here?"

"No, he's gone," the youngster said. "He and mama went to the train station to see Mr. Lenin. Mr. Lenin is coming tonight by train."

Philip stood motionless, stunned by what the boy had just said.

"You mean tonight Mr. Lenin is returning to Petrograd and to Russia? What time will he be here?" Pavlenko asked.

"I'm not sure," the child answered, "but I heard papa complaining about how late Mr. Lenin would be arriving."

"Well, you go back to bed. My friends and I are going to the station to meet your papa and Mr. Lenin," Pavlenko replied. "Good night, Sasha."

The men ran from the house. "That's less than a mile from here. I know a shortcut. We can leave the horses here and get to the Finland Station on foot almost as fast—and we won't have to worry about watching our animals," Pavlenko commanded.

It was 11 o'clock when the winded men arrived to find hundreds of people crowded outside the railway station. This was historic: the return of Lenin from exile in Switzerland. Philip knew that for the Russian Left it was almost religious in its connotation. The intellectual and political leader was coming home to organize and champion their goals at a time of national desperation. And in a stroke of incredible coincidence, he was arriving in the final minutes of Easter Monday.

Shoving and weaving through the crowd, Pavlenko eventually found his friend, Mikhail Korotkin.

"Dmitri. Is that you? What great timing you have," bellowed Korotkin when he recognized his confederate. Squeezing their ways toward each other, the two men finally met and embraced. "This is the greatest night in Russian history," said Korotkin. "And here you are in Petrograd with your Army buddies to experience it. How did you know Lenin was coming home tonight?"

"I did not know until my friend Comrade Jean-Luc Corbière from Switzerland told me," Pavlenko replied. He then introduced the two men.

"This gentleman from Geneva knew when Lenin was arriving?" Korotkin asked his old friend. Turning back to Philip, he continued. "Then you must be one of us," he concluded as he hugged Philip and kissed him on both cheeks. "Did you personally arrange the return?"

Philip, still amazed at the situation, continued his great bluff. "No, I didn't arrange the journey," he replied laughingly. "That was handled from Berlin. But my contacts at home told me that the return from exile was going to happen soon—even as early as this evening."

"That's wonderful, just wonderful," exuded Korotkin.

"Yes, it is truly wonderful," added Pavlenko as he patted Philip approvingly on the back.

At 11:10 the train carrying Lenin pulled to a stop at the railroad platform. Soon, he and a group of other exiles walked through the

Finland Station and into the cold Russian night. Smiling broadly, they all appeared happy to be safely in Petrograd. They also seemed surprised and impressed that so many people had come to greet them.

Pavlenko and Korotkin smiled with satisfaction as they spotted Lenin and more than two dozen other Bolshevik leaders who had accompanied him. "There's Karl Radek, the Austrian," shouted Korotkin. "There's Gregory Zinoviev. And there's Lenin's wife, Krupskaya. Hello, Nadya," Pavlenko yelled as his waved toward Mrs. Lenin.

People at the front of the welcoming crowd became so excited that a few of them hoisted Lenin on their shoulders and carried him toward a welcoming platform. A loud "hurrah" erupted among the onlookers. The excitement of the event, the multitude of colorful banners containing defiant Socialist political slogans, plus a group of military musicians playing the French national anthem all contributed to the festiveness.

And there was Vladimir Ilyich Ulanov—popularly known as Lenin—standing on the raised platform ready to address the throng. He spoke not of thanks for his safe arrival. Instead, he charged the crowd to reenergize the revolution, ending dramatically with "Sailors, comrades, we have to fight for a socialist revolution, to fight until the proletariat wins full victory! Long live the universal socialist revolution!"

Philip was struck by the defiance and inflexibility in Lenin's words. Even Bolshevik leaders in Petrograd were softening their radical views. Some like Lev Kamenev and Josef Stalin, co-editors of the party newspaper *Pravda*, suggested continuing the war and finding points of compromise with the moderate wing of the Social Democrats, the Mensheviks. But here was Lenin hitting the ground running, stridently proclaiming that his goal was to reinvigorate the Russian Revolution. He called again for social rebellion worldwide to usher in a modern perfect world. To that end, he ordered his supporters to begin constructing the Red utopia.

Philip knew that in less than ten minutes Lenin had evolved from a returning exile to the chief advocate for continuing the revolution, a principal precondition of which was Russian withdrawal from the war. It was exactly what the Germans hoped for when they escorted him through their country in a railroad car. It was the worst fear of American and the Entente leaders.

Surprisingly, Lenin waded into the crowd when he spotted Pavlenko. "Dmitri Pavlenko, my old Cossack buddy. I have missed you. How are you?" he said as he pushed through his boisterous greeters. When they finally reached each other, Lenin grabbed his friend's hands. "You appear healthy, if not prosperous. It's been ages since we sat together talking political philosophy and sipping vodka. We must do it again, soon. Oh, it is good to be home and to see true comrades like you."

"Ilyich, it's wonderful to welcome you back. You have been missed here," Pavlenko replied. "We are all so happy that our leader has returned from the mountains. We await your call to action."

"I see you're still wearing that battered old Mexican sombrero," Lenin observed mirthfully.

"Well, I paid a lot for it. At least I paid the madam a lot of rubles, and then 'borrowed' it on my way out of that beaten-down Odessa 'riding academy.' There must have been a Mexican freedom fighter in another room," he said laughingly. "I never stuck around to find out."

Lenin found that hilarious. Indeed, both men laughed heartily and embraced in renewed friendship.

In short order Lenin recovered his composure. "But how did you know I was coming?" he asked. "I know the Party headquarters here in Petrograd organized this welcome, but you and your men operate far from Petrograd."

"Ilyich, let me present the man who told us you were coming home," said the Cossack leader as he and Lenin walked toward Philip. "This is Comrade Jean-Luc Corbière. He is a petroleum broker from Switzerland. He knew exactly when and where you would be arriving. Without him, we would have missed this momentous occasion."

"Well, a Swiss recruit—and a businessman as well," said Lenin somewhat cautiously as he embraced Philip.

"Yes, Comrade Lenin, I am a petroleum broker. I'm here in Russia seeking oil contracts for clients in Latin America," Philip responded.

"You must have interesting contacts. I'd like to speak with you about them. How about this afternoon? Why don't you join me for lunch when we can talk at length? Krupskaya and I are staying with my sister Maria. But I'll meet you at 2 o'clock at Party headquarters in the Kshesinskaya Mansion. Anyone in the city can tell you how to get there."

Lenin leaned over and whispered something into Pavlenko's ear. Whatever he said caused Dmitri to peer back at Philip, then slowly return his attention to the Bolshevik leader.

"We will meet later for food and conversation," Philip said to Lenin as the Red philosopher-politician turned to acknowledge again the adulation of the multitude of well-wishers.

Because he was trusted by his Bolshevik friends, Philip had no trouble leaving them and returning to the Hôtel de l'Europe. Fortunately he had dragged his valise with him across the steppes on horseback, then on foot to the Finland Station. At least he would be able to shower and shave before his rendezvous with Lenin.

That afternoon as he walked up the front steps, Philip was struck by the beauty of the Kshesinskaya Mansion. It was a striking, bright example of art nouveau architecture, a style that emerged in Europe at the end of the 19th century. The Mansion was built eleven years ago for the renowned prima ballerina Mathilde Kshesinskaya. At age seventeen she had become the mistress of the future Nicholas II. She continued in that capacity for three years before he married a British princess. The marriage ended her relationship with Nicholas.

Because she openly continued to associate with the Imperial court, both socially and sexually, Mathilde lost her property in the earliest days of the anti-Tsarist revolt. Her mansion was looted, and she was exiled and allowed to relocate to France. Her elegant residence was confiscated by the Bolsheviks to house their political offices.

Philip was taken to Lenin's room on the second floor where he was warmly greeted. "I hope you don't mind, Monsieur Corbière," Lenin said, "but I've taken the liberty of ordering lunch to be brought to us here. I prefer the quiet intimacy of the office. If I go outside to eat we will be mobbed, as you saw last night. Thousands of people yelling does not make for proper digestion of Baltic salmon. That's what I've ordered for our meal. You do like fresh salmon?"

"Oh, yes, that will be excellent," answered Philip.

"And we'll share a bottle of Riesling," added Lenin. "When we moved into this building, we found a wine cellar stocked with fine vintages. Wait until you taste this German Riesling from the Mosel region. It's from 1897, a very good year for German white wines, I'm told."

The meal proved Lenin to be not only a generous host, but also a connoisseur of good food and drink. As they ate, the radical leader became more serious, asking Philip for details about his clients' interest in oil contracts. "No matter how this revolution turns out, Russia will need foreign capital, and foreign capitalists will need petroleum," he explained.

Philip explained that his clients had abandoned their interest in Russian oil because of the unstable political situation. He also mentioned the recent development of Mexican oil fields and how this had also influenced their decision to suspend the overtures he was making in Petrograd.

Lenin became testy when he asserted, "But Dmitri said you were one of us. If that's so, you must persuade the South Americans to reconsider Russian petroleum. In the name of radical socialism, it's your duty to make the effort."

Philip figured it was time to be straightforward. "I appreciate your faith in my persuasiveness, but I'm sure they've made up their minds. They won't spend millions in Russia at this explosive time. They will not risk such large sums of money in this explosive atmosphere."

"Would peace in Russia change their minds? If the Bolsheviks took complete power and left this predatory capitalist war the next day, would that make them see things differently?" Lenin asked.

Philip hesitated. "Are you talking about a second revolution? A revolt against the Provisional Government and all those politicians trying to create a Russian republic with a democratic form of government?"

"Nonsense," Lenin replied sharply. "They're trying to create a bourgeois structure that's out-of-date before it's ever born. No, I'm talking about the future of governments everywhere in the world. I'm speaking of the international socialist destiny: a worldwide classless society based on proletarian values as envisioned by Karl Marx and Friedrich Engels.

"You obviously haven't read the newspaper. While I was on that cursed trek from Zurich to Petrograd, I sketched out my ideas on what needs to be done. They're published today in *Pravda* under the title 'April Theses.' These ideas, Comrade Corbière, are a roadmap to socialist triumph over piratical capitalism and revolutionary defeatism. Here, here's a copy of the article," Lenin said thrusting a newspaper toward Philip.

After skimming the document, Philip looked up. "Well, sir, it's a daring plan. You're placing your historical reputation—and maybe your life—on the line."

"I will be forty-seven years old next week," Lenin said emphatically. "If I don't make my stand now in these historic circumstances, when will I? I know the Germans brought me here to take the Empire out of the war. But I will have the last laugh when the social transformation being born now in decadent Russia sweeps over Germany and destroys that rotten regime and all other bourgeois political arrangements."

"But your plan goes well beyond what Marx and Engels envisioned," Philip responded. "You've written in praise of them in the past. They saw a proletarian victory evolving from the inherent shortcomings of industrialization. But Russia is still a peasant country. The proletariat, that industrial working class that would lead the revolution, is miniscule here."

"Comrade Corbière, that master plan is seventy years old. If you are familiar with my writings over the years, you know that I have long advocated updates in Marxist orthodoxy," Lenin explained. "Sometimes theory needs to be reevaluated. And sometimes a human push is required to change thought into action.

"I am not a Marxist, Corbière, I am a Marxist-Leninist. I believe Russia is now the ripest of nations from which to launch the movement to bring radical socialism to power globally. But theory is not enough. Instead of letting Russian industrialism evolve naturally toward bourgeois domination and eventually to proletarian conquest, I am advocating direct action. We need to catalyze Russia's economic development by injecting the political might of the Bolshevik Party flowing through local soviet councils. Instead of waiting for the proletariat to mature into a proper anti-bourgeois force, I am urging an immediate dictatorship of the proletariat, with proletariat redefined as exploited people from the industrial to the agrarian sectors of society. Think of it: factory workers and poor peasants and everyone else disaffected by exploitative capitalism, now amalgamated under the leadership of the Bolshevized soviets. That's the catalyst that will catapult Russia to world leadership in creating a new workers' world.

Lenin continued his explanation. "I am not so theoretical that I would let slip a historic moment that cries out for initiative," he remarked. "So, we shove Marx and drag Engels ahead by a few decades, maybe even a century. Who cares? We alter the original recipe and add human organization and armed force to the formula our founders originally described. Who's going to stop us?

"Tactical compromise when necessary, strategic inflexibility always. That's the way wage this conflict," he added. "Occasionally, we may have to take a step back, but only after taking two steps forward. Remember this: accomplished enough times, two steps forward and one backwards results in victory.

"And while we're at it, we need a new name, something aggressive and different. No more Bolsheviks; it's too Russian. No more Social Democrats because that sounds too parliamentarian. We need something electrifying.

"I've given this a lot of thought. I think that from now on we must refer to ourselves as the Communist Party because we are communists and we're about to reformulate the world, not just Russia."

"I have a question about your vision," Philip interrupted. "What happens to the people who don't agree with you? I mean, Marx argued that people would evolve, they would come to agree that capitalism was evil and in need of replacement by socialism. But your plan allows no time for evolution; you anticipate, even demand, immediate consensus. So what happens to the unconvinced in your world?"

With a cynical grin Lenin was blunt: "They must be purged as enemies of the people," he remarked. "Are there deviationists in the Christian Heaven? Of course not. Heaven's is a dictatorship. If someone says God is wrong, God has that sinner eliminated. In the same spirit, if there are subversives in the classless Communist paradise, they will not be accommodated. They will be liquidated.

"This is not about democracy, comrade. We are moving beyond bourgeois liberalism and democracy. This is about creating a heaven on Earth. What the great philosophers of the 18th century envisioned, what Marx and Engels reinvigorated, the new Communist Party is about to achieve. Disloyalty will not be tolerated."

The philosophical discussion continued well beyond lunch. Finally, Lenin broke it off. "I must apologize, Monsieur Corbière," he stated while rising from his chair, "but I am scheduled to present my April Theses this evening before the All-Russia Conference of Soviets of Workers' and Soldiers' Deputies. I have to gather my thoughts for a while.

"But, please contact your South American clients," he added. "I am most interested in acquiring hard currency for the struggle ahead. It may be a step backward for a Communist, but it's taken in anticipation of two—or maybe three or five or ten steps forward. Can you get back to me in a few days?"

Philip agreed, and after thanking him for the delicious lunch and the stimulating conversation, he left the Mansion. But there was new urgency in Philip's stride as he walked toward his hotel. He felt the pressure mounting. Sooner or later the Bolsheviks would learn that he was not one of them, perhaps even discover that he was working secretly for the President of the United States. It was time to fold his Russian operations.

The rest of the evening Philip placed his conclusions on paper. He added this final document to the reports he had already written, carefully placing them in a large envelope. He even included the issue of *Pravda* containing Lenin's radical agenda.

Philip remembered the instructions he received when he entered Russia. He was to place his reports in a safe-deposit box at the State Bank where he would find his next assignment. The bank was located close to his room. But, he figured, Bolshevik agents would surely be following him as soon as he walked through his door. That meant that any sign of imminent departure—checking out at the front desk, carrying a suitcase, going directly to the Finland Station—could generate suspicion and even arrest.

In the morning he found his key to the safe-deposit box. He had hidden it in a soiled sock and mixed it inconspicuously in a pile of clothing that needed laundering. He poked the large envelope containing his reports next to his bare back but covered by his shirt and suit coat. Everything was strapped in place by the belt on his trousers. Through his room window he observed that the spring weather seemed to be warming, so with his top coat draped inconspicuously over his well-traveled suitcase he went to eat.

Philip saw no one following him, but he could not be really certain. The situation reminded him of his railroad trip to Rome when caution paid dividends.

After a leisurely breakfast, he walked outdoors and headed in the direction of the bank. On the crowded street he moved slowly, peering through store windows and staring at the architecture, just as any tourist might admire the shops and buildings of Petrograd on a warm morning.

Philip positioned himself at the side of a large group of office workers who were walking fast, as if they were all late for work. As they passed the State Bank, he used them as a screen to dart through the doors, hopefully unseen by any pursuer on foot. Quickly, he found the department containing safe deposit boxes and produced his key.

The bank official dithered a bit, then took him to a private room and presented him with the box. Carefully, Philip opened it and withdrew a small envelope from inside. He then placed his own set of reports inside the box, locked it, and returned it to its proper place.

He smiled as he read his new assignment. "We respectfully request that you proceed to Egypt near the Arabian areas of the Ottoman Empire. A room has been reserved for Walter Kaplan at Shepheard's Hotel in Cairo."

He was going to North Africa and the Near East. To facilitate such a long trip he found an open-ended railroad ticket through Helsinki to Turku on the Baltic Sea. And there was sufficient cash—this time in United States dollars—to purchase passage on a neutral freighter headed toward the eastern Mediterranean.

There was also a new U. S. passport in the name of Walter Kaplan. An enclosed biographical summary described Kaplan as a foreign correspondent for the *Chicago Tribune* on assignment to cover the war in the Near East.

The President was asking a lot. But to Major Belmont it was an order from the Commander-in-Chief. He could not refuse the directive.

Carefully, he emerged from the bank and was alert to anything threatening. After proceeding for several blocks without incident, he hailed a droshky to take him to the railroad station.

As the carriage crossed a bridge spanning the Neva, he asked the driver to stop for a moment. Confident now that he was not being followed, Philip left the carriage and walked to the bridge railing. From here he cast the bank key far into the river. Satisfied that he had followed instructions completely, Philip returned to the droshky and continued his trip to the Finland Station.

15

The trek to Cairo was long and frustrating. Just getting to neutral Sweden involved railroad travel to Helsinki and then to coastal Turku. From that city in western Finland, Philip found a boat captain willing to take him almost 170 miles across the Baltic to Stockholm—but only for a hefty fee.

Then there was Stockholm. It took him several days in the Swedish capital to find a freighter scheduled to carry a cargo to the eastern Mediterranean. Unfortunately for Philip, the ship was a coal-burner that made stops, sometimes for a week or more, to load and unload commodities and to replenish its fuel supply.

Although the freighter was Swedish, the captain took no chances with safety. Because there was always the possibility of encountering German mines in the Baltic and the North Sea, he proceeded slowly, carefully watching for these treacherous bombs drifting in the ocean currents. To inform submarine commanders of his neutrality, he flew the Swedish flag; and on both sides of the vessel he painted the word "Sweden"—in large block letters and in French, German, and English—to announce the ship's affiliation. At night, spotlights were employed to illuminate these identification markings.

Although Philip wasn't seeking a leisurely voyage to the cities of neutral Europe, he found himself spending time in Norway, Denmark, the Netherlands, and Spain before disembarking several weeks later in decidedly non-neutral Alexandria, Egypt. Although no German submarine ever approached the freighter during its cruise, the possibility of a U-boat attack, even on neutral shipping, was continually on his mind.

Landing in Alexandria meant relief for Philip. His lengthy journey from Russia was finally finished. No more worry about torpedoes and floating mines. No more fear of being shelled by a belligerent warship, or being boarded by hostile forces.. From here he had only a train ride of 130 miles on the Egyptian State Railways to reach Cairo.

This was a new assignment, but no one from the U. S. government had approached him with specific instructions. All he knew was that there was an open reservation in his new name waiting at the fashionable Shepheard's Hotel in the Egyptian capital and that he was to report on the struggle against the Ottoman Turks in the deserts of the Near East.

The train trip gave Philip time to develop his new character. As Walter Kaplan, he would pose as a foreign affairs journalist for the *Chicago Tribune*, who was assigned to examine British efforts versus the Turks. He was pleased that this time he could carry out his pose in English, a language with which he was growing increasingly unfamiliar. Sometimes he was convinced that his French and Russian were now much better than his native language.

In the Near East Philip was entering an area of chronic combat. Diplomats may have historically referred to the Ottoman Empire as "the sick man of Europe," but efforts to defeat this invalid had proven costly. Over the decades defeats and victories from the Black Sea to Persia had convinced European military leaders that Turkey was not to be taken lightly.

But "the sick man" was weakening. Throughout the 19th century the Turks had battled many European nations, often losing strategic portions of an Empire that once spread as far west as the outskirts of Vienna. Even before 1914 Constantinople had lost control of Albania, Serbia, Greece, Bulgaria, Rumania, Bosnia, Herzegovina, Montenegro, and Macedonia. At the same time in North Africa, it lost control of Egypt, Tripolitania, Algeria, and Tunisia. And the growing importance of oil to European economies made Ottoman control of Persia, Mesopotamia, and the Arabian Peninsula increasingly precarious.

Since 1908, however, the Ottoman Empire had been improving politically. Led by a cadre of junior officers, the army revolted that year against the repressive Sultan Abdul Hamid II, compelling him to restore the Constitution he had abolished. These so-called Young Turks became a political force demanding reforms. The following year they engineered the replacement of Abdul Hamid with Mehmed V, a new Sultan who was more sympathetic to their plans.

Militarily, too, the Ottoman army by 1914 was an improved fighting force. This was primarily the result of German officers who had helped reform and train the Sultan's troops. The Germans brought discipline, training, weaponry, and renewed morale to Turkish forces. They also brought fidelity to Berlin which resulted in the Empire joining the Central Powers in declaring war on the Triple Entente. Practically speaking, the Ottoman Empire probably would have joined any nation willing to fight the hated Russians who were perched menacingly in the Black Sea and on its northern border.

By the time he arrived in Cairo the weather was hot. Unlike the freeze that prevailed during much of his Petrograd assignment, morning temperatures in Egypt were already approaching ninety degrees Fahrenheit. Philip was not unthankful. He read that in Egypt and the nearby Sinai desert summer temperatures often reached 120 degrees—with only slight overnight cooling.

Cairo stood in remarkable contrast to the other cities he had visited. Although there were several ornate mosques and oversized royal palaces, most buildings in this metropolis of a million residents were plain and functional. Everything in the city seemed to be built of Egyptian sand and the color of most Cairene architecture matched that of the surrounding desert.

There were exceptions to such sameness, none more striking than the foreign quarter which attracted British civil servants and rich visitors from Europe, Australia and New Zealand. Here is where the non-natives frolicked in prewar days amongst luxurious hotels, gaudy night clubs, boutiques selling the latest Paris fashions, jewelry shops with pricey baubles, and other caterers to conspicuous wealth. Although war and the recent imposition of martial law diminished nightlife excesses, among expatriates this part of the city remained vibrant.

Philip went immediately to Shepheard's Hotel in the middle of this Western excess. He was greeted at the entrance by an Egyptian porter wearing a fez and a uniform rich with native embroidery, even though the establishment was owned and run by Europeans. It struck Philip that the manager, the concierge, and even the reservation clerks were from Europe or the richer British dominions. When he ate lunch at the Hotel's famous Terrace, it was populated overwhelmingly by European women wearing their finest outfits—and gentlemen in proper British suits—sipping midday cocktails.

To Philip, this was a cloud-cuckoo land, a bizarre enclave that seemed to deny there was a savage war going on. Like Jonathan Swift's Laputa floating above the actual world, wartime restraint in this little playground of tourists and expats was nowhere to be seen.

As he returned to his room, Philip chuckled to himself about the absurdity he had just witnessed. When he walked in, however, reality awaited him. On the floor was a white envelope that had been shoved under the door while he was dining.

A letter inside began with in a familiar manner: "I can't wait for the spring weather to arrive." The phrase convinced Philip that this was an official communication. It ordered him to make contact with the British commanders of the Egyptian Expeditionary Force, and to prepare a report on the conditions of Entente forces in their war against Constantinople. Specifically, the note asked whether the President should consider sending U. S. troops into the Sultan's lands.

Philip already had made preliminary conclusions on the matter. Diplomatic relations between Washington and Constantinople had been severed since Congress declared war against Germany in April. Philip figured that eventually the U. S. would declare war on the other Central Power, Austria-Hungary. From his viewpoint, hostilities involving the Turks would be a natural next step. Whether or not that happened now seemed to depend on his final assessment.

The only part of his instructions that irritated Philip was a change in Walter Kaplan's mission. Kaplan was now to present himself as the author of travel books who was in Egypt to write about how the pyramids and other ancient structures were surviving the war. It was to be part of an effort to build interest among Americans to tour this part of the world once the war ended.

However, Philip preferred the Kaplan personality he developed on the train ride from Alexandria. Patterned according to his original instructions, he had prepared himself to be a journalist dealing with foreign affairs and military matters. He thought that a serious Kaplan would be more effective than a tourism writer. He dismissed Kaplan's revised persona and went with his own characterization.

More familiar to Philip, the envelope contained the address of the Royal Bank of Scotland and a key to a safe-deposit box there. There was no explanation of what to do with it and when to do it, but he knew the pattern. Only this time the Nile would receive the key when he finished his assignment.

On June 30 when Philip finally presented himself at the General Headquarters of the Egyptian Expeditionary Force, it was as a war reporter seeking an interview with leading British military officers.

GHQ was located in a large, first-class suite in the swank Savoy Hotel, another monument to European extravagance planted in the midst of Egyptian deprivation. It was an unusual venue for a GHQ since the hotel was filled with foreign tourists, wealthy Arab sheiks, and beautiful women bejeweled and provocatively clothed. Philip walked by British, New Zealander, Australian, and Indian military brass sitting in the saloon in mid-afternoon. With a war going on outside, he was not impressed by the relaxed, alcoholic practices he observed as he walked toward the office of the General in charge of Egyptian operations..

Philip explained to the junior officer stubbornly governing access to offices of the Egyptian Expeditionary Force that his newspaper had assigned him to report on British activity along the Ottoman Front. The young soldier was unmoved. He put down his gin and tonic and addressed Philip directly. "Look, Mr. Kaplan, the EEF has no time for you. We're busy commanding troops on several fronts. Why don't you just go away and leave us fight the war. Come back when it's all over and we'll share our stories with you and your readers."

Philip tried for several minutes to stress the importance of the assignment, but the officer remained resistant. This intransigence frustrated Philip. He would have to return tomorrow or another time when this soldier was not on duty.

As he turned to leave, however, the door to the Commandant's office burst open and a tall mustached British General in his mid-fifties walked into the reception area. He was loud and assertive. "Lieutenant Bryson, I thought I told you I needed that Palestine report as soon as possible," he blurted out. "Now, where the hell is it? And pour out that drink. I told everyone, including you, there'll be no alcohol consumed while on duty"

"Sir, I apologize. I'll get the file immediately, General Allenby—and I'll dump the G & T immediately. Meanwhile, I've been trying to get rid of this nosey reporter for the past few minutes," Lieutenant Bryson explained. While he went to another room searching for the tardy paperwork, the Commandant turned toward Philip. "Who are you? And what do you want?" he asked, somewhat annoyed.

Philip explained his predicament and pleaded for a chance to interview senior British officers. "There are millions of Americans anxious to learn of your campaigns in the Near East," he remarked.

The explanation apparently worked. The General smiled. "You're absolutely correct," he said. "I think it's a brilliant idea. Why don't you begin by interviewing me? I'm still getting acquainted here, but I have some fresh ideas about the situation. Come into my office while my assistant is looking for that infernal report."

Philip was stunned at his reversal of fortune. But he entered the office and began interviewing with the obliging officer.

"Let me introduce myself first. I'm General Edmund Allenby, the new Commander of the Egyptian Expeditionary Force. In fact, I've only been in Cairo for two days—just sent out here to replace General Murray who ran this operation for the past year."

Philip extended his congratulations. "Can you tell me, then, what London expects from you that General Murray did not accomplish?" he inquired.

"Ah, you're sharp, Kaplan. No small talk. The first question goes directly to the heart of the matter," the General commented. "I can't get personal, but I can tell you this: things are going to be different. From the conduct of men stationed here at GHQ, to the tactics and resources we use in battle, there will be changes made very soon."

Allenby suggested that his background as a cavalry officer probably accounted for his assignment to the desert theater since when it came to combat in the sand mounted soldiers remained critical. He mentioned that he was at Mons in 1914, Ypres in 1915, and Arras earlier this year. "I've seen where cavalrymen are impractical. They were mowed down by German machine guns. But I'm here to show that in the Middle East man and horse—and sometimes camel—are indispensable to victory."

Philip was amazed at the coincidence of the General's experiences with his own in France. For a fleeting moment he wanted to sit back and share memories of those battles against the Germans.

"But, I am not just a cavalry officer, Mr. Kaplan," Allenby continued. "I know what modern technology has done in Europe, and I'll emphasize that when we make our push toward Gaza and Palestine and then Syria and Turkey. Tanks don't work here very well, but the airplane is a wonderful instrument for spotting the enemy's location. Johnny Turk can't escape the gaze of a good pilot trolling the skies in a Sopworth Pup or an S.E. 5a.

"We also need to intensify our use of machine guns and long-range artillery," he added. "Our infrastructure needs improvement. We need to extend our rail lines. We need new pipelines to deliver water for the men and for our horses and camels. We also need better roads for our trucks.

"In short, we need changes. And changes there will be. Morale will be unified and focused on the tasks at hand. And the EEF will start employing the lessons of the European frontlines. One of my first moves will be to leave the flesh-pots and other decadent distractions of Cairo and move GHQ closer to the fighting in Gaza. In the next few days this whole circus will be moving 300 miles northeast of here. You can't expect regular soldiers to risk their lives on the battlefield while their leaders are drowning themselves in liquor and beautiful women far from the fighting."

THE HEADLONG FURY

When Lieutenant Bryson returned, he seemed surprised to see Philip sitting and chatting with the General. "Lieutenant, please come in and I'll take that file, thank you," Allenby said. "This is Mr. Walter Kaplan. He is from the United States. He's writing a series of articles on our battles. Please allow him access to all EEF officers. And if he wants to meet with me again—be it here or in the Sinai when we move our headquarters—afford him every courtesy in making the proper contacts." With that unambiguous order, Philip concluded the interview and departed.

He retired to the Savoy bar for his favorite drink, a Ramos gin fizz and a chance to assess what had just happened. He left the conversation certain that he had struck a responsive chord with the new head of the EEF. Philip didn't care that Allenby might be using him for personal or professional advancement in London, he was happy that his Near East assignment had not been stifled by the defiance of a narrow-minded junior officer.

The fact that the Commandant had urged him to speak freely with other officers assured Philip that this was an unusual leader, a man who was confident in the support of his staff and in his own exercise of authority.

"Hello," said the man sitting at the bar next to him. "You must be the American journalist I just saw leaving General Allenby's office. I'm Lieutenant Colonel G. E. Badcock."

"Nice to meet you, sir," replied Philip. "Yes, that was me with your new boss. He's a striking fellow."

"You don't have to tell me. We all love him—and he's only been here for two days," Badcock remarked. "Our previous Commandant, General Murray, was aloof and ineffective. To a man, we all think Allenby is smashing. You can bet on it: he'll change the tide of battle in the Middle East. Just wait and watch."

"How so?" Philip inquired.

"Well, he's immediately changed morale around here. As soon as he reached GHQ he came to visit each officer under his command. He actually shook my hand and asked how I was doing. Now that's a simple act, but General Murray never did it. And Allenby doesn't forget names. It's as if he really cares about his officers and men. There's a different atmosphere here. And it's been accomplished in jig time.

"I understand that Allenby is commandeering every bottle of beer in Egypt and sending it to the front for thirsty non-Muslim troops and laborers building roads and laying rails in the hot sun. That's what kind of a leader he is. Everyone here is ready to fight for this man."

"But how do you feel about moving from Cairo to the Sinai?" Philip asked.

Badcock stared squarely at Philip. "What am I supposed to say: 'I'll miss the parties and the call girls?' It may come as a shock to you, Kaplan, but first, last, and always I'm a trained soldier. That's why I'm here. I didn't join the Army to have wild flings in the Egyptian desert. No one really prefers Cairo to being home. So, let's end this bloody war as soon as possible and get back to England, Australia, New Zealand, India, or wherever home is.

"Did you know that earlier this month Arthur Henderson of the British War Council estimated that seven million men on all sides have been killed thus far in this war? Seven million! That's a staggering number. He also calculated that at least another seven million have been wounded, many crippled for life. That's fourteen million casualties, and there's no end in sight. How much more can our civilization withstand?"

Several days later Philip took General Allenby's suggestion and headed for the frontline in the Sinai Peninsula. From the Cairo Station he caught the Egyptian Railways morning train to the Suez Canal. Immediately across the Canal was the town of El-Kantara. Once a lethargic oasis, it was now the vibrant center of EEF activities in the area.

Here men and materiel were assembled and sent north on the Sinai Military Railway or by transport truck to the village of Rafah, the deepest EEF penetration thus far into Palestine. From the opposite direction, wounded soldiers flowed into town for advanced medical attention, while Turkish prisoners of war were funneled through El-Kantara in open box cars headed for internment elsewhere in Egypt. And from the east camel caravans flowed continuously into the city bringing everything from foodstuffs to firearms.

El-Kantara was alive with foot- and hoof-traffic. EEF soldiers and Bedouin camel herders competed for space on the crowded dirt streets. Columns of pack horses also stopped traffic. As he walked toward the main offices of the relocated GHQ, Philip had to stop several times to allow camel caravans to pass. Similarly, military automobiles and trucks, which were plentiful, also had to wait impatiently for the vital caravans to pass by. It didn't take Philip long to figure out the pecking order in El-Kantara: pack animals did not stop for anyone or anything; automobiles were next in line; and human beings, whether walking alone or marching in formation, were at the bottom of the priority list.

Inside headquarters Philip learned that ranking EEF officers were attending a ceremony and were not expected back for another hour. Impatiently, he retired to the empty waiting room. While he passed the time he thumbed through a pile of old American and British magazines stacked on a small table. Most of the publications were well worn, a testimony to the many people who had sat for countless hours to keep their appointments.

Most of the publications were interesting, but one monthly caught his attention. It was the American news magazine, *The World's Work*, from September 1914. This particular issue was entitled "The War Manual." The cover presented its contents as "Facts Everyone Needs to Know About the Causes of the War, the Armies, Navies, Finances, and Principal Characters of the Countries Involved."

As he read through the thick publication, he was struck by some of the expert analyses offered in the earliest days of hostilities. For a man who had recently left Russia with its military in shambles, it was interesting to read one expert declaring that "The Russians impressed me as a magnificent fighting force. They are heavy and slow in movement, but their rank and file knows no thought but that of obedience."

The prognosticators were enthusiastic about the Austro-Hungarian military, too. One asserted "Austria will surprise the world in her preparedness in aviation." Another contended "The Austrian soldiers form an ideal military force. They are as strong and hardy as the Germans, but they have all the active mobility of the French. The Hungarians are of the same type and are, if that were possible, even more patriotic and more greatly imbued with the war spirit."

In actuality, the Austro-Hungarian forces were fairly ineffective after the early months of war. Invading both Serbia and Rumania, only massive intervention by the Germans saved the Hapsburg forces and turned defeat into substantial victory. Still the experts in 1914 lauded Austro-Hungarian prowess. "The Serbians will be no easy task for Austria, but the result...is inevitable, for Austria must conquer with her superior force, her superior equipment, and her splendid training," proclaimed one writer.

Another misguided expert assured readers that "Rumania is strictly for peace, but I have never seen a more magnificent force of men that constitute her Army. Her aeronautic corps is highly advanced and her artillery equal in efficiency to that of France." In reality, Rumania was practically knocked out of the war by the time Philip was reading this article.

In an article concerning the Ottoman Empire, another expert argued that the Sultan's military would prove decisive. "Turkey must be seriously considered in this conflict," he wrote. "Her arms might easily be the balance of power. There is no better fighting force in the world today than the Turks."

Next to that last comment, some British reader had penciled in the comment: "PREPOSTEROUS!" It was obvious that this unsolicited commentator had made his one-word critique before February to November 1915. That's when the Ottoman military slaughtered a Franco-British force—augmented by soldiers from Newfoundland, India, New Zealand and Australia—that had invaded the Gallipoli Peninsula in an attempt to wrest from Turkey this strategic site overlooking the Straits of the Dardanelles.

But perhaps the most stunning miscalculation by the observers in *World's Work* had to do with battlefield casualties. According to one medical expert assessing the nascent war, "Soldiers who escape death on the battlefield in the great conflict now going on will have a far better chance of returning home alive than any soldiers ever had before." In a conflict with at least seven million combatants killed by 1917, this prediction did not strike Philip as particularly accurate.

As he continued to read, Philip was oblivious to the men who joined him in the waiting room. When he finished with the magazine and began choosing another, one of those sitting near him spoke out. "Sometimes I've waited as long as four hours," he remarked. "Patience is your only weapon when waiting for the Commander—any Commander."

Philip did not raise his head when he replied. "But while you sit, curiosity can be richly rewarded by some of these magazines," he said as he continued to rummage through the reading materials. When he finally selected a new journal and turned toward the man who had commented, he was amazed by what he saw. Here was young man whose accent betrayed him as being British. Yet, he was dressed like a Bedouin sheik fresh from the Negev desert. Despite the dark turban and a flowing gown that covered him from neck to feet he was obviously not Arabian. Philip was baffled.

"Sorry I interrupted your search," the stranger said. "My name's Lawrence, Tom Lawrence. Even before this place became the GHQ of the Egyptian Expeditionary Force it was the office of the local officer corps. I've been through this waiting game too many times. But don't give up, your officer will always get here—just never on time."

Philip knew that he was talking to the renowned Lawrence of Arabia, but he acted normally. "Nice to meet you," he responded. "I'm Walt Kaplan from the *Chicago Tribune*. I'm on assignment for my newspaper—writing about the EEF and the Turks. What do you do here in the desert?"

"Well, I used to be an archeologist," said Lawrence. "I loved digging up historical artifacts for museums. But London impressed me into this man's army and designated me as a commissioned officer. So now I fight Turks and their assorted friends.

"What's your rank," Philip asked. "I can't see any stripes on the clothing you're wearing."

Lawrence smiled. "I'm a Captain, or is it a Major. Perhaps I'm a Lieutenant? I can't keep up. It depends on what GHQ thinks of me at the time," he added. "That's why I'm here today. I have to introduce myself to General Allenby and get back to my troops as quickly as possible. I'll have to ask him what my rank is."

"In that case, please take my place in the queue." said Philip. "I'm waiting for Allenby, too. I was the first person in the room, so as soon as the General returns you may go in. I'll take your position in line."

"That's very courteous of you, Walt," Lawrence remarked. "I appreciate it very much."

The conversation continued as Philip explained further his journalistic assignment, and the unassuming T. E. Lawrence talked about military matters.

When the Commandant finally arrived from his ceremony, Lawrence immediately entered his office. Philip and the others sat there for another half-hour or more. When the office door finally reopened, Philip was surprised to see Lawrence waving him into his conference with the Allenby.

Philip responded to the invitation and walked into the ongoing meeting.

"Mr. Kaplan," said the General with an attitude of authority, "you're here to assess the EEF and its capacities. I'm glad. I was impressed with you when we met in Cairo last week.

"But now I have an idea that could win you some great journalistic prizes back in the States. In the spirit of Entente cooperation and informing the American public, how would you like to be an actual observer of the history of this Middle East campaign?"

"How so?" asked Philip with great curiosity.

"Captain Lawrence is ready to deliver a strategic blow against the Turks. He and his Arab irregulars are going to hit a key enemy site, the port of Aqaba. He says you might learn something about us if you went along for the experience. I can't give any more details than that, but he will fill you in should you wish to join him."

It didn't take Philip long to decide. "I'm game, sir," Philip said. "When do we leave and on what train?"

Lawrence of Arabia laughed out loud at the idea. "We leave as soon as I walk out of this office. And we don't go by any smooth train; we're going on backs of very uncomfortable camels."

"By camel? Across the God-forsaken desert? In this heat? There must be another way, Lawrence" Philip asked in desperation.

"No other way to get there," the Englishman remarked. "There's no highway or railroad to Aqaba. We could travel by the Red Sea, but that would be too risky. Ottoman long-guns are situated all along the eastern shore of the waterway. They would blow our boat apart in short order.

"But if you could fly an airplane, we could get there in a few hours."

"You're pulling my leg?" said Philip incredulously.

"No, not at all," answered Captain Lawrence. GHQ has a reconnaissance aircraft, a two-seater, parked at a landing strip just outside El-Kantara. It's on loan from the Royal Flying Corps. I rely on it for aerial photography. I mean I order an RFC pilot and his photographer to take pictures of areas we plan to hit. It gives us a great advantage. I've used it a lot to scout the terrain around Aqaba."

"Well, we're in luck. I do know how to fly. Back in Chicago, I'm a licensed pilot. Haven't done it for a while, but let's go by air instead of camel," Philip responded.

Lawrence was momentarily speechless. "Well, I am stunned. You're a pilot? Then, Tallyho! Let's get going!" he said excitedly.

Before the two men left, however, General Allenby reminded Lawrence that he would be in the Egyptian capital for the next several weeks. "I want to know directly from you what happens in Aqaba. So, when the battle is over, come immediately to Cairo and let me know the details."

"Will do, sir," agreed Lawrence as he and Philip left the GHQ building.

Philip was pleased that he would be flying again. Still, he played down his piloting skills for fear his passenger might question him about his background. He had never flown a British machine, but the bi-plane waiting outside town looked much like the Nieuports with which he was familiar.

"This is a dandy," said T. E. Lawrence. "It's an Armstrong Whitworth F.K. 8. We call it the Big Ack. As I said, we use it principally for aerial photography. But we have firepower capacity on this baby—Lewis machine gun mounts on the both sides of the fuselage, and a Vickers machine gun bolted in front of the pilot. And the plane can be used as a bomber. All this versatility, and at a swift 95 miles per hour!

"Our route will be to fly in a southeast direction toward the port town of Aqaba which is located at the top of the Gulf of Aqaba. Our landing site is about twenty miles from the target. You'll recognize the site by the large number of men, horses, and camels we've assembled for our final push. Because Aqaba is about 200 miles from here, and the Big Ack has a range of 270 miles, we should have no problem getting there. Coming back may be another matter."

"Look at that," Philip remarked in jest as he entered his cockpit. This aircraft has dual controls—one located in each passenger compartment. That means that if anything happens to me while I'm flying, you can land the plane and save our lives."

"Are you crazy, Kaplan?" Lawrence exclaimed with sincerity. "I don't fly airplanes, and I certainly can't land one. All I know is automobiles and motorcycles. If something happens to you on this flight, then it happens to me. Please don't fall out or have a heart attack or get shot by a Turkish combat pilot!"

Philip smiled broadly suggesting that he was simply joking.

"Oh, so you think this is funny," Lawrence answered. "Just wait until I get you on a camel. Then we'll see who has the upper hand."

It took Philip only a few minutes to adjust to the unfamiliar control panel. After that the flight proceeded without incident. Lawrence had worried that the Ottoman Air Force based in nearby Ma'an might have fighter planes in the air when he and Philip neared the Gulf. Lawrence didn't want to engage the Turks in a dog fight, especially since in the interest of weight and speed, Philip had detached the machine guns and left them at the airstrip. Fortunately, this threat never materialized.

It was a noisy flight, but from their conversations that afternoon Philip learned that Lawrence was playing a significant role for the EEF in this theater of the war. As a civilian archeologist laboring in the Arabian wastelands years before the war, he had built a rapport with local populations and tribal leaders. He spoke Arabic, understood and respected Islam, and appreciated the history and culture of the native population. To most Arabs he was "El Aurens," a name of esteem and affection.

In 1916 as a junior officer in the British Army he helped spur the various Arabian tribes in the Near East to rise in nationalistic rebellion against Ottoman rule. It was called the Arab Revolt, and Lawrence helped to trigger it by appealing to ethnic pride. He urged Arab leaders to take command of their own destinies in the same way Balkan peoples were fighting for their own lands and for national independence.

Lawrence worked closest with Hussein-ibn-Ali, the Sharif of Mecca and protector of the Holy Sites in Mecca and Medina. Hussein was also governor of the Hejaz region, a large and strategic desert area located along the eastern shore of the Red Sea from the Gulf of Aqaba southward to Yemen. A few months after the Arab Revolt erupted, Lawrence persuaded Hussein to reorganize his lands as the Kingdom of Hejaz and to install himself as its monarch. Subsequently, he helped King Hussein to organize a formidable army of Arab warriors to confront the hostile Ottomans.

The Royal Army was commanded by Hussein's son, Emir Feisal, who dispatched his cousin, Sharif Nasir, and forty Hejaz fighters to await Lawrence's return to from El-Kantara. Lawrence, however, had recruited substantially more troops from the Howeitat tribe of Bedouins led by Auda ibu Tayi. If this contingent could capture Aqaba, the harbor could become the strategic for supplying Entente soldiers in their campaign to wrest Palestine and Syria from the Turks.

By manpower standards of the European fronts, the Arab force was miniscule. Feisal's contribution, plus the Howeitat units and fighters from several other sedentary and nomadic peoples of the region—Kawakiba, Shararat, Haywat, and Rwalla—totaled fewer than 1200 men. Most were cavalrymen mounted on horses and camels. But they were quick to dismount and become guerrilla foot soldiers. On such a meager contingent of warriors rested Emir Feisal's political dream of creating a pan-Arab state as an expression of Arab dignity and newly-appreciated nationalism.

In British military circles Arab soldiers were generally ridiculed. Too few of them, too undisciplined, too untrained; maybe good for hit-and-run raids in the desert, but not really prepared to take on the forces of a powerful country. El Aurens, however, never accepted such criticism. To him, this mobile army was a potent and stealthy fighting force, the military vanguard of a national movement that would inevitably alter politics in the Near East and Mesopotamia.

The Arab soldiers became masters of guerilla warfare. They blew up random rail lines, attacked outposts throughout the sandy wasteland, and generally disrupted the Ottoman forces in an unpredictable pattern of harassment. Such unsystematic attacks never failed to send Turkish troops in all directions in a fruitless search for the Arab perpetrators. They, however, were already miles away and never found.

After hours of uneventful flying at top speed, Philip reached the Arab encampment. Lawrence pointed toward a long stretch of hard sand that was perfect for landing.

Once the plane touched down and taxied to a halt, a crowd of joyous irregulars rushed to surround it and began chanting "El Aurens! El Aurens!" It was obvious to Philip that Lawrence of Arabia was more than a battle leader, he was a genuine hero to these native fighters. But he was also a humble man. He accepted the gratitude of the troops, but he insisted that Feisal was the head of this force and this was an Arab struggle to win or lose.

The final push toward Aqaba was on schedule. It began with preparatory raids on a series of Turkish outposts. These attacks lessened Ottoman resistance and bred confidence among the Arabs. The subsequent skirmish at Aba al-Lissan resulted in 300 Turkish killed and 160 captured. Arab forces suffered two deaths.

Importantly, these victories also delivered a message to the Ottoman enemy: resistance was futile, fight at your own peril. By the time of the final assault on July 6 the message had obviously been received. When Arab forces entered Aqaba the town and port were empty, the Turkish defenders scattered—in part because of the fierceness of the invaders, in part because of shelling from a British gunboat which had joined the battle earlier that morning.

Philip was an eager spectator at these events, but for diplomatic and personal reasons he was careful not to participate in the fighting. He was, however, pleased with the performance of the victorious troops. To those who felt that the Arabs lacked discipline and shooting accuracy and resembled a band of desert raiders more than a formal army, the Battle of Aqaba suggested otherwise. What Philip observed that day was purpose and bravery.

"We did it, Kaplan. We won!" Lawrence exclaimed. "Do you realize the significance of this victory? This is historic. July 6, 1917 will go down as the first defeat of a major nation's military by a modern Arab army. It opens a vital port to EEF shipping and assures Allenby a safe harbor for supplying his campaign of liberation in northern Arabia. It also opens an unlimited political future for these abused people. This is the day Arabia changed. The Arab Near East will never be the same."

THE HEADLONG FURY

That evening the happy troops celebrated. Camp fires were lit; sheep and cattle were slaughtered and roasted; the tensions of battle gave way to merriment. In the midst of the revelry, Lawrence, Philip, and Sharif Nasir sat by a bonfire and discussed the implications of the day's events.

"This victory proves the effectiveness of your guerrilla tactics, El Aurens," Nasir remarked. "By attacking the Hejez Railway at various points we kept garrisons of Turkish soldiers preoccupied hunting for us in places we were not. The Hejez Railway is vital to supplying Ottoman forces. But bombed tracks here, destroyed locomotives there, a bridge demolished somewhere else: your actions distracted the Turks who went in all directions trying to find us. And that was not only your idea, it was your activity. You designed and led most of these raids, El Aurens. For your leadership and faith in us, we thank you very much."

"I appreciate the compliment, my friend, but Arab men still had to win the fight. Arab commanders had to keep them in line and inspire them. And Arabs had to stand up to the mighty Turks, which they did spectacularly," the British officer responded.

"We have to defeat the Ottomans before it is too late," Nasir added. "The weaker the Turks become, the more they are dominated by Germany. If they win this war, the Germans will dominate Constantinople, and the Ottoman Empire will become a vassal state to Berlin.

"Can you imagine that? Infidels controlling us! The Holy cities of Mecca and Medina under the Kaiser's authority! At least the Turks are Muslims; the Germans are Christians, mostly rebel Protestants at that. That would be intolerable."

"I understand your concerns, but where do you go from here?" Philip asked. "I know how important Aqaba is. But it's yours now, and the Royal Navy will make sure it's not recaptured. But what's next? Do your forces and the Bedouin raiders fade back into the mountains of Hejez—go back to their sheep and their crops—or are there other political and military objectives ahead for them?"

"Until the Ottomans are driven out of Arab lands, there will always be other objectives," answered Nasir. "On that matter I am sure my cousin, Feisal, agrees with me. In our coastal lands Palestine must be freed; Syria is unliberated; Lebanon remains controlled from Constantinople; and the various Trans-Jordanian territories are still occupied by Turks.

"The eastern regions of Arabia, too, are not fully cleansed of the Ottomans. The British took Baghdad and Samarra a few months ago, but are these cities truly secured? I think not. Then what about the rest of Iraq and the rest of Mesopotamia? Every place where the Arab population predominates must be permanently rescued from the Turks if we are to create a proper Arab state.

"And the Sultan understands the threat we pose to his authority. He has called all Muslims to wage *jihad* against you Westerners. He hopes to use religion to reunite Arabs and Turks in holy war against the British and French—but, of course, not against the Germans and Austrians and Hungarians. But we see through his actions; they will not work. Arab nationalism is not a political lever to be used for Turkish interests And Islam cannot be manipulated to augment the temporal power of the Sultan."

Lawrence interrupted Nasir's explanation. "But what about the non-Arab peoples living in your lands—many there for generations? What will their fate be in an Arab state?" he asked Nasir. "What about people with religions other than Islam? What about people who don't speak Arabic? What will you do with these infidels?"

"These are good questions that demand answers," Philip said to Faisal. "For instance what is your viewpoint on the Armenian situation? Armenians are Christians—is there room for them in an Islamic Arab state?

"Or, what do you think of Zionism?" he continued. "You have read the holy books. You know that Judaism has its ancestral roots in the Near East. Jewish people remain numerous in Arab lands, and there are many Jews in Europe who would migrate here in an instant if a protected Jewish settlement or state were established. That would be Theodore Herzl's dream come true. But it's not an Arab dream or even a Muslim consideration."

Philip continued his effort to get Nasir to be specific. "The Hebrew people may be Semitic just like you, but their language is not Arabic. They couldn't become Arabs if they wanted. What do you do with the Jews in the great new Arabic domain?"

Nasir chose his words carefully. "We Arabs are peaceful people," he began. "We have endured domination for centuries without demanding our independence. Our lands and our souls are vast enough to welcome all of the children of Abraham. Like Muslims and Christians, Jews are People of the Book. Let them come to Palestine. Let them establish their own Jewish areas. As long as they respect our religion and our rights, I say, 'Welcome, my brothers.'

"But there is one caution" added the Arab leader. "What I'm saying can happen only if the European Powers don't interfere with our new country. We Arabs want friends, not masters. Already my cousin and I are hearing of secret plans to divide Ottoman lands between France and Great Britain. Palestine, Trans-Jordania, and Iraq for the British—Syria and Lebanon for the French. We will not accept such an arrangement. If that happens, all Arab promises are cancelled."

"Speaking of the British reminds me I need to reach Cairo and report to General Allenby as soon as possible," interjected Lawrence. "Plus we have to return the airplane. It's too uncertain to fly at night, but we can leave at daybreak."

Philip was still thinking about Nasir's warning when he and Lawrence met early the next day. On camels they retreated the twenty miles to retrieve their aircraft. After refueling with Turkish gasoline seized at Aba al-Lissan, they were able to take off for the Sinai Peninsula.

Once again it was what a defenseless war pilot desires, an uneventful flight with clear flying weather, no enemy fighter planes in the skies, and a safe landing at home. Lawrence and Philip quickly returned the airplane at the airfield. They then jumped aboard an EEF truck for a short ride to the ferryboat dock. Here they crossed the narrow expanse of the Red Sea and raced to the railroad station. The men arrived in time to board the last train of the day to Cairo.

Relaxing in a passenger coach speeding toward the Egyptian capital, Philip had several hours to probe Lawrence's ideas about the war. The most interesting insight he gained was the Englishman's view that the battle was a racial showdown with Germans out to reshape the world. "It's so obvious to me that Germany is fighting to gain control of a swatch of territory stretching from Berlin to India," Lawrence explained. "The British—along with the French, the Italians, the Slavs, and now the Americans and the Arabs—must stop the Huns. It's as simple as that.

"Surely you can see the Germanic plan as it unfolds," he continued. "The alliance of Berlin and Vienna conquers poor but strategic Serbia. And through military threats and secret agreements the Dual Powers soon dominate Bulgaria and Greece. This effectively turns the Balkans into a Germanic corridor leading directly to Constantinople.

"With such a commercial corridor, consider the position Germany has acquired in the decaying Ottoman Empire. Already there are German troops in Turkey. German advisors train Ottoman fighters and sometimes lead them into battle. German loans finance the Sultan's feeble economy. Supplies of food and war materials from Berlin keep the Empire alive. Turkish politicians, especially those aging Young Turks, rely on German advisors and German bribes.

"And let's not forget the Berlin-to-Baghdad Railway. Germany has been building it for years. Much of it is already in operation. But imagine this: a single German railroad running from Berlin through Austria to the Balkans and Constantinople, then across Anatolia and Syria to eastern Iraq and the Persian Gulf. What an economic and military asset that would be. Mesopotamia in the hands of the Germans would be a cannon pointed directly at British Empire.

"Soon German power would extend eastward across Persia to the Indian border—southward through Arabia to Egypt and Hejez, and northward into the oil-rich lands of Moslem Russia. This would be the fullest realization of the German policy of *Drang nach Osten*, the 'push to the East' that rabid nationalists in Berlin and Vienna have been advancing for decades.

"Let me ask you something, Kaplan. Do you know how long it takes for a British freighter to sail from London through the Suez Canal to Karachi, India?"

Philip had no answer.

"Let's face it, you don't know. Well, it takes fifteen days. More than two weeks! But a land journey using the Baghdad Railway and a paved highway to Karachi would take eight days. That's a full week saved. That would be mean death for British interests in Central Asia, and a monumental victory for German commerce and militarism. And if, as some speculate, the Berlin-to-Baghdad Railway expands to become a Berlin-to-Bombay railway, the British Empire would be severely undermined, perhaps destroyed. Overnight, the Suez Canal would be obsolete. Our dominant position in Mediterranean commerce would be weakened, our alliances and trade agreements shattered, and our naval and military prowess undermined throughout the colonial world. Germany would be ascendant, while Britain, I'm sorry to say, would be in rapid decline.

"You can see now, I hope, how a Germanic victory would mean Berlin's dominance of Europe, the Near East, and much of Central Asia? I am speaking of nothing less than creating and controlling a worldwide German empire. In fact, let's call it what it really would be: the Caliphate of Berlin"

"Point taken," Philip replied.

He thought for a few seconds then asked Lawrence, "There's a question that has bothered me about the war for a long time. Do you think the entire struggle is based on racial and cultural differences that date to the 5th, 6th, or 7th century? Do you think the war councils in Vienna and Berlin seriously believe that one race of mankind is superior to another, so much so that they are willing to see perhaps ten million people killed—many of them Germans—to assert the preeminence of their race?

"Imperialistic expansion, I'll buy that. Economic advantage, I'll accept that, too. But it's difficult for me to believe that racial preeminence is an underlying factor in this war."

"I know, it sounds preposterous, old man," El Aurens answered, "but beneath the thin crust of civility we Europeans have built, you'll find aggressive man—brutal and emotional, certain that his way is the true way, eager to believe in destructive myths, and forever justifying intolerant prejudices as expressions of the will of his God."

"That's a gloomy picture," Philip remarked. "I'm not sure I totally agree. Maybe you've been around those Bedouin tribes too long. The West has so many civilizing forces at work, from religious institutions to universal education to representative government. Civilization is the byproduct of taming the savage breast."

"Ha! You miss the obvious," Lawrence remarked. "The priests of civilization sprinkle holy water on all sides fighting this war. Many of our most educated citizens want more death, more expansion. From Kaisers to elected Presidents, the thirst for blood goes unslaked. Civility is a costume, Kaplan, and it can be changed very quickly."

Lawrence continued. "Here's an analogy: in your mind's eye assume a man dressed splendidly in a tuxedo and a silk top hat. How dapper and regimented he appears, the perfect *gentle*man. But when he catches his finger in a carriage door his emotions instantly erupt. Despite his clothing and breeding and sense of decorum, he screams and curses and runs around writhing in pain; perhaps he even sheds a tear or smashes a vase in anger because of the discomfort.

"Now, think of wartime emotionalism as a finger slammed in a carriage door. All your learning and praying and voting can't stop the emergence of a man's primal character. All the Savile Row suits you can ever wear can't cloak the incivility brought forth by the pain. That's why men kill easily in war but abhor murder in peacetime. War reintroduces us to our instincts. It brings us back to our original animal selves. And, when it has the seal of approval from our countrymen who endorse it as patriotic and heroic, sanctioned by God, defensive of Good and destructive of Evil, killing becomes irresistible.

"Damn it, man, before I became a warrior celebrated for murdering Turks, I was an archeologist, an academic ditch-digger. How tame can a man be? Kaplan, you haven't had your finger pinched in the carriage door yet. You've been safe in America for the first three years of this struggle. But you're in it now, friend. You'll soon discover that I'm right."

When the train arrived at the Cairo station, Philip and his British companion parted ways. Lawrence left for his de-briefing with General Allenby, and Philip took a taxi to Shepheard's Hotel to begin packing. He also hoped to finish his report that evening and file it at the Royal Bank of Scotland in the morning. Although he was tired, he was actually anxious to receive his next assignment from Washington. He tried to guess where he might be headed next. Perhaps here was going to German East Africa or Ethiopia where the war was marked by occasionally fierce clashes between British and German forces.

He hoped he wouldn't have to travel all the way to the Orient where Japan was an Entente ally conducting naval operations against German colonial interests along the coast of China and in various German islands in the South Pacific. Maybe he was headed for the Balkans, or perhaps Italy. After all, this Great War was an international conflict, not just a struggle in Western Europe with France and Great Britain on one side and Germany on the other.

In the morning he checked out and made his way to the bank. With no secrecy or high drama this time, he deposited his commentary and found new instructions and another unmarked key to a safe-deposit box. This time he was ordered to Venice to analyze the Italian war against Austria, a conflict fought mainly in the mountainous regions of northeastern Italy. There was also more cash—some Italian lire, but mostly convertible American dollars. Interestingly, there was no new passport. He would continue to be Walter Kaplan, a *Chicago Tribune* journalist.

This was an assignment Philip was eager to pursue. He had seen much of the western Italian coast and Rome when he journeyed to the Farnese Palace several years ago. But ever since he was a youngster glamour photos of Venice made him want to visit this "floating city." He would not be going there as a tourist this time, but he welcomed any opportunity to experience *Venezia* as well as the Alpine regions to the north of this singular city.

He hailed a taxi and headed for the Cairo Station to catch the next train to Alexandria, stopping only to throw his old key and his shredded instructions into the Nile. It was time for a change of scenery.

Philip found a comfortable window seat, pulled several British magazines from his luggage, and prepared himself for hours of restful reading while the train rolled toward the Mediterranean coast.

He paid no attention when he felt someone sit next to him. "Hello, I'm Agnes Hightower," said the woman now seated on his right. "I'm from Des Moines, Iowa—that's in the United States," she added. When she received no response, she nudged Philip's elbow and repeated her self-introduction.

Reluctantly, Philip turned to reply to his fellow traveler. "Hello, Miss Hightower, I'm Walt Kaplan from Chicago. That's not too far from Des Moines." He smiled and returned his gaze to the journals he was anxious to read.

"Oh, I'll bet you're a journalist. I can tell by the way you devour those magazines," she said. "I'm a journalist, too. I write for a newspaper syndicate that provides stories to papers from St. Cloud to Sioux City. Not very big, but we keep the Midwest up to date on what's happening."

Again, Philip smiled and nodded politely. He returned to his reading materials hoping this intrusive woman would no longer bother him.

No luck. For the first twenty-five miles of the railroad trip Agnes Hightower peppered him with questions to which he responded minimally. Finally, Philip surrendered to her talkativeness. He folded his magazines and placed them at his side, then fell into fluid conversation with her.

For the next few hours Philip tested his acting skills. Without volunteering anything personal or accurate, he explained his profession, made up fake details about stories he had never covered, discussed his coverage of the World War, and otherwise danced around the truth.

Agnes Hightower, as she explained herself, was actually a crime reporter for a newspaper syndicate. But she finagled an Egyptian assignment from her editor who wanted an on-the-ground perspective on the war. The editor sent her to Cairo because Turkey was not at war with the United States. He felt it would be safer than assigning her to France or Great Britain. Now, after two weeks in Egypt, she was on her way back to Iowa.

Philip explained that he was headed for Rome and would travel by boat from Egypt. He asked for recommendations on vessels departing today or tomorrow.

"I already have my ticket home. I'm booked on a Dutch liner going to Amsterdam and then to New York. But I arrived here on a very nice boat that I hired in Athens. Wonderful captain. His name is Vasalakis, Konstantin Vasalakis. He's a garrulous man with a fetching personality. But he is also a great seafarer. His boat is the *Star of Hellas*.

I think he's based in Alexandria. I suggest you contact him when you get there. You won't get any discount if you mention that I sent you, but tell him anyway, please. Tell him I had an excellent trip and I still talk flatteringly about his skills as a mariner."

"I'll do that," said Philip. "Maybe I can hire his boat for an impulsive trip to Italy. And, I will mention your name, even though I shouldn't expect a discount. But, who knows?"

Once at the harbor in Alexandria, Philip began his search for a "Mediterranean cruise" to Venice. Several boats were not leaving for days. Others would take him only as far as Sicily at the tip of the Italian boot. Many captains were fearful of being attacked by Austrian warships based on the eastern side of the Adriatic, or worse, by German submarines operating throughout the Mediterranean.

When he inquired about Vasalakis, several of the boat owners knew him and confirmed that he might be a good man to contact. "Vasalakis likes risky assignments," said one Egyptian captain. "He should be tied up farther down the dock."

Eventually, Philip found his way to the *Star of Hellas*. He mentioned Agnes Hightower and her positive experience with his boat. The captain actually recalled bringing her to Egypt. "I remember her," he said. "She was a lovely passenger. I need more clients like Miss Hightower."

Vasalakis was a friendly man. As he explained himself, "I was born in Crete sixty years ago, but I live on the sea, so I am owned by no country. I am a citizen of the sea." He added that his steamship delivered varied cargoes throughout the Mediterranean. "I won't go beyond the Pillars of Hercules. The ocean is too rough beyond Gibraltar, and I'm afraid my old ship will break apart. But on these waters I'll go anywhere anytime. So, I would be happy to take you to Italy."

Philip smiled and handed the captain $300 in American currency.

Forty-five minutes later the *Star of Hellas* puttered out of Alexandria harbor and headed into open waters. Philip was happy to be leaving Egypt. He figured the voyage would take about twenty-four hours. This was not a cruise liner, however, so for food and drink he brought aboard his own supplies. He poured himself two fingers of Scotch and sat back to watch the eastern Mediterranean pass by.

After a few hours of smooth sailing, however, Philip detected something peculiar. The *Star of Hellas* was not heading west toward Italy. Instead, it was bearing due north. When he asked Captain Vasalakis about the direction he was traveling, the old man just shrugged his shoulders and answered in Greek. Philip tried French and Russian, but still the answer came in Greek—this from a man who a few hours earlier had negotiated this voyage in satisfactory English.

When the captain bolted the door to his chambers and refused to hear further complaints, Philip recognized that he was in danger. He decided on a physical confrontation with Vasalakis. But when he picked up an axe to break down the locked door, he was greeted from behind by two burly men with pistols in their hands.

"Sit down, Mr. Kaplan, or I'll blow your brains out," said one of the gunmen in blunt English. "I said sit down. NOW!"

16

All night and morning stiff breezes out of southern Turkey roiled the Mediterranean. Large crashing waves bounced the steamer in all directions. The splash filled the air with salt water. Yet Philip was forced to sit on deck, his hands and feet bound, and his mind searching for answers.

From the boat's course and what he could see, Philip calculated that the *Star of Hellas* was headed for the coast of Turkey. The captain was Greek, but the two armed men spoke in a language he didn't recognize. They might be Ottoman agents, he concluded, but he couldn't be certain. Their guns, however, made it clear that he would comply with whatever they ordered him to do.

Off the port side in the distance Philip could see a large landmass, not big enough to be the Turkish mainland, but too large to be one of the tiny Greek isles dotting the Aegean Sea. Philip decided it must be Cyprus, the large strategic island close to the Turkish mainland. Once an Ottoman possession, the island was now part of the British Empire, appropriated in 1914 by England during the early days of the war. Perhaps that was why Captain Vasalakis stayed several miles away from it.

He was all the more convinced when his captors came on deck and placed a gag in his mouth and dragged him below. He figured that they feared a British ship might spot him bound and gagged and then make inquiries.

Several hours after passing Cyprus the Captain eased his boat into a nondescript Turkish harbor. At gunpoint Philip was ordered to stand up and prepare to disembark.

"Follow me," said a voice from inside the Captain's cabin. When he turned to see the source of the command, he was facing Agnes Hightower.

"What are you doing here?" he inquired in amazement.

"Oh, you poor fool," she answered. "You simple American fool. You've been arrested as a spy, Walter Kaplan. You're a prisoner of the Turkish government. I didn't buy your war-correspondent story for a minute. We know you conspired with General Allenby and Captain Lawrence. We know that you fought in and around Aqaba and killed Turkish soldiers who were defending Ottoman territory. Who are you, Walter Kaplan? What are you doing in this war?"

"A simple fool? You bet," Philip confessed. "I bought your story—all of it. But I can see you're no newspaper woman from Iowa. Who in the hell are you?"

"You're right. I've never been in Des Moines, but I did live for several years in Detroit. When the war broke out I returned to Constantinople to work in the Sultan's secret police. I am Colonel Rana Osman. And that large brown building you see on shore, that is where you will be living for a long time—if you don't die there. Take a good look: this is your future, Mr. Kaplan.

With that Colonel Osman led Philip and his burly captors down a rickety walkway toward a large non-descript building situated near the shoreline. Fenced off from the world around, the old earthen structure was clearly a prison. Philip saw tall gun towers and armed guards carefully perusing the grounds. Electric spotlights were protection against nighttime escapes. Philip couldn't understand the writing on its walls, but he assumed it identified the facility and warned people away.

Inside, he was treated rudely. He was also stripped naked and thoroughly searched for weapons and contraband, then issued a prison uniform. His clothing and his suitcase as well as his money and passport were confiscated and placed in a storage room which, as Philip saw, was filled with other suitcases. Clearly, he was not alone here.

No matter how many ways the interrogator asked him about his activities in Egypt, he answered with variations on the same theme. "My name is Walter Kaplan. I'm a citizen of the United States. I was in Egypt as a journalist investigating a story for a Chicago newspaper. I request a meeting with someone representing U. S. interests in Turkey. And, I demand to be released immediately."

"Mr. Kaplan, we are not wrong," the inquisitor said in English. "Our agents saw you conferring with British military officers. We know you flew an RFC aircraft to Aqaba and were part of Arab attacks on Turkish installations in the area—attacks that killed many of our soldiers. We know that you collaborated with T. E. Lawrence, the butcher the British romantically call Lawrence of Arabia. I can assure you that we Turks do not call him that."

The Turk was crystal clear. "Tell us everything, Mr. Kaplan. We need to know about British operations in the Near East. Tell us the truth, or you will die."

After three hours of such rhetorical banter, the questioner was exasperated. "Take him away," he said to the guards watching the prisoner.

Philip was marched to an underground cell that can best be described as medieval. Straw strewn on the floor, a hard cot for sleeping, a metal bucket in the corner for accumulating human waste, the occasional rat running along the wall, no daylight visible, and a dim electric lamp hanging from the ceiling. Philip recognized the scenario; he had encountered just such a place in an Alexander Dumas novel he read years ago.

The cell was crawling with fleas and lice, and it didn't take long for his body to become covered in bite marks. Although he spent hours picking the pests from his clothing, his hair, and his skin, it made little difference. No matter how many creatures he plucked from his body, they returned once he fell asleep.

Soon it became a game for Philip. He began to count the number of fleas and lice as if there was a competition between the vermin for dominance over his body. At least it broke the monotony of days—or was it weeks?—of solitary confinement. Without seeing the sun or the moon, a man can lose his bearings. It then becomes impossible to gauge the passage of time. Even scratches on the wall are unreliable indicators as time becomes anachronistic.

Feeding time, too, was irregular. But the food, itself, was predictable: cabbage soup with an excess of pepper, stale bread that was sometimes moldy, and weak coffee three times a day. It seldom varied no matter how hungry or disoriented he became.

Eventually, Philip's mind began to weaken. He spoke to himself, laughed uncontrollably sometimes, and frequently cried. He was smart, he told himself. He would wait them out. He would not be broken by any torturer. In the meantime, deprivation affected his psychology as well as his physical well-being

At this low point, the jailers began administering cold showers. At bayonet point he was marched to a shower room when he was forced to stand naked under icy water until he was near fainting. As he stood shivering and unclothed, the questioning would begin again. This form of torture happened several times a day until someone must have decided it was a fruitless technique.

Then they began tying Philip to a post and leaving him standing for hours until his head drooped and he eventually collapsed. That method of torture also proved ineffective.

Somehow, he was able to provide the same evasive answers. He might cry out for Millie and baby Elizabeth—for Chicago and his parents, for happier times. But even under such duress his mind refused to release the name Woodrow Wilson. He continued to repress the truth about his activities, saying nothing the Turks could find informative.

One day two guards came to his room and pushed him upstairs. The brightness of sunlight through the windows was momentarily blinding, but Philip soon adjusted. Almost immediately, he could feel his sanity returning.

He was also placed in a room that contrasted strikingly with his subterranean chamber. This was a tidy chamber with its own sanitary facilities, a proper bed, and a wooden floor that was cleanly swept. In a perverse way it reminded him of his apartment at the Two Swans Hotel in Paris.

He also received better food, and he was served at the same time every day, week after week.

Philip stayed in this glamour cell for a long time. By the scratch calculations he made on the wall, he was there for almost six weeks. It may have been more comfortable, but it was still solitary confinement. He was still cut off from human contact and left alone with his thoughts. No one attempted to interrogate him, and no one ever spoke to him. He was effectively alone with his thoughts.

He tried exercise as a diversion. He sang every song he could remember. In his mind he tried to write his book about Louis XVI. And he slept a lot, always hoping to dream of Millie and Elizabeth.

Then one day for no particular reason the scene shifted. Again two jail guards appeared and returned him to the basement cell with its debased conditions. Philip wept as he was shoved into the room and the door was locked behind him. Time soon became irrelevant as he drifted inward toward his primal instincts. He was going crazy, losing his mind—and he knew it.

A week or so later, the guards returned. This time, however, they dragged him into an interrogation room where a new Torquemada tried to unlock his secrets. But now indignation was gone from Philip's responses. Without hesitation he answered the fundamental questions, elaborating with addresses and relationships, details from conversations, personal matters that were really beyond the scope of the interrogation. However, his mind would still not open its Woodrow Wilson file; and he was unwilling, even unable, to provide details of his interactions with Lawrence and Allenby. For all practical purposes, he had erased from his memory everything specific about his time in Egypt.

The unsuccessful questioner left the room exasperated.

Philip had been in detention for months and still refused to explain his crimes. Since psychological aggression proved ineffective on the prisoner, the Turks switched to an older approach. A muscular man was brought in to question him. Each time Philip gave an unsatisfactory reply, the strong man whacked him with a heavy stick or smashed his fists into Philip's face. Time after time, whack after whack, punch after punch he pummeled the prisoner.

The interrogator wanted to know everything about events in Egypt, but Philip could recall nothing. He wanted to know if Philip was a military advisor or a rifle marksman, a gun-runner for the Arabs or an *agent provocateur*. Perhaps he was a bomb maker, a Bolshevik, a would-be assassin, a social activist organizing protests. Maybe he was a spy or a double-agent for Russia, France or England, Serbia or Rumania or Greece, perhaps for the United States—or possibly Germany, Austria, or Bulgaria.

The important questions kept meeting with silence or evasive answers while the stick and fists continued to pound Philip to the point of collapse. This kind of questioning happened multiple times over a period of weeks until he was removed from the room unconscious and bleeding. He was shipped to the prison's hospital ward for observation.

The hospital was a joke. It was a large barn with dirty mattresses on the floor and a ceiling that dripped when it rained or the snow melted. He stayed here for several days of recuperation before the authorities placed him in a barrack among the general population.

"Wake up. Wake up before they think you're dying." Philip heard the voice speaking French, but through his swollen eye lids it was difficult to see who was talking. "If they think you are injured and near death, they will kill you. Few people who lie down with injuries ever get up," the voice warned him.

"*Oui, oui.* Yes, I'm getting up. God, help me. I don't want to die here," Philip said.

He spent the next quarter-hour walking back and forth near his bed. Even this minimal movement helped to clear his head.

"You must have put up lots of resistance to the Brute. That's what we've named the thug who beats prisoners," said the man leaning down from the bunk above. "He's pretty tough, especially when a guy can't hit him back. We've all felt his fists and the stick he carries."

"By the way, my name is Movses Mirakyan, but you can call me Moso," he said. "I've been in this place for a while. When you're in better health, I'll give you my advice on how to survive this rat's nest."

"Thanks. I'm Walter Kaplan from Chicago, U. S. A.," Philip answered weakly as he continued to pace the barrack.

"Oh, U. S. A.!" Moso blurted out. "I have a cousin in America. In California. He owns a big grape ranch near a village called Fresno. There are many Armenians like me in Fresno. Do you know that village? Maybe you've heard of my cousin?"

"No, I'm sorry. I've only visited California once. I don't know anyone in Fresno, and I've never been to a grape ranch there, either," replied Philip.

"That's too bad. They would like to know a brave man like you," said Moso. "Maybe all Americans are brave like you. Maybe Americans will rescue us from these murderous Turks."

"So, they're all Turks," Philip remarked. "That's what I figured. I remember being arrested by Turks. Then we must be in Turkey, right?"

"You don't know where you are, Walter?" asked Moso incredulously. "Yes, you are in central Turkey near the coastal town of Alanya. And this is the most notorious Ottoman prison for people suspected of being spies and subversives. They call it Prison 29. They couldn't even give it a real name. Just a number," he said as he spit defiantly on the floor.

"So, everyone here is accused of being an enemy of the Ottoman Empire," remarked Philip. "Well, even if we came here as innocents, imprisonment in this disgrace to humanity would make all of us ready for revolution."

"I don't need an excuse to be a subversive in this decadent country," Moso said. "I am Armenian, and the Turks are out to eliminate all my people. That's reason enough.

"They raid our villages and shoot everyone, women and children included. They herd us into rivers and drown us. Sometimes they sell us—especially our young women—as slaves to wealthy families. Other times they simply drive us northward out of their lands and into Russia.

"They have relocated thousands of us, marching us for as many as a hundred miles southward into the Anatolian wilderness with armed troops guarding us. The unlucky ones are those who are not shot or who do not collapse by the roadside and die from thirst or exhaustion or fever. With no crops planted and no animals to breed, we starve to death in the winter. With no homes and poor land, we are forced into the mountains to survive in caves, or we try to build shelters in the open fields.

"They hate us because we are Christians, because we are more cultured, better educated, and more successful. They hate us because we want political autonomy within their corrupt Empire," the Armenian continued.

Philip interrupted him. "Is this a new development?"

"No, the Turks have been killing us wholesale since the middle of the 1890s," answered Moso. "A massacre here, a pogrom there—but we are now in the midst of a new wave of killing that began two years ago, and it's much better organized. Turkish defeats in the war have unbridled the brutality of the Sultan and his Young Turk allies. The massacres are cheap victories over defenseless people.

"They even kill Armenians who are soldiers in the Ottoman Army—thousands of them. Sometimes they only take away their rifles and turn them into trench diggers and stable cleaners—then they shoot them. The Turkish goal is simple: get rid of the Armenian Question by exterminating the Armenians."

Philip interrupted Moso's explanation. "I've heard that in eastern Turkey other ethnic groups are being massacred by Turks and Armenians and Russians," he said. "They say the Kurds have murdered many Armenians, and Armenians have done the same to the Kurds. As you well know, Armenians did join the Russians to make war on the Empire because it served their ambitions for political autonomy and independence. Maybe ethnic murder is normal in that part of the Empire?" Philip inquired.

"True, the Turkish military has killed hundreds of thousands of citizens from many different groups," Moso answered. "True, also, invading Russians recently sparked the wholesale killing of Turkmen, as well as Sunni and Shia Moslems in Georgia and the Caucasus—anyone loyal to Constantinople. But I've heard figures as high as 300,000 to 600,000, perhaps a million Armenians killed in a planned, deliberate way by the Sultan's men.

"One of your last ambassadors in Constantinople—what's his name?—Henry Morgenthau, that's it. Ambassador Morgenthau said—and I heard it with my own ears when I was a waiter at the U. S. Embassy a few years ago—that in this war our Empire has probably killed two millions of its own citizens. And he specifically named my people, the Armenians, as the main target.

"I am from Harpoot. Let me tell you the story of a neighborhood family in my home town," said Moso as he began a tale of suffering. "The father of the family was a very successful rug merchant selling Oriental rugs around the world. The wife was a loyal mother of four beautiful children: two girls and two fine, strong boys. Wonderful home, good food, respected, successful, a happy life. They had it all.

"Enter the Turks. First, the father was ordered by the police to close his business. Then he was taken away to perform manual labor as a road builder. We heard later that he was shot after a few days.

"The mother was next. The police took her in a wooden cart, and she was deported along with many other women and children. She was one of thousands forced by Turkish soldiers with whips to march across Anatolia. To this day we do not know if she survived. But I fear the worst.

"Before mama left, she cut her thirteen-year-old daughter's hair short and thinned her eyebrows. It was her attempt to make the girl less attractive. Mama knew what would follow, and she needed to protect her child from sexual slavery. On the same day, she placed her money in a cloth sack and buried it in the family vineyard. Only the older son was with her when the coins were hidden.

"But this was not all of the suffering endured by this family. A few weeks later the children were among the 25,000 other Armenians who were deported from Harpoot in one massive evacuation. These poor souls were marched across the desert in the scorching heat. Despite her mother's attempt to make her ugly, however, the older daughter was taken by a military officer to be sold into a rich man's harem. The other children continued the march.

"Fortunately, God be praised, this thirteen-year old girl managed to escape before the harem deal was completed. She started walking toward Russia alone, hoping to find support among Armenians living there. It was a miracle, but along the route she found her siblings. They, too, had escaped and were headed to Russia.

"By this time, however, the younger brother was already blind from starvation, and he soon died. The other children secretly returned to Harpoot to retrieve the buried coins. That they eventually found sanctuary in Russia was because the hidden money allowed them to buy food from local Kurds, and on two occasions buy their freedom from Kurdish men who had captured them.

"The saddest part of this, my friend, is that it's typical of what has happened to my people."

"That's a terrible story," Philip remarked.

"I think ever country has its history of secret slaughters and state-sponsored mass murders," Moso remarked. "History shows that even your wonderful United States has killed countless native Indians, Negroes, and others—even white Americans.

"But these Armenian Massacres are special," Moso continued. "They are the most brutal repressions of a single people in the history of the world. Even Ramses did not annihilate the Hebrews when they made their exodus from Egypt. Whatever the Sultan perceives our crimes to have been, he has no right to murder us or drive us out of our communities while facing the point of a sword or the barrel of a rifle."

Philip felt helpless about the Armenian situation, but at least Moso had survived. He was also pleased that his new acquaintance was so strongly anti-Ottoman because, he suspected, the prison must be filled with informers, men eager to tell what they overhear in order to gain favor with their captors. But to be safe, he resolved to trust no one with his secrets—not even the Armenian.

The following day, Philip was physically ready to walk outside into the prison yard. This was the first time he had seen the entire place. The facility was much larger than he had imagined. The central gathering area was about seventy-five yards long and fifty yards wide. Around it were four shabby barracks in which prisoners were housed. A small square building at the far end passed as the hospital. Philip discovered that he had been living in Barrack 1.

On warm days the prisoners had nothing to do except gather together outside and exchange small talk. A few men liked to run around the grounds for exercise, but there were no sports teams or organized recreation. So, mostly, being outdoors meant sharing idle chatter. On cold days, however, the men simply stayed indoors.

Politics didn't seem to be a divisive issue since all prisoners were considered enemies of the Empire. Except for Moso, Philip, and a few Arabs, the inmates were from the Balkans. Serbs were most plentiful, but there were Montenegrins, Macedonians, several Greeks—and even a handful of Bulgarians who opposed Tsar Ferdinand I for allying his kingdom with Germany, Austria, and the Ottoman Empire.

The most troubling problem confronting the prison population, Philip learned, was the high incidence of sickness in the camp. Dysentery and malnutrition might be expected, by there was typhus from the bad water supplied to the prisoners, and most alarming, an expanding incidence of influenza. Several men had already died because of the flu.

The Turks didn't offer real health care, just a medical assistant who could apply poultices and give inoculations whenever serum was available. There was no surgery, no professional diagnostic capability, and no certified doctor for that matter. Further, no prisoner could remember Red Cross personnel from the outside inspecting or even visiting Prison 29.

This did not reassure Philip who did everything he could to avoid becoming ill. Through a varied group of translators who understood French or Russian, he cautioned the men to cover their mouths and nostrils with cloth whenever in contact with a diseased person. Then destroy the used cloth, he urged, by burning or burying it in a pit dug for this purpose.

He ordered them to boil all water, even water used for bathing. And he explained germ theory, a relatively new concept in medicine. These were the only ways he knew to fight typhus.

As for the influenza affecting Prison 29, in especially strong terms Philip warned that this strain of the flu was obviously lethal and needed to be treated with great caution. For many days he trained the inmates, especially those who volunteered to care for colleagues when they came down with high fevers or crippling stomach pains.

When he was called into the prison's central office, Philip figured it was for a commendation for his lay medical advice. Instead, it was for another interrogation. Just when the wounds from the last brutal questioning had healed, Philip feared he was about to be mauled again.

As it had been in his transfer from bad cell to good cell and back to bad cell, the Turkish strategy appeared to alternate between friendly questioning and physically brutal interrogation. Again, however, Philip was resolute. He refused to admit or divulge anything.

Somehow social involvement with the other prisoners had strengthened his resistance. It was easier this time to avoid direct answers and protect his identity because he had become a man with immediate medical responsibilities. Nothing would break him. He was convinced that even if he were struck repeatedly, he would not talk. Not even beatings or possible extraction of his fingernails, he assured himself, would alter his resolution.

In those painful sessions with his torturers, Philip concentrated on trying to figure out the date. As a mental exercise, it preoccupied his thoughts and provided some detachment from the body blows he endured. Ironically, he honestly wanted to know what day, month, and year it was. The other prisoners, however, had all lost track of time, and the guards and administrators remained silent.

But the weather was bitter and he saw a dusting of snow on the ground when he was outside. He guessed that it was about January 1918, but he couldn't be certain.

Whatever the exact date, Philip did know that his timely medical advice had saved lives. The incidence of typhus had been reduced, and the spread of the killer flu had stalled for the moment. The prisoners appreciated his medical intervention. In the words of Nikolas Bronkovich, a tall and athletic Serbian college student who had left his studies in Belgrade to fight Austrian invaders, "You are a wonderful man, Walter Kaplan. You have saved our lives. We will always love you for it. To us you will always be Doctor Kaplan." It made Philip tear up whenever he thought of Bronkovich's praise. He knew it represented the opinions of more than a hundred prisoners who remained healthy despite being caged with infected colleagues.

For the next several weeks the cool weather persisted. A light covering of snow remained on the prison grounds, but it was melting and the temperature was becoming more tolerable. To Philip it meant that spring was coming—if it weren't already here. The men ventured out to the central campus area for conversation and minimal physical exercise. A few jumped up and down to fight the cold, but most had dirty blankets wrapped around their shoulders. This allowed them to stay in the open a little longer. Anything was better than remaining in the foul-smelling barracks to which they were confined.

During one typical outdoor day several dozen inmates came together for their usual conversations. It was another uncomfortable day with accumulations of filthy snow still not melted and a breeze that made exposure even chillier. Philip and Mojo had just left Barrack 1 and were talking with other prisoners about insignificant matters. As the men conversed they felt movement below their feet. "Earthquake!" screamed one of the Balkan prisoners. "Get the men out before everything collapses! Do it now!"

It began as a subtle tremor but escalated in intensity and duration. At its peak, the ground shook so violently large cracks appeared in the campus area. It was one of those powerful shifts deep inside the Earth which frequently destroyed entire towns in an earthquake belt that extended from Italy eastward to Persia.

This was a big one. The ground trembled strongly for about two minutes. To Philip and the others it felt like at least a half-hour. In short order, most of the men were in the open yard because the entire prison was disintegrating. Barracks, central office, external walls and guard towers: the earthquake was levelling Prison 29. More importantly, the panicked guards fled the crumbling edifice, some running to the Mediterranean shore, others scrambling into nearby hills and valleys.

It didn't take the prisoners long to seize the opportunity. Immediately, they scattered in all directions. This was an unanticipated chance at freedom, and everyone who could walk took it. Philip ran across a clearing and headed up a steep hill. He figured the mountains had the best hiding places should the guards return to search for escapees. Climbing over rocks, fallen logs, and unseen gullies he sped up the hill. He tripped several times slicing his legs and arms in the process. But he raced on. Winded and bleeding, he finally paused to catch his breath near a forested area that was thick with pine trees.

Philip then sprinted into the pines, dodging branches left and right, careful not to twist an ankle or sprain a knee. If he ever wished to see his wife and child again, this was his opportunity, possibly his only one. He had to make it. Onward he ran. Even when he felt exhausted he ran. Deeper into the woods, farther away from the prison, closer to Millie: this was life against death, and Philip was determined to live.

The earthquake had ended an hour ago, but aftershocks continued to rattle the area. Philip didn't care, he was free. He rested by a stream he discovered in the forest and was reinvigorated by its fresh cold water. He now needed to plot his next move. He was, after all, in the middle of hostile territory, a prisoner on the run, and probably a target for Turkish police and military sharpshooters. But the odds were with him. To capture a single runaway was not overly difficult. But to roundup a hundred or more escapees was a problem of extraordinary size.

While he sat near a hilltop devising a way to resolve his predicament, Philip heard a rustling noise coming from below. The crunch of fallen leaves and breaking twigs told him someone was approaching. His heart raced with fear. He was frightened that it might be an armed guard or a Turkish soldier.

Instinctively, he rolled into a small ditch on his left and pressed his body close to the ground. Perhaps the intruder wouldn't notice him in the ravine. He was also careful not to break his silence, but this was difficult because he felt like screaming out in terror.

As the climber reached the crest of the hill, Philip heard him walk by. He was relieved that he was not seen. A quick glance upward also reassured him that the pursuer wasn't carrying a weapon. Indeed, he immediately realized that it wasn't a pursuer at all. It was Nikolas Bronkovich, the Serbian college student and fellow ex-prisoner. "Nick," Philip said softly in French. "Nikolas, behind you."

The young man stopped and swung around defensively. He was ready to fight the man who had just recognized him. For the Serb this was also a life-or-death confrontation. But when he saw Philip he smiled and ran toward him, embracing him in a bear-hug and kissing him on each side of the face. "Dr. Walter Kaplan, it is wonderful to see you. I thought you and the others might be recaptured or even dead by now. But what are you doing up here? Are you alone?"

"Yes, I'm alone. You scared me. I thought you were a Turk ready to shoot me," Philip said. "I am so happy it was you. You're the only person from Prison 29 that I've seen since the quake."

"I do not think we have to worry for a while," explained Nikolas. "When the prison collapsed, the staff lost all communication with Constantinople. It will take the army at least a day to send troops here. And the prison guards, they totally disappeared. They must have figured the military would blame them for our escape. So, we have until morning to get out of here."

"Sounds good. But I can't think of any way out of this place," Philip confessed. "If we had an airplane we could fly out. That would be nice."

"It would be excellent. But, I have a plan; and I think it will work," Nikolas remarked. "It takes place tonight. I came up the hill to hide until later this evening."

"What's the plan? Can you share it?" asked Philip.

"After all you did for us when we were prisoners, Doctor Kaplan, of course I can. We can do it together," he replied. "This is what happened. When we all ran away, I stayed close to the shoreline. I was hoping to find something—a log, a wooden crate, anything—to float me to Cyprus. It's not very far from here, and Cyprus is British.

"While I was hiding there I saw several small boats trolling the beach. They were about one hundred yards off shore. From one of them I heard a Navy officer speaking through a megaphone saying that any runaway who wished to reach Cyprus should be on the beach at low tide tonight. He spoke in English, so I figure he was British.

"Apparently these boats can get closer to the shore at low tide. So, I'm planning to be down on the beach tonight. I want to get out of here. I suppose you do, too."

"I definitely want to reach Cyprus," said Philip joyously.

"I don't understand English very well," Nick continued. "But I could recognize some of his words. Escape, beach, low tide, tonight: I can put them together. I think it means freedom for anybody who can get aboard.

"I think you're right, Nikolas Bronkovich. You have a future as a translator," remarked Philip as he happily slapped the young man on the back.

Philip continued. "We can stay up here for a few more hours and make our move when it gets dark. But first, are you hungry? I found some apples frozen under the snow. They've been in my pockets for a while so they must be edible by now. These should help until we get aboard the rescue boat. If you're thirsty, there's a flowing stream in the forest not far from here. Come on, I'll show you."

The sun had set and night was falling when the two men made their descent to the Mediterranean. From the bottom of the hill they sprinted toward the rocky beach. "Over here, Nick, we can lean against these cliffs until the Navy arrives," Philip said softly. "You don't want to stand in the middle of the rocks and sand. It's not a bus stop, you know. Standing in the open would make us perfect targets for snipers."

It becomes very dark in southern Turkey where the moon falls behind the clouds. Only the white foam of the ocean hitting the beach reflects the heavens. And at ebb tide, the foam is thinner and visibility is diminished. In this darkening world, the two escapees sat in anxious anticipation.

It was pitch black about 11 pm when they heard the noise of an engine offshore. It was moving in their direction, getting closer to the beach. "This is it," said Nikolas. "We can signal with our shirts and let them see where we are."

With the tide out the men waded close to the vessel. When they saw its spotlight panning the area, Philip and Nikolas waved their shirts frantically and yelled for help. The pilot responded by cutting his engine. He was trying to pinpoint where on the beach they were. Eventually he spotted the pair and trained his light on them.

"Stand back and we'll shoot a tow line to you," he said through his megaphone. "Hold on to the line and we'll haul you aboard."

Using some kind of mechanical launcher, the crew launched a lengthy rope toward them. Philip and Nickolas grabbed the line and twisted it around their wrists. They were preparing to signal the boat to drag them aboard when a desperate voice from behind pleaded, "Wait a minute! Please! Wait a minute! I want to go with you! Take me, too!"

Philip didn't have to turn around to recognize the voice of Moso Mirakyan. "Come on, you old Armenian carpet seller," he yelled back toward the sound. "Hurry before the Turks shoot you from both sides."

THE HEADLONG FURY

Out of the dark Moso materialized, panting and frantic to be saved. He ran into the water to claim his place on the tow line. As this drama unfolded, three more escapees emerged from the darkness. They jumped in front of Moso and latched onto the rope.

"Take it away," Philip yelled in English toward the boat. "Ready to be brought aboard."

Slowly at first, then more rapidly the captain rewound the tow rope now with six desperate men clinging to it. Like so many fish hooked on a jig line, they were dragged toward the naval vessel. They were overjoyed to climb up the ladder extended to them. On his way into the rescue boat Philip noticed that there were two similar boats behind this one. He hoped that they would have as much luck fishing for prisoners as this present sea craft had been.

When he came aboard, the first question Philip asked was the date. "What month and day is this? What year" he questioned one crewman.

"That's the first time anyone we just rescued posed that question. What's the date? It's February 8, 1918. Why do you ask?" the sailor inquired.

"Just wanted to know," Philip replied. "I don't want to miss sending out my Valentine's Day cards this year," he added with a wink.

Safely aboard and dried off, the captain approached his evacuees. "Welcome, gentlemen. You're all guests of the Royal Canadian Navy. You're now aboard Naval Drifter *CD-9*," he said. "This little tug may resemble a fishing trawler, but underneath she's one tough cookie. She can tow minesweepers, fight it out with surfaced U-boats, and generally harass enemy ships of any class and size. Plus, as you will appreciate most, she can get very close to shore to retrieve friends when they break out of Turkish prisons."

The men, at least those who understood the subtleties of English, laughed then applauded.

"You are not British? I am surprised," Nikolas said in halting English.

"Same language, same Empire; but we're all Canadians aboard this vessel," said the captain. "You'll meet enough Brits when we get to the big island."

He continued, introducing himself as Captain Angus Simpson from St. John, New Brunswick. He then asked each man to identify himself.

Philip considered introducing himself as Major Belmont of the United States Army. But he remembered the importance of not breaking cover. When it came his turn, he presented himself as Chicago journalist, Walter Kaplan.

"We're already on the way to Cyprus," Simpson announced. "We should be there in a few hours. The island is only fifty miles from where we found you. But we're headed to the British naval base at Famagusta on the east coast. That's a little farther away. Once we arrive the Royal Navy will decide what to do with each of you. Until then, relax and enjoy the ride. We have fish sandwiches, potato salad, plenty of beer—enough for a late night picnic at sea. Enjoy yourselves, fellas. And if you want to wash up and get rid of those beards, you'll find everything you need in the shower room."

As the *CD-9* made its way toward Cyprus, Philip grabbed a share of the food and drink and considered his own course of action. He had several alternatives now. The Italian assignment seemed inappropriate because almost eight months had passed since he was ordered to Venice. Another move might be to expose his true identity and seek directions from Washington. Or, he could continue his assumed identity as a newspaperman and see where it led.

As he contemplated his alternatives, Philip remembered the secret code given to him last year by Agent Roger Macray. That seemed the best course for the present circumstances. But it left an enormous task before him: he needed to get to an American diplomatic post to make his situation known.

As the naval site most responsible for protecting the Mediterranean side of the Suez Canal, Famagusta was home to an array of British and Dominion ships of war. When the Canadian drifter entered the harbor in the early morning, Philip passed a line of destroyers, cruisers, one battleship, and several smaller war boats. To Philip, who knew little about modern seamanship, this fleet was impressive.

Once on land, the men were escorted to a debriefing room. Here Canadian and British officers met privately with each of the runaways. Philip explained to one interviewer that he had to reach his editors in Chicago immediately. After months of incarceration he wanted to reassure them that he was still alive. He also needed to learn his next assignment. He asked for access to the international cable to contact his newspaper.

The officer smiled and explained that Cyprus lacked such sophisticated technology, and that he didn't have the authority to afford him such a privilege. For that kind of clearance he would have to visit the U. S. diplomatic office in either Cairo or Athens.

Philip was also ordered to visit the base doctor for a physical examination which, despite his poor treatment in Prison 29, he easily passed.

Later that morning the base commander agreed to transport Philip to Athens on the next ship heading for Greece. However, that would not happen until Sunday the 10th. Meanwhile Philip was invited to clean up, have a good night's rest, and spend a day exploring the capital city.

Following the best breakfast he had eaten in a long while, plus a refreshing change of clothes courtesy of the base supplies office, Philip was ready for his ramble. It was completed fairly quickly, however, because Famagusta was a small place. Only the busy Navy base that had been opened eleven years ago gave it the appearance of being a sizable town. Few sites of importance, no massive mosques or cathedrals, little historical mystique, but lots of smelly fishing boats: it pretty much lacked attractiveness.

Only one building was of interest to Philip, the town library. He had been away from war news for so long he wondered, whimsically, if the struggle might be nearing its end. The library held a modest collection of old newspapers, and there were news magazines and pamphlets that also helped Philip catch up with world events.

He discovered to his disappointment that the war was still raging—all over the world. In France, however, familiar names persisted. He read now of the Third Battle of Champagne, the Second Battle of the Aisne, the Third Battle of Ypres, and the Second Battle of Verdun, all sites of fierce conflict he had experienced in lower-numbered manifestations.

But for dogged repetition nothing compared to the Italian and Austro-Hungarian bloodbaths fought along the Isonzo River in northeastern Italy and in the Slovenian area of Austria-Hungary. Philip read about the Eleventh Battle of the Isonzo where in August-September 1917 the Italian military fought the Austrians to a draw—although there were 30,000 Italians dead and more than 100,000 wounded; and 20,000 Austro-Hungarian soldiers dead, 45,000 wounded, and 50,000 taken prisoner or missing.

Less than a month later in a Twelfth Battle of the Isonzo the unprepared Italians were pushed back, and fighting became intense in and around the village of Caporetto near the Italian border with Austria-Hungary.

Ironically, Philip read assessments that suggested that these confrontations on or near the Isonzo accomplished little in terms of advancing Italian goals of acquiring the strategic coastal city of Trieste on the northern Adriatic; or, more fancifully, conquering Slovenia and marching victoriously into Vienna. But the dozen enumerated battles along that river took their bloody toll. Italy lost 300,000 men—fully one half of all Italian war casualties thus far. The Austro-Hungarian military suffered 200,000 dead and wounded. Such brutality reminded Philip of the horrific fighting he had witnessed at Verdun—or as that confrontation was now called, the First Battle of Verdun.

Not only was the war still raging, but as he read more accounts Philip realized that it was expanding. In the months he was out of touch, new countries declared war on Germany or Austria. These included Greece, Liberia, China, Costa Rica, Cuba, Panama, and Siam. Significantly, on December 7, 1917 the United States expanded its European commitment by declaring war on Austria-Hungary.

As he read more journals, Philip became convinced that imprisonment had removed him from a critical stage of the war. His friend General Allenby finally took Palestine. The pro-German King of the Hellenes, Constantine, had been deposed, and Greece was now a Republic fighting alongside the Entente forces. By October of 1917 German submarine attacks had destroyed a total of eight million tons of British shipping, although Germany lost about fifty U-boats in the process. In this naval war of attrition, German U-boats seemed to be steadily losing.

Even the war in East Africa continued. Philip knew that German colonies in the west such as Cameroon, Togoland, and German Southwest Africa had been overrun by Entente troops in the first year of the war. But in German East Africa a tenacious commander, Paul von Lettow-Vorbeck, with a guerrilla army of German officers and native troops, successfully resisted all efforts to drive the Germans out of the area.

Combat had begun in August 1914 and, as Philip read, Lettow was still fighting here in early 1918. Tens of thousands of men had died in East African combat, mostly on the Entente side. Interestingly, in confrontations with numerically-superior British, South African, Indian, and Portuguese troops, almost four years later Lettow's battalions remained undefeated. Even the British press seemed in awe of the victorious record the German general was creating.

While these developments interested Philip, no event was more striking or significant than the Bolshevik revolution that had occurred in Russia several months ago. The old newspapers were filled with the story. Gone was the Provisional Government; gone, too, were the reformers planning for democracy and a parliamentary Republic of Russia. The land of the Tsars was now vehemently anti-capitalist and in the midst of formalizing a controversial peace treaty with the Central Powers. What the Entente and the United States had feared, a unilateral Russian withdrawal from the war, was now an accomplished fact. The final terms of withdrawal were being negotiated in peace talks in the Belorussian city of Brest-Litovsk.

The mastermind of this second, more radical stage of revolution was Vladimir Lenin, the Communist leader whom Philip had visited in Petrograd. Philip was intrigued at the time by Lenin's self-assuredness, but he feared the revolutionary's rigidity in matters of dissent.

In fact, the more he read, the more Philip recognized that a civil war was underway in Russia. In the euphoria of political and philosophical victory, the new Communist government declared that self-determination of all nations was a right and secession was now acceptable. In rapid order Ukraine, Finland, Latvia, and Moldavia/Bessarabia declared themselves independent republics no longer under Russian control. Reports Philip read in the newer periodicals suggested that other parts of greater Russia would soon follow suit, notably Lithuania, Estonia, Armenia, and several provinces in the Caucasus region.

Philip knew that, political ideology aside, these territories were vital to the survival of the new Russian regime. Ukraine, for example, was rich in wheat and other agricultural products and was often called the breadbasket of Russia. The Baltic provinces were strategically located, and their independence rendered the unpopular Bolsheviks vulnerable to international navies. Philip wondered how long Lenin would take before Red military forces were assembled to drive these new nation-states back into the Communist paradise.

A more recent newspaper story showed him how long: Lenin had just appointed Leon Trotsky to be Commissar of War with the duty of forming a Red Army from enthusiastic volunteers flocking to support the new revolutionary government. Clearly, the Communists were preparing to defend, and possibly expand, their early gains. It sounded less like a welcome to a Leninist heaven on Earth, and more like an oppressive military maneuver to expand and solidify power—another Tsarist Empire, only veiled by a different name.

On Sunday morning Philip boarded a British destroyer, the HMS *Tigress* for the voyage to Athens. He felt honored because this ship was the talk of the base. *Tigress* was being lauded for her successful engagement less than two weeks ago with the finest ships in the Ottoman fleet: the battle cruiser *Yavuz Sultan Selim* (formerly the German warship *Goeben*), and the Turkish light cruiser *Midilli* (formerly the German ship *Breslau*). The Royal Navy was already terming it the Battle of Imbros.

Philip learned from the sailors that the battle began at the British naval base on the Aegean island of Imbros situated near Constantinople. When enemy battle cruisers with their German commanders and crews attacked British vessels anchored in Imbros, they sank two British monitor warships—small armored vessels with shallow drafts used primarily for bombarding enemy shore positions. The Ottoman ships precipitously retreated when they were confronted by the *Tigress* and another Royal Navy destroyer, HMS *Lizard*.

In their retreat the *Midilli* ran into a minefield and sunk. *Tigress* actually stopped to pull 162 survivors off the sinking Turkish warship.

As they pursued the *Yavuz Sultan Selim,* the two British destroyers had to avoid artillery barrages fired from Turkish guns on shore; they also had to fend off four Ottoman destroyers dispatched to protect the distressed battleship.

According to accounts Philip heard, the damaged *Yavuz Sultan Selim* ran aground near the Strait of the Dardanelles. *Tigress* and *Lizard* continued firing.

What especially struck Philip was that British aircraft from the seaplane carrier HMS *Ark Royal* bombed the stricken Turkish vessel inflicting even further damage. The implications of large ships becoming floating air bases carrying warplanes into battle were enormous and frightening. To Philip, it was another irretrievable step taken along the path to mechanized wartime death, another unfortunate marriage of engineering and science to produce killing machine that were efficient as well as indifferent.

Although *Yavuz Sultan Selim* was eventually towed to safety by the Ottoman Navy, the British sailors seemed confident that the battleship would not see combat for a long time.

Aboard the *Tigress* and now sailing for Greece, Philip was able to congratulate the ship's captain, Lieutenant Commander Joseph B. Newill. "There seems to be no rest for the weary," he said to the Commander. "You go from a tough sea battle to a lone voyage through waters infested with enemy U-boats. Isn't sailing through the Aegean a bit harrowing?"

"It can be risky," Newill responded. "But we make this trip once a week and haven't had a loss—not even a skirmish, thus far. The Germans have tried to block our use of the Mediterranean, but it hasn't worked. Besides, the Royal Navy has developed some effective ways to counter subs. But let's hope you don't have to see them in action on this trip."

"That's interesting," Philip remarked, "before the war most people felt the dreadnought class of modern battleships would change naval warfare. They're bigger, faster, and better armed than the any pre-dreads. The British and the Germans put lots of money into building fleets of them. This naval race went on for more than a decade. If this war is any indicator, the real change in naval warfare is being made by lighter vessels, particularly submarines that sink supply ships, and destroyers like yours that protect supply ships and even dreadnoughts."

Newill agreed—to a point. "It's funny how things work out. The monster battleships seem to have balanced out each other. But it was those bloody subs that altered war at sea. They can sink millions of tons of cargo because supply ships are not equipped for combat. And it's especially painful when they sink cargo ships filled with food. Food is the most underappreciated vulnerability in this war. All sides need it, but with military manpower demands and the loss of usable farmland, it's becoming increasingly difficult to grow crops or raise livestock in Europe. And no one can wage war on an empty stomach—just ask the Russians.

"German and Austrian submarines can also sink our big, slow warships. That's because these giants sit so low in the water and U-boat torpedoes fired from underwater are unstoppable. But a destroyer, like the *Tigress*, sits higher in the water. Subs have to surface or come very close to the surface in order to torpedo us. And when they come up, they expose themselves. Then we can bombard the hell out of them from a safe distance. We also have a smaller, faster, lighter sea craft—the submarine chaser—that can inflict great damage on U-boats. It's almost impossible to torpedo these pesky boats when they're scooting around the surface searching for underwater vessels.

"Destroyers: we are the future," said Commander Newill with obvious pride. "We are fast and we can deal with submarines.

"But so, too, can seaplanes on carriers like the *Ark Royal*. If you had seen how those aircraft belted that Turk cruiser with machine guns and bombs, you would better understand what I'm saying. Just think of it: seaplanes on pontoons are stored in a ship, then hoisted by cranes into the water from which they take off to strike enemy targets. Then they return to the mother ship and are hoisted out of the water and stored for the next encounter. If I weren't well into my career, I might consider training for naval aviation. Those seaplanes really did a job on the *Yavuz*."

17

From the moment he arrived in Athens, Philip could sense deep political tension among the residents. This may have been the birth city of Western democracy, but its pinnacle was reached 2300 years ago. It had been downhill for Greece since the end of the Age of Pericles. Today, following years of conflicting political rivalries, the city seemed to be a tinderbox of popular resentment and divided loyalties, a city on the verge of social explosion.

Greece was in the midst of the third war in the Balkan Peninsula since 1912. The First Balkan War featured a Russian-sponsored Balkan League comprised of Greece, Serbia, Bulgaria, and Montenegro in a struggle with the disintegrating Ottoman Empire in 1912. This struggle was no idealistic crusade for freedom or justice. It was a land-grab in which League nations sought to expand their territories, especially at the expense of the amorphous Ottoman province of Macedonia.

When the first war ended in 1913 the Bulgarians were disgruntled. Arguing that they had suffered the largest share of casualties, the government in Sophia demanded a larger portion of Macedonia than its League allies were willing to concede. The disagreement rapidly led to a Second Balkan War. This time Bulgaria attacked its former partners, Serbia and Greece. A new combatant looking for land, Rumania, joined the fight against the Bulgars. And Turkey changed sides, allying now with the anti-Bulgarian nations. Although this confrontation lasted only one month, it shifted the territorial alignment of the peninsula.

The Greeks received an enlarged share of Macedonia and soon began calling their new acquisition northern Greece. Its main city was Salonika. The Serbs also received a larger slice of Macedonia, much of it originally intended for Bulgaria. Sophia was awarded Macedonian land, but the size and strategic value of this prize were considerably diminished. For their short involvement, the Rumanians obtained important territory along the Black Sea. And the Turks, on the winning side this time, reacquired the important city of Adrianople in Thrace, the ancient European area situated between Constantinople and the Ottoman border with Eastern Europe.

Before the governments could fully integrate their new holdings, however, the Great War erupted over another Balkan event: the assassination in Austrian-controlled Bosnia of the heir to the Hapsburg crown, Archduke Franz Ferdinand. In essence this murder in Sarajevo triggered a protracted and uncontrollable Third Balkan War.

Riding in a carriage from the harbor to the United States Legation in town, Philip saw graffiti on the walls that suggested popular discontent. The name Venezelos was scribbled in Greek and English on many buildings. So was the name of the monarch who was deposed eight months ago, Constantine.

In perfect French, the driver explained that Eleftherios Venizelos was the prime minister who had pledged to bring Greece into the war on the Entente side. For this, the British were willing the cede Cyprus to Greece when the war ended. Opposed to the prime minister was the King who favored neutrality until a winning side became apparent. Then Greece could join the winner and demand even more Ottoman territory in the peace settlement.

"Many of us feared for Greece," the driver explained. "The fact that the King had been educated in Germany and was the brother-in-law of Kaiser Wilhelm led us to believe our King was not neutral. When Constantine ordered our army not to oppose Bulgarian and German troops when they occupied a key town in northern Greece in 1916, people were certain our monarch was sympathetic to Berlin and that Greece would soon become an ally of the Central Powers."

"It sounds like the ingredients for a civil war," Philip added.

"Indeed, things seemed headed that way, especially after the King dismissed Venizelos. But with support from Britain and France, our dismissed prime minister moved his government to the island of Crete and declared that he was now leading a provisional government with powers superseding the monarchy. Several days later on a visit to Salonika, Venizelos announced that Greece was now in a state of war against Germany and Bulgaria. To that end he raised three battalions of Greek soldiers and joined the Entente forces. The Greek islands and parts of the mainland stood with Venizelos. The remainder of the nation backed the king. Greece was, as you suggested, near civil war.

"But there is more," the driver continued. "To this political tension add the fact that Greeks on either side were not fully in control of the Greek state. Under terms of the treaty that created our nation in 1830, the French and British established a military presence at Salonika in 1915. Entente naval bases were also installed on several Greek islands where they supported the war against Bulgaria and the Ottoman Empire.

"But Salonika is the crown jewel. It's the premier city in northeastern Greece. It stands directly in the Germanic route across the Balkans and into Turkey. Without this strategic city, Germany and Austria can never win the East."

"You certainly are an informed observer of politics," Philip volunteered. "But you haven't told me where you stand personally now."

"Me?" the carriage driver asked. "I am for Venizelos and a republic. Constantine may be gone now, but as far as I am concerned, you can ship all our imported royals back to Denmark where they came from. Battenberg or Mountbatten—their family name depends if you're speaking German or English—send them home to Copenhagen on the next cargo ship. I care nothing that our new King Alexander was born in Greece. He is Constantine's second son and that means he's a Dane. He is also the Kaiser's nephew, and that worries me, too."

Philip had obviously touched a sensitive nerve. "I get the sense that Athens is still close to social explosion," he said to the coachman.

"Ah, not so much today," he replied. "But last year I would have bet big money on it—if I had big money. Only when the French and British ordered Constantine and his heir-apparent to abdicate, only then did the tension break. But we're still left with young Alexander.

"And we continue to have problems. Tens of thousands of Greek troops who backed Constantine are now refusing to fight for the Entente. They won't even wage war against the hated Turks. Two Greek units mutinied a few days ago when they were ordered to Salonika. The French have arrested them and may execute the officers. The new monarch says he supports the crackdown. He claims he favors France and Great Britain.

"My final assessment?" proclaimed the driver, "Matters are peaceful now, but they could get worse in a hurry. Let's see what happens to those rebellious Greek soldiers being held by the French."

As informative as the coachman was, Philip's attention was inevitably diverted to the beauty of Athens. Entering the city he gazed in awe at the Acropolis, the high hill on which rested the world famous Parthenon. That ancient temple dedicated to the goddess Athena was one of the most celebrated sites in world history. It stood in beautiful symmetry, a stunning vision and homage to human accomplishment. But if it survived as a grandiose testament to the era of Pericles, Socrates, and democracy, it was no longer architecturally perfect. Instead, it was neglected and apparently crumbling toward extinction.

For Philip the Parthenon was a metaphor for contemporary Europe: glorious in many ways, but imperfect and uncared for. The disintegrating temple was also a victim of war since its current disrepair began when Venetian warriors in 1687 fired on the temple knowing that its Ottoman protectors used it as a storehouse for gunpowder. When Venetian artillery hit the explosives, the ancient site was blown apart leaving only its base, most of the marble pillars that surrounded the temple, and part of the roof.

"It's sad that we haven't repaired our most important relic," said the carriage driver, "but we apparently prefer investing in armies and expanding Greek territory."

When he reached the United States Legation, Philip paid his driver and went in search of Garrett Droppers, officially known as the Envoy Extraordinary and Minister Plenipotentiary of the United States of America to Greece. As the highest ranking U. S. diplomatic officer in Greece, Droppers was the only person who could authorize Philip's use of the trans-Atlantic cable.

Philip presented himself as Walter Kaplan, but he dropped the pretense of contacting his newspaper editor because it sounded too self-serving and commercial. Convincing the Minister to allow such a transmission was difficult as access was highly restricted and Droppers was unwilling to accommodate unofficial request.

"But I was told that in a time of crisis, I would have access to international transmission by identifying my coded address," Philip explained to the Minister.

Again, Droppers was unrelenting. However, once Philip wrote down the actual code and handed it to the Minister, everything changed. "Excuse me, Mr. Kaplan, I am truly sorry for any lack of cooperation," he said apologetically. "You may have complete access to our telegraphic facilities. In fact, we'll be pleased to send and receive cables for you."

Philip was amazed by the power in the secret line of numbers and letters he briefly showed to the Minister. Now, the legation staff couldn't do enough to assist him. To keep his code confidential, Philip preferred to send the message himself. After being shown how to operate the transmission machinery, he informed Washington of his escape from Prison 29, and his desire to be assigned to the Macedonian Front. He also requested a French passport in the name of Laurent Montfort, whom he described as a professor of sociology conducting a study of what motivates soldiers to risk their lives in wars. It was the first time he requested a specific assignment, but he felt it was an excellent topic for his next report to President Wilson. He hoped the State Department might endorse his request as compensation for the harrowing months in that horrid Turkish prison.

"If you return tomorrow morning," Droppers said, "everything should be taken care of. Meanwhile, how are you fixed for cash?"

THE HEADLONG FURY

"Well, now that you mention it, I am flat broke," responded Philip.

"We can take care of that," said the Minister reassuringly. He explained that the legation had a petty cash fund for the financial emergencies of American citizens. "You are an American citizen, aren't you," he asked.

"Proudly so," Philip replied.

Droppers left the room for a moment and returned with $500 in Greek drachmas. "I trust this will tide you over for a while," he said.

Since Philip had almost a full day before his reply would arrive, he decided on a walking tour. For a historian of any specialty, Athens is a thrilling experience. From ancient amphitheaters and museums to modern architecture, Athens fascinates and informs as few other cities can.

He visited Athens as a tourist. The Parthenon, of course, most intrigued him. But wherever he wandered, he was excited to think that he was where Plato and Aristotle and Euripides once lived. But after several hours of traipsing around the city, he began looking for a decent restaurant. As much as he felt like roasted lamb with green beans and a splash or two of roditis, he was intrigued by the Irish pub he spotted in the middle of a narrow side street. O'Malley's Public House had a large crowd of diners, but not so large as to discourage one hungry American.

As he sat eating his traditional boiled dinner washed down with a pint of pale ale, Philip felt as if he were dining in Chicago or Dublin. He became so involved with his nostalgic meal that he failed to notice the British officer coming toward the table. "Excuse me, but are you Phil Belmont, the pilot from the Lafayette Escadrille?" the intruder asked.

Philip froze for a moment. "Why do you ask me that?" he cautiously answered.

"You don't know me, but I'm Franklin Briggs, captain in the Royal Flying Corps. I've been stationed in Salonika for a couple of years.

"I was a close friend of Paul Pavelka of Squadron N391. I can't tell you how many times Skipper bragged to me about the Lafayettes. And he mentioned you many times. He was forever rummaging through a box of snapshots he took while he was with you lot. Some pictures he received from old friends still with the Squadron. You're in a few of those, too. That's how I recognized you. You've lost some weight, but I know you through Skipper and his snaps."

"You're talking in the past tense a lot," Philip responded. "What's happened to Skipper? Isn't he here anymore?" Philip inquired. "I always liked Paul. He was the pilot who took me to and from my first meeting with the *Escadrille*. In fact, I hope to catch up with him while I'm in Greece."

"Well, I'm sorry to report that Skipper is deceased," said the Englishman.

Philip was stunned to hear such news. "Paul is dead?" he exclaimed. "That's horrible. He was such a likeable guy. How did it happen?"

"I'm truly sorry, Phil," said Captain Briggs. "He was killed a few months ago in a freak horseback-riding accident. He was trying to tame a bucking mare. No doubt you knew that Skipper used to work on cowboy ranches in Montana. Well, when the horse couldn't throw Skipper, she fell to the ground and rolled on top of him. He died of internal injuries three months ago. On November 11th to be exact. Skipper's friends will always remember the date: 11/11/17."

"That's awful, Captain," Phillip said. "Please sit down. Tell me more."

"Not much more to add. He's gone just like so many others in your little Squadron," Briggs replied.

"How do you know so much about the Lafayettes?" asked Philip.

"I don't know that much, but Skipper was always talking about who was transferred or who was killed or injured or captured. He didn't keep up a regular correspondence with his Lafayette pals. But somehow he always learned about what had happened to them.

"Skipper used to say that most of the flyers from his days in France were either dead or getting ready to fly someday for Uncle Sam. Since the Yanks finally got into this fight only a few Americans stayed with the Lafayette Flying Corps. Most have opted to join the U. S. Aero Service—in the 103rd Aero Squadron to be precise."

Captain Briggs continued to bring Philip up to date on the fate of his former comrades. "If I can remember Paul's words accurately, he spoke about Jimmy McConnell dying about a year ago," Briggs explained. "He was shot down in a dog fight over Germany, but he managed to get his Nieuport back to France before he crashed. He wouldn't give the Boche the satisfaction of dying in the Fatherland.

"Then there was Lieutenant Al de Laage, Captain Thénault's adjutant. He also died. De Laage's SPAD VII stalled during a takeoff. It crashed and killed him. There were others he used to mention, but I can't recall their names or what happened. I think many of these others were pilots who joined the Squadron after Skipper came to Salonika."

"More terrible news," Philip said sorrowfully. "I liked the flyers you mentioned. I knew Jimmy back in Chicago long before the war. He was a brick. And Al de Laage was always nice chap and one brave pilot. Of course, everybody loved Skipper. What a wonderful pilot and great friend he was."

"I'm devastated, Captain. This is very sad for me." Philip paused for an instant to steady his emotions. "If you don't mind," he finally said, "let's raise a glass to these pilots—to all the pursuit flyers of the *Escadrille Lafayette* who've left us. For that matter, let's raise our glasses to every American who ever served in the damnedest French flying corps in this whole hellish war. Here's to the Lafayette Flying Circus!"

Philip and Captain Briggs solemnly touched glasses and drank to the memory of departed colleagues, and all those Yanks who had served France in the skies.

"Wait a minute," interrupted the Englishman. "I have a clipping in my wallet. Let me find it. I tore it out of a magazine and decided to keep it with me always. It's very touching and appropriate."

As he fumbled through his billfold, he explained that Jimmy McConnell had written a letter to be read only if he died in the line of duty. "It's one hell of a letter. Every Entente pilot should have a copy," the British officer remarked. "Here it is. Let me read the best part of it to you."

> My burial is of no import. Make it as easy as possible for yourselves. I have no religion and I do not care for any service. If the omission would embarrass you, I presume I could stand the performance. Good luck to the rest of you. God damn Germany and *vive la France*.

Instinctively, Philip and Briggs raised their right hands toward their foreheads and again saluted their fallen brethren with another swig of Irish beer.

Philip gathered his emotions. "I remember the day Skipper was transferred to the Army of the Orient. He was happy beyond words. He wanted to fight the war on all its fronts. Like a box of mixed chocolates—a war sampler, you could say," noted Philip. "But I also think he was depressed by the recent loss of close friends from the Squadron."

"Kind of a romantic, wasn't he?" Briggs replied. "But you're right. He left the Lafayettes when the Frenchies sent him to the Balkans. He'd been with Squadron N391 ever since he arrived."

"I supposed he would have joined the new 103rd Aero Squadron that the Americans are putting together," Philip inquired.

"Tell you the truth, I don't think so. He loved it here in the East. He liked the mix of nationalities in the Army of the Orient," explained Captain Briggs. "God knows, we have a heavy responsibility here. Some people call us a sideshow to the main act in France. But, I can assure you, fighting in Macedonia is no act and we're not clowns. We just don't get the publicity you receive when you fight in northern France."

"Nor the number of battle casualties," Phillip added.

"Right! But we get enough," said Briggs. "There are thousands of casualties in the armies and navies battling here in the Balkans. We've got Bulgars, Rumanians, Serbs, Montenegrins, Albanians, Greeks, Turks, Austrians, Slovenes, Croatians, Americans, Germans, and probably a few ethnic types I've omitted. These guys are bleeding and dying every day. And that adds up over a period of years."

"Then what are you doing here in Athens?" Philip asked.

"I'm still based in Salonika. I'm here today because I flew a bigwig officer down to Athens for a special meeting" Captain Briggs answered. "They gave me a three-day leave. The general is staying, but I'm flying back tomorrow afternoon to continue saving the world from Bulgarians and Turks.

"Maybe you'd like to join us on the Macedonian Front," Briggs added wryly. "The weather's better in northern Greece—even in wintertime. But before you commit yourself to the Balkans, let's order another round and we can talk about what you've been up to."

THE HEADLONG FURY

The officer's friendliness put Philip in an awkward position. He needed a plausible explanation fast; he couldn't be honest about his work. Fortunately, however, Briggs seemed to know nothing about the phony dead-or-captured scenario Captain Thénault concocted to get Philip out of the *Escadrille*. Or was this British officer just being courteous, waiting to ask about what had really happened in the woods near Germany early last year.

Once the barmaid replenished their drink supply, Philip told a story that wasn't total prevarication. "Well, after I was shot down by a Boche fighter," he began, "I was taken prisoner. The next two months were rough. You don't want to be a prisoner in the Fatherland during the war. It's a wretched experience.

"Then I was transferred to an Austrian jail for eight months. You don't want to be caged in one of these places either. Finally, when they decided I wasn't worth beating anymore, I was sent to a Turkish prison for a respite. But no one told the Turks I wasn't worth beating. I spent a total of a year and a month being tortured as an enemy prisoner. I really don't like to talk about what happened in these venues."

"I understand," said the Captain. "I can imagine the painful memories you must have."

"I was able to escape the Turkish prison a few weeks ago when an earthquake destroyed the entire place," Philip continued. "The quake leveled everything: no walls and no guards, so no Phil Belmont. And now—well, I just arrived in Athens. Now I'm getting emotionally ready to return to Paris."

"Well, relax, old chum" responded Briggs. "Athens is a great place to recuperate. Get yourself back in gear before you start that deadly dancing in the sky again. There's a lot of war left to be fought. You'll still get your share."

While the men conversed, Philip tried to size up the British flyer. "Tell me about yourself. Where do you come from and why are you here?" he asked.

"Well, as I said, I'm Franklin Briggs. Middle name is Oglethorpe, but that's a secret; please don't tell anyone. They usually call me Crash. I was born in Wolverhampton in the West Midlands and educated at several excellent universities. The family hoped I would become a chemical engineer. But I was crazy about aviation from the beginning. I always wanted to fly. My folks practically disowned me for my treason against the British class system.

"I got the moniker Crash because I have always been fascinated with Greek mythology, and especially with Daedalus, the master inventor. He's the bloke who built the wings of wax and feathers that first allowed humans to fly. In fact, I have his name written in block letters on the side of my Sopwith fighter.

"I've been careful to emulate Daedelus, but not his scatterbrained son, Icarus. That nipper flew too close to the sun and had the wax in his wings melt and the feathers fall off. Poor laddie. Left flapping his arms in space as he fell to earth and was killed. Nowhere on my plane will you find the name Icarus—no hint of him whatsoever.

"Regardless, in flight training school people started calling me Crash as a reminder of what happens to the pilot who soars beyond the capacity of his wings. It's served me well for all these years of aerial combat. I still haven't flown too close to the sun."

As the men spoke, Philip mentioned that he didn't have a room for the night. "That should be no problem," said Briggs. "A bunch of us are staying at the Athena near here. It's cheap, and cootie-free. I'm sure they'll have a room—or at least a folding cot in the hallway that they could rent for the night."

The Athena was a dive, and it was overbooked with soldiers from all over the world. However, the night clerk managed to find an extra folding bed and set it up in a hall. It was not the Crillon in Paris or Shepheard's in Cairo, but it was warm and manageable.

The next morning Philip was awake and dressed early. He left the hotel before saying goodbye to his new friend. He was more anxious to get to the United States Legation which was located about two miles away. Unfortunately, he arrived twenty-five minutes too early. The offices didn't open until 9:30. So, he sat on the hard steps of the building and watched the parade of people passing by.

Already the sidewalks and streets were filled with men and women on their way to work. This was Tuesday morning, but even with wartime uncertainties Athens was vibrant with pedestrians who had places to go and important things to do.

Hundreds of Athenians streamed up and down the sidewalk. From the finely dressed to those in military uniforms and others clothed in tatters—a diverse and fascinating procession of civic life passing by his gaze.

One character especially caught his Philip's eye. He wasn't sure if it was a man or a woman because the person was dressed like a circus clown—right down to the big red nose and floppy oversized shoes. The clown walked slowly toward the U. S. Legation, jesting with people he encountered on the sidewalk. As he flopped up the sidewalk, the clown distributed flyers and nodded humorously at each person who accepted one. Philip figured that there was a circus in town and this was advertising for its Big Top attractions.

When the brightly-attired clown spotted Philip sitting on the concrete steps, he ambled toward him with exaggerated gestures that made the burgeoning street crowd erupt in laughter. He even rubbed his rear end as if to suggest how sore Philip must feel after sitting on the unforgiving stairs. The swelling crowd of bystanders chuckled knowingly at the gesture.

While his followers awaited the next comedic gesture, the clown spoke to Philip in a buffoonish voice. "I can't wait for the spring weather to arrive," he said. Philip sat stunned for a few seconds then responded with "It's the same all over Europe."

"Yes, but I don't live in Europe; I live in Greece. And it's too damned cold here," he quipped, turning then to his street audience for approval. The crowd roared loudly at the repartee. In the middle of the reveling, however, he handed Philip a flyer. In grasping it, Philip felt an envelope under the single-sheet circus handout.

With a comical nod of his head, the clown skipped down the street followed by avid onlookers waiting for his next entertaining gesture.

Philip was impressed by the audaciousness displayed in the delivery of his instructions. A clown! On a crowded avenue in the center of Athens! He had been so swept up in the messenger he almost missed his line in the identifying verbal exchange.

Nonchalantly, Philip folded the advertisement over the envelope and placed the items inside his shirt. He walked away from the steps to find a private place to read the contents. A nearby park that was quiet and unoccupied on this warm morning afforded him the solitude he needed.

In the envelope Philip found more cash and, as requested, a new French passport. His name this time was Laurent Montfort. His assignment was simply described: "The Balkan situation."

Two items in the envelope, however, were unusual. First, there was a formal letter written to General Adolphe Guillaumat, the Commander-in-Chief of the Army of the Orient. It requested his full cooperation with Dr. Montfort in his research endeavors. The letter was signed by General Ferdinand Foch, Chief of the General Staff of the French Army. Philip was struck by the quality of this clever forgery from Washington.

The second item was the key to a safe-deposit box. Surprisingly, however, it was for use in the Banca d'Italia on via Nazionale in Rome.

Even before he fully read the instructions, Philip was devising a plan for accomplishing the assignment. If he was expected in Rome, he would investigate political and military conditions in the Balkan Peninsula by moving steadily westward from northern Greece toward the Western Adriatic coast and eventually make the jump to Italy.

First, however, he had to get to Salonika about 200 air miles from Athens. He recalled that Crash Briggs was scheduled to fly home later this afternoon. If it weren't too late, he hoped to fill that second seat.

It took an hour to locate Crash who, fortunately, was still at the Athena. By mid-afternoon Philip was sitting in the bombardier seat of a Bristol F.2, a British two-seater that Crash affectionately called a Biff.

As he and Captain Briggs flew northward, the temperature began to change. Instead of the warm conditions of an early spring in Athens, Philip felt the cold grip of winter. New to this part of the world, he soon discovered that in Greece the mountainous regions to the north were colder and less hospitable than Athens and southern Greece. Even before they arrived in Salonika it began to rain slightly, something he obviously felt as the Biff had an open cockpit. Philip crossed his fingers that the weather would not further degrade and produce a lightning storm or even a snow shower before they could land.

"I thought you told me you had better weather in northern Greece than they have down in Athens," Philip yelled to Captain Briggs.

"I did, and it's true," said the Englishman. "It's just that I prefer a cold climate to a hot one."

The landing was harrowing. Rain and melting snow made the field muddy and slippery in places. When the wheels touched down, the aircraft bounced a few times then skidded to the left as it passed through a squishy spot on the runway. For two experienced flyers, however, this was nothing out of the ordinary. Philip recalled similar landings when he was in training and when he was with the Lafayettes.

As for the Captain, he was nonplussed. "Don't worry, Phil," he said reassuringly, "you and I have made tougher landings than this. A muddy field in Greece can't compare to the shell holes, tall grass, snow drifts, and sneaky puddles in France. And don't forget the sniper fire.

"At least you know you're alive when you come down like this. The old heart beats like mad, blood races through the veins—that's real living, mate."

"Maybe I forgot the thrills that come with being a pioneer in aerial combat," remarked Philip. "I forgot all about the snipers who shot at us when we had to land near the German border. I forgot about the deadly dog fights in the clouds. I forgot about all the friends I lost to combat and the crash landings."

"Hey, come on, don't get morose on me now" Briggs said. "It's getting dark. You can stay in our barrack tonight. Whatever you have to do in Salonika will keep until tomorrow morning."

"Thanks for the invite. I accept," replied Philip. "But there's a matter I have to discuss with you before we get to your quarters."

Carefully, Philip described his predicament, explaining that any mention of his real name might lead to his imprisonment again in Turkey. "I'm sure they've placed a bounty on my head," he said. "It might be tempting for someone to turn me over to the Sultan just for the reward. So, if you can call me Joe Smith or something else. No, I've got it. Introduce me to your pals as Jimmy McConnell. I'll be Jimmy for tonight. Then, I'm gone in the morning. Besides, it'll dust off Jimmy's name. It'll be a rebirth of sorts."

"I understand," Briggs replied. "This will be Jimmy's final wartime appearance. From the way Skipper Pavelka described his Lafayette colleagues, it sounds like something the Squadron would approve of. Definitely, the guys would be touched by it."

That evening Jimmy McConnell was reincarnated. Philip enjoyed meeting the combat flyers in the Army of the Orient. It was a mixed group with French and British, Serb and Greek, Italian, Rumanian and Yank pilots. As the flow of liquor increased, the polyglot din increased in loudness. The barrack became a veritable concert hall offering a symphony in discordant foreign languages. Philip loved it. To him it was a friendly merging of nationalities—men respectful of one another, exchanging stories, enjoying each other's company, at peace together.

In the morning he left Briggs and the other flyers. He was headed into town to find a decent room, then to command headquarters to meet General Guillaumat.

By Balkan standards, Salonika was one of the peninsula's more modern cities with a population above 150,000 and an ethnic mix of residents that for the most part were Sephardic Jews, Turks, Greeks, Bulgars, and Gypsies—plus a recent influx of war refugees from Macedonia, Serbia, and other danger zones. The place was an important trade center with an excellent harbor situated at the head of the Gulf of Salonika on the Aegean Sea. Trade between the southeastern Balkans and the Near East flowed through its busy port.

By 1918, however, the city was shabby and overcrowded. Some referred to it with words such as squalor and decadent. It lacked proper sanitation. Many of its streets were foul with the smell of decomposing garbage. An abundance of fish markets enhanced the social aroma. Salonika had the appearance of an old town that had recently expanded—too rapidly and without a central plan for growth. Like many ocean fronts in wartime, the stream of military personnel into and out of town also took its toll. The stationing of more than 100,000 troops from Entente and allied nations—men with no ties to the city—only compounded its urban distress.

THE HEADLONG FURY

The raggedness of Salonika was worsened by indifferent management and surrender to civic decline. Moreover, Salonika had not yet recovered from the great fire that swept through most of the city in late August 1917. Flames from the accidental blaze destroyed one-third of the town. About 9500 homes burned down as did more than half of the city's 7700 shops. An estimated 70,000 people were left homeless. One-half of the Jewish citizens lost their businesses and possessions in a conflagration that burned unchecked for thirty-two hours, leveling structures from the northwestern residential area down to the harbor.

In addition to such urban despair, Salonika was sullied by an array of dingy cafés, shops selling a variety of colorful and unnecessary trinkets, and beggars and prostitutes soliciting on the streets. To compound its instability, the city was situated only thirty-five miles from the Greek-Bulgarian boundary line. And the Bulgars were still resentful that in 1912 a Greek army entered and claimed Salonika only hours before their own troops arrived with the same intention. By 1918 this was not a city in which to raise a family.

Finding a decent place for the night might have been an arduous task had not one of Crash Briggs' friends mentioned the Hotel Alexander the Great. "It's the best in town since the Hotel Splendide burned to the ground last year," he explained.

Philip found the Alexander the Great a few blocks from the electric streetcar line that ran along the waterfront. He tipped the concierge to show him the best room in the hotel. It wasn't luxurious, but he couldn't be choosey. Philip booked it for three weeks with an option to extend his stay. He then took a taxi to the Anglo-French military headquarters.

At first General Guillaumat refused to see Laurent Montfort, this unknown French professor of seemingly no importance. But when Philip produced his letter from General Foch—authentic or not—things began to happen. The entire base was put at Philip's disposal. Without prior clearance he was permitted to interview anyone or participate in any non-classified activity. Should he want to see combat up close, he was authorized to accompany any foot patrol, air mission, or infantry assignment. The Commander-in-Chief also presented him with a small card. "This will explain your status. Just show it to any doubting officer," said Guillaumat. "It will open closed doors immediately."

"Thank you for granting me such access," Philip said. "I want to learn why men fight; why they're willingly face great danger for a cause; why they're willing to kill for the state, even prepared to give their lives for the state. I want to learn how men experience physical trauma or even imminent death. Do they sing local patriotic songs? Do they curse the enemy soldier who fired the rifle or dropped the bomb that maimed them or killed their friends? Are they loyal to King and country to the end, or do they blame the government that ripped them from their routine lives and trained them to slay other men?

"I also want to know why men desert. Is there a point at which the human spirit says I've had enough and a soldier simply walks away? Does a man desert the military because of fear? Maybe it's exasperation or disgust or disillusionment that pushes him. Perhaps he is moved by thwarted idealism or religious faith desecrated by the realities of organized warfare. And what then happens to a deserter? Is he forever ashamed of his action? Does society shun him, even imprison him? Or, does he easily justify desertion and move on with his life?

"For that I would first like to visit your prisoner-of-war detention center. I'll probably need translators who can handle languages other than French and Russian. And, of course, I'll need an armed guard or two."

The General made several phone calls and in less than thirty minutes, Philip had a contingent of translators and guards—plus full access to the enemy prisoners. The first men he interviewed included a Turk and two Bulgarians. They were hesitant at first, even hostile. Eventually they warmed to the unthreatening questions Philip posed. To each man he asked simply: Why did you fight in this war?

"I fought for the land of my fathers," said the Turk. "We Ottomans have ruled the Balkans for centuries, and now our lands are being stolen by these new Crusaders from Europe. I am a Muslim, and this is a holy war for what is rightfully ours.

"For generations my forefathers ruled in the Balkans. They governed well for almost 500 years. Balkan agriculture fed millions; our commerce flourished; we lived in harmony alongside people of all cultures. And we Turks accomplished this through compassion, not oppression. But now the Slavs and the Greeks and the Germans covet our territory. They proclaim that Balkan lands will be theirs for the rest of time.

"Enough, I say. It is time to reverse the flow of history, to assert our rights and restore what is rightfully ours.

"And let us be honest," he continued, "these Christian rebels and invaders have their eyes on grabbing all of Turkey, not just the Balkans: Thrace, Constantinople, Anatolia, all of it. Can you imagine the rejoicing in Athens and Petrograd—in every Christian capital—when our Hagia Sophia mosque in Constantinople has its crescent replaced with a cross? That is their goal, and that's why I fight to stop them.

The Turkish soldier continued. "I fight also because the Western world is corrupting my people. You bring your religious prejudice and your capitalism. Already we have Germans running the Empire. And soon you hope to have a German railroad running from Berlin directly through Turkey and into Mesopotamia. What bad influences will that rail line bring to our civilization? I can only imagine."

Philip recognized the historical inaccuracies in the man's statements, but he was not here to argue. He only wanted to hear the reasoning of soldiers willing to wage war.

The two Bulgarians had been in the Salonika internment facility for more than a year. They were young peasant boys barely twenty-two years old. But they offered reasons that were more nationalistic that those of the Turkish prisoner. "Why do we fight? Because our homeland must be strong and secure," one soldier explained. "Bulgaria only became independent forty years ago. Or, so you believe. But have you ever heard of Tsar Samuel? Nine hundred years ago he built a great Bulgarian Empire that extended from the Danube to the Black Sea to the bottom of Greece?

"Ever hear of Tsar Symeon who lead mighty Bulgarian armies against the Byzantines and defeated them a century before Samuel was our Tsar?" asked the other prisoner. "We were a great Christian people, a people of culture and civilization and accomplishment long before we were resurrected in 1878.

"But for five centuries we struggled under the Ottomans who destroyed our lands and our homes. They raped our women, killed our people, and tried to erase our civilization. But Bulgars remember. And since we were reborn as an independent Kingdom, we have sought to reclaim greatness by reconquering our lost lands. Macedonia should be ours. Thrace should be part of Bulgaria. Much of northern Greece should belong to us. Salonika should be ours, too.

"So, you ask why I fight. I fight for lost majesty, to honor it and to reclaim it. I fight also for Symeon and Samuel and our present Tsar Ferdinand. Our allies are Turkey, Germany and Austria, not because we love them or even support their goals. We fight beside them because they have pledged to help us regain what has been stolen over the centuries."

Philip knew that anecdotes did not prove trends. Such personal stories were individual instances, single examples that usually expose more about the teller than overall conditions. Still, as samples of opinion they can be indicative of broader sentiment. It would be foolish to believe that the opinions of two Bulgarians or one Turk represented the feelings of all Bulgars and Turks. Conversely, Philip understood that it would be wrong to conclude that these were random instances with no validity beyond the particular men expressing them. In other words, where there's smoke there may only be a smoke machine—but, based on experience, there's a good chance that the smoke comes from an actual fire.

The next group of prisoners included a Croatian, a Slovene, and an Albanian, diverse men whose shared support for the Hapsburg dynasty led all of them to fight in support of the Germans and Austrians.

"My Croatian friend and I fight because we are part of the Austro-Hungarian Empire," confessed the Slovenian prisoner. "We are Slavic peoples, but we are Roman Catholics. We are not Orthodox Christians like the Serbs and the Bulgarians. Our model is Vienna, not Belgrade or Sofia—and especially not Petrograd. We have seen the magnificence of Austria. Have you ever visited Vienna? It is beautiful. We are comfortable with Germanic leadership. We fight to preserve our Austrian identity and our Slavic roots.

"We are not part of peasant Serbia. We are sophisticated, people of dignity and achievement, not cabbage-growers and shepherds. We are also not Italians who dream of conquering Vienna by marching through Croatia and Slovenia like we were so many weeds on their pathway to greater glory. But we are not weeds. And we will kill any scruffy Latins who parade through our lands seeking to destroy Austria-Hungary."

The Croatian embellished his friend's argument. "Austria-Hungary is the oldest empire. Our roots go back to Charlemagne and the creation of the Holy Roman Empire. That was in the year 825, more than a thousand years ago. We are valuable to Europe because we hold the geographical center in a single citizenship. We remain loyal to the Empire as embodied by Kaiser Karl, Emperor of Austria-Hungary since the death of our beloved Franz Joseph two years ago.

"Unlike most of Europe, we are cosmopolitan, not tribal. We have about a dozen different peoples speaking as many languages in our lands. German may be the official language, but neither my Slovenian friend nor I can speak the language. Most Hungarians and Poles, and Czechs and Slovaks don't know German. The same is true of the Bosnians and the Ruthenians. But we are all proud to be citizens of our Empire. And that is what we will protect."

The Albanian prisoner also praised Austria-Hungary, not because it was sophisticated and a European linchpin. He felt obliged to the Vienna government because it defended his country from bordering nationalities. "Everyone has been trying to slice off pieces of Albania. The Montenegrins come from the south and the Serbs attack us from the north. From the East the Greeks are the aggressors, and from the West the Italians cross the Adriatic to claim towns and ports along our coast. The Bosnians and even the Muslims of Bosnia-Herzegovina, the Bosniaks, want portions of my country. But the Austrians are our benefactors who will never allow another nation to steal our land.

"That is why, when my government in Durrës asked for volunteers to protect the nation and our declared neutrality, I was honored to join the cause.

"Today the Austrians and their Bulgarian allies have occupied much of my country—not to conquer Albania, but to defend us until the war is finished. Then we will be a free and independent kingdom again."

Through much of the day, Philip heard variations on the same themes as he confronted a stream of prisoners. Two of the most interesting captives that afternoon were a German lieutenant and a Jewish private from Bulgaria.

"We did not start this conflagration," asserted the German officer. "We are fighting a defensive war against the nations that would destroy us. Great Britain and Russia have been planning for a long time to destroy the Fatherland. And France joined in their plans. The tension mounted, and by 1914 we had to take action or be destroyed.

"And now the Americans fight us. President Wilson has brought the United States into this conflict. He is nothing but a British puppet. The world will soon learn this when American blood flows on the battlefields of France, and when we invade the British Isles," he continued with anger etched in his face.

"But be assured, Dr. Montfort, Germany will never be defeated. Just look at what we did to Russia. I think the Frenchies and the Brits know now that they are finished. We have always desired peace, and we await any responsible overture from our enemies that will lead us to that goal. Until then, we will continue to slaughter you and your allies."

The Jewish private from the Bulgarian infantry told a unique story, perhaps the most honest of the testimonies Philip heard all day. "I fought because I was drafted into the national Army. I didn't want to go. I had to go. I have no love for Tsar Ferdinand, nor do I hate the Russians or the Serbs or Greeks so much that I would kill them.

"As for Bulgaria, I love its countryside. It's beautiful. My family has lived there for centuries. But the Bulgars, themselves? That's a different situation. Most of them are so filled with antipathy toward Jews that I cannot respect them. They despise Jews, so I fear them.

"The other Hebrew boys in my village were smarter than I. They figured they were most likely dead if they went to war—either killed by enemy bullets, or murdered by Bulgarians who hated them more than they disliked Serbs and Greeks. Do you know what these men did when they were called to the colors? They had the village *mohel* cut off a segment of their little fingers, or they asked him to scratch an eyeball to ruin their sight in one eye. They were wise: they knew they would not survive if they joined the army, but with a physical injury, carefully inflicted by an expert with a small blade, they would be rejected by the army as physically unfit. But they would be alive. How's that for a choice?"

Philip had no reply. He sought pure answers uninfluenced by follow-up questioning or his own reactions. He also wished to avoid intimidating the prisoners, some of whom might be reluctant for fear of further punishment. Personally, Philip winced at many of the revelations. He was also angered by some and touched by others. But externally, he just took notes and avoided comments.

The final prisoner Philip met that day was a Russian foot soldier. That was unusual since the Russians, at least until the Bolshevik coup last November, were part of the Entente's military alliance. But this young man had deserted from the Tsarist army and was now in prison for murdering a British officer who tried to detain him.

"Yes, I deserted," he confessed. "It was during a hopeless campaign in Rumania. You know the Dobruja area? That's where we fought Bulgarians and Germans. Why? To rescue the poorly-trained Rumanian army that was being slaughtered. We were hungry and tired and in need of weapons and ammunition, but our commanders ordered us to continue fighting. Then after we lost and were retreating, we were ordered north to Bessarabia—the eastern part of Moldavia—to defend it from German conquest.

"That's when I decided to leave. A group of us simply walked out of camp one night and headed back to Russia. Was I expected to die for the Tsar and the Motherland, neither of which still existed then? The Tsar and his family were deposed and imprisoned; the government in Petrograd was crippled by inaction; the Bolsheviks were threatening a second revolution; the Motherland was moving toward civil war. I may only be an uneducated peasant from the Ukraine, but I want to live. I had avoided death on the battlefield for years; I decided not to gamble with my life again.

"Then I met a British officer along the road. He was in a big black automobile with little Union Jack flags on it. He stopped me and threatened to arrest me and send me to jail. I could not allow that. To survive on the battlefield I had killed. I had no hesitation in shooting an English soldier who also menaced my existence. In this endless war, what's one more death? As long as it's not mine.

"In normal times, I would never think of murdering anybody. But in wartime, the state has trained me to shoot in defense of my life and the lives of my fellow soldiers. I responded as a trained fighter. Now, I'm in this rotten Salonika cell because I killed an ally of yours instead of an enemy. Tell me, professor, what's the difference when your life is at stake?"

In a base tavern that evening Philip was haunted by the confessions he had heard. Even the noisy group of soldiers drinking next to him noticed his quiet withdrawal. "Hey, bud. You all right?" asked one young soldier with an American accent.

"Oh, yes. I'm OK," Philip replied in English with an affected French accent. "Just a little tired, that's all."

"We thought you were about to fall off the bar stool," the Yank remarked. "Too many pints, eh?"

"Me? Nah, I can hold my balance up here. I think I was falling to sleep," Philip joked. "Hello, I'm Laurent Montfort from Paris, he said in introducing himself."

"Nice to meet you, Larry. I'm Private Rico Tramonte from New Orleans," the American responded.

"How long have you been over here?" Philip inquired while shaking the young man's hand.

"I joined last August, got my training, and arrived in Salonika a week ago," Tramonte responded. "I don't know why I'm here right now because I'm on my way to Italy. I'm part of a force supplementing the Italian military in the northeast. How's that for destiny? An Italian guy going back to rescue the ancestral homeland."

"Been in combat yet?" asked Philip.

"Not yet, but I can't wait," Tramonte answered.

"Then, can you answer one question for me?" asked Philip. "I don't mean to invade your privacy, but I've been talking to people about why they're in this world war. There is no right or wrong answer. If I may, let me ask why are you fighting in this war?"

"Wow, that's a deep question," the soldier responded. "I guess I'm an idealist. The other nations seem to be fighting for territory or loot or glory, but I joined up to help the world. I guess I'm fighting to bring democracy to everyone. You know the bromide: government of the people by the people and for the people. That's what I hope to bring or preserve here.

"And when we fight, we Americans won't be stopped by barbed wire or poison gas, tanks or even machine guns. Americans fight for freedom, and because of that we demoralize liberty's skeptics and convert its foes.

"That's about the size of it," he concluded in a matter-of-fact manner.

"Thanks," Philip said. "I appreciate your perspective."

As naive and facile as it sounded, Philip recognized himself in the soldier's answer. From the American Ambulance to the *Escadrille Lafayette*, Millie's human sympathies and Gene Bullard's struggle for equality and respect, Americans understand world affairs in idealistic terms. Philip concluded that with time and experience—if Rico Tramonte from New Orleans, Louisiana survived the battles ahead of him—he might become jaded and less accepting of romantic wartime rhetoric. But at this point in the game, he was typical U. S. A.

Throughout the next weeks Philip revisited the prisoner-of-war facility to enhance his study. Although his report would not be statistically valid, he wanted President Wilson to know why these soldiers acted as they did. Philip's conclusions, as might be expected, suggested that there was no dominant reason for taking up arms. There was a wide variety of rationalizations for why people battled to the death, but the largest variable was national citizenship.

He encountered Germans who argued that their nation was the dominant European power. As one soldier summarized it, "Germany now controls the destiny of Europe and, therefore, the world. Our culture and values and laws are restructuring the future of mankind. A century ago the great philosopher Hegel explained that the driving force of history was the Spirit of Freedom moving through time. He was right to recognize that

Prussia under the royal house of Hohenzollern embodied that Spirit. Now update Hegel to the early 20th century and your conclusion must be that Kaiser Wilhelm, who is a Hohenzollern, is leading the most important nation on Earth; and he must be allowed to shape the world according to superior German standards. History demands nothing less!"

Then there were the soldiers who in the prewar years were avid socialists. Typical of their arguments was the captured Austrian officer who was unembarrassed when he spoke of abandoning the collectivist notion of the brotherhood of proletarian workers, a class solidarity that renounced nationalism and national borders as well as it denounced the exploitation of workers by bourgeois capitalism. "It was extremely disillusioning," explained the Austrian. "By August 1914 socialism had no explanation for the world war unfolding before me," he remarked. "Only nationalism made me understand that the French and the British and the Russians were warrior tribes—Franks, Angles and Saxons, Slavs in Russia and the Balkans, all intent on dismantling the great civilization that we Teutonic people created.

"Where industrial socialists proclaimed the primacy of labor's brotherhood and claimed that soldiers from the working class would never fight each other for the benefit of capitalists, nationalism said take up arms because the barbarians—many of them from the laboring classes—are coming at us from all directions. Don't believe leftist mythology; fight to save yourself and your people from the invaders.

"Today French socialists kill German and Austrian socialists. How can we honor class sameness when proletarians from Paris and London murder us and call it a noble act? That's why I say Death to France, Britain, and Russia. Death to Italy, Serbia, and all enemies of the great Germanic people."

Religious faith, other than the pseudo-religion of nationalism, also crept into several of the justifications Philip heard. Typical was the Bulgarian sergeant who saw the war as a practical continuation of the Counter-Reformation. But he fought not only against Protestant deviation from the true Christian faith; he still felt the Pope as Bishop of Rome should concede to the moral superiority of the Eastern bishops of the Orthodox Christian Church.

"I don't care if the Ottomans are our allies, not until the divide between Eastern and Western Christianity is healed can Europe reunite and defend itself from the real threat which is Islam," he declared. "We have seen the cruelty of the Moslems in the repression carried out by the Ottoman Turks. The only way to counter such Oriental evil is to crusade in unity against the unholy East. Nothing less than our civilization is in the balance.

"I know the Ottomans are supposed to be my allies," he continued. "But I am not fooled. That only means that we fight side by side because we have a common foe, the Entente armies and their allies. The true enemy is Islam, and the impediment to Christian solidarity is the Pope in Rome. When he submits to the primacy of the Eastern Orthodox Church, only then can we defend our culture and triumph over the Mussulmen. If Christianity is to endure, the Roman Church must accept the leadership and interpretations of the Eastern hierarchy."

Gathering testimonials for his report was a laborious task. The diversity of responses convinced Philip that it would be impossible to deduce one or two dominant lines of thought. With so many perspectives motivating a continent at war, how could a few categories of justification explain the passion and historical ignorance he detected in almost every interview?

Moreover, Philip felt it necessary to broaden his perspective. He needed to interview Entente soldiers, and preferably those stationed on the frontlines.

18

When Philip proposed expanding his investigation by visiting the battlefront, Guillaumat cautioned him. "You are certainly welcome to speak with my troops about the war. It would be more informative to compare the attitudes of fighters on both sides. But if you seek to understand the war in its fullest expression of human reaction, are you sure that you are asking the widest range of questions?

Philip admitted his confusion over the General's remarks. "I've been addressing the motives and fears among of soldiers. Now I want to compare those responses to what our own troops say," he replied.

"Understood, Dr. Montfort. Your interviewees are men reacting to war and its battlefield culture of victory or death. But is it enough to register these opinions without more fully understanding the environment in which these warriors have operated? Your interviewees may think their greatest peril is our firepower. And make no mistake, our arsenal is deadly. But there is another killer at work, Professor. And it has influenced attitudes on war, too.

"Have you given much thought to the lethal influence of disease?" Guillaumat asked. Here in Macedonia we have malaria, elsewhere it may be typhus or polio or influenza—there are so many deadly illnesses to be considered. The men you've met all know about disease. They've live with it and around it for months, even years. Have you asked how exposure to sickness may have influenced their attitudes toward the war?"

He went on to explain how malaria along the Macedonian Front was ravaging both sides. "When future historians evaluate human loss in this Great War," he suggested, "they will use gross statistics of battle deaths and injuries to assess the importance of our various confrontations. They will ask: how many were shot, killed, or were wounded in particular battles? How many deserted or were captured or simply disappeared?

"These are valid questions, Professor. But if only scholars would delve a little deeper they might discover that the true victor on both sides was the mosquito, or perhaps the rat, or the humble louse. That's because these tiny carriers of disease are often more deadly than enemy bullets or long-range artillery shells.

"Even civilian populations have been ravaged by wartime diseases," the General added. "And what makes it all the more frustrating is that we know the proper procedures and the right drugs and serums to prevent and even cure most of these vicious illnesses. But we have insufficient supplies and an inefficient distribution system for what we do have.

"God, do I hate to see robust soldiers with fatal sicknesses. Death in armed combat is much easier for me to deal with. But watching the slow agony of a young man dying because of typhus or malaria is terrible," he added.

"With that proviso you are welcome to accompany me on a visit to the frontlines. I have only been Commander-in-Chief here for a few weeks. I'm trying to meet all our troops to reassure them that the officer corps cares about their safety and successes. But, in all fairness to the troops you'll meet, consider the impact of disease as well as conflict on morale and attitudes in general.

"If you would like to come on my visit tomorrow morning, be sure to get your quinine pills from the medical officer before we leave. You'll need them to help fight the potential of contracting malaria."

Philip was pleased that General Guillaumat was so interested in his research. And he was correct, Philip had been giving no attention to the role disease was playing in affecting the psychology of soldiers on all sides. Dutifully, he visited the base hospital to pick up preventive medicine. He was ready the following morning to visit the frontlines.

A convoy of trucks and troops left Salonika at 7 am headed for the Struma River in southwestern Bulgaria. Here they stopped at a small military outpost overlooking the waterway and guarding the strategic road that ran from Salonika into the Bulgarian interior.

While the General spent the afternoon meeting with his officers, Philip took the Commandant's suggestion and sought out the camp physician. He wanted to learn more about the effect of microbes and disease on both military and civilian populations.

Dr. Luigi Falcone was a trained internist from Milan, not exactly the epidemiological background for a man fighting contagions, but at least he was formally-educated and a licensed physician. Speaking in French, he was happy to share his observations with Philip. Besides, it gave him a chance to vent his rage at the stubborn ignorance he regularly confronted while trying to save lives from disease.

"When I joined the Italian medical corps in 1915," he explained as he visited patients in the encampment hospital facility, "bullets, artillery bursts, grenades, even aerial bombs were the principal causes of death and injury among our troops. But over time, disease has become a major reason so many soldiers die or become war casualties.

"Nowadays, the war has slowed. The great offensives are not as frequent as they were three or four years ago—even a year ago. But the death rate is not diminishing. That is because killer illnesses attack everyone's troops without a shot being fired."

"Are you suggesting that environment—I mean, where the troops live and fight—may play a role in the attitudes soldiers develop?" Philip inquired. "If so, I would think that living in the dirt in narrow trenches would contribute to wartime medical problems as well as opinions about the war."

"To a great degree that's true," the Italian physician replied. "But life in the trenches is a misnomer. You can't label a hellish existence in deplorable conditions as 'life.' These below-ground refuges are found on every battlefront—from the Germans in France to the Rumanians in Bessarabia and the Turks in Syria. Everyone digs these holes in the ground and endures the squalor that inevitably comes with them.

"Below the earth's surface, men live like moles. Soldiers pop their heads above ground, and are lucky if they're not killed. They take exploratory night patrols, but always return to their protective pits before dawn. Charges with guns blazing are so risky that most of the fighting is now done while hunkered down, buried in the earth on bended knees. But it's so difficult in the trenches. Many soldiers welcome going over the top as a relief from the tedium of being buried alive. Some even look forward to hand-to-hand combat because at least it's invigorating.

"And what wretched places these trenches are. Dug by men with shovels, they're narrow slits in the ground in which armies hide to avoid being slaughtered. Monotony occupies much of the trapped soldiers' lives. They converse with each other about mundane matters. They spend hours pressed to the trench floor or walls avoiding enemy bombardment. They eat cold, tinned food because it's usually too dangerous to start a cooking fire.

"The entrenched man may be buried alive, but he is still exposed to the elements from freezing winters to springtime flooding to sweltering summer days. Sometimes they contract trench foot from the germs that float on the mucky bottoms of these holes in the dirt. Often in very cold weather troopers knowingly risk their lives by sitting on the edge of trenches to keep their cold feet out of the frozen liquids that inundate the floors of these foul places.

"But don't stop there. There is still the problem of human waste. Sure, in the maze of trenches the warriors construct latrines at the far ends of their earthen lines. But these toilets need constant cleaning and frequent re-digging. So, what happens in the midst of battle when a soldier needs to visit the latrine but cannot leave his position? He stays at his post and relieves himself there. And what about dysentery, a very common bowel condition that can drive a fighter to the latrine ten or more times a day? When fifty to eighty percent of your men are afflicted—thanks to tainted food or hordes of flies carrying germs from decaying corpses nearby—how do you handle demand for access to toilets?

"This is living?" Falcone asked rhetorically. "In the trenches men become accustomed to death. It no longer fazes them. Sure, they all want to live; but they see buddies killed and maimed every day, and over the months this inures them to normal feelings. They become fatalistic, even indifferent to the potentialities of combat. Some even wish for death. Maybe that's where bravery originates—when indifference to dying emboldens a man to undertake heroic feats.

"But men have been boxed in trenches for so long they are now dying from the germs that infect them in those holes," the doctor asserted. "Compared to the diseases a rat can carry, poison gas is child's play. And the trenches are crawling with vermin and their parasites. Rats scurry along foul trench floors, nesting in discarded clothing, seeking the warm bodies of sleeping soldiers; and all rats carry deadly lice.

"Some call them cooties, nits, pants rabbits, or seam squirrels. The French named them totos; to the British they're coddlers. But whatever they're called, one thing is for certain: lice love people. They thrive in the hair on a man's head and pubic areas. They invade the hair on the legs, chest, back, and arms. And they crawl everywhere on the body. When they bite—and they do that frequently, leaving small areas of open skin in the process—they will often defecate. So, when you scratch, you rub louse defecation and its deadly bacteria into the open bite mark. This causes typhus with diarrhea and high fevers that can lead to pneumonia or swelling of the heart muscles and the brain. In short, Professor Montfort, the louse is a mighty killer.

"Let me give you an early example. Six months after Austria attacked Serbia in 1914, the Serbs experienced an epidemic of typhus. Some people believe that the Austrians first contracted it and then spread it to the Serbs. From a total population of three million Serbian citizens, 500,000 came down with typhus. More than forty percent of the infected died—70,000 were members of the Serbian Army. Even 30,000 Austrians, prisoners of Serbia, died of the illness.

"To fight the epidemic, Serbia had only 400 doctors. Many of these were in the Army where typhus killed more than one hundred of them. The contagion was so bad that Austrian generals, fearing further exposure to the disease, refrained from attacking Serbia several months."

"I had no idea that parasites could be so lethal," Philip remarked. "No one talks about it. I don't read about it in the popular newspapers or magazines. Soldiers must learn about it during military training, but how effective is the prevention program on the battle lines? General Guillaumat mentioned that it's difficult to get sufficient serums and drugs to fight these germs."

The doctor just smiled sardonically. "You prove my point. Even if I were the greatest research epidemiologist in the world, winner of science prizes for medicine, discoverer of the cure for all diseases, if I don't have sufficient medical supplies I can't protect my patients. I can't, and the German, Bulgarian, Turkish, and Austrian doctors can't either. No physician can cure without good medicines sufficiently available.

"But I understand that typhus is not the most urgent threat to the Army of the Orient," said Philip, "at least here in northern Greece—or are we in southern Bulgaria? I guess that depends on the outcome of the war and the trading of territory that will inevitably follow."

"*Touché*, Professor Montfort. I see you can be as cynical as I," the doctor responded.

"In the Balkans we are fighting a trench war in a place that is already a swamp," Falcone explained. "Can you imagine what that does to a soldier's physical condition? Add the insufficiency of medicines and you are talking about disease that is almost epidemic.

"Here, in the Balkans," he explained, "our greatest problem is malaria. Sure we have rats carrying lice, but those damned Anopheles mosquitoes and the bacteria they implant when they bite exact a morbid toll. Do you know that Anopheles is from classical Greek meaning 'worthless?' What an irony that the worthless mosquito carries vicious malaria that causes incapacitation and even loss of life.

"These flying menaces breed in the bogs and swampy marshes near the river. They become infected by ingesting contaminated blood, then invade our trenches and military installations and spread their pathogens. Look around you, Dr. Montfort. At this moment you are standing in one of the worse malaria sites in Europe; it's the valley of the Struma.

"The mosquitoes here infect everyone, but they especially enjoy biting light-skinned men like those from Great Britain. And the commanders in Salonika have given the Tommies the lead role in defending the river. Among their forces, we treat ten times as many men for malaria as for battle wounds. In the summer when the disease is rampant in the valleys, the Brits relocate to higher ground where there are fewer flying bugs. This creates a No Man's Land nine-miles wide that separates the warring armies. Wisely, enemy officers refuse to occupy the evacuated territory.

"How can our soldiers fight when they're incapacitated with malaria? Luckily, it is not a guaranteed killer like typhus, although it can prove fatal by causing brain damage and kidney failure. But malaria can be treated with quinine and cinchona bark. The disease, however, will take you out of commission for weeks.

"And it's recurring," Dr. Falcone added. "Periodically for the rest of your life you will come down with the sickness because it never fully leaves your system.

"If malaria and typhus aren't discouraging enough," he continued, "there's cholera. Troops everywhere have been killed by cholera. Its cause is poor sanitation and specifically consumption of water contaminated with fecal matter. Cholera moves fast. In a matter of hours—instead of days or weeks—it can cause renal failure and death.

"The Italian Army in the winter of 1915-1916 fought cholera as much as it fought Austrians. In fact, we doctors believe that outbreak spread accidentally from sources in the Austro-Hungarian Army. The Turks have been plagued by the disease. Throughout the war—even dating back to the First Balkan War in 1912—cholera epidemics swept Constantinople, Ankara, and villages throughout the Ottoman Empire. Soldiers and civilians suffered; we'll never know how many Turks died.

"But we do know the cure. Ottoman doctors—as few as there are in the Sultan's lands—know how to treat it. But with all the nations of the world—not just those at war, mind you—scrambling for the same antidotes to cure and protect their citizens, supplies are scarce."

"Now that I've turned your stomach and made you afraid to touch or drink anything ever again, do you have any questions?" the doctor asked.

"Well, you opened my eyes," Philip admitted. "These are three major diseases with horrible potential. I'm afraid to ask if there other wartime sicknesses."

"Oh, I should have mentioned disorders that are less prevalent," Falcone interrupted. "You may not read about it, but we military doctors treat scurvy, trench foot, trench fever, influenza, and amoebic dysentery. We've also encountered cases of syphilis, typhoid fever, diphtheria, spotted fever, plague, and sometimes even smallpox. Every disease could quickly spread if we didn't intervene.

"And keep this in mind: every infection has epidemic, even pandemic potential. From the common cold to polio: when you have thousands of people jammed for months in cramped quarters such as in those squalid trenches, the possibility of mass inflection rises dramatically."

Philip interrupted the doctor. "Let me stop you there," he said. "You've just reminded me of something. Five or six weeks ago I had the opportunity to witness the spread of influenza among a group of abused prisoners held by the Turks. Now, I have considerable experience with battlefield medicine. I worked with the American Field Service Ambulance a few years ago. But I never saw anything like this flu. I did what I could: separated the infected from the healthy; advised the other prisoners to keep their hands clean and to cover their mouths with masks or gauze; and above all avoid close contact with the infected. That stopped the spread. But many of those who had the disease died—some in great agony."

The doctor grew tense. "Where did you witness this?" he inquired with a serious look on his face. "Did you report it to the Turkish authorities? To the French or Greek medical officials when you got to Salonika?" he asked nervously. "Influenza is an amazing disease. It mutates very rapidly. As soon as we find the cure for this year's strain, next year's version arrives and is resistant to the previous cure. And if the newer influenza has a high fatality rate and remains unchecked, nothing can stop it from spreading rapidly around the world. Then we're talking about a pandemic and global devastation!

"Most of our flu varieties come from the Far East and move through Asia to Europe and then across the Atlantic to North and South America. But it can originate and spread from anywhere. It could even start in North America and move to Europe and then to Asia. If what you experienced is an untreatable kind of flu, you may be describing a global contagion which, in modern wartime circumstances, could have catastrophic consequences for public health."

"Should I have reported it?" asked Philip.

"Without a doubt. And if you fail to do so, I will do it first thing tomorrow morning," replied Falcone. "Where did this occur? How did you happen to be there? What happened to the other prisoners when you left? Were Turkish doctors alerted?"

"Wait a minute," Philip interjected. "Let me sit down and write out a full report. I'll give it to the chief military physician in Salonika. Let me think about it; there are details I may have omitted. I'll put it all down on paper."

"That would be the responsible thing to do," Dr. Falcone responded. "When it comes to matters like this, even war must stop and react to the implications. The world has already lost millions of lives in the conflict. I don't know if human civilization can withstand countless more millions dead because of an unchecked strain of killer influenza."

The conversation with the physician diminished Philip's enthusiasm for further interviews that day. Instead, he sat down and began searching his memory for every detail of the sickness he encountered in Prison 29. He wrote precise descriptions on everything he could recall.

Philip continued to write his testimony as the military convoy was assembled and headed back to Salonika. Hours later when the caravan reached headquarters, he completed his observations. He immediately presented a copy of the report to General Guillaumat and urged him to send it immediately to the proper officials in Salonika, Paris, and Constantinople. He also planned to include a copy with his final assessment for President Wilson. If this strain of flu could leap oceans, he wanted the health community in the United States to be aware of what he had witnessed.

THE HEADLONG FURY

The following day Philip was awakened by an excited concierge rapping at his door. "Hurry, Monsieur Montfort, get up! Everyone's driving over to Mikra. The Serb Volunteers Second Division is arriving this morning. They're throwing a big party to welcome home the soldiers. Lots of Serbian music and food, a big parade with a marching band. Everyone needs a morale boost. This should be just the tonic. Come on, get up. The hotel bus will be leaving in ten minutes."

This was a big day for everyone in Salonika. A new contingent of 6000 Serbian fighters had made it to Greece after weeks of grueling travel. It was now time to celebrate.

As he learned from others on the way to the welcoming festivities, these Serbia troops followed an unconventional route to get here. Many months earlier these Serbs came to pre-Bolshevik Russia as liberated prisoners, freed from Austrian captivity by the Tsarist army. There were so many that the Russians created two divisions of so-called Serbian Volunteers. Salonika was their gateway to the Balkans and a return home, but the Volunteers were still stuck in Russia in November 1917 when the Communist overthrew the Provisional Government and seized power.

A month later the First Division, 20,000 strong, arrived in Salonika. They left Russia through the far-northern port of Archangel. Their evacuation route took them by ship past northern Finland and Norway, then southward into the Atlantic and to Italy. From Italy they reached Greece.

The smaller Second Division, however, was less fortunate. It was detained by the Reds. Specifically, by Communist officials who blocked the Serbs from leaving through Archangel which by now was frozen over until late in the following spring.

This move forced the 6000 men of the Second Division to take a much more demanding route: they had to travel eastward across revolutionary Russia on the Trans-Siberian Railroad and the Chinese Eastern Railroad to the Pacific coast city of Port Arthur in Japanese-occupied China. From there, British ships transported them to Hong Kong and then around Asia, past India, and through the Suez Canal to Port Said in Egypt. From Port Said the Volunteers finally reached Salonika. This journey of almost 14,000 miles lasted eleven weeks.

Throughout the first days of April the Second Division straggled into Mikra, a dingy village five miles outside Salonika. Serb military forces had been quartered in Mikra for several years. Today, however, the town was decorated to celebrate the arrival of both Divisions.

Philip hurriedly dressed and prepared himself for what sounded like a street party. He well understood the plight of the regular Serbian Army. It had been in combat since the opening day of the hostilities. This was after already enduring grievous wounds during the two Balkan Wars. Further, because of wartime strains—including partial occupation by Austrian and Bulgarian troops and bouts of disease—agricultural productivity declined and the nation faced the possibility of mass starvation even if the Serbian side won the war.

But there would be no hunger in Mikra today. Salonika was preparing to welcome its new heroes, and food was the medium of celebration. Local residents and ethnic Army cooks spared no expense in honoring their brethren with food for everyone. Fragrant loaves of freshly-baked bread; the delicious aroma of grilled pork and lamb; limitless rolls of stuffed cabbage and grape leaves rolled thick with fresh minced meats and spices; baked beans in tangy tomato broth; moussaka, goulash, and other Balkan specialties, all lubricated with cold beer and slivovitz. There was music and dancing, men and women dressed in fancy national fashions, even a beauty pageant glorifying the most beautiful Serbian women in the area.

The highlight of the event, of course, was the military parade. Units of weathered Serbian troops stationed for months in northern Greece were followed by the honored Volunteers. The infusion of new blood seemed to energize the older soldiers. Everyone marched with an attitude of confidence and authority. The determination shown by the Volunteers to reach the Macedonian Front and liberate their homeland seemed to imbue all Serbs with renewed self-assurance.

The image of brave infantrymen marching eight abreast to the stirring rhythm of martial music thrilled the bystanders. As the Volunteers moved down the main street, they were a throwback to the idealism and pride of the earliest weeks of the war. There was swagger in their step, and smiles of excitement on their faces. These were fighters who were going to save Serbia from being destroyed by the greedy interests of Vienna, Berlin, and Sofia. The troops and their roadside supporters seemed unwilling to accept any other result.

For Philip this was a perfect context in which to probe the psychology of war. One nationality, various levels of experience: what was the interaction when they meet? What did fresh troops mean to the experienced soldiers? How did the veterans of Macedonian fighting impact the Serbian Volunteers? And what about idealistic and inexperienced non-combatants? What was their reaction to the veterans and the Volunteers? Conversely, how did civilians affect the men in uniform?

He had heard that the Volunteers were scheduled to leave tomorrow by truck for the frontline Serbian town of Monastir. He hoped to join them when they departed in the morning. When he showed the Serb commander the note General Guillaumat had written, he was granted immediate permission to join the convoy that was leaving before sunrise.

But for this afternoon in Mikra, it was time to hail the Serbian heroes and enjoy the food and drink offered in their honor.

The dirt road to Monastir was bumpy with occasional places where the Vardar and the Struma rivers had overflowed. Here the roadway remained flooded, but the large tires of the transport vehicles slowly rolled their human cargoes through deep waters and toward their destination near an encampment of Bulgarian soldiers protecting holdings they captured in southern Serbia.

During the motor trip Philip and General Guillaumat discussed the Balkan situation. The fact that he was seated next to the General led Philip to believe that the letter from General Foch bolstered his image with the local officer corps. Guillaumat urged Philip not to discount Monastir even though it seemed battered and neutralized by the proximity of troops from both sides. This town remained an important launching point for his plan to drive Bulgaria from the war, he assured Philip. He hoped to revitalize the Army of the Orient—especially the Serbian contingents who considered Monastir a Serb city—and use their energy to rally all his troops. At this point, however, he was only willing to carry out random thrusts into enemy territory, probes that would season his men and gauge the response of the opponents.

By the autumn, he told Philip, he would execute a military push along the entire Balkan frontline stretching from Albania eastward to Thrace. Such an expansive line of battle, the General argued, would thin Bulgarian defenses and any Austrian or German participation that might materialize. This would allow his international forces to push the enemy totally from the peninsula. It was a bold vision for an army unfamiliar with victories. Guillaumat, however, was determined to accomplish his goal.

When the caravan reached Monastir, there was apparent excitement as soldiers on the ground welcomed the reinforcements, in particular the Volunteer divisions. A large percentage of the new troops were from Bosnia, and they were greeted especially warmly by the veteran Bosnian soldiers stationed at Monastir.

"Welcome to the end of the world," said a young French lieutenant, as he reached out to shake Philip's hand. "I am Lieutenant Marcel-Pierre Blondel. I am your liaison here. Anything you want, just ask me."

Philip smiled and thanked the French officer for his assistance. As the two men conversed, however, the friendliness of the meeting was interrupted by a massive explosion. Strangely, only the newcomers ducked for cover. The others went about their business, some of them even laughing at the reaction of the neophytes from Salonika.

"Ah, that's only the Bulgarians reminding us that it's time for lunch," said Lieutenant Blondel. "No need to dive for cover. They send over a few artillery rounds every day. They're not trying to hit anything. It's just a friendly soldier-to-soldier greeting. They hit a pig pen once, and an old barn another time. But they miss us on purpose. They know that if they killed any of our soldiers, we would retaliate in kind. The Bulgars don't want that. They are content to sit in occupied Serbia a few miles on the other side of town. From there they can send periodic greetings of *bon jour, bon appétit,* and *bon soir.* The next time you hear a shell explode, check your wristwatch; you will find it's time to get up, eat, or go to bed."

With that assurance, Philip determined to be indifferent to the next explosions. It wasn't an easy adjustment, however. In the meantime he grabbed his notebook and translator and began to search for people to interview.

The several Serbs he encountered all told the same story. They were filled with nationalist fervor and hoped to push the enemy out of Greater Serbia. The men also strongly supported the creation of a Kingdom of South Slavs that would unite Serbia with Montenegrins, Croatians, Slovenes, and even some Bulgars. Their choice for the new monarchy was venerable old King Peter I of Serbia. "But," cautioned one of the soldiers cynically, "how long will it take for Roman Catholic Croatians and Slovenes, Orthodox Serbians, plus Jews, Protestants, and Muslims in such a mixed kingdom to begin fighting among each other? Five years? Ten years? Twenty? Maybe only a few months."

Philip found it bizarre that only one of his interviewees mentioned the Ottoman Empire as a reason for making war. This was a young sergeant who saw the problem as the result of Ottoman collapse after centuries of occupation. "We have to finish this Balkan business once and for all. Boundaries in the peninsula have been shifting back and forth for too long," he told Philip.

"Did you ever notice how the Balkans quiver whenever the Turks loosen their grip and surrender territory? When the Russians attack the Turks, all the little countries here feel the aftereffects. When the Austrians annexed Bosnia in 1908, everything was shaken in our lands. A few years ago in the Balkan Wars we fought each other, everything changed again: Greece got fatter; Bulgaria added only a little; Serbia and Rumania expanded their territories; not so much for Albania and Montenegro, but they did grow a bit. And poor Macedonia? It lost plenty of land.

"We need a fixed map," he explained. "We need someone to come along and say 'You own this, and you own that. No changes are permitted ever again. Enjoy your land, but don't try to take another nation's territory or you will be punished.'

"They say politics abhors a vacuum. With the Turks in retreat, this part of Europe is a perpetual political vacuum. It must be rearranged once and for all or these wars will go on forever."

Philip was impressed by the sophistication of the answers he was now receiving. Most of the men were of peasant background, lacking in formal education; but they were trained soldiers. And despite a lack of formal educations, their responses demonstrated a basic understanding of the history and geopolitics of the Balkans.

But Philip was taken aback when another Serbian raised a point he had not yet heard. "I am a Serbian soldier. I'm part of the Second Division recently arrived from Russia. I have seen the world. But I have not seen anyone willing to admit that Macedonia should be for the Macedonians. By what right do the Bulgars bite off chunks of this land? Who asked the Greeks to grab a large section? Did anyone check with the Macedonians to get their approval? Were they even at the peace talks?

"I must admit that my own country is equally guilty. Serbia has demanded and taken its own large portions of Macedonia. Thousands of poor souls like me have died or been injured protecting the land stolen in my name by my government in Belgrade.

"The name Macedonia is famous in history. Alexander the Great was Macedonian. He was born in Pella, not that far from here. He didn't speak classical Greek—maybe no Greek at all because he was not Greek.

The Macedonians' problems are that their language is too much like Bulgarian; their culture is also Bulgarian. This allows their rivals to say these people are nothing but a group of Slavs who live there now with no ethnic or cultural ties to ancient Macedon.

"Modern Macedonians also lack an effective nationalist movement. Although they have political and cultural leaders who call for self-determination, who listens to them? They've fought no great battles to liberate themselves. They have robbed no banks to finance their revolutionary schemes. They haven't assassinated one king or prime minister to publicize their goals.

In other words, they have been weak players in the political game. One must be assertive or be forgotten. Just look at the Ruthenians and the Tartars, the Basques, Kosovites, Gypsies, Circassians, Cossacks, Jews, and so many other nationalities destined to be absorbed into a someone else's country."

Philip wasn't certain of the soldier's factual accuracy. But when he congratulated him on being perceptive, the Serb explained that before joining the army he had been a school teacher in Nish, once the second largest city in the Kingdom of Serbia. "I used to teach history. Now I'm living it," he quipped.

"I fought the Austrians, the Germans, and the Bulgars when they invaded my country. I even survived the horrendous Great Retreat of

THE HEADLONG FURY

1915-1916 when 250,000 soldiers with family members and enemy prisoners crossed the snowy mountains while Bulgarians, Germans, and Austrians bombarded us. They were trying to massacre the entire population of Serbia, and we had to run from them in order to save our nation.

We traveled along icy paths barely wide enough for an ox cart. We squeezed through jagged passes with steep cliffs from which countless humans and pack animals plunged accidentally to their deaths. And often we fled while under attack from two sides.

"It was a long slog: from Serbia through Albania and Montenegro to the Adriatic coast where we found eventual refuge, mostly on the Greek island of Corfu. As well as the enemies at our heels, we faced starvation, disease, freezing temperatures, massive deprivation, hostile Albanian tribesmen, and great tests of will and strength. But like our precious Serbia, we proudly survived. Or, at least 150,000 of us survived the Great Retreat—but only 70,000 that number were physically able to fight in our next offensive in Macedonia the following summer.

"So, as I said, I have lived history; and it has been brutal. As much as I appreciate people recognizing me as a Serbian hero, I would rather have remained a school teacher," the soldier concluded.

Philip spent the next several days interviewing men with compelling stories and interpretations. One English sergeant quoted Rudyard Kipling's poem, *Tommy Atkins*, in explaining why he was a Tommy. "I got very little respect back home before the war. But now everyone loves me. Especially the birds, the girls that fly around me like I was some kind of posh millionaire. You remember the ending of Kipling's ditty, don't you?

> For it's Tommy this, an' Tommy that,
> an' "Chuck him out, the brute!"
> But it's "Saviour of 'is country"
> when the guns begin to shoot;
> An' it's Tommy this, an' Tommy
> that, an' anything you please;"
> An' Tommy ain't a bloomin' fool—
> you bet that Tommy sees!

"Well, I sees, Professor, and a lot of what I sees I don't like" he continued. "But why do I fight, because I ain't a bloomin' fool. I fight because I'm a proud British Tommy. And I sees a lot worth saving. Tommy Atkins, that's me, and this is me life."

A French soldier, a *poilu*, seemed almost happy that he was in Macedonia. "I could be in a trench in Champagne, with rats and rotting corpses all around me. I could be ducking Boche machine gun bullets and dodging poison gas. But I am in Macedon. Do you understand the significance? I am in the place that bred Alexander. If I am going to fight and possibly die, let me do so in the land of *Alexandre le Grand*.

"I am just a plain farmer from Anjou. My life is not spectacular, not like what I see in the magazines and at the cinema. But now I walk where the greatest warrior in history once strode. His spirit is here! If I die, maybe my blood will fall where he once bled; maybe our essences will mix. My wife and children can then be proud that I, a simple rifleman from Central France, perished and became one with Alexander of Macedon. Now, that would be spectacular."

Only on that afternoon did Philip have a chance to probe the health conditions facing the average soldier. Speaking to a young Greek private, the conversation switched to sanitation and its importance. "You need to know, Professor Montfort, that whatever Army a soldier fights, his greatest enemy is the pestilence that surrounds him at all times. No infantryman can maintain his patriotism when he is up to his ankles in the putrid mud of a stinking trench. Sloshing around in this mix of urine and excrement, be it human or otherwise, will not make a soldier feel honored to be part of this horrific war.

"And this inhumanity does not discriminate. Turks and Frenchmen die from the pox. German and Italians die the same way from cholera. And, I imagine that Chinese and Japanese, Africans on both sides of the fighting, Indian conscripts, Portuguese, Canadians, and even non-combatants suffer the same deadly results when disease is in their air.

"But what is done about it? Very little! They just carry away the corpses and restock the trenches with fresh conscripts who have no idea about the role of sickness in their new environment. These young guys are worried about their heads being blown off, and that's understandable. But the more virile killer is in the muck covering their feet, in the vermin that reside in the trenches with them, in the fecal matter that pollutes their underground living quarters."

It was a startling summary, reminiscent of what Dr. Falcone had explained yesterday. In fact, most of the answers he encountered in Monastir were similarly expressive. But after days of collecting testimonies, Philip was ready to return to Salonika, to complete his report to President Wilson and move on to his assignment in Rome. As he waited in the officers' tent for the next returning truck, a Serb soldier he had already interviewed approached him. "I know you're about to leave, Professor Montfort, but there's a soldier I think you should speak with. He has a unique story for you because he's the only Pole I've met fighting for us. We don't get Polish guys this far south."

Philip's interest was piqued. "Well, let me unpack my equipment. You bring him here," Philip replied. "Wait. What languages does he speak? I have no translator for Polish."

"Here he is," the Serb said as he reached outside the tent and dragged in a young blonde soldier dressed in a Serbian uniform.

"Hello," he said in Russian. "My name is Anton Oleska. I am a private in the Serbian Third Army. I am a sharpshooter, and I speak Polish and Russian—and I've learned a little Serbian in recent months."

Philip introduced himself in Russian and explained the interview project. "So, if you're ready," he said, "let me ask the question I have asked dozens of men on both sides of this war: why do you fight?"

Private Oleska gathered his thoughts. "I fight for the Entente," he began, "because I am Polish and Poland must exist again. Only through the free democracies can Poland become independent. I love France and Britain, Italy and America. They allow their citizens to be free. If they win, they will bring their kind of freedom to us, and Poland will be reborn.

"I always had problems with Tsar Nicholas being part of your Entente," he continued. "You had the most repressive government in Europe sleeping in a bed of democracy. That was hard for Poles to understand.

"But now the Tsar is gone. Russia is out of the war. Our only enemies are Austria and Germany—and we Poles hate both of these empires. When the Entente crushes them, Poland will be liberated and we will emerge as an independent nation."

"Now, you might be thinking, why does Oleska fight in Serbia and Macedonia? Isn't that far from Poland?' But everything is close in this war, Professor," said the young soldier. "A victory here has implications in northern France. Destruction of the Austrians in Serbia is as good as destroying them in Italy. If we attack across the Struma, we will hammer the Bulgarians and that will force Austria and Germany to send more troops into our battle. And where will these new troops come from? From reserves originally headed for France or Italy or Poland. So, wherever I battle Poland's enemies my contribution has significance at home."

"Poland must be free. We must become an independent, free nation-state like so much of Europe will be once the war ends. We are a sizable people who fit the definition of a nation-state. We speak one language, worship through one Roman Catholic Church, and are many millions strong. Also, we share a history in which we were once the greatest power in Europe until our neighbors through many wars sliced us apart.

"The final butchering of Poland occurred at the Congress of Vienna, the conference in 1815 where the forces for change from the French Revolution and the Napoléonic wars were stifled by the reactionary winners. Prussia, now the heart of modern Germany, took Great Poland with more than three million Poles. The Austrians were given Galicia with three and one-half million Poles. The Russians incorporated our eastern borderlands into their empire. All that was left was called Congress Poland; it is the heartland of our country. That was supposed to be constitutional and autonomous, but the Congress of Vienna made Russia our protector. Ha! It didn't take long before our protector became our oppressor."

The Polish soldier continued his explanation. "Until the outbreak of this present war Congress Poland was dominated by the Tsars. Technically, Congress Poland was the Kingdom of Poland—but the Tsars made themselves our kings. Is that independence? I spit on that type of national freedom.

"Our language was forbidden in schools. Our culture was corrupted by Russian influences. Our sense of self-worth was shattered by foreign occupation. The Russians even dissolved the frontier between themselves and Congress Poland. Poland ceased to exist—on paper, at least.

"In our southern region, Galicia, the Austrians carried out a similar policy. Although Vienna eventually shared power with the Hungarians, they never bestowed such authority on the Poles or the Czechs—or any other minority peoples living within Austria-Hungary. Practically, we were all slaves in our own land.

"This war is a pivotal point in history," Oleska concluded. "In a few years you will find many new nation-states, independent democracies carved from the old empires. I fight to make certain that one of those new countries is the Republic of Poland. We don't want another Kingdom with a foreign prince imposed on us as king. We struggle for democracy, our own democracy. We want nothing less than what you have in France. What others have in the Entente nations and in America."

19

Returning to Rome was both nostalgic and a reminder of frightening times. Philip loved this city. From historic monuments surviving from the age of the Caesars to the pace of modern street traffic, Rome was rich in history and contemporary importance. He recalled vividly his excitement when arriving four years earlier. Then he was on a bicycle with his life in peril. Today he came by train from the Adriatic town of Bari; still, after months of torture in a Turkish prison, he remained cautious.

In the safe deposit room of the Banca d'Italia he carefully placed his reports on conditions on the Macedonian Front and looked for his latest instructions. This time, however, he found no key. He inspected the steel box carefully, but it was empty save for a thin, sealed envelope which he had withdrawn. He returned the box to its place in the vault and left the bank.

In the envelope, he found only a single sheet of paper containing a simple message: "Ambassador Camille Barrère, Embassy of France, Palais Farnese."

He smiled. One of his fondest memories of his initial visit to Rome was interacting with the distinguished ambassador. Although he had no idea of why Washington wanted him to seek out Barrère, he looked forward to visiting the Farnese Palace again.

THE HEADLONG FURY

It was a short and pleasant springtime walk from the Banca d'Italia to the French embassy. Philip enjoyed being normal again. He put aside his frightening memories of Rome and strolled comfortably toward the Piazza Farnese. He loved to watch the people passing by, and he enjoyed the public sights of the magnificent Eternal City. He was simply happy to be alive and whole as he walked in the warm sunshine.

His entrance into the embassy was different this time: no automobile trying to run him over, no gun aimed at his head, no exhaustion or fainting in front of the French guards. Although Philip remained unsure why he was ordered to come here, he presented himself to the receptionist as Professor Laurent Montfort from Paris. He produced his passport to prove his identity.

Several minutes later a young official appeared and escorted him to a second-floor office. "The ambassador will see you soon," the receptionist promised. "Please make yourself at home."

He had entered the embassy with confidence, but as the minutes passed and Barrère failed to appear, Philip grew increasingly unsure of what this appointment was about. But all misgivings vanished when he finally appeared. "My dear friend, Philip Belmont, how wonderful to see you again," the ambassador said enthusiastically. He embraced Philip, then grasped his hand and led him toward the inner rooms. "Come upstairs to my office," he said. "There is so much to talk about. Follow me. We'll order some wine and have a leisurely conversation. I have so much to learn from you."

"It's a pleasure to see you, Monsieur Ambassador," said Philip. "You seem healthy and vigorous in spite of the pressures you must be facing with this war. And how is our mutual friend, Minister Delcassé. I've not read his name in the newspapers recently."

"Théo, poor man, has never been the same since his only son, Jacques, died while a prisoner-of-war," Barrère replied. "Jacques was tortured by the Germans and died at age twenty-six in a hospital in Switzerland. That was two years ago. I don't think Théo will ever be the same."

As they walked toward his office, the ambassador ordered a servant to bring wine and cheeses for him and his guest. "I hate discussing politics on an empty stomach, don't you?" he asked with a smile on his face.

Philip nodded in genuine agreement.

"It is wonderful to see you again," the ambassador reiterated. "We've been following your exploits for several years. I've read all your reports, except the latest one. They have served both Washington and Paris well. Some of our best strategies came from insights you provided."

"But I thought I was working exclusively and confidentially for President Wilson," said Philip in bewilderment. "Why do you—and I presume the Quai d'Orsay, too—know so much about my activities?"

"Ah, Philipe-Michel Belmont, we know everything about you. Your journey was always a collaboration between France and the United States," explained Barrère. "We've done meticulous research on you. And don't forget, you were a member of the *Service Aéronautique*. You were in the French Army. We had to approve your release before President Wilson could recruit you. So we've been involved with you from the beginning of your odyssey."

"Then you knew about my endeavors in Petrograd and Cairo, Athens, Salonika?" Philip inquired.

"We certainly did. In fact, many of the arrangements made for you in those cities were made by the Ministry of Foreign Affairs, not the State Department," Barrère revealed. "We made all your travel reservations. Remember the clown in Athens? He was a French agent who had studied mime before entering government service. It was an unusual use of a preexisting talent, if I do say so myself.

"On some occasions we made contacts at the highest levels for you. In Cairo for example, we had to speak to General Allenby directly and reveal that you were working on a Top Secret project. We insisted to him that France and the United States expected complete cooperation from Great Britain.

"We relied on your intelligence to approach only safe contacts when you were abroad. But after the unpredictable way you performed in bringing the Schlieffen Plan to Rome, we came to trust your maturity to adjust to meet changing circumstances. We have always appreciated your adaptability, Professor."

Philip smiled. "Here I thought my life was often threatened, but at least I had two nations secretly protecting me," he said.

"Oh, no, no, my friend, that wasn't the case at all," responded the ambassador. "France made the arrangements and even some of your assignments. But, believe me, your life was in real danger. Neither France nor the United States had any way to keep you alive if someone decided to murder you. You were on your own all the time.

"We just made life a little less complicated for you. Call us your *agent de voyages*, your travel agent. But you never had a bodyguard from us or the Americans.

"And that reminds me," Barrère continued. "We lost contact with you for seven or eight months last year. Some people thought you were dead, other said you were bought off and moved into obscurity with millions in German gold. There were some on both sides of the Atlantic who speculated that you might resurface as a double agent. I was not among such cynics.

"Then out of the blue, we received a cable from the Royal Navy in Famagusta, and then from you in Athens. But, tell me more. What happened to you during those lost months?"

Philip laughed as he explained that he didn't *go* anywhere, instead he was *taken* and held by Turkish authorities suspicious of his activities. He explained his capture, his torture in Prison 29, his escape, and his rescue by Canadian sailors.

"I knew you didn't fail us," Barrère remarked. "I can read a man's character fairly well. I've always been impressed with your integrity and selflessness. Not many men would commit themselves to carry a secret message for a foreign government—and at such a great risk to their own lives. Honoring a commitment, that's a test of a man's virtue."

"Thank you for your confidence," replied Philip. "Meanwhile, I'm sitting here in Rome; it's April 26, 1918, and I presume the war is still going on. By the end of July this conflict will be four years old. That's four years of death and destruction. Will it ever end?"

"It has been long and bloody, there's no doubt about that," the ambassador agreed, "but we must have patience. We've been fighting a foe with tremendous military skill and weaponry, great manpower reserves, and substantial financial resources.

"The public may be growing weary of the killings and devastation, but there is still a public desire to win this war. Two days ago I attended an inspiring display of popular support for Italy and the Italian military. It was the third anniversary of Italy's entry into the world war. Hundreds of thousands of people crowded the streets of Rome to commemorate the day with a great procession. There were troops and delegations from all the nations fighting against Austrian and German aggression.

"A highlight of the day was a parade by old soldiers, revered men who were veterans of Giuseppe Garibaldi's *Camicie rosse*, the famous Red Shirts who fought to bring Italy into nationhood in 1860. They were cheered by onlookers, many of whom had tears in their eyes. Some of the old vets also wept as they swaggered past, their arms swinging triumphantly. Flags from the northern cities where Austrian militarism has caused such suffering were also applauded when wounded soldiers and sailors carried them into the center of the Piazza Venezia.

"But nothing was greeted with more affection than the young men of the contemporary Italian military who marched with obvious pride. This was civic endorsement, not disapproval. Yes, the Italian public wants the war to end; but not if it means defeat at the hands of a savage enemy.

"But, between you and me, I think this will be the final year," Barrère suggested. "The Germans have pretty well closed down their Eastern Front. Look at the present situation. Russia has left the war and is now fighting a civil war. Rumania has been beaten again, its territory shrunken and its oil fields under German control. Poland is totally under Germanic control and threatened by the Red Army of Communist Russia. In Macedonia, the Bulgarian Army and our Army of the Orient have stalemated, while Serbia has been militarily battered.

"The only problem in the East is the impending collapse of Constantinople. It has been a long-time coming, but Turkish nationalism has finally supplanted loyalty to the Sultan. The myth of a harmonious multinational Ottoman Empire has been exposed. The British and the French are strangling Turkey. The question is just how much political power and territory Constantinople will retain when the war concludes.

"The focus in Berlin today is on Germany's Western Front. For months Germans have been shifting troops from the East through the Fatherland and into France. Trainloads of soldiers have been arriving daily in German cities to prepare for a final offensive against us. Others have been brought directly to France to bolster the troops already waiting for the push to begin.

"In fact, I believe the big show is already underway. Five weeks ago the Germans launched a massive operation to divide French and British forces permanently. They hope to maul the British so badly that London will evacuate its soldiers from the continent. And, to be honest, they've been somewhat successful; at least in pushing the British back toward the Atlantic. But, we French are now deploying our reserves and the extra manpower is helping to blunt the enemy offensive.

"But we have a not-so-secret weapon this time. And that's why we will win the war in 1918. That weapon is the Sammies from North America. We have the United States of America and all the manpower and supplies that represents. One year after the U. S. declared war on Germany your countrymen are at last engaged in major battles across northern France.

"Now we must teach the Boches that they can't simultaneously defeat three of the greatest military powers on Earth. When they learn that lesson—and, I'm afraid, it will have to be written in German blood for them to understand it—the democracies will have won the war."

Philip was encouraged by the Ambassador Barrère's optimism. "You really think victory is that close?" he asked. "I'm embarrassed to say it, but I've lost contact with developments in France. I've been so focused on Macedonia and Serbia—and before that, Egypt and the Near East. And in between, of course, there was my little excursion to Prison 29."

"Yes, this will be the last year," Barrère assured him. "I can't imagine another long cold winter with Germany drawing up plans for a Spring Offensive in 1919. How many failed seasonal offensives does it require until you learn you can't win? How many young Germans have to die before the Kaiser's government admits that military triumph is impossible?"

"So you believe the American presence has shifted the balance in France?" Philip asked.

"Oh, most definitely," said Barrère.

"Then you must be very proud of your accomplishments here in Italy," Philip continued. "Your diplomatic efforts broke the Triple Alliance and led the Italians to join France and Britain against their former allies."

"Thank you for the praise," Philip, "but I feel terrible about my accomplishments. My diplomacy has been a disaster. I never worked for war; I always used my talents to ensure peace."

Philip sat chagrined as the ambassador further clarified his perspective.

"How many French men and boys have died because of this war? How many Italian young men have perished? Or Germans and Austrians for that matter? And how many innocent civilians have been killed, wounded, or dispossessed by the invaders? War is not a competitive parlor game with results recorded on a score sheet: 'Oh, I win. You only killed two million on my side; I killed three million on your side!'

"No, war is real and horrendous. It is the unleashing of base human instincts that civilized societies do not tolerate—except, perhaps, by their own heroic warriors in wartime. But in this modern age where military technology has appropriated science to create monstrous weapons of slaughter, war is more than the loosening of base human emotionality. Today, war is lunacy. And millions are dead or crippled in a lunatic calamity that my diplomatic failure helped to produce.

"No, Professor, I cannot take pride in what has happened during the past few years. Nor can any of my diplomatic colleagues throughout Europe. We've all failed our profession and the people who trusted us. They trusted us to keep the balance, to preserve the peace, to solve the problems in international relations; and in those endeavors we were decidedly unsuccessful."

As Philip contemplated Barrère's apology, the ambassador changed the tone of his remarks. "Before I become morose, let's get back to your question about the American contribution to the war. But before telling you why your Sammies—or, as they like to call themselves, doughboys or Yanks—have made such a difference, let me call our cook. I remember how excited you were about his *steak au poivre* the last time you were here. With your permission, I would like to repeat that dining experience."

Philip smiled appreciatively. "I thought you would never ask," he replied with a hint of familiarity, "I would very much enjoy revisiting the adventure."

The ambassador phoned the kitchen and ordered the finest cuts of beef filet. "The maestro of meat says it will be ready in thirty minutes. So, let's retire to the parlor and continue our palaver. "Our chef is always a little tardy delivering his meals," the ambassador explained. "He said a half-hour, but I'd guess forty-five, Genius, you know, cannot be rushed."

As they walked toward the parlor, Barrère delivered news Philip was not expecting to hear. "There's one Entente victory that should interest you very much," he commented. "We finally stopped the Red Baron. Baron Manfred von Richthofen was shot and killed several days ago near Amiens."

This news astonished Philip. He was at once pleased that this formidable enemy was gone, but saddened that so honorable a fighter pilot had been killed. "He was the Ace of all Aces," Philip noted somewhat sadly. "Even if you wanted to shoot him down, and we all did, you had to respect the man's skill and bravery. For him aviation seemed to be a form of principled athletic competition.

"Every pursuit pilot hoped to be as good as the Red Baron—and as gentlemanly. I remember how he once allowed a flyer in the *Escadrille Lafayette* to land safely rather than shoot him out of the air. Our man was out of ammunition and unable to defend himself, and von Richthofen didn't think it was a fair fight. That was style and class—and he possessed both in abundance."

"According to my reports," said Barrère, "he had eighty kills to his credit when he was shot by either a Canadian or Australian soldier standing on the ground. We are not certain yet who fired the fatal shot. But the Red Baron was in the middle of a dog fight seeking his 81st victim. He was not quite twenty-six years of age when he died."

"Did he crash? Was he mangled or incinerated in the wreck?" Philip inquired.

"Not at all, and that's an amazing thing," said Barrère. "He apparently bled to death from a bullet wound. But, he still had time to land his airplane carefully. He expired just as French soldiers were coming to apprehend him."

"Sounds like something he would do as a curtain call, a final swooping bow to his audience. I hope they gave him a funeral worthy of his status. He was the greatest pilot of this whole insane war," Philip said.

"Indeed, France afforded him a full military service, and he was buried in a cemetery near Amiens," noted Barrère.

"But, to return to your question about how the Americans have shifted the military balance on Germany's Western Front," the ambassador added. "First, your people are fresh to the fight. They bring enthusiasm and confidence that will sustain them and bolster our morale as well. We've been at this business for four years; we are tired of combat as are the British and the Germans. Yet, short of unconditional victory or defeat, there is no way to stop the killing. We need new energy, and your Yanks have lots to spare.

"The most obvious reason is your numbers. The war has killed or injured sizable percentages of every participating nation. We can't use children or women at the front, but the pool of men of military age is shrinking. We are down to our reserves, the last line of our military defense.

"But the United States has millions of fighters. I have heard predictions that at least two million Sammies may actually come to fight in France. That's a massive number of reinforcements. Imagine that you're a German at the point of national exhaustion and now you have to face two million well-trained, fresh soldiers from a country that was formerly neutral. That has to terrify Berlin. Plus, since America declared war on Austria-Hungary, strategists in Vienna have to be frightened as well.

"And the final reason, Philip, is your president, Mr. Woodrow Wilson. He is an idealist preaching to an audience of skeptics here in the Old World. We Europeans have been made cynical by the barbarity we've endured, and to be honest, the violence we've inflicted on others.

"We scowl at Wilson's simplistic goals: 'The war to end all wars.' 'The world made safe for democracy.' 'Open covenants openly arrived at.' Ha! There's so much fantasy in these words. They're almost juvenile.

"Yet, secretly we love them. They renew the hopefulness that is too often banished from the minds of us toughened Europeans. And then Wilson proposes the creation of a League of Nations: a cooperative, global institution through which all international problems would be settled by negotiation instead of conflict. The notion of such a League is utterly naïve—it's unrefined balderdash. But if it works, just think of its wonderful impact!

"So, let's give your President a chance. Let's see where he and his idealism take us. It can't be as bad as what we have now. In fact, the notion of maintaining world peace through a parliament of nation-states is the first new idea since the Concert of Europe in 1815. And the Concert was only an informal agreement among a few conservative monarchies."

Philip expressed his agreement with the ambassador's interpretation. "But there is a massive problem underlying your interpretation," he said respectfully. "And that's the issue of nationalities. The destruction of three massive empires means the unleashing of dozens of nationalities, most of them already agitating for independence. How will the victorious Powers handle that situation?

"Some, I know are obvious. There must be an independent Poland when the war is over. Turkey will remain as a nation-state, but its imperial Ottoman days will be finished. But what do you do about Arabia: one massive Arab state or several smaller Arab countries? Free or under European control?

"Then there are the Jews: where do they go, if they go at all? Is Zionism to be respected, or dismissed as wispy Hebraic make-believe?

"Do Estonians, Lithuanians, and Latvians get their own separate countries? If so, what about the Gypsies? Do they get their own nation-state? Where would it be located? Which nation will cede its land to carve out a Roma homeland?

"Albania has been independent on paper since 1912, but in practice it stands ready to be consumed by Italy and Serbia. Can Albania survive? Will its citizens retain their own free country, or will they be folded as an ethnic minority into someone else's nation-state? Then, there are a million ethnic Albanians living in the district of Kosovo. Will they be merged into an expanded Albania, or will Serbia add them and their land to its great South Slavic state even though Albanians are not Slavs?

"I have just come from Macedonia. Will it be incorporated as a Balkan nation-state? Or will it be parceled out to its strongest neighbors—even some of it given to Bulgaria which has killed many thousands of Entente soldiers. And regardless of Macedonia's fate, what happens to Bessarabia, Bohemia, Ukraine, and other areas where the ethnic population doesn't match those holding political power?"

Philip continued his questioning of the ambassador. "Then there's the question of how far the Great Powers go in redesigning the map. Is Armenia to become a free country? Or will you allow the Bolsheviks or the Turks to overrun the Armenians? Just how much of the world map needs redesigning? Do you go as far as China and, with the help of the victorious Japanese, redraw that massive nation's boundaries?

"Similarly, if you rearrange the lands of the losers, do you also redraw the lands of the winners? Will France allow Brittany to become a free nation-state? Will England allow Ireland and Scotland and Wales to determine their own destinies? Will internal tensions force Italy to become two countries: northern and southern Italy?

"Finally," Philip wondered, "with all this national liberation occurring and losing empires facing extinction, what about the nations held as colonies by the victorious imperial Powers. Like the Russian, German, and Austrian Empires, will the French Empire be shattered into a collection of independent countries? A free Indo-China? Guyana, Algeria, Morocco, and Tunisia as self-governing republics? Mozambique and Martinique granted their independence?

"The same holds for the British Empire, especially in the case of India. How can tiny Lithuania become free and independent while massive India remains a subservient colony claimed by a small island halfway around the world? How can Egypt be an independent country on paper but remain under British occupation and control?

"On the other hand, Mr. Ambassador, boundary drawing can be addictive. Can France and Britain resist acquiring new holdings when maps show dozens of unclaimed territories that are unprepared for national sovereignty? This will be especially true if France and Great Britain are the architects of the new global arrangement."

"Excellent questions, all of them," Barrère conceded, "and I don't know the answers. But, to your point, I can recognize hypocrisy. Last January in the so-called Fourteen Points speech, President Wilson several times mentioned that nationality must be the basis of rebuilding the state structure of postwar Europe. That's a noble idea. But will your President allow such self-determination in Puerto Rico? The Philippine Islands? The Hawaiian Islands?

"Just last year your government purchased the Danish West Indies from Denmark. Now you call them the Virgin Islands. But the United States did not buy a vacant atoll, Professor Belmont. Real people lived in the Danish West Indies. Am I supposed to accept that the United States can simply purchase these islands like buying so much Danish cheese at a *fromagerie*? Buying people from another country: isn't that a bit like buying slaves from the auction block? Did America call for a plebiscite to learn if the citizens of the Danish West Indies wanted to be owned by the United States?

"Will President Wilson do anything about freedom for the American Indians? Or, the Mexican nationals who were acquired through the absorption of the Republic of Texas, the territories of Arizona and New Mexico, and the Republic of California into your union?

"Ultimately, which is the better model for assuring lasting peace: the creation of many free nation-states organized around ethnic identity? Or, large empires that integrate many nationalities into a single, cosmopolitan state? A Balkanized world or one of oversized multinational states: what's the answer?

"I know that nationalism is a powerful human emotion," added Barrère. "But hasn't this war dealt a fatal blow to nationalism? Or, has it rekindled, even intensified the demand for self-determination by ethnic nations. We must choose the correct formula if we are to make it better for those who come after us. We must get it right this time, and we won't have much time to decide once the war is over and the inevitable peace conferences begin."

It was a compelling discussion that touched on some of the most perplexing political problems awaiting the end of hostilities. Although dinner finally arrived, these questions commanded the interest of the ambassador and his guest throughout the meal, and for the rest of the evening. Both men agreed upon one thing: the resolutions finally reached would determine the course of postwar politics.

At one point in their after-dinner discussions, Philip raised the matter of the influenza he had seen in Prison 29. "Have you heard anything about a strain of flu that is highly contagious? I encountered it in Turkey, and I'm concerned. I have already alerted Entente military and medical leaders. I have written about it in my last report, the one deposited at the Banca d'Italia."

"How perceptive of you," Barrère replied. "There is an unstoppable influenza that is starting to move across the world. It is manifesting itself in Spain right now. Existing drugs are ineffective against it.

"We have to be vigilant. Everywhere public health officials are watching for it very carefully. Hopefully, it will be contained, but it could rapidly become a pandemic. Then we could be facing a new global plague. I look forward to reading you report after dinner."

"What a warning to our so-called civilized society where we have massacred so many people," added Philip. "Nature is stronger than you; and if she wishes, she can destroy all of human society with one tiny weapon: a germ."

After further conversation about disease and its potential impact on the course of the war, Philip finally found the opportunity to bring up the matter of his future. "I'm sorry to burden you with my personal business," he said to the ambassador. "But since France had so much to do with my life for the past year, and because my latest instructions only ordered me to meet you here in the Farnese Palace, do you have an idea about what I'm expected to do now?"

"Oh, I apologize. I should have mentioned that matter myself. It slipped my mind. How time flies when you're in a stimulating discussion," Barrère responded. "Following our meeting you are to return to Paris and meet as soon as possible with the American ambassador, William Sharp. I have your tickets for the Paris Express which leaves, in fact, later this evening. There is a private room waiting for you, this time at the Hôtel Ritz in the Place Vendôme. Nowadays much of the Crillon is used as a British military hospital, so the Quai d'Orsay thought you would be more comfortable at the Ritz. That hotel is in the 1st arrondissement, not far from the Place de la Concorde.

20

Two days later Philip entered the U. S. Embassy in Paris and asked that he be announced to Ambassador Sharp. Within five minutes he was ushered into a small inner office where the ambassador was working at his desk.

"Come in, Professor Belmont. Come in and sit down, please. I'm Bill Sharp. It's a pleasure to meet you at last," he said. "I've heard about you and the exploits you've undertaken for our government. Most impressive work."

"Nice to meet you, too," Philip responded. "I didn't expect such speedy service. I barely announced my name before I was entering your office."

"That's because we've been anxiously waiting for you," Sharp explained. "I told my staff to bring you directly here once you arrived."

"That probably means you have something for me to do," said Philip. "Just when I was getting used to civilian life."

"No one said you weren't perceptive, Professor. You're right. We do have an important assignment for you," the ambassador responded with a grin. "Professor Belmont, you have become a significant asset. Your unique undertakings over the past year or so have made you one of our chief experts on the war. So, whenever a situation requires knowledge of wartime foreign and military affairs, you're the authority we turn to."

"I'm flattered you think so highly of my work. I'm curious about what my next project might be," Philip responded.

"Before we proceed," the ambassador interrupted, "I am required to remind you that this conversation is classified. Under penalty of law you may not divulge any of its details to any person not authorized to receive such information."

"Understood and agreed to," said Philip.

"Good. Here's the situation. Since the United States has been landing troops and actually fighting in France, we've become a kind of broker in the minds of the Central Powers. German and Austrian leaders really distrust the British and the French. I guess four years of punishing warfare will make that happen. Because we're new to the scene, the enemy nations apparently trust us more.

"Ever since last winter we've been receiving overtures from the Austrians about negotiating a ceasefire or a separate surrender. Even Kaiser Karl seems to be supporting such proposals. Several weeks ago the British held a short meeting on the matter with an Austrian official in Switzerland, but nothing happened. I've heard that the British representative actually walked out after three minutes of evasive answers from the Hapsburg representative.

"I'm not sure what Vienna is signaling by these gestures. But Washington wants certainty.

"The State Department has ordered me to meet with Austrian officials in Geneva to get to the bottom of this diplomatic dance, to flesh out any authentic offers they may be making, or to expose their peace-talks suggestions as a charade. I would like you to accompany me to the meeting next week as my senior political advisor. We'd be in Switzerland for a few days of bilateral conferences most likely. But before then you'll need to do background research on why Vienna might be dropping these hints."

Philip pondered the offer. "What about the French and the British? Do they know about this?" he asked.

"They know all about it, but they won't be with us in those meetings. They'll be kept up to date on everything that transpires. We won't be doing anything without informing them," Sharp promised. "The Austrians no doubt will do the same thing with their puppet masters in Berlin.

"This may be a chance to end the war diplomatically. Every complicated international agreement begins with low-level talks where areas of difference are discussed and resolved. Our meetings in Switzerland could be such a contact—ambassadorial level, to be specific. It may well be the first step toward restoring peace in the world soon."

"I'd be honored to work with you on the project," responded Philip.

"That's excellent. We've scheduled our first meeting with the Austrians for June 11. That's next Tuesday. You'll need to leave Paris on June 9. My secretary will book a room for you at the Excelsior Hotel in Geneva. The meeting shouldn't take a long time, but if this is a genuine request to make peace, we could be there for a week or more. You can never tell about these things. We'll have to play it by ear.

"Meanwhile, your train tickets will be sent to the concierge at the Ritz. By Saturday afternoon, I'll need a report from you on possible Austrian motives. You can deliver it to the embassy. I'll be forwarding it to the State Department.

"One more thing," Sharp added. "We've prepared a new passport for you. No more Laurent Montfort. Are you ready for this? This time you'll be Philip Michael Belmont. How does that suit you?"

Philip smiled. "Maybe this war is ending, after all. Why, I already feel like my old self again," he joked.

For the next several days, Philip pored over news magazines and journals. He read every article he could find about contemporary conditions in Austria-Hungary.

On the advice of a friend who once told him "Don't say you can't read Italian if you haven't tried," he even perused Italian publications in search of insights. These proved interesting because, with the exit of Russia from the war, Italy had emerged as the principal enemy of Austria-Hungary. But they certainly were not new enemies. Their murderous battles in the Alps in northeastern Italy had drained both nations of money and manpower for three years.

As he sat at his desk Friday evening compiling his findings, a clearer picture of the Austrian dilemma made itself apparent to Philip: the Hapsburg Empire was in the middle stage of political disintegration. The death of Franz Josef in 1916 had been a devastating blow for wartime Austria-Hungary. More than King or Emperor, the man who had headed the Empire since 1848 was an adhesive who bound together its various segments through personal loyalty. Prime ministers and parliaments may have taken unpopular steps in the past, but Franz Josef remained the beloved and blameless Imperial grandfather. The new monarch, Kaiser Karl I, commanded no such devotion. He was a dynastic replacement, not an adored successor.

Austria's strong relationship with Germany was also being undermined by the cost of the war. It was one thing to list casualty figures, numbers that can be easily discounted or forgotten. It was quite another to discover that by May 1918 the war was costing Germany $935 million per month, and that the cost to the Central Powers of almost four years of combat had reached $45 billion.

Importantly, in Germany the bill was totally paid by the German citizenry through war loans, taxation, and a "conscription of wealth." The recently-concluded Eighth War Loan had raised $3.6 billion from the German people. Still, matters had deteriorated to the point where the Berlin government was selling plunder from Russia—horses, seeds, farm carriages—with payment accepted only in war bonds. If the credit of the German government was this stretched, he concluded, the budget of Austria-Hungary must be similarly strained, if not worse.

Domestic unrest was also unraveling the Dual Monarchy. Famine had become an everyday part of life in areas such as Bohemia where Czech and Slovak residents had publically demonstrated their preference for Woodrow Wilson and the Entente over their current arrangement. In fact, in the West there were rumors about creating a Czecho-Slovak state even before the war ended, a state that would be recognized as independent by the United States and Western European nations.

The citizens of the North Tyrol were also upset with curtailed food supplies so much that Berlin was compelled to combine that Austrian region in its own food distribution program for southern Germany.

In the Balkan Peninsula—the ultimate goal of Austro-Hungarian entry into total war in 1914—Slavic politicians were discussing the creation of a nation of South Slavs, or Yugoslavs. Informal plebiscites had shown the desire of a majority of Balkan Slavs to join Serbia in forming such a nation.

There were also disruptive military matters facing Vienna. Czecho-Slovak regiments of deserters and emigrants were assisting Italian troops wage war against Austria. Disaffected Rumanians and Slovenes were also being organized as foreign units assisting the Italian military.

Then there was the success of the Bolsheviks in Russia. In February 1918 their socialistic rhetoric inspired naval mutinies within the Austrian fleet stationed at Pola and Cattaro on the Adriatic coast. Six cruisers and a number of destroyers flew revolutionary red flags until order was restored. Armed resistance, arrests, and executions quelled the impulse toward mutiny, but authorities in Vienna now had reason to doubt the steadfastness of their own military.

When he finished his report, Philip delivered it on Saturday. But he was not finished. He continued to gather materials and study them until his train left the Gare de Lyon the following morning. He spent much of the trip to the Alps writing a supplement to his original findings, a document he presented to Ambassador Sharp when the two men met in Geneva the following day.

Official talks with the Austrian representatives commenced on Tuesday at 10 am. The chief enemy negotiator was Count Adam Tarnowski, the former Austro-Hungarian ambassador to the United States. He had not done much in that ambassadorial role, principally because of his short tenure. Tarnowski had arrived in Washington at the end of January 1917 and departed on May 4 because Vienna severed diplomatic relations with the United States when Congress declared war on Austria-Hungary's ally, Germany.

In Geneva Tarnowski was accompanied by an entourage of bureaucrats drawn principally from the foreign offices in Vienna and Budapest. The American delegation consisted of Ambassador Sharp assisted by Philip.

The diplomats wrangled over issues most of the first day, but it was immediately clear to Philip that the Hapsburg diplomats were not seeking a separate peace that would leave the Germans fighting alone. The vulnerability of the Dual Monarchy to every disruptive nationalist pressure tied Vienna closer to Berlin. This was not a Germanic brotherhood; Austria-Hungary now needed Germany as a bulwark against nationalism, militarism, liberal democracy, economic weakness, food shortages, and Bolshevism. There was no way Tarnowski would weaken the one relationship that kept his country intact.

In this light, it was difficult to understand the Austro-Hungarian overtures. Unless, of course, the Hapsburg Empire was operating as a surrogate for Berlin.

The American team spent three days trying to pin down the specifics of the enemy's peace gestures. In the middle of the second day, an exasperated Ambassador Sharp bluntly asked Tarnowski if he was acting as a proxy for the Germans.

After a few minutes of evasive rhetoric, the Austrian admitted that he might have that ulterior purpose in mind. "Many times your President Wilson has stipulated the terms of ending the war," he stated. "His Fourteen Points clearly address some of these terms: Alsace-Lorraine must be returned to France; Italy's borders must be readjusted along ethnic lines; Poland must become a free state; conquered areas of Rumania, Montenegro, Serbia, and Belgium are to be evacuated and prewar borders reinstated.

"But what does Mr. Wilson envision for the Hapsburg Empire?" asked Tarnowski. "How can we plan for peace if we don't know our options? You must give us more information. If we surrender, it's because you have won. But is there an incentive for surrendering before complete defeat? Or, must we fight to the last man before you tell that final soldier what is expected of him?"

The Austrian response frustrated Sharp. He asked for a short break to confer with his political advisor. "Good. I need a good cup of coffee, *mit schlag*. Let's meet back here in twenty minutes," said Tarnowski sounding much friendlier that he did when negotiating.

In a small adjoining room, Philip explained why he felt the Austrian's statement was essentially a confession that the Hapsburg and Hohenzollern Empires were near collapse and the war would soon end. "It's impossible that he's asking these questions solely for the sake of Austria-Hungary," Philip concluded. "The Germans want our answers, but they don't want to ask the questions to our face. It would be too suggestive and humiliating for Berlin. Plus, if it became known that they were secretly seeking peace terms, it might precipitate greater unrest within the Fatherland. So Germany gets Tarnowski to act as its proxy and make the inquiries."

"Possibly. But before you settle on this interpretation, consider what's happening while we sit here and negotiate," commented Sharp. "We know from secret communications that the Austrians are assembling a large force to launch a coordinated land campaign in northern Italy and a sea assault against Italian naval installations at the mouth of the Adriatic. That assault will begin any day. I think they will be slaughtered this time because Rome knows the plan. Already there are Italian, French, and British units assembled, waiting for the Austrian High Command to issue the order to strike. From what I hear, there may even be American units deployed to assist the Italians in this battle.

Does that sound like the Austrians are getting ready to give up? They may be ready to quit if this campaign is crushed. But not right now. They still see themselves sitting triumphantly in Milan or Florence or perhaps even Rome.

"Then there's Germany's Western Front. The Boches are in the middle of a powerful drive led by General Ludendorff. It resembles the early campaigns of 1914-1915. It's a do-or-die effort to defeat Great Britain and France before the Yanks are fully involved in the fighting. If you ask me, I think it'll be a tremendous loss of life and treasure for the Germans, possibly a defeat from which their Empire cannot recover.

"It hasn't been easy, but we Americans are tipping the balance," the ambassador continued. "In last few weeks alone Marine and Army units of the U. S. Expeditionary Force have been fighting next to French troops, stopping German advances at Seicheprey, Cantigny, Château-Thierry, and Belleau Wood. The Germans must know by now that they can't win when they suffer defeats like that."

Philip listened intently. "I agree with everything you just said," he remarked. "But, do we really know why the Austrians brought us here? Will you recommend to the Washington that talks continue at a higher level?"

"Let me ask you, professor. You're the historian. What do you think we should report?" Sharp countered.

"Well, it could be a feint, an attempt to make us think the Central Powers are weakened while they regroup and launch powerful offensives against our allies," Philip answered. "But my research tells me the Hapsburgs want to end the war, and they are in league with German leaders in this effort. They are anxious to find a way to maximize their inevitable capitulation—and that's no misstatement. I think both nations want to get as much as possible out of surrendering. If the Entente offers to forgive the billions of dollars the two empires owe for starting this war, I'll bet they'd end the war tomorrow morning—possibly tonight."

"That sounds logical to me, too" Ambassador Sharp said. "In that case, my recommendation to Washington will be that channels of communication be left open, but until something significant develops there's no need to schedule further talks at any level.

"But we won't tell that to Tarnowski," Sharp remarked. "We'll let him find out for himself."

On the train returning to Paris the following day, Philip sat in his private compartment working on his conference report. He never realized that being a senior advisor entailed so much research and writing. Sipping on a cup of warm tea, he was summarizing the final meeting with the Austro-Hungarian conferees. Philip was confident that he and Bill Sharp had drawn the proper conclusions following three days of talks.

At first the tapping on his compartment door was faint, impossible to hear over the noise of the speeding train. As the caller grew more impatient, however, the sound grew louder. Philip now tried to ignore the knocking, but it continued. Exasperated, he relented and brusquely opened the door. Before him stood a man and woman, both in their early 30s, who appeared startled when he opened his compartment door so brusquely. "Excuse me," Philip said, "but I'm in the middle of important work. I can't be disturbed."

When the callers stared dumbly at each other, Philip switched to French, but still no reaction. Finally he tried Russian. Russian was the correct language.

Again he explained why he could see no one at this time.

"Pardon us, Professor Belmont," the young woman implored him, "but we did not know you were so busy. We have come with an urgent request. Lives are at stake, and we desperately need your help."

"I'm sorry, but I'm working at the moment," Philip reiterated.

"Please, sir, we need your help. Won't you assist us?" the man pleaded.

Grudgingly, Philip gave way and invited them into his compartment. "But I can only spare you a few minutes, no more," Philip stated as he gestured for the pair to sit down. "All right, you've got me curious. Just what is it you want from me?"

"My name is Zbigniew Janowski—please call me Zbig. This is my sister Tatiana Wojda. We are members of Free Poland, a citizens committee advocating for Polish liberation from tyranny. You are an American. In the past your President Wilson has expressed sympathy with our cause. This encourages us to ask you to present our case before your people. In your newspapers and magazines, in your work, in your private life we would like for you to become a champion for Poland."

"A champion for Poland? I already favor creating an independent Poland," Philip said with bewilderment. "I know that Poland has been ruthlessly controlled by others for a century. I know that Germany and Austria-Hungary recently grabbed large chunks of Poland and now plan to create a Kingdom of Poland—of course, with a dynastic relative installed as your new king."

"But a champion is someone who writes and speaks out for truly free Poland," Tatiana interrupted. "We cannot leave our independence in the hands of the emperors in Vienna and Berlin—or the new madmen in Petrograd and Moscow. But this may be our last chance for another century to allow Poles to live in freedom."

"She's right. The window is now open, but we fear it will close very quickly," Zbig explained. "We would like you to help us keep that window of opportunity open long enough to create a Polish republic with democratic institutions such as those in your own nation."

Tatiana continued her appeal to Philip. "There are many Poles who live in America," she argued. "They write letters home and tell us about the United States. Even if things are difficult there, they say their lives are so much better than when they lived in occupied Poland."

THE HEADLONG FURY

Philip was confused. "But why me? Why do you come to me?" he asked.

"Because you are an influential man, a man of responsibility. You are a Professor and a writer. You can present our case to America. We need a man like you," implored Zbig.

"How did you find me? And how did you know I would be on this train?" Philip inquired.

"One of our colleagues remembered you from his military days in Monastir," Tatiana responded. "He said you once interviewed him about Poland. He left the Serbian Army and is now in Geneva where I live. He recognized you several days ago walking on the street and, well, here we are asking for your help.

"It's funny, but he knew you by a different name. He said you were a French professor. But we investigated and discovered your real name and citizenship. That pleased us very much."

"Yes, we know you are a good man, Dr. Belmont," Zbig added. "But innocent people are dying right now because the Germans and Austrians—and the Communists—are trying to destroy the nationalism that stirs in the Polish people. Poland will be free one day, that we know. It is inevitable. But people die every day we postpone this inevitability. Please, will you help us?"

"Look, I have great sympathy with your cause. If I were a Pole I'd be in the underground myself," Philip explained. "But what you ask is not possible. I have work to do that would interfere with commitments to your Free Poland movement."

"Are you certain? Can you check with your employer? We need you. Here is my card. I live in Paris, and my sister is visiting me from her home in Geneva. Please see if there is some way you can assist us," concluded Zbig.

Once the Polish visitors left his room, Philip sat down in amazement. He tried to comprehend the implications of what had just happened. He never thought of himself as a propagandist, but that was the essence of the role urged upon him by these activists. He decided to mention the incident to Ambassador Sharp when he submitted his final report in the morning. But he would advise against cooperating with any political movement.

"I think it's a wonderful idea for you to work with the nationalist movement," exclaimed Ambassador Sharp. "Its political goal is completely compatible with the positions expressed by President Wilson. He called for a united, independent and autonomous Poland in his address to Congress in January of last year.

"Your acceptance of this role would give us insight into the dynamics of Polish activism. And it would allow us to influence the direction of the movement should it veer toward the Central Powers or toward the Reds. I'll check with the State Department immediately. But I don't see any problem.

"One thing, however," he continued, "you can't accept a salary. It must be voluntary. Otherwise, your secret status here would complicate our diplomatic ethics."

Several days later Philip contacted Zbig to set up a meeting. They arranged to confer that afternoon in a bistro on the Boulevard Saint-Michel near the Luxembourg Gardens.

Philip was already seated in the restaurant when Zbig came up to him excitedly. "Did you read the papers this afternoon?" he asked. "The Austrians have been obliterated along the Piave River in northern Italy. The Italians, with French and other foreign troops—including Czecho-Slovak military contingents—have decimated the invaders. The papers are saying this battle could end with as many as 100,000 Austrian casualties."

"That's amazing. People thought the Italians were finished last year after Caporetto. Today they have the most successful army in the Entente," said Philip.

"This battle was supposed to be Vienna's great solo campaign: no Germans to pull the Austrian chestnuts out of the fire this time. Well, those chestnuts just got roasted and served as *antipasto*."

Zbig was beside himself with excitement. "This will drive another nail in the Hapsburg coffin," he emphasized. "The Empire must perish so other nations may live. Not just Poles, but everyone suppressed by the brutes in Vienna and Budapest. And when Austria goes, Germany will not be far behind."

It took Zbig a few minutes to calm down. He kept clenching his fist and striking the table with enthusiasm. Finally he confronted Philip

THE HEADLONG FURY

with the question he asked on the railroad trip from Geneva: "Now, will you help us?"

Philip explained that his boss had agreed to let him work with Free Poland. His only stipulation was that it be a voluntary position with no salary, stipend, or honorarium paid or expected.

Zbig immediately agreed. He stood up and grasped Philip's hand, then embraced him enthusiastically. "That's wonderful news. I can't wait to tell Tatiana. Great news! As good as the Italians on the Piave," he said. "Maybe better!"

He calmed down enough to detail what the Committee needed from Philip. "We would like you to give speeches and publish articles for us. We think your voice is important for everyone to hear. Maybe you can also bring other American voices into the Free Poland movement.

"You will be your own boss, and you can come to us for information and direction should you need either. We want you as our spokesman."

Philip explained his own perspective on the matter. "I've been thinking it over and I have an idea that may be more effective. Have you ever heard of a man named George Creel?" he inquired.

Zbig shrugged his shoulders in ignorance. He had never encountered the name.

"I thought not," Philip said. "Most people don't know George Creel. I learned only recently of his activities. But someday everyone will be familiar with his work. Creel is an American journalist and former Police Chief of the city of Denver. At the moment he is in charge of a government office called the United States Committee on Public Information. You've probably never heard of that group either. The Committee is a well-organized propaganda agency of the U. S. government. That makes Mr. Creel one of the first official government propagandists in modern history. His job is to keep national morale high during this war, and he does this through the information he regulates.

His strategy includes creating and distributing posters and motion pictures that promote government policies. His group writes articles favorable to the American war effort and gets them published in prominent magazines and newspaper. Plus, the Committee writes negative articles about America's enemies and has them published wherever possible. Creel has also created a network of public speakers who appear everywhere to support American activity in the war.

"To assist him in all these endeavors Creel and his Committee have recruited scores of men and women who share his view on the war and the U. S. role in it. With his speakers bureau he has a cadre of civilian orators who appear before clubs, churches, civic organizations, and other public groups. Here, they explain present government policies. He insists on short speeches, no long-winded orations, just curt presentations. He calls these speakers his Four-Minute Men because their lectures don't last more than four minutes. Creel believes the average person's attention span lasts only four minutes, hence the time limit on his spokesmen.

"I explain all this because with the help of you and your friends, I want to use the Creel model for Free Poland. We'll need artists and printers, writers and publishers, and speakers who can sway a public audience in short order.

"I want an army of propagandists, men and women, focusing on Polish freedom. They can speak and write in any language because we want to engage people everywhere. But French, English, and Italian are the preferred languages for obvious political reasons. Can you organize such an army?"

Zbig saluted and clicked his heels. "Yes, sir," he said dutifully. "Free Poland has contacts everywhere in Europe. Your plan is impressive. And, I think, it's achievable."

"Well, let's start with France, Britain, Italy, and the United States," announced Philip. "I would add Poland to the list, but we don't want to get anyone killed, especially patriots who might organize demonstrations or rebellions inside the country. We want every Pole alive to witness the eventual birth of the new Republic."

"That's excellent. We will have fifty volunteers for you by tomorrow evening, and double that by the next week," Zbig pledged. "We can gather at the Polish Union Hall. It has a large meeting room. In fact, we can use the Polish Union as our home site. My brother-in-law runs the place. He will agree.

"The Polish Union Hall is at 31, boulevard du Temple, a few steps from the Métro station at Place de la République. It is very convenient to get to. The first fifty volunteers will be there at 8 o'clock tomorrow evening ready to launch the Free Poland Committee on Public Information—the FPCPI."

The following evening the Union Hall was packed with people ready to work for the common goal. Philip was slightly intimidated by the response, but he pressed forward with the organizational ideas he borrowed from Creel. "First of all, we'll need money. I want half of our Four Minute Men and Four Minute Women to speak at fund raisers. The rest will speak wherever we can place them. If you are offered cash for appearing, bring it to the Treasury here at the FPCPI. You may be tempted to buy a dinner or two with your earnings, but every franc you keep or spend on yourself means five more of your countrymen will die. So, go ahead, dine on the profits if you wish. But think of what you're doing to people inside Poland.

"Next, I want one leader for each of our three divisions of communication: public speeches, poster production and distribution, and print publications. Each division leader will manage the functioning of his or her area. For the speech-makers, the Committee will provide daily sheets of points we want you to make. No presentation will exceed four minutes, with questions and discussion following. If they want eight minutes, give the speech twice, then answer their questions for the rest of the time. We'll be converting a few people every time, but, more importantly, we'll be reaffirming the commitment of hundreds each time as well. Convince and Reaffirm: that must be the motto of the Public Speakers division.

"As for your artists and printers of posters, we want anguish. We want pain. But we also want smiling, happy Poles—individuals, children, families, old people, priests and nuns—projecting the happiness inherent in future independence. Who are our national heroes? Copernicus, Pulaski, Chopin, Paderewski, Pilsudski, and others you may think of. We want their images approving the Republic of Poland

Also place Woodrow Wilson, as well as Georges Clemenceau, David Lloyd George, and Vittorio Orlando on some posters. Show these Entente leaders as pleased and embracing the idea of a new

Poland. These four men hold the key to your fate because they will be the chief negotiators at any future peace conference. Flatter them. Treat them nicely. Although they're elected heads of state, most have been reluctant to support Polish independence because they were tied to Tsarist Russia. Well, Nicholas and his wife and children are now dead—overthrown last year and murdered by the Communists a few months ago. No amount of reactionary White Russian troops, German schemes, or invasions of Russia will bring the Romanovs back to power. The Reds will hold on in Russia, and the European democrats will come around to Wilson's position regarding Poland. So, let's speed them in that direction now.

"For purposes of raising money, we need broad international outreach. We must organize. Solicit donations from abroad, especially from Polish émigrés, but from anyone anywhere willing to support the cause. Make your speeches, your articles and posters, promote this theme: everybody wants to see a free Republic of Poland—everybody needs to donate.

"Propaganda for us is advertising with a political purpose. It's not a new idea, but with the methods of communication we have today, it is more powerful than ever. Use it to sell national aspiration. Manipulate human emotions—guilt, happiness, anger, a sense of justice, hatred, whatever. Persuade people to your side.

"Finally, I want to thank all of you who are here this evening. You must want an independent Poland very badly. Well, let's go and grab it before someone decides to impose another arrangement on your homeland. Poland will be a democratic Republic only if you persuade people to make it free."

The enraptured audience broke into applause even though he had spoken more than four minutes. While the crowd expressed its approval, Philip leaned over and whispered briefly to Zbig. Philip then announced to the gathering that "future details of this plan will be handled by the Director of the FPCPI, Zbigniew Janowski." One of the first rules of successful propaganda, Philip understood, is don't trust a Polish patriotic organization if its leader doesn't have a Polish last name.

With the Committee on Public Information organized and providing direction, Philip's job was to suggest themes and encourage production. Meanwhile, Tatiana spearheaded the global aspect of the Committee by establishing a nascent group in Switzerland and acting as a clearinghouse for Polish nationalists in other countries.

Zbig focused on the Paris operations, especially on the Speakers Bureau which provided propagandists to a wide variety of groups wishing to hear and spread the Free Poland message.

The FPCPI wasn't much as a money-maker, but it did manage to cover its expenses. By late August the group was fully functional and expanding. A rising number of contacts outside of France confirmed that the message was being absorbed internationally.

"I think it may be time to introduce specific suggestions into our propaganda," suggested Philip one day. "I'm thinking about naming people who would be appropriate leaders in the new Poland."

"Don't you think such a move might make us appear partisan within Polish politics?" Zbig asked. "It is one thing to push for independence; it is quite another to tell people whom to support as their elected leaders."

"Correct," Philip conceded, "but that's why we must choose people who are unassailable, people nobody would oppose. I'm thinking about the Czecho-Slovak independence movement. The embodiment of that campaign is Tomas Masaryk, a distinguished scholar and editor, a Professor of Philosophy in Prague and at the University of Chicago. He has political experience, but fundamentally he is a man of culture and reason, a scholar. Who can see the image of Professor Masaryk and say the Czechs and Slovaks should not be free? We need someone that iconic for Poland."

"Then the obvious choice is Ignace Jan Paderewski," responded Zbig. "He is a world-respected classical composer and pianist, a man of culture, the arts, and achievement. He has been a political spokesman and organizer for Poland in the United States for years, so he has a political background and international contacts—although, frankly, he's more at home in a concert hall than a parliamentary congress."

"You may be right about his lack of experience, but he sounds like a man no one could assail. Let's start pushing Paderewski as the type of person the Republic of Poland will put forward on the world political stage: honest and fair, non-threatening, culturally accomplished, intellectual, humane. That should be an easy sell," Philip remarked.

"Personally, I think General Josef Pilsudski would emerge as the first President of the Republic if a vote were held today," Zbig noted. "He is not a cultural giant like Masaryk or Paderewski. Pilsudski is our George Washington, the great military leader organizing and leading his Polish Legions against the Russians, then resigning from command and going to prison in Germany because he would not support the invaders from Vienna and Berlin. No to the Russians! No to the Huns!"

Zbig thought a moment. "But we don't want a political clash between a man of action like Pilsudski and a man of thought like Paderewski. How about Pilsudski as President and Paderewski as Prime Minister? How does that sound to you?"

"I like it very much," Philip said. "The General's past is a little controversial. He was a radical socialist. He fought the Russians in cooperation with the Germans and Austrians."

"But that was because he couldn't fight all three tyrants simultaneously," Zbig explained. "He was supplied by Austria-Hungary and did well fighting the Russians. After the Russian Revolution in March 1917 he was ready to turn against Austria. But he was thrown in a German jail a year ago when he and his men refused to swear an oath of loyalty to Kaiser Wilhelm. He's still rotting in that prison."

"No argument, Zbig. I agree with you," interrupted Philip. "Pilsudski is the perfect Polish patriot: a successful military man as well as an imprisoned martyr. From now on Pilsudski and Paderewski will be more than just men of achievement in our messages: we'll feature them as destined for political leadership in the new Republic of Poland."

Clearly, Philip was showing a side of his personality never exploited in his earlier wartime experiences. But he was not acting beyond the scope of his work for President Wilson. Every Monday he presented Ambassador Sharp with a summation of the previous week's developments. Any new campaign or important change was coordinated with the State Department and checked for its compatibility with Washington's foreign policy objectives. The change of emphasis in presenting Pilsudski and Paderewski, for example, was cleared by Washington before Philip ever discussed it with Zbig.

By late September the FPCPI had become an influential player in Polish émigré politics. Philip was consumed with its operations, and Zbigniew continued to find people in Paris and other urban centers willing to commit their time and money to the effort. Philip marveled at the dedication of these people. Clearly nationalism was the unconquerable force that neither Entente diplomacy nor German bullets could quash. The rest of the new century, he now firmly believed, would be marked by the romance of nationalism and its political consequences.

Philip was also pleased because of the maturation of the Free Poland Committee. Demand for Free Poland speakers and materials was rising dramatically, especially in France and Great Britain. Zbig and his sister in Geneva continued to attract recruits to the ranks of Four Minute Men and Four Minute Women. Lower-level organizers were trained and now operating in important European cities. Many were long-time nationalists dedicated to independence. They spoke in churches and synagogues, social gatherings, large or small political rallies, street corners, civic halls, wherever people would pay attention to the message.

There was also an expanding demand for newspaper features and magazine articles about the Polish condition. Philip wrote several of these under the pseudonym "A Polish Patriot." The FPCPI also provided authoritative men and women for press interviews, university lectures, and roundtable discussions. At least two short histories of Poland were being written by Polish professors while a translator was converting their manuscripts into several languages.

As for the political posters, these were actually becoming collectors' items. In Rome and Paris small exhibits of FPCPI poster art were scheduled at museums for late November, several bookings involved appearances by the artists who created the posters. Significant civic and university libraries also requested copies for their research collections.

The only thing outshining the accomplishments of the Free Poland Committee was the pattern of Entente military victories in northern France. One after another efforts by the Central Powers ended in defeat. It was late October of 1918 and already the endless world war seemed destined to end soon in triumph for the Entente.

In the Champagne region of northern France, a rout of the German Army was well underway. In August the Germans were turned back by French, British, and American troops at the protracted Second Battle of the Marne. At St. Mihel the following month 650,000 American troops and 100,000 Entente soldiers, mostly French, won a decisive victory that helped secure the area and opened the door for a major offensive—the Meuse-Argonne campaign—that General Foch and his commanders organized.

Commenced on September 23, the campaign was designed as a wide pincer attack against entrenched German troops. With French forces in the middle to hold ground and assist both sides of the pincer, a British-French-Belgian force to the north drove toward Cambrai and the industrial city of Lille. To the south a force of 600,000 doughboys led by General John J. "Black Jack" Pershing attacked northward into the Argonne Forest and toward Sedan.

Although the Meuse-Argonne offensive was still underway, German troops were being crushed by the Americans and the reenergized Entente armies. The Germans offered stiff resistance, but they continued to lose towns and villages as the fell back toward the Fatherland.

In Germany there was political disarray. On October 4 the conservative cabinet resigned and was replaced by a new government headed by the liberal Prince Max of Baden. Leaders in Berlin and Vienna immediately appealed to President Wilson for an armistice and peace talks based on his Fourteen Points. This time, Philip sensed, the enemy was serious about surrendering.

Victory over the Central Powers was not limited to northern France. An Italian offensive against Austrians in late October was a complete disaster for Berlin and Vienna. Although outgunned, the Italians—assisted by a small number of French, British, Czecho-Slovak, and American regiments—obliterated the Hapsburg forces. When a truce was eventually called in this Battle of Vittorio Veneto, it was reported that Entente forces took a half million Austrian prisoners. Press accounts claimed the Italians also seized 250,000 horses, 5000 guns, enough provisions for a full winter campaign, and about one billion dollars in cash. The victory followed by almost one year the disastrous Italian defeat at Caporetto.

In action that was particularly gratifying to Philip, the Army of the Orient finally launched its decisive campaign for Macedonia. It was the attack for which General Guillaumat had prepared his forces before being brought back to France to head the prestigious Second Army. Led now led by his replacement, General Franchet d'Esperey, the multinational Balkan force engaged the enemy from Albania to the Struma River.

The results were stunning. The Serbs were especially successful, driving forty miles into enemy territory in one week. Within ten days the Army of the Orient was through Macedonia and capturing key towns inside Bulgaria. The routed Bulgars buckled and surrendered. On September 30 in Salonika, they agreed to a complete armistice. Four days later Tsar Ferdinand abdicated and Bulgaria was out of the war.

Philip knew well that Bulgaria was the underappreciated linchpin in the assault against the Balkan Slavs. Without military support from Sophia, Serb and Entente troops were too strong for the small number of Austrians and German troops stationed in the Peninsula. Rectifying the situation would require a massive commitment of fresh manpower and materiel from Germany, something Berlin and Vienna could not afford at this time. The capitulation of Bulgaria also shattered Pan-German dreams of a Balkan corridor with access Turkey and the markets of Central Asia. It also encouraged the Entente forces and pushed the Central Powers close to military collapse.

By this time in the Arabian theater of action British troops led by General Allenby were destroying the dispirited Turks and their German reinforcements. At the Battle of Megiddo in mid-September, the British expanded their conquest of Palestine, capturing thousands of Turkish troops in the process. By late October Allenby's soldiers had already taken the Syrian cities of Damascus, Homs, and Aleppo. The occupation of ancient Aleppo effectively cut the Berlin-to-Baghdad rail line thereby isolating Constantinople from eastern Ottoman provinces and Mesopotamia.

The Sultan's Empire was in a death spiral. The surrender of Bulgaria now opened the way for Entente troops to move eastward to invade Constantinople. The Turks lacked sufficient manpower to stop such an assault. They also lacked the ability to dispatch reinforcements via railroad to either Baku where British Army units were battling for control of valuable oil fields, or to Iraq where British forces were hammering Turkish forces and threatening to ride the Berlin-to-Baghdad Railroad back toward the Ottoman capital. These developments created the perfect military scenario for the Entente: troops from British Mesopotamia, augmented by Allenby's Egyptian Expeditionary Force up from Palestine and Syria, now moving west toward Constantinople—while the Army of the Orient rolled eastward from Salonika to the Turkish capital.

Facing total destruction, the Sultan on October 14 implored President Wilson to arrange an armistice. Terms of a ceasefire were not yet finalized, but clearly a Turkish nation-state would be all that remained of the once-vast Ottoman domains.

"I can't believe everything is falling in place so fast," Philip said to Ambassador Sharp during one of his weekly visits to the embassy. "We've been fighting these criminals so long, and now they're collapsing. Bulgaria, gone; Turkey, out of the war; Austria, Hungary, and Germany now pleading for an armistice and peace talks: let me pinch myself to see if this is all a dream."

The ambassador was pleased. "It's no dream, it's actually the end of our long nightmare," he said.

Despite the disintegration of the opposition, Philip was still uncertain about Poland's fate. Unlike the Czech pattern in which the Entente nations and the United States recognized Czecho-Slovak independence even before the Czechs and Slovaks formalized their own independence, Polish fortunes remained tied to unfolding military results in these apparent final days of conflict.

By the first week in November the postwar world was beginning to materialize. On November 1, the Austro-Hungarian Empire crumbled with the declaration in Vienna of a Republic of Austria. In Budapest negotiations toward creating an independent Republic of Hungary were nearing a successful conclusion.

It was in this atmosphere that Philip and Zbigniew Janowski continued to press for Polish democratic unity. It was reassuring that in early June the Entente powers had declared their support for an independent and reunified Poland, but nothing guaranteed this commitment.

Matters began to coalesce in October, however, when a Polish Regency Council announced that Poland would be a free and independent country. As exciting as this declaration was, Zbig was panicked by the end of the month. Factionalism was starting to undermine Poland's greatest chance for freedom since the 18th century.

"Can you believe what's happening?" he asked Philip with fear in his voice. "The Regency Council set up a free government in Warsaw on October 26 and a week later they dismissed it!

"In Galicia another Polish government was established on October 28. Then the socialists and the Peasant Party in Lublin declared still another government on November 7. And in Congress Poland, leftist radicals are now forming workers soviets and preparing a Communist revolution.

"We Poles have been apart so long we can't come together as one people, even when the possibility is staring us in the face! I'm afraid we're headed for civil war or continued dismemberment," Zbig lamented.

Philip was worried over these divisions, but he tried to mask his doubts from the Free Poland activists. "It's much too early to panic," he cautioned. "Let's wait and see what develops. Just keep our people out there repeating the message, Convince and Reaffirm. Remember that. And keep pushing our formula for success: Pilsudski and Paderewski. Promote them in every speech and all our writings. These are the most critical times. The Germans are near surrendering and will have to release Pilsudski from prison very soon. Don't lose hope. We've come this far. Keep on believing, and work for the dream."

That evening Philip asked for a special meeting with Ambassador Sharp. He needed to discuss his fears about the Polish situation. Interestingly, the ambassador didn't seem upset. "I think matters will work themselves out very soon in Poland," he said calmly to Philip. "The Germans released Pilsudski this morning. I've heard from the State Department that tomorrow some of the rival governments will step aside and recognize him as the provisional head of state for a united Polish Republic until a formal state structure can be established."

"That's wonderful news," Philip said. "The Free Poland people will be delighted."

"There are a lot of loose ends everywhere. They have to be tied down," Sharp added. "The establishment of borders that rearrange Europe according to nationalities is one of the most important. Almost every national boundary needs reevaluation. We even have frontier disagreements involving Luxembourg that need to be resolved," he remarked with frustration.

"With respect to Polish aspirations, we need to amalgamate ethnic Poles. They and the land they occupy in Prussia, Austria, and Russia need to be integrated into a single national state. We also need to resolve Polish territorial disputes with Lithuania, Czecho-Slovakia, and Ukraine. And this new Poland must also be provided access to a port on the Baltic; she can't be left landlocked. Now multiply these problems by the number of countries involved in this war and you'll see what is facing us.

"Ah, but I'm not finished. Overriding all these quandaries," the ambassador continued, "we have a problem that demands immediate attention. Europe and parts of Asia are facing starvation. Almost everywhere the Germans and Austrians went, they devastated the infrastructure. They pillaged northern France. In Picardy in the town of Laon, for example, they pressed the population into forced labor. They compelled the citizens to pay almost $1.2 million in fines and taxes. The Germans even stole furniture from city hall and private homes when they retreated. The population in Laon is now 6500; it was 16,000 before the war.

"The city of Lens, near the Belgian border, was similarly ravaged: 10,000 houses were destroyed in the fighting. The town is in a coal mining region, but that livelihood is threatened because the Germans flooded the mines and smashed the pit machinery. Some mines were simply blown up. The British ambassador has told me that it might take two years to get them in working order, and as long as five years to get them back to normal. And winter is coming very soon.

"This is not just happening in France. In Belgium unoccupied homes were stripped of their valuables. Food supplies were confiscated from the local population. Able-bodied men and boys were deported to Germany as slave labor. The Belgians estimate that since August 1914 the Germans extracted as much as a billion dollars from their nation in machinery, raw materials, and fines and taxes.

"The Germans did this before," Sharp added. "When they were retreating earlier this year under attack from the Entente forces and the Yanks, they robbed as they fell back toward the Fatherland. President Wilson warned them in stiff terms that we would not tolerate wanton pillaging. The German Army has agreed to stop the practice. Some people are now saying that industrial Lille and the Belgian city of Bruges would have been severely damaged and looted had Wilson not sternly warned the Boches.

"Then there's the global agricultural situation: ruined farmland, crop failures and insufficient harvests, inadequate manual labor, and the need to conscript armies of men.

"With men away at war much of the farming in France, for example, fell increasingly to struggling women. I imagine it was the same everywhere," Ambassador Sharp continued. "As men became warriors womenfolk—who already had substantial household responsibilities—were pressed into tilling the earth, seeding the fields, and eventually harvesting the crops. Understandably, they fell behind schedule. It's now mid-November and winter will be here soon. In many countries the fields have not been fully seeded, and it's now too late to plant for the spring harvest.

"These problems extend throughout Europe, into Africa and the Middle East, and across much of Russia and Central Asia. Where will the food come from to feed all the hungry people—be they civilians who never left home, or millions of war survivors who will soon return from battle?"

"I can see where this is headed: to world famine," interjected Philip. "The damage has been done. People must feel hopeless whether famished at home or in a survivor camp. Wherever they're sheltered, their futures are grim."

"Now we have an added misery: that influenza you first recognized in Turkey is sweeping the globe," Ambassador Sharp further explained. "That's a recipe for human catastrophe. The world population is at risk of completely dying."

"What can we do?" Philip asked.

"President Wilson has anticipated this food tragedy—but not the flu pandemic," Sharp answered. "You've heard of Herbert Hoover, right? He was in charge of the United States Food Administration during the war, and before that he headed Belgian Relief that fed as many as nine million people a day in Belgium and northern France early in the war. Well, Mr. Hoover will now coordinate the global distribution of emergency food supplies to any country in need.

"This will be a monumental undertaking. Some nations are worse than others. But as a general guide, wherever the Germans and Austrians went, there you'll find the worst famine. Ironically, Germans are hungry, Austrians and Hungarians are starving, and the Balkan Peninsula lacks sufficient food. Finland, Poland, Armenia, Serbia, and Czecho-Slovakia are famished; and much of the rest of Europe and the Near East are near that point.

"Mr. Hoover and his staff have a big job ahead of them. If they fail, the consequences will be horrendous. Wish him luck and Godspeed."

All Philip could say was "Amen."

November 11, 1918 was one of the most important days in history. Philip was excited to read the morning Paris newspapers, all proclaiming that an armistice had been signed by the Germans and Austrians. General Foch accepted the document on behalf of the Entente and the United States. It ordered the end of all combat effective at 11 am. It was not a peace treaty; that document would be negotiated at a later date, but the armistice could be renewed periodically until an actual peace treaty was arranged and signed.

The war was over. Still, much remained unsettled. Newspapers reported mutinies, rioting, and political demonstrations throughout Germany and Austria. Kaiser Wilhelm had abdicated yesterday and was searching for a new home. Kaiser Karl stepped down this morning, renouncing his participation in matters of state, but refusing to abdicate. His goal was to become a figurehead such as the King of England. But that was academic. He was an anachronism with the emerging Austrian and Hungarian republics.

Reading the newspapers, Philip was reminded that the armistice would not end all the fighting sparked by the war. Italian troops had designs on strategic segments of the Turkish interior. Russia was locked in a civil war pitting the new Red Army against reactionary White forces. Furthermore, American, French, British, and Japanese troops remained in control of several strategic Russian cities occupied in mid-1918 in hopes of destabilizing Red power and thwarting German plans to overrun strategic parts of Russia. The armies of Lithuania, Estonia, and Latvia were still anticipating an invasion by Russian Communists who coveted their strategic Baltic locations. Albania, which fought on the Entente side, continued to protect itself from armed incursions by Serbians and Italians. And Poland had to contend with German troops still active in the western provinces, while Leon Trotsky's Red Army threatened to invade from the east.

Philip was uncertain about the timing of the armistice. Certainly, Germany and Austria-Hungary lost the war. People living in the Fatherland lost loved ones or had relatives and friends injured or maimed. They knew young soldiers who had been emotionally wracked by battle, and they had seen their personal savings evaporate as Imperial German war bonds were now worthless.

But the average German, Hungarian, and Austrian never knew the full physical and emotional destructiveness of war. Before the victors could march deeply into Germany or Austria-Hungary—with howitzers blazing, machine guns slaughtering soldiers and civilians, and bombs falling on urban centers—the governments in Berlin and Vienna surrendered. When foreign troops did arrive, they came as occupiers, not belligerents.

The losers never felt the anguish of having homes destroyed, cherished cities and cultural monuments blasted apart, farmlands ruined, property and cash confiscated by murderous invaders, and the myriad other indignities inflicted upon Serbian, Belgian, French, British, Italian, and other allied nationalities. They never faced slave labor deportations; never had their ways of life shattered by artillery shells fired from seventy-five miles away, or by enemy soldiers looting and torching their hometowns. They never had groups of innocent friends and neighbors rounded up and executed by enemy firing squads. In other words, the surrendering enemies never experienced what they had imposed on those they invaded and subjugated. The war was one thing in Louvain, Verdun, and Belgrade; it was quite another in Berlin and Vienna.

Had the Germans learned a lesson? Did the average person in Augsburg or Munich or Bremen realize what devastation had been wrought in his or her name? Did those living in Leipzig or Magdeburg, Vienna or Salzburg, Budapest or Szombathely know just how much suffering they had inflicted on people everywhere when they gave their sons to kill for their respective governments?

Philip wondered, too, if somewhere in the future a new generation, made eager for war by another Emperor or his equivalent, would employ destructive combat to resolve problems. Would another rapacious worldview, like that of the Hohenzollerns, the Hapsburgs, and the German General Staff disrupt the peace and threaten civilization? Would the losers of 1918 recognize their defeat as an admonishing moral failure, or might it become a nationalistic rallying point for reenergized warfare?

There were so many unresolved difficulties confronting the Central Powers, among them economic instability; reparations for damages inflicted by the invaders; demilitarization; the demarcation of territorial boundaries; industrial reform; the Jewish situation; Marxist-Leninist civil war; and the assumption of guilt for starting the war. It was easy for

Philip to imagine how German social weakness could be manipulated for political advantage if the upcoming peace conference failed to craft a judicious rearrangement of national and international politics.

Still the streets of the world were filled with revelers on November 11. They were ecstatic that the ghastly struggle had finally ended. With the guns along Germany's Western Front silenced millions of soldiers could begin thinking of discharge and a return to normality.

As Philip explained it in his first letter to Millie in the last two years, "Perhaps the Europeans just became bored with peace. Like that crazy Futurist art that influenced Italy before the war, maybe they just longed for something visceral to get their hearts pumping, something combative that would be different from the rational way of living they found so predictable and dull.

"Well, they got it, and it almost devoured them. The monster that is war must never be turned loose again. Hopefully, as President Wilson said, this was the war to end all wars."

He signed the letter with the promise to be back with her and Elizabeth before the year ended.

21

A letter sealed in an embassy envelope and anonymously slipped under his door was a strange reminder to Philip of his days of spying. But this was postwar 1918, and the Armistice had been in effect for more than a month. He was still in Paris with no expectations or desire to be assigned to another war zone for purposes of keeping President Wilson—or the French Ministry of Foreign Affairs—informed about events in the streets.

In fact, all he wanted now was passage back to the United States and the chance to rejoin his family. It had been almost two full years since he was with Millie at the New Willard in Washington. And the more he thought about her and Elizabeth, the more anxious he became to say *adieu* to Paris and hello to Baltimore.

Nevertheless, he had business to complete while he was still in France. Most importantly, he needed to contact the University of California to see if his position in the Department of History was still available next term or in the Fall. If he did face hesitancy from the University, he figured a letter of recommendation from Professor Woodrow Wilson or Ambassadors Sharp, Herrick, or Barrère might help make his case for reinstatement.

There were other minor matters he needed to settle, but his mind was focused on his primary concern: getting home. He hoped to visit

Chicago to reconnect with his parents. He wanted to travel in peace throughout the United States on a leisurely vacation; to visit museums since most of them in Europe had been closed for years, their artifacts moved to rural storage sites for safe keeping. He hoped to meet with friends and not use an alias or speak a foreign language or worry about being tortured in some miserable prison.

In sum, he wanted to be with his wife and child and become social and whole again: no more solitary hotel rooms for weeks at a time; no more fear of artillery shells, bombs, or gunfire. No more spies and would-be assassins. Just a happy, productive life. That's all he hoped for.

But when Philip opened the envelope and read the letter, he was crushed. In a most cordial way, he was being invited to join President Wilson's staff at the upcoming Paris Peace Conference. He was asked to come to the U. S. Embassy that afternoon to discuss this "exciting opportunity to be a seminal participant in history."

He felt guilty. He had given his word to the President to honor his requests. But the war was over and like so many Yanks, he simply wished to return to the States and let the rest of the world go by.

Nonetheless, later that morning Philip walked to the embassy on Avenue Kléber to meet Bill Sharp and discuss the "exciting opportunity." It was a chilly day under a gray Paris sky. Clearly, winter was beginning to show its angry face. He steeled himself for the tough sell he would face. But his mind was made up.

"Phil, nice to see you again," the ambassador said, "Come in and let's talk. Sit down. Anything to drink? Coffee or tea? A soft drink? Water?"

"No, thank you," Philip replied. "I'm fine. I just had breakfast."

"Then, let's get to the reason for this meeting," Sharp continued. "The President was so impressed with your work that he wants you as part of his team during the peace negotiations with Germany that begin here in January. He'll be arriving in France in a day or so, and he can tell you then how informative and influential your reports were to his policy making."

"I'm very sorry, Mr. Ambassador," Philip interrupted, "but I'm going home. I've served my time in Hell. I want to be with my family again. I want to be normal."

The ambassador was taken aback. "But Phil, the Paris Peace Conference will be historic," he pleaded. "Centuries from now people will speak of it. You can have a role in shaping its conclusions. Especially with your background in history, you understand what has to be done. The way you handled the Free Poland committee was brilliant. Just consider who's in charge in Warsaw today: General Pilsudski. And who is also prominent and ready to join the General in governing: Ignace Jan Paderewski, the man who will undoubtedly become his prime minister. You helped make that possible because you knew what would work.

"Before you definitively say no, think of the exciting proposals the President is going to be bringing to reality. New countries will be established and validated. New rules for the freedom of the seas will be written. A League of Nations will be created to guarantee world peace. Imagine, all the nations of the world coming together to resolve problems and outlaw war. Permanent institutions will be established in Geneva where global issues such as hunger and disease can be resolved. Rules for international labor can be written and enforced. It's the dream of the old philosophers come to fruition. It's Wilson's wisdom placed in long-term service to humanity. And you will be a voice in defining its structure and outcome. Wouldn't you rather help draft the parameters of the League of Nations than write a monograph about Louis XVI and the Revolutionary War?

"Accepting the assignment could be a career-maker, too," Sharp continued. "This is a singular opportunity for someone interested in public service. With this under your belt, I can see you sometime in the future as an ambassador, or a member of the Senate, or even another Woodrow Wilson. Damn it, man, by working at the Paris Peace Conference you'd be establishing the ground rules for the next century. That's better than sitting in the faculty Club in Berkeley sipping wine and discussing how many angels can dance on a hairpin plucked from Marie Antoinette's wig?

"I love your sales pitch, Bill. No wonder you were such a successful businessman before becoming ambassador to France," Philip responded. "I'm really flattered, and I understand what a marvelous opportunity you're placing before me. But I can't accept it. No, I *won't* accept it. I'm too set on returning to the United States.

"I don't resent the two years spent serving my country. I feel like a foot-soldier who's lucky he didn't have to spend his time in a putrid trench ducking machine-gun fire. I also feel like a weary *poilu*—and like most of them who survived, I'm tired and I want to go home."

"Damn. I was afraid you'd be this way," said the ambassador. "You do realize that as a Major in the United States Army, the President can order you to accept this offer.

"Honestly, I doubt he'd do that! But this is once-in-a-lifetime, Phil. However, if you're determined to end your relationship with the President, I can't stand in your way.

"The embassy actually anticipated your refusal so we booked you a spot on the USS *Leviathan*, a troop transport sailing Friday for Norfolk," Sharp said as he handed Philip an envelope with the requisite documentation to board the vessel. "You're scheduled to leave a few hours after the President and his entourage dock in France. He'll be coming from England where he's now on a state visit. He will disembark in Brest. If you're lucky, you may see him when he arrives. Just make sure you're in Brest on December 13. Your ship sails at 7 o'clock in the evening."

"Thanks for being so understanding," Philip said. "I am really exhausted and ready to go back to my life in the States."

Returning to the Ritz, Philip was surprised to find Zbig and Tatiana sitting in the hallway waiting for him. "Philip, I'm so glad we caught up with you. We were afraid you might have left for America already. So many Sammies have already shipped out," Zbig said as he embraced his friend.

"Tatiana and I needed to see you before you departed. We wanted to tell you how vital you've been to Free Poland."

"Today we are building a new nation because of the Public Information Committee you set up for us," Tatiana added. "We have no doubt that the FPCPI played a crucial role in persuading public opinion to settle for nothing less than an independent and democratic homeland for our people. We have a long way to go to perfect our freedom, but we are on the way."

Philip expressed his thanks for their kindness, but added ominously, "You've achieved a victory of quantity: you have helped forge your nation into a representative republic. That is an admirable achievement. But now you must work toward the achievement of quality: creating a good state, one that respects all its citizens and treats them equally and honestly.

"I say that because I read a story about Poles a few weeks ago conducting a pogrom against Jewish people living in Lemberg. It was so disappointing to read of Polish troops sacking and burning ghetto shops and homes. A synagogue was torched with hundreds of Jews inside seeking protection. I read reports of people shot in the streets, girls raped and thrown from windows. There were three days of massacres that reportedly killed anywhere from a few people to four thousand civilians. The Polish officer in charge justified the event by blaming the victims. He said they poured boiling water on his soldiers.

"Thousands of people dead because someone poured hot water on a few cavalrymen! Contemplate that number. Is this how the military of a great and good nation—with hostile German and Russian armies on its borders—handles its own citizens who may or may not have been running around their ghetto throwing hot water at the troops?"

"I haven't heard of this event," Tatiana said. "But if it's true, it's despicable."

Zbig added, "Clearly, Free Poland can't quit now. We need to focus on the qualitative goal you mentioned."

"I wish you the best of success in improving Poland," said Philip. "As for me, I am leaving for Brest tonight where I will be boarding a ship for America. I am going home. I've enjoyed working with you. You have accomplished a great goal; now make your new republic noble and admirable."

With that final admonition, Philip took leave of his patriotic friends. It was time to leave Paris.

The train trip to the Atlantic coast lasted eighteen hours, but Philip was happy all the way. He was oblivious to the uncomfortable seating and the bouncy ride because he was going home. He arrived in Brest at 1 o'clock in the afternoon and began the boarding process.

THE HEADLONG FURY

Shortly after having his papers stamped and his ticket validated he heard the crowd along the dock beginning to shout. In the distance was a virtual armada of American warships headed into port. A printed program for the day explained that this impressive assemblage was comprised of seven battleships, including the USS *Pennsylvania*, the flagship of Admiral Mayo, Commander in Chief of the Atlantic Fleet; and the USS *Wyoming*, flagship of Vice-Admiral William Sims, Commander of U. S. Navy ships in Europe. Other battleships in the President's fleet included the USS *Arkansas, Nevada, Utah, Florida, Texas, Arizona*, and *New York*. There were also fifteen destroyers in the flotilla.

It was a stunning display of naval strength, perhaps the greatest accumulation of U. S. large ships since President Roosevelt placed sixteen battleships in his Great White Fleet that sailed around the world more than a decade ago. Philip was excited to witness this extraordinary event.

The President arrived aboard the USS *George Washington*, a German-built ocean liner that had been interned early in the war, then seized in 1917 and converted into a U. S. Navy troop carrier. Mr. Wilson walked onto French soil at 3:15 pm greeted by spontaneous applause from the large crowd gathered along the shore and on the pier.

His arrival in France was greatly anticipated. Even when Philip was going to the train station in Paris last night, he saw people camped on the sidewalks waiting to see President Wilson when he arrived from Brest around mid-morning on December 14. Philip knew then that the President's visit was going to generate a welcoming response of massive proportions.

About fifteen minutes after the *George Washington* docked, Philip was aboard the *Leviathan* waiting to leave for Virginia. As he stood watching the spectacle on the dock below, he felt someone tapping on his shoulder. "Excuse me, but are you Major Philip Belmont?" asked a young officer whose hat identified him as a crew member of the USS *Wyoming*. "I'm looking for Major Belmont."

"Yes, that's me," Philip answered.

"Excellent. Will you please come with me, sir," the sailor said.

Philip followed him down the gangplank of the troop ship and toward a crowd of people gathered around someone on the pier. As the officer pushed his way through the throng, Philip followed dutifully until he found himself standing opposite Woodrow Wilson.

"As you requested, Mr. President, here is the Major," the young man announced.

"Well, it's my wonderful information specialist, Professor Belmont," the President responded warmly and he shook Philip's hand. It's been almost two years since we made our little pact. And how well you've upheld your part of the bargain."

"Thank you, Mr. President, or should I say Professor Wilson," Philip replied jokingly. "It was a pleasure to serve you and the United States—although I could have done without those seven months as a guest of the Sultan."

The President laughed. "We let you down on that one, I'm afraid," he added.

"Well, at least I survived," Philip jested. "I'm thrilled to see you, sir, and to watch this overwhelming display of France's affection for you. All Europe is in love with you and with the United States. But I guess you knew that already."

Wilson smiled. "I only wish the Republicans in the Senate were half as appreciative. You know, I actually heard from Congressional supporters that some GOP Senators will oppose the League of Nations we propose to create because they think it will lead to a world government; and with all this popularity, they fear I would be elected President of the World. Utterly foolish is what I say to that cockamamie conclusion. I just hope they see through their own nonsense and ratify the League when we finish our work in Paris.

"Meanwhile, I wanted to meet with you to express the gratitude of the nation and of this old soul for all you've done. I know you've made many sacrifices to perform your job. And although you won't be working with me on the peace treaties, I think you've earned a release from our agreement. I truly wish you a happy and productive life, Dr. Belmont. You deserve it. I am honored to have worked with you. And I would be happy to read and review your first academic book when it's published."

Philip was deeply moved by the President's kind words. It almost made him feel embarrassed for rejecting Ambassador Sharp's recruitment pitch. He shook Wilson's hand again and wished him many successes at the peace negotiations scheduled for Versailles and other cities surrounding Paris.

Several hours later as his ship loaded with American troops and nurses sailed out of sight of Brest, Philip reflected on his experiences. It was a horrific war that engaged the planet. Its toll on human life and property was incalculable. Its effects on civilized society were yet to be fully realized. That's what the peace talks were all about.

But as a human adventure, he understood that his own wartime biography was singular—and yet it was only one of countless narratives. Everyone associated with this conflagration had a tale to relate—although many millions were no longer alive or able to share the details of their particular odysseys through perdition. No war as worldwide as this had ever happened. No conflict had ever killed so many people. It was Philip's prayer that a crime—and that's what he felt this war to have been—such as this should never occur again.

As night fell and his ship moving through the open sea, Philip sat in the officers' bar casually sipping on a glass of sherry. Near him was a group of junior Army officers sitting around a table playing poker and talking loudly enough about the war that everyone in the saloon could overhear their conversation. When their talk drifted to the topic of the origins of the Great War, Philip listened intently to hear their interpretations.

"There's no doubt that Germany caused the war," said one officer with a broad Texas accent. "The Huns hoped for full control of Europe, and the only way to accomplish that was to knock out Russia and France. When the Russians mobilized against them, the Germans had to hit France fast because France was weaker than Russia. But the French took the hit and didn't fold. The Germans soon found themselves with a prolonged two-front war that they could never win."

"I don't know," said another man. "For my money the Austrians started the war. Their move against Serbia in late July was irresponsible, even foolish. They basically wanted Serbia to cease being an independent country. And when that didn't happen they invaded the Balkans and tripped the switch on a maze of interlocking diplomatic arrangements. It's a simple formula: no Austro-Hungarian invasion of Serbia, no World War."

"I can't accept that," replied the Texan. "I'll bet when they go through the German diplomatic papers, they'll find that Berlin urged Vienna to invade Serbia. I'll bet the Germans wanted this war in order to destroy Russian power and to discipline the French who were outspending them on war preparations in the years before 1914."

A third poker player, identified by a name tag as Lieutenant James Frazier, interrupted the argument. "You're overlooking the obvious, guys. The Balkan Peninsula was the problem, and Serbia was the provocateur. I've studied the politics of this area. I know Balkan politics pretty well. Serbia was a young country on the make. Belgrade was making economic and military moves that threatened to upend the delicate balance in southeastern Europe.

"For one thing, Vienna virtually controlled the Serbian economy. Almost all Serb exports were sent to markets inside the Hapsburg Empire or overseas through Austrian ports on the Adriatic. Whenever the Austrians didn't like what the Serbs were doing, they could impose new tariffs or limit ocean access to Serbian shipping. Political autonomy is nothing if you don't have economic autonomy; and the Serbs resented Austria's stranglehold on their economy."

"That sounds logical to me," admitted another of the players. "But what were the Slavs doing that angered the Austrians and, in your opinion, made Belgrade the cause of the war?"

"Easy. Serbia was upsetting the apple cart," Lieutenant Frazier replied. "The Serbians found new routes and new markets for their exports. Instead of shipping north to Austria, they began shipping eastward, down the Danube River to Bulgaria and the Black Sea, or through Salonika to the Aegean Sea. In the process, the Serbs were finding new markets of the Near East with no Austrian strings attached.

"But that's not all. In recent years Serbia had expanded its size by almost half when it seized Slavic territories from Turkey during the two Balkan Wars. Serbia even came close to acquiring its own harbor on the Adriatic.

"You can imagine how that upset Vienna," the Lieutenant continued. "An economically- and politically-successful Kingdom of Serbia might excite the three and one-half million Slavic people living under Austro-Hungarian control. These were mostly Serbs, Croats, Bosnians, and Slovenes who had few rights or privileges inside the Empire dominated by Austrians and Hungarians.

"What if one day the Serbs decided that citizenship in the Kingdom of Serbia was preferable to subjugation within the Hapsburg state? What would be the fate of Austria-Hungary? Internal unrest, rebellions, loss of territory, enormous costs to maintain civil peace, the rise of a powerful Serbia on their southern flank, the end of Austrian dreams of controlling the Balkans—how long could Vienna and Budapest withstand such pressure?"

The Texan interrupted with a question. "Let me get this straight. You're saying that the war was the fault of the Serbians because they wished to escape oppressive controls imposed by the Hapsburg Empire? That doesn't make sense to me."

"It does to me," Frazier answered. "The Serbian moves were dangerous. There were no negotiations, no collaboration with Vienna. Just out of the blue, Serbians decided to upend the status quo: to lessen its ties to Austria-Hungary and aggressively pursue territorial expansion and self-reliance. Where I come from in Indiana, that's called throwing down the gauntlet. What else could the Austrians do but respond?

"Maybe so," said another officer, this one with a pronounced New England accent. "But I've heard it said that the British were actually behind the maneuvers leading to the outbreak of the war. It all started with the dreadnought naval program in 1904 when the British started building super-battleships. This forced the Germans to respond with their own stepped-up naval programs. The British also diplomatically encircled Germany via an Entente with France in 1904 and an agreement with Russia in 1908. If you were a German, wouldn't that convince you that the British meant to throttle your nation's development—arrest its colonial expansion, stunt its economic development by compelling Germany to spend millions on naval expansion, and inject a sense of doom in the Germanic mind by encircling the Fatherland with unfriendly neighbors.

"Put yourself in Germany's situation," he suggested. "Then you can understand the invasion of France and the attack on Russia as defensive maneuvers. Germany had to protect itself. Berlin didn't want global war; it just wanted to be free from the perils inherent in that naval race with Britain."

"You must be kidding," exclaimed the Texan. "By 1914 the Germans were falling behind. The French were ahead of them in military spending and in the number of trained men in arms. In terms of military size, Russia's land forces were much larger than those of Germany. But instead of seeking new alliances or solving international troubles, the Germans decided to make war on their neighbors. What was Luxembourg's sin against Germany? How did legally-neutral Belgium warrant invasion, brutal suppression, and long-term occupation? This was naked militarism, not innocent defense—unmitigated aggression, not an act of self-preservation."

"Now wait a minute," interrupted the man dealing cards. "I have studied this war, read the literature, and analyzed the data. The Russians are the causal factor in this war. Backward, regressive, retrograde Imperial Russia with its massive size and population couldn't keep up with modernity. Russia was a gigantic stumbling block to European development.

"Consider how decadent the Tsarist Empire was," he continued. "It didn't have any kind of elected legislature until the Duma in 1906, and that didn't have much power. It was so militarily weak that the nation lost a war to tiny Japan—that country of little Oriental people—a decade before the outbreak of this World War.

"You can't be that big, that full of resources, that militarily imposing, and be so weak. Russia was a war waiting to happen, a political void inviting attack. The Russians may as well have worn a sign on their foreheads saying 'Invade Me.' There's your cause of the war: backward Imperial Russia!"

As each officer reiterated his interpretation in increasingly strident tones, tempers began to fray. Soon the men were yelling at each other. Bitter invectives flowed and fists were clenched in preparation for an all-out brawl.

At this point Philip left his seat at the bar and approached the feuding poker players. "Excuse me, gentlemen," he asserted loudly. "I'm Major Phil Belmont and I've been listening to your rational discussion evolve toward a fistfight. So I'm telling you once and once only: calm down or else Army guards will be in here to arrest all of you."

Grumbling and embarrassed, the men lessened the anger in their voices. They returned to their chairs around the poker table and looked sheepishly at Philip.

"Now, that's more civil," Philip said. "I'm impressed that you've been talking about such an important question as the origins of the Great War. I suspect it'll be discussed for centuries with no definitive answer forthcoming. But let me tell you, every one of you is wrong."

The soldiers were stunned by Philip's bluntness. A few even snickered aloud. "What do you mean we're all wrong? Surely one of us is correct, said the soldier from New England. Maybe you want to argue that Italy caused it all because she failed to honor her treaty obligations to Germany and Austria-Hungary? Or, maybe you blame the Greeks because they were politically divided and weak. Maybe the Rumanians caused it. Or even the Spanish caused the war because they never fought in it."

"No, not at all," Philip responded with patience. "And I don't want to suggest that Woodrow Wilson started the war in 1914 as a long-range strategy to get reelected and to make United States the richest and strongest nation in the world in four or five years.

"I've been involved with this war since the summer of 1914 when all of you, I assume, were more concerned with the Mexican Civil War and characters like Carranza, Zapata, and Villa. No amount of book learning will get you to the real truth behind the war, at least not until government documents are opened for public scrutiny and a lot more research is completed by the professionals.

"I'm here to tell you that the war was caused by no nation. No country could have wanted the bloodbath we just ended. No individual could have planned the deaths of as many as twenty million people—maybe even more.

"No, gentlemen, the World War resulted from a delicately-arranged balance of power which by 1914 was precariously held together by a patchwork of secret alliances and obscure military agreements. Into such a fragile system, introduce six dynamic nations—France, Russia, Britain, and Italy on one side; Germany and Austria-Hungary on the other—each scheming to outmaneuver and surpass one another on a multitude of fronts: economic and financial, industrial and imperial and, of course, military.

With so many potential trip-wires ready to activate this hodgepodge system of treaties and commitments, even a drunken dancer could have accidentally triggered global warfare. Maybe you should be discussing which government was drunker while politically dancing in the summer of 1914?

"No single country caused this, gentlemen. Yet, all nations have some degree of culpability. But the question is ultimately irrelevant. The real question is: How do we arrange international relations so that a well-ordered balance of power maintains stability worldwide and makes war difficult to cause because the arrangements between nations are well-considered, publically known, and filled with political safety-valves and abort mechanisms?'"

"Well, Major, do you think that's possible?" asked the Texan.

"I don't know. Does anyone?" Philip answered. "Maybe President Wilson's dream of a League of Nations will work. But I haven't read its terms. I don't know what it will or won't do. It seems to me, however, that every country would have to accept the concept and live up to its terms. Does any of you think that could happen—even in our own country? Frankly, it's difficult for me to see that occurring. But I hope that I'm wrong. Only the future will tell."

With that Philip returned to his bar stool to continue drinking alone.

One of the officers gathered the playing cards then reshuffled the deck. And a new game quickly began.

ABOUT THE AUTHOR

J. Fred MacDonald was a history professor for twenty-seven years; he earned his PhD from UCLA after writing his doctoral dissertation on French diplomacy from 1898 to 1902. He is the author of several books on the cultural history of United States radio and television. Now retired, he enjoys writing fiction as a means of fostering an appreciation of history. He currently lives in Illinois.

CPSIA information can be obtained at www.ICGtesting.com
Printed in the USA
LVOW13s0500130514

385474LV00001B/12/P